THE STORY OF ALL OF US

MANKIND

TABLE OF CONTENTS

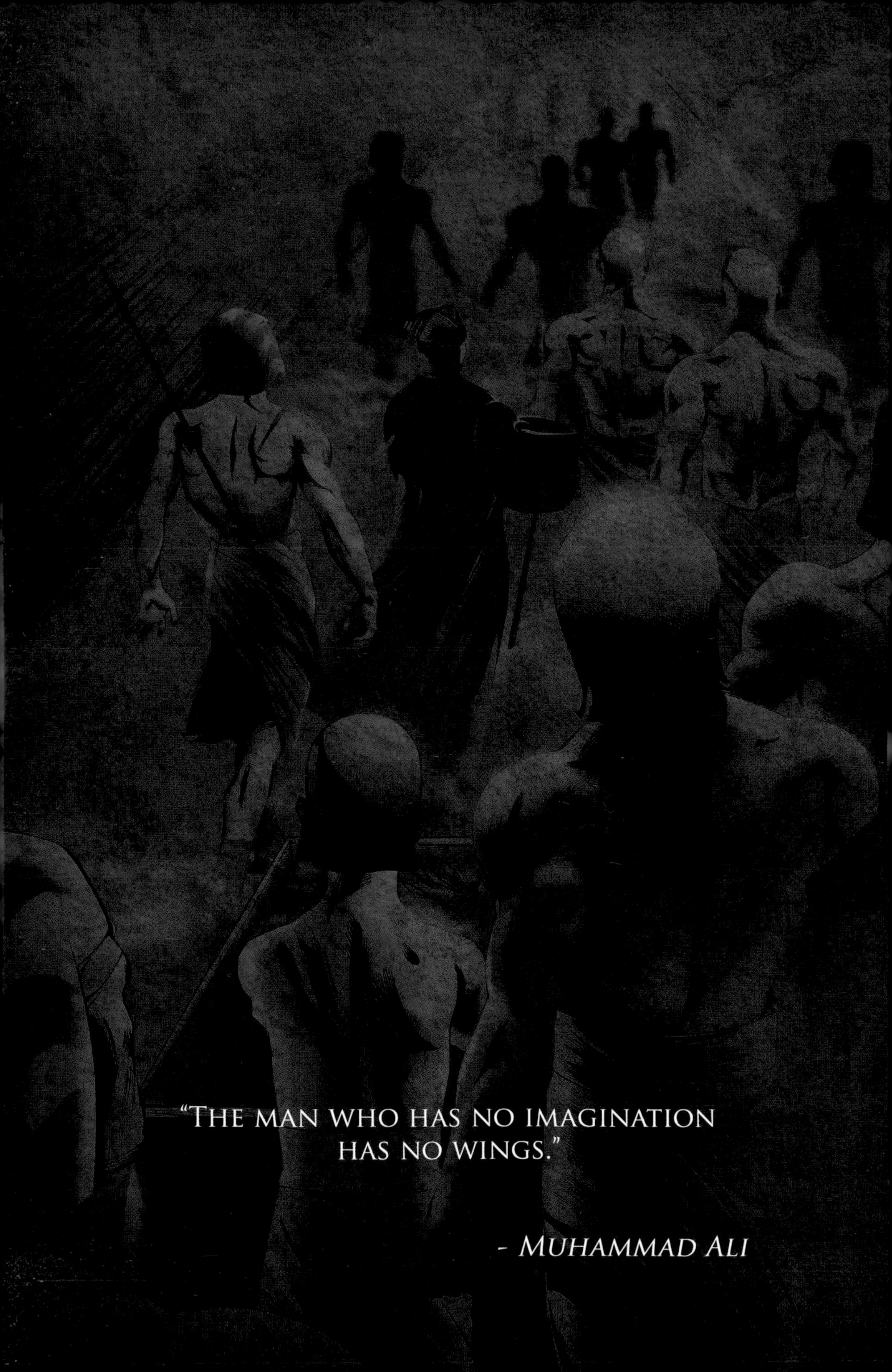

"THE MAN WHO HAS NO IMAGINATION
HAS NO WINGS."

- MUHAMMAD ALI

INTRODUCTION

You are about to begin an epic journey, one with a most unlikely hero: us. It is a gripping tale that is stranger than fiction: how one species rises against all odds to dominate a planet. In the great science fiction film *2001: A Space Odyssey*, an ape hurls an animal bone to the heavens, which metamorphoses into a space ship. This striking image captures mankind's story. Bound by the earthly forces from which we are birthed, we reach for the heavens.

Mankind arrives incomplete. Our fate is a riddle and a race: can we decode the keys hidden within our hostile environment in time to ensure our survival? Ninety-nine percent of all species on earth have gone extinct. What armed homo sapiens with the tools to prosper? Powered by our brain, the most complex structure known in the universe, we are hard-wired with the ability to transform the world through thought. It is this power of imagination that is a game-changer. Thinking bigger gives mankind a unique edge. It fuels our ability to harness the powers embedded in the universe to enhance our own strength.

The story of mankind's ingenuity and ambition is told again and again across many cultures through the use of myths. Take the ancient Greek mythological tale of Prometheus. It begins with a mind game (imagination!). Prometheus, a mortal, tricks Zeus, ruler of the gods, into eating the bones of a slain bull, thus preserving the meat for man. For this transgression, Zeus withholds the element of fire (no way to cook the meat!). Going undercover, Prometheus enters the realm of the gods, stealing fire and bringing it back to empower the mortals. Prometheus's bold act unleashes the powers of the universe in the service of man: writing; agriculture; the domestication of animals; the ability to track the seasons by the star; engineering; the power to make medicines; to sail the seas; to unearth the secrets of mining. Myth rubs up against history in this story. *MANKIND THE STORY OF ALL OF US* is the real story of those who dared to change the world, to unlock the keys that would transform our destiny.

We share a common destiny. Adventure is in our DNA, we seek new powers, we innovate and thus transform our world and our fate. The graphic novel you hold in your hands is based upon the television series produced by Nutopia for HISTORY® called *MANKIND THE STORY OF ALL OF US*. It presents history's greatest adventure, the biography of who we are. We mortals start here. Mankind takes flight.

Julian P. Hobbs

Executive Producer, *MANKIND THE STORY OF ALL OF US*

SEEDS OF CHANGE

WRITTEN BY
MARV WOLFMAN

ART BY
TOM DERENICK

INKS BY
BILL SIENKIEWICZ

COLORS BY
DASH MARTIN

LETTERS BY
JIM CAMPBELL

ONE FAMILY'S JOURNEY IS TRACKED FROM THE ICE AGE TO THE WORLD'S FIRST EMPIRE AS THEY UNLOCK THE KEY TO SURVIVAL IN THE SOIL.

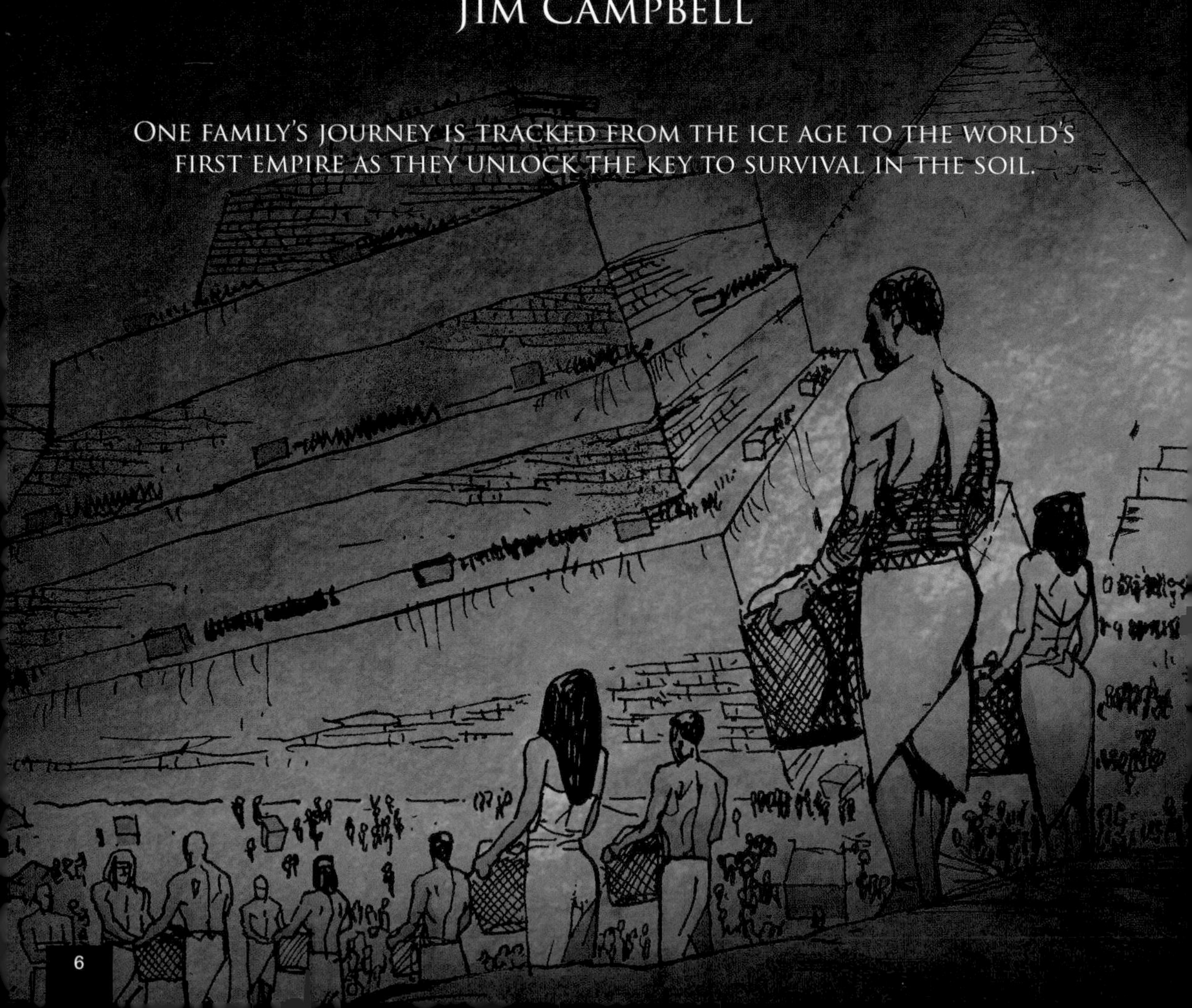

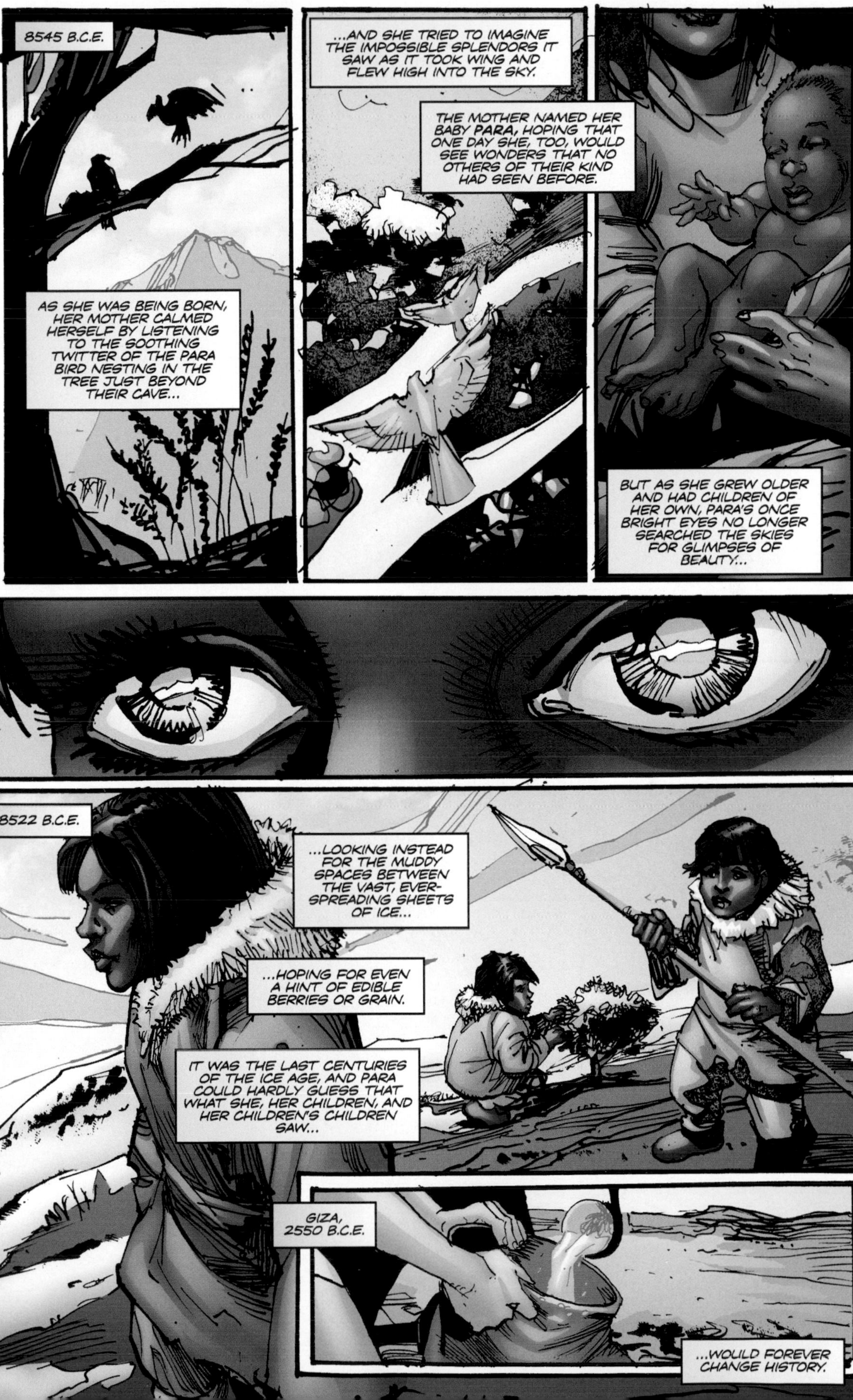
8545 B.C.E.
AS SHE WAS BEING BORN, HER MOTHER CALMED HERSELF BY LISTENING TO THE SOOTHING TWITTER OF THE PARA BIRD NESTING IN THE TREE JUST BEYOND THEIR CAVE...
...AND SHE TRIED TO IMAGINE THE IMPOSSIBLE SPLENDORS IT SAW AS IT TOOK WING AND FLEW HIGH INTO THE SKY.
THE MOTHER NAMED HER BABY PARA, HOPING THAT ONE DAY SHE, TOO, WOULD SEE WONDERS THAT NO OTHERS OF THEIR KIND HAD SEEN BEFORE.
BUT AS SHE GREW OLDER AND HAD CHILDREN OF HER OWN, PARA'S ONCE BRIGHT EYES NO LONGER SEARCHED THE SKIES FOR GLIMPSES OF BEAUTY...
8522 B.C.E.
...LOOKING INSTEAD FOR THE MUDDY SPACES BETWEEN THE VAST, EVER-SPREADING SHEETS OF ICE...
...HOPING FOR EVEN A HINT OF EDIBLE BERRIES OR GRAIN.
IT WAS THE LAST CENTURIES OF THE ICE AGE, AND PARA COULD HARDLY GUESS THAT WHAT SHE, HER CHILDREN, AND HER CHILDREN'S CHILDREN SAW...
GIZA, 2550 B.C.E.
...WOULD FOREVER CHANGE HISTORY.

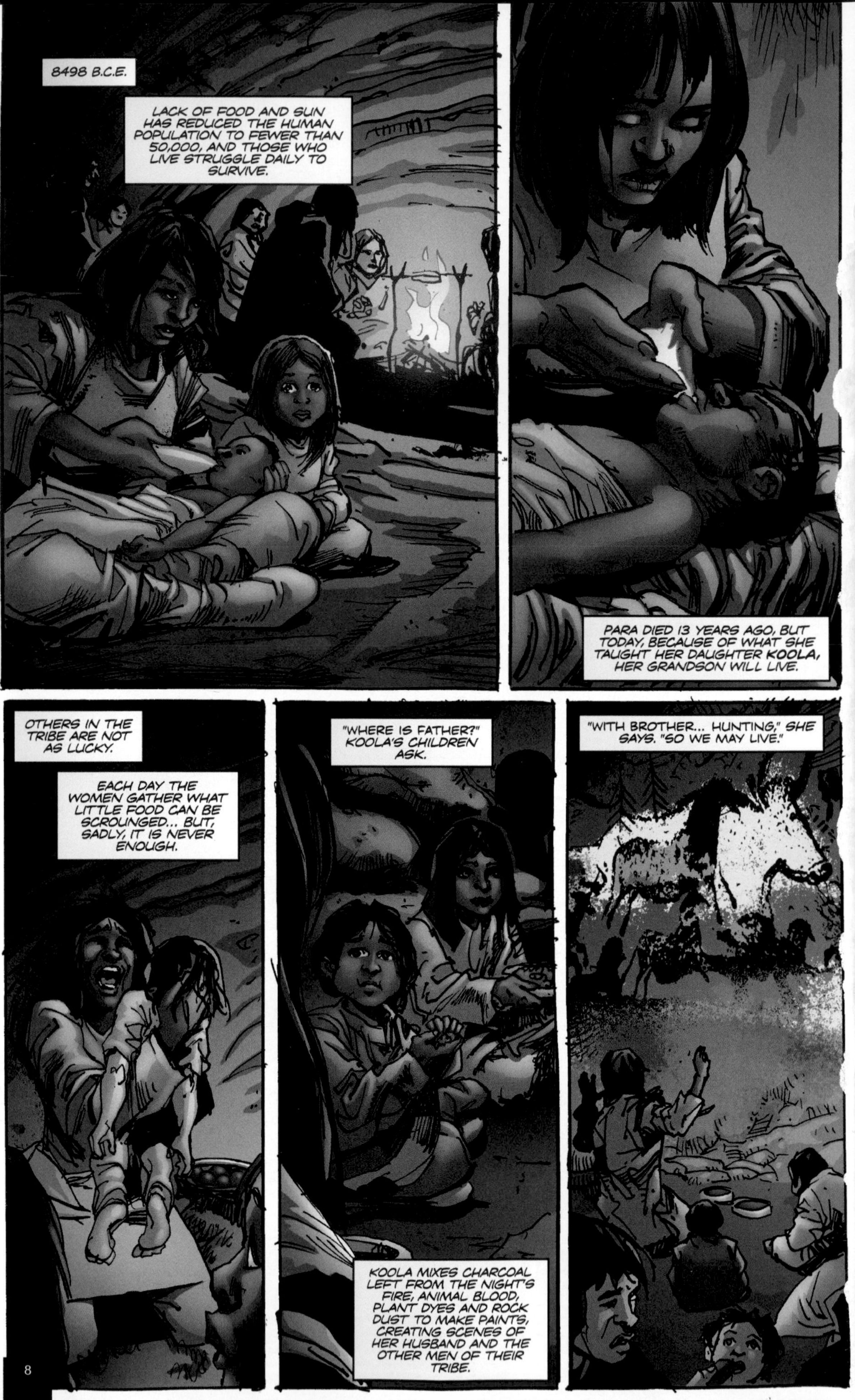
8498 B.C.E.
LACK OF FOOD AND SUN HAS REDUCED THE HUMAN POPULATION TO FEWER THAN 50,000, AND THOSE WHO LIVE STRUGGLE DAILY TO SURVIVE.
PARA DIED 13 YEARS AGO, BUT TODAY, BECAUSE OF WHAT SHE TAUGHT HER DAUGHTER KOOLA, HER GRANDSON WILL LIVE.
OTHERS IN THE TRIBE ARE NOT AS LUCKY.
EACH DAY THE WOMEN GATHER WHAT LITTLE FOOD CAN BE SCROUNGED... BUT, SADLY, IT IS NEVER ENOUGH.
"WHERE IS FATHER?" KOOLA'S CHILDREN ASK.
KOOLA MIXES CHARCOAL LEFT FROM THE NIGHT'S FIRE, ANIMAL BLOOD, PLANT DYES AND ROCK DUST TO MAKE PAINTS, CREATING SCENES OF HER HUSBAND AND THE OTHER MEN OF THEIR TRIBE.
"WITH BROTHER... HUNTING," SHE SAYS. "SO WE MAY LIVE."

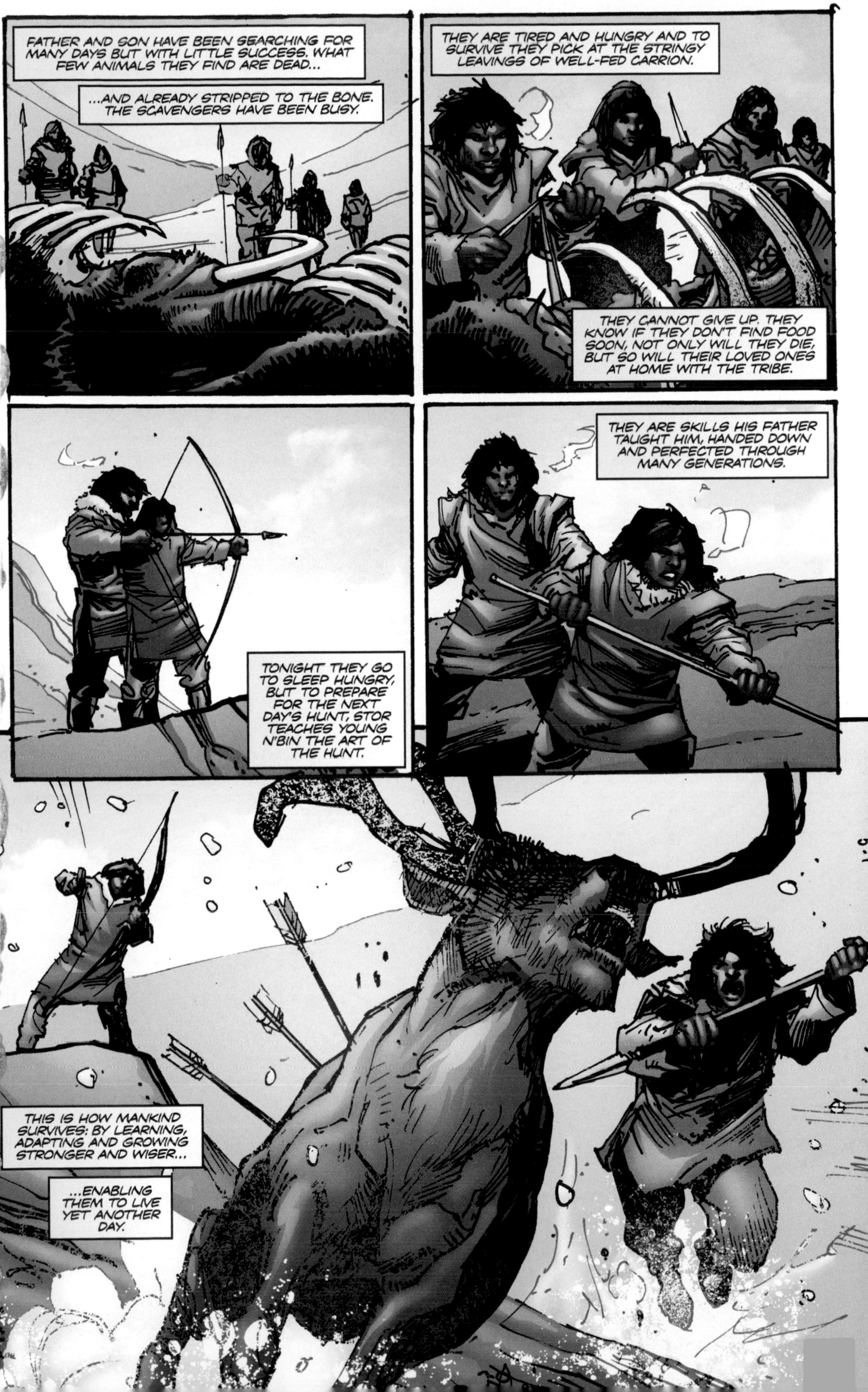
FATHER AND SON HAVE BEEN SEARCHING FOR MANY DAYS BUT WITH LITTLE SUCCESS. WHAT FEW ANIMALS THEY FIND ARE DEAD...
...AND ALREADY STRIPPED TO THE BONE. THE SCAVENGERS HAVE BEEN BUSY.
THEY ARE TIRED AND HUNGRY AND TO SURVIVE THEY PICK AT THE STRINGY LEAVINGS OF WELL-FED CARRION.
THEY CANNOT GIVE UP. THEY KNOW IF THEY DON'T FIND FOOD SOON, NOT ONLY WILL THEY DIE, BUT SO WILL THEIR LOVED ONES AT HOME WITH THE TRIBE.
TONIGHT THEY GO TO SLEEP HUNGRY, BUT TO PREPARE FOR THE NEXT DAY'S HUNT, STOR TEACHES YOUNG N'BIN THE ART OF THE HUNT.
THEY ARE SKILLS HIS FATHER TAUGHT HIM, HANDED DOWN AND PERFECTED THROUGH MANY GENERATIONS.
THIS IS HOW MANKIND SURVIVES: BY LEARNING, ADAPTING AND GROWING STRONGER AND WISER...
...ENABLING THEM TO LIVE YET ANOTHER DAY.

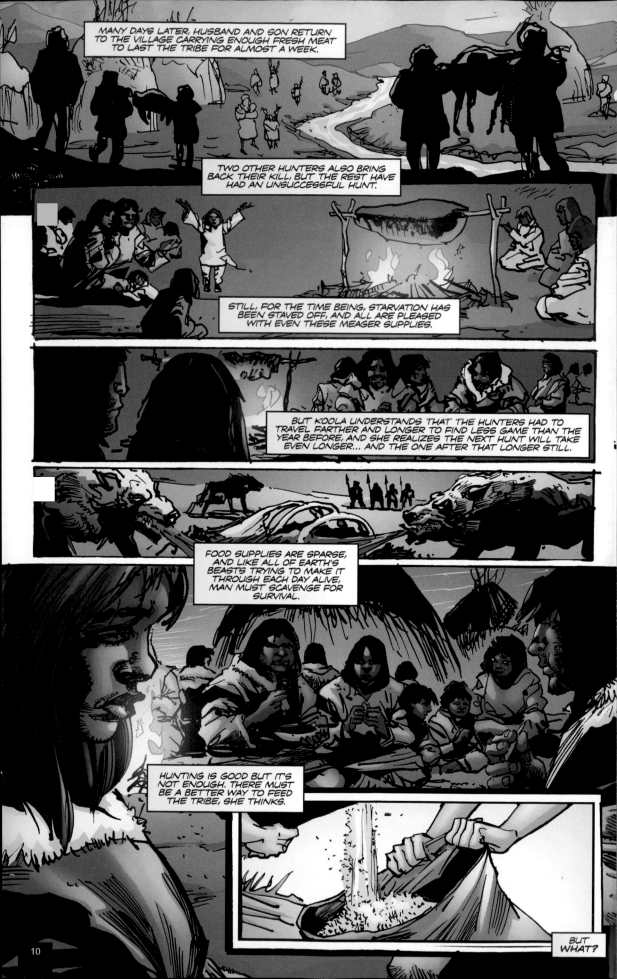

MANY DAYS LATER, HUSBAND AND SON RETURN TO THE VILLAGE CARRYING ENOUGH FRESH MEAT TO LAST THE TRIBE FOR ALMOST A WEEK.

TWO OTHER HUNTERS ALSO BRING BACK THEIR KILL, BUT THE REST HAVE HAD AN UNSUCCESSFUL HUNT.

STILL, FOR THE TIME BEING, STARVATION HAS BEEN STAVED OFF, AND ALL ARE PLEASED WITH EVEN THESE MEAGER SUPPLIES.

BUT KOOLA UNDERSTANDS THAT THE HUNTERS HAD TO TRAVEL FARTHER AND LONGER TO FIND LESS GAME THAN THE YEAR BEFORE, AND SHE REALIZES THE NEXT HUNT WILL TAKE EVEN LONGER... AND THE ONE AFTER THAT LONGER STILL.

FOOD SUPPLIES ARE SPARSE, AND LIKE ALL OF EARTH'S BEASTS TRYING TO MAKE IT THROUGH EACH DAY ALIVE, MAN MUST SCAVENGE FOR SURVIVAL.

HUNTING IS GOOD BUT IT'S NOT ENOUGH. THERE MUST BE A BETTER WAY TO FEED THE TRIBE, SHE THINKS.

BUT WHAT?

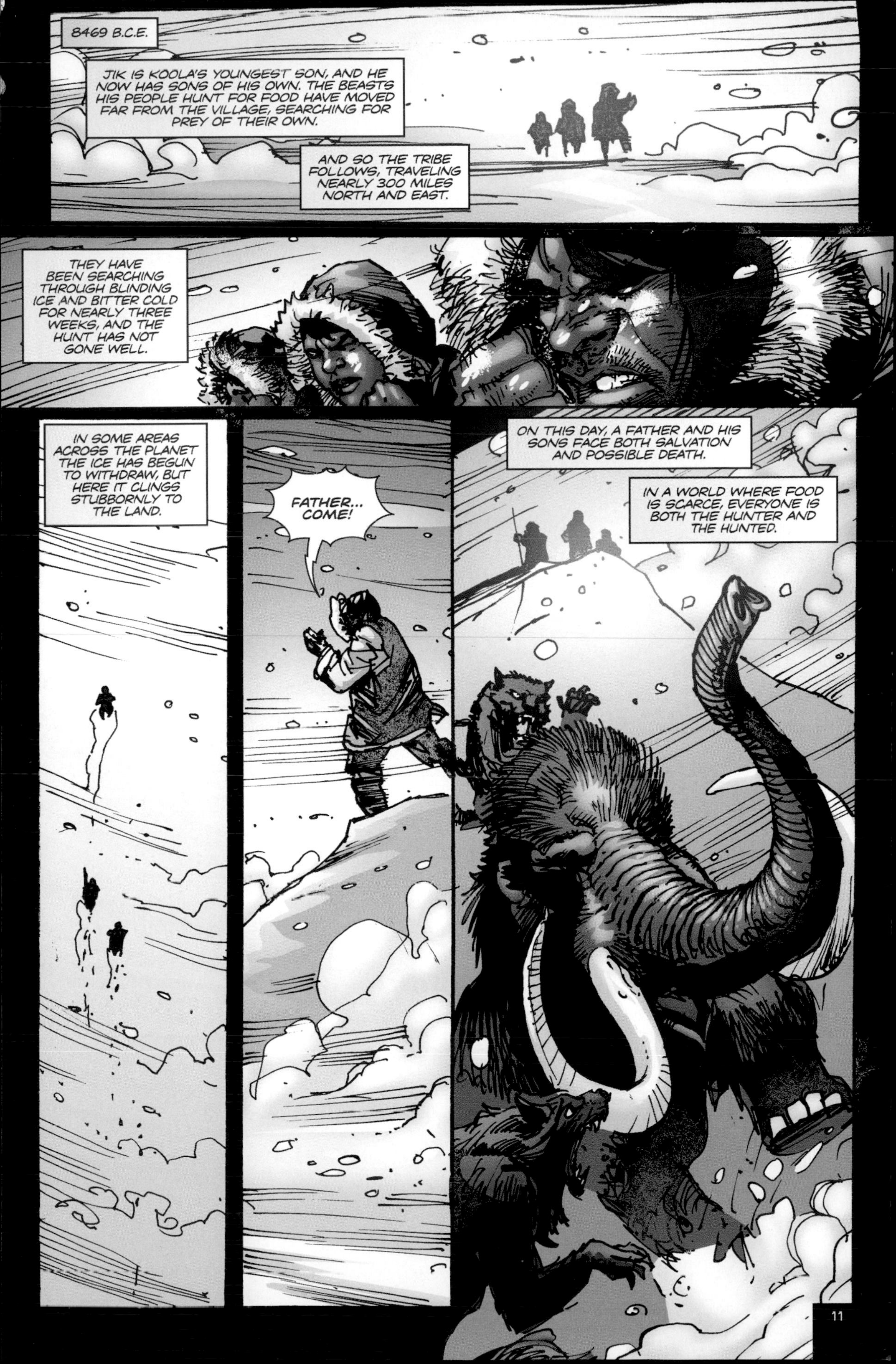
8469 B.C.E.
JIK IS KOOLA'S YOUNGEST SON, AND HE NOW HAS SONS OF HIS OWN. THE BEASTS HIS PEOPLE HUNT FOR FOOD HAVE MOVED FAR FROM THE VILLAGE, SEARCHING FOR PREY OF THEIR OWN.
AND SO THE TRIBE FOLLOWS, TRAVELING NEARLY 300 MILES NORTH AND EAST.
THEY HAVE BEEN SEARCHING THROUGH BLINDING ICE AND BITTER COLD FOR NEARLY THREE WEEKS, AND THE HUNT HAS NOT GONE WELL.
IN SOME AREAS ACROSS THE PLANET THE ICE HAS BEGUN TO WITHDRAW, BUT HERE IT CLINGS STUBBORNLY TO THE LAND.
FATHER... COME!
ON THIS DAY, A FATHER AND HIS SONS FACE BOTH SALVATION AND POSSIBLE DEATH.
IN A WORLD WHERE FOOD IS SCARCE, EVERYONE IS BOTH THE HUNTER AND THE HUNTED.

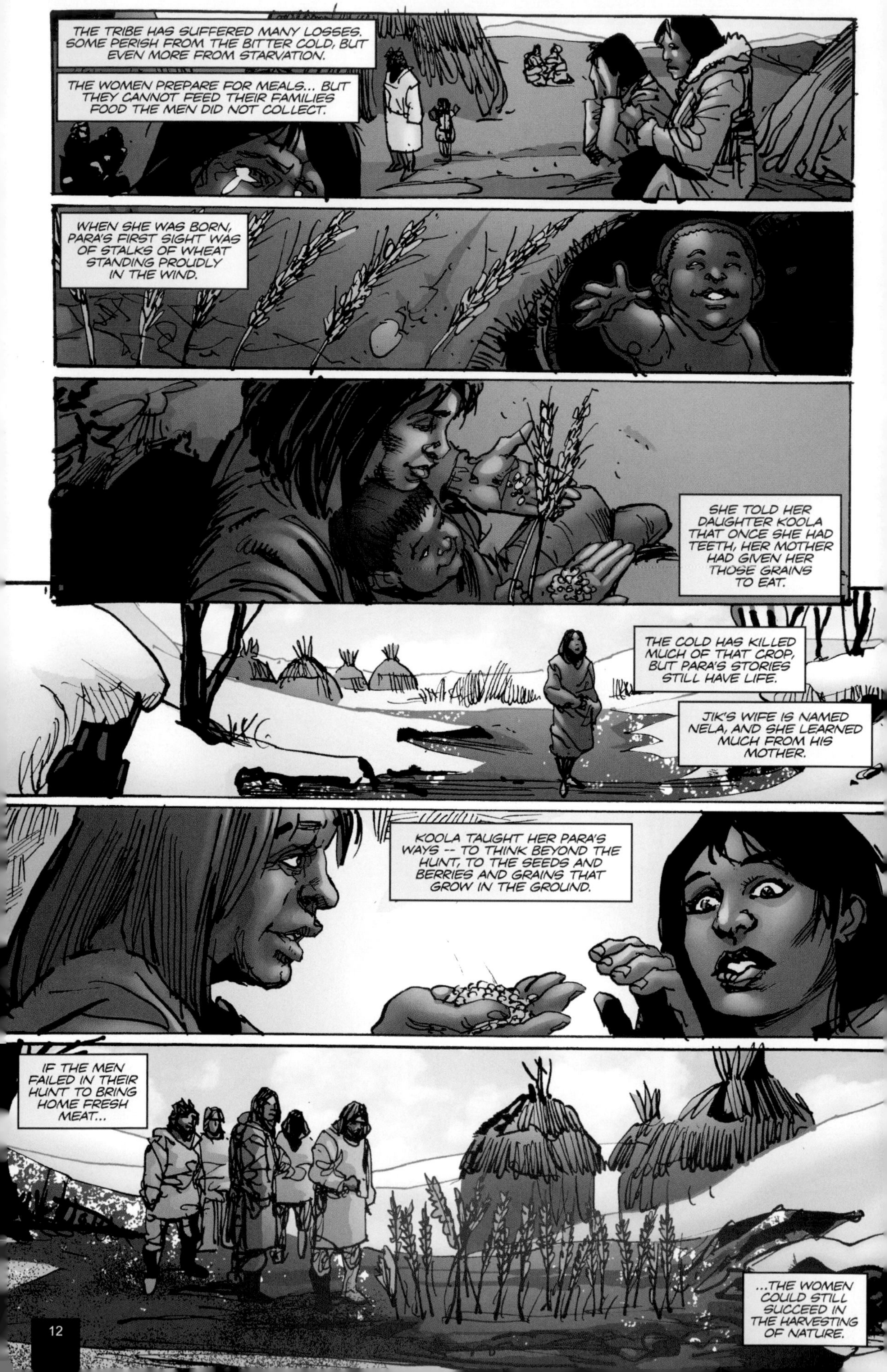
THE TRIBE HAS SUFFERED MANY LOSSES. SOME PERISH FROM THE BITTER COLD, BUT EVEN MORE FROM STARVATION.
THE WOMEN PREPARE FOR MEALS... BUT THEY CANNOT FEED THEIR FAMILIES FOOD THE MEN DID NOT COLLECT.
WHEN SHE WAS BORN, PARA'S FIRST SIGHT WAS OF STALKS OF WHEAT STANDING PROUDLY IN THE WIND.
SHE TOLD HER DAUGHTER KOOLA THAT ONCE SHE HAD TEETH, HER MOTHER HAD GIVEN HER THOSE GRAINS TO EAT.
THE COLD HAS KILLED MUCH OF THAT CROP, BUT PARA'S STORIES STILL HAVE LIFE.
JIK'S WIFE IS NAMED NELA, AND SHE LEARNED MUCH FROM HIS MOTHER.
KOOLA TAUGHT HER PARA'S WAYS -- TO THINK BEYOND THE HUNT, TO THE SEEDS AND BERRIES AND GRAINS THAT GROW IN THE GROUND.
IF THE MEN FAILED IN THEIR HUNT TO BRING HOME FRESH MEAT...
...THE WOMEN COULD STILL SUCCEED IN THE HARVESTING OF NATURE.

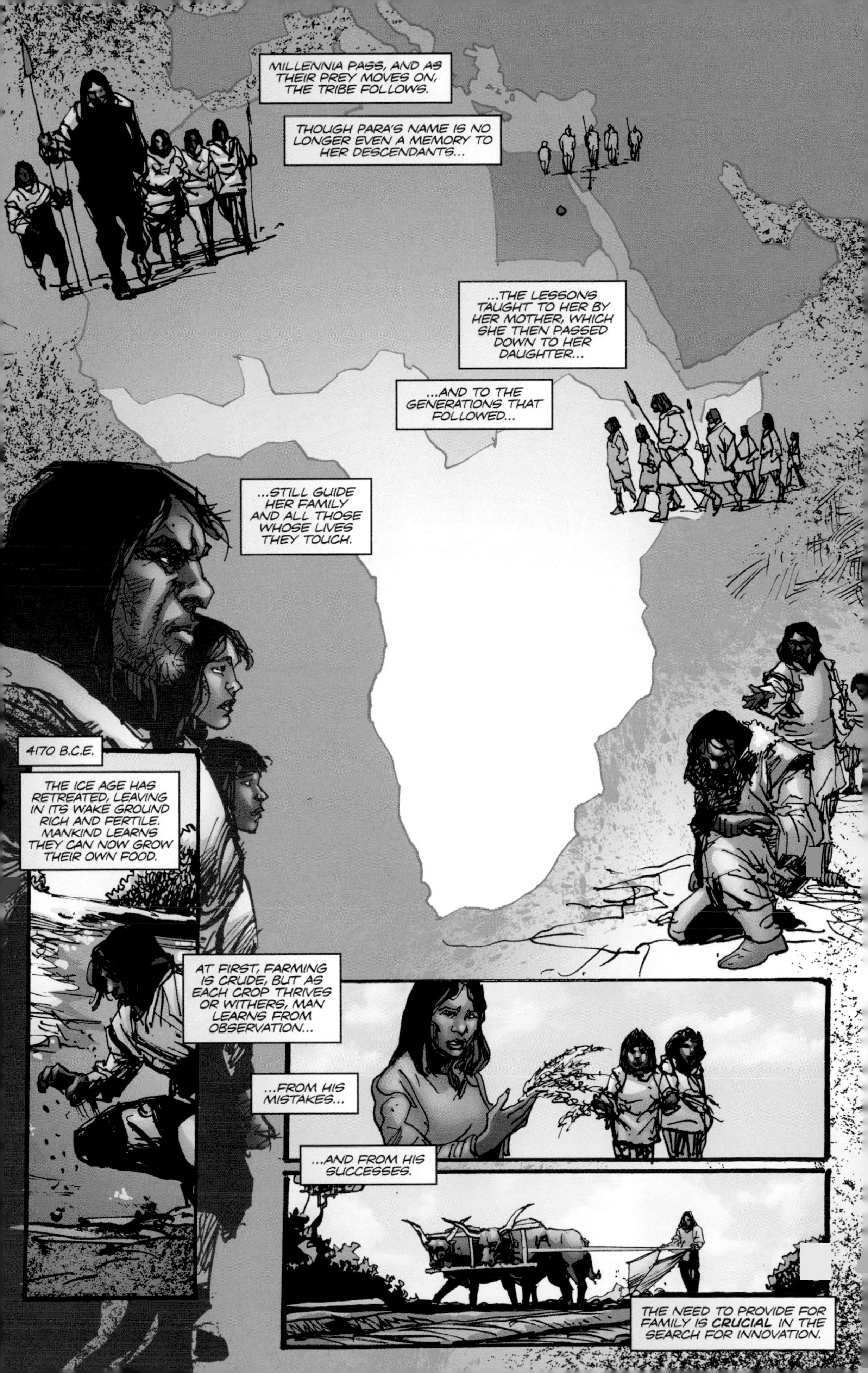
MILLENNIA PASS, AND AS THEIR PREY MOVES ON, THE TRIBE FOLLOWS.
THOUGH PARA'S NAME IS NO LONGER EVEN A MEMORY TO HER DESCENDANTS...
...THE LESSONS TAUGHT TO HER BY HER MOTHER, WHICH SHE THEN PASSED DOWN TO HER DAUGHTER...
...AND TO THE GENERATIONS THAT FOLLOWED...
...STILL GUIDE HER FAMILY AND ALL THOSE WHOSE LIVES THEY TOUCH.
4170 B.C.E.
THE ICE AGE HAS RETREATED, LEAVING IN ITS WAKE GROUND RICH AND FERTILE. MANKIND LEARNS THEY CAN NOW GROW THEIR OWN FOOD.
AT FIRST, FARMING IS CRUDE, BUT AS EACH CROP THRIVES OR WITHERS, MAN LEARNS FROM OBSERVATION...
...FROM HIS MISTAKES...
...AND FROM HIS SUCCESSES.
THE NEED TO PROVIDE FOR FAMILY IS CRUCIAL IN THE SEARCH FOR INNOVATION.

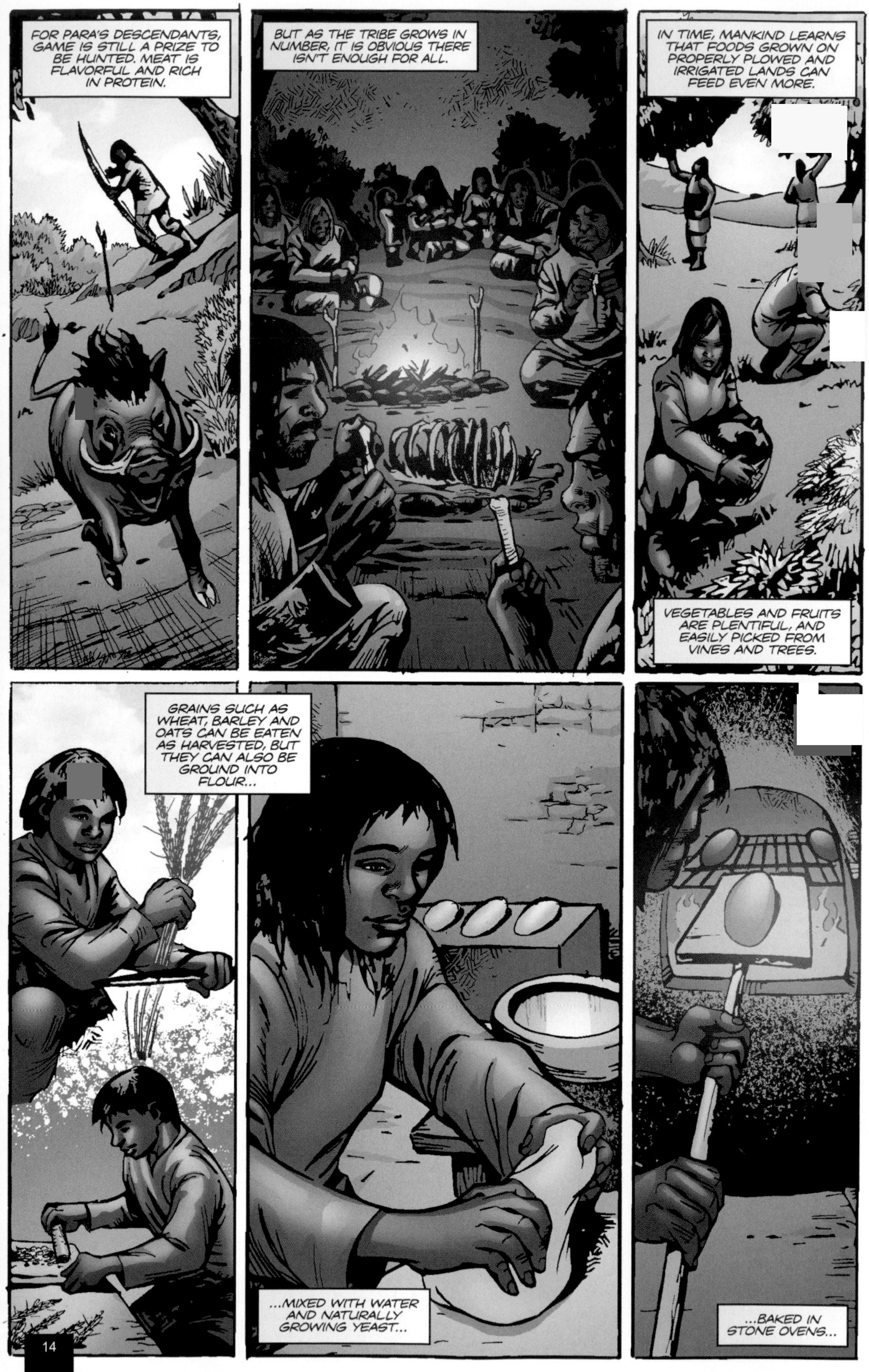
FOR PARA'S DESCENDANTS, GAME IS STILL A PRIZE TO BE HUNTED. MEAT IS FLAVORFUL AND RICH IN PROTEIN.
BUT AS THE TRIBE GROWS IN NUMBER, IT IS OBVIOUS THERE ISN'T ENOUGH FOR ALL.
IN TIME, MANKIND LEARNS THAT FOODS GROWN ON PROPERLY PLOWED AND IRRIGATED LANDS CAN FEED EVEN MORE.
VEGETABLES AND FRUITS ARE PLENTIFUL, AND EASILY PICKED FROM VINES AND TREES.
GRAINS SUCH AS WHEAT, BARLEY AND OATS CAN BE EATEN AS HARVESTED, BUT THEY CAN ALSO BE GROUND INTO FLOUR...
...MIXED WITH WATER AND NATURALLY GROWING YEAST...
...BAKED IN STONE OVENS...

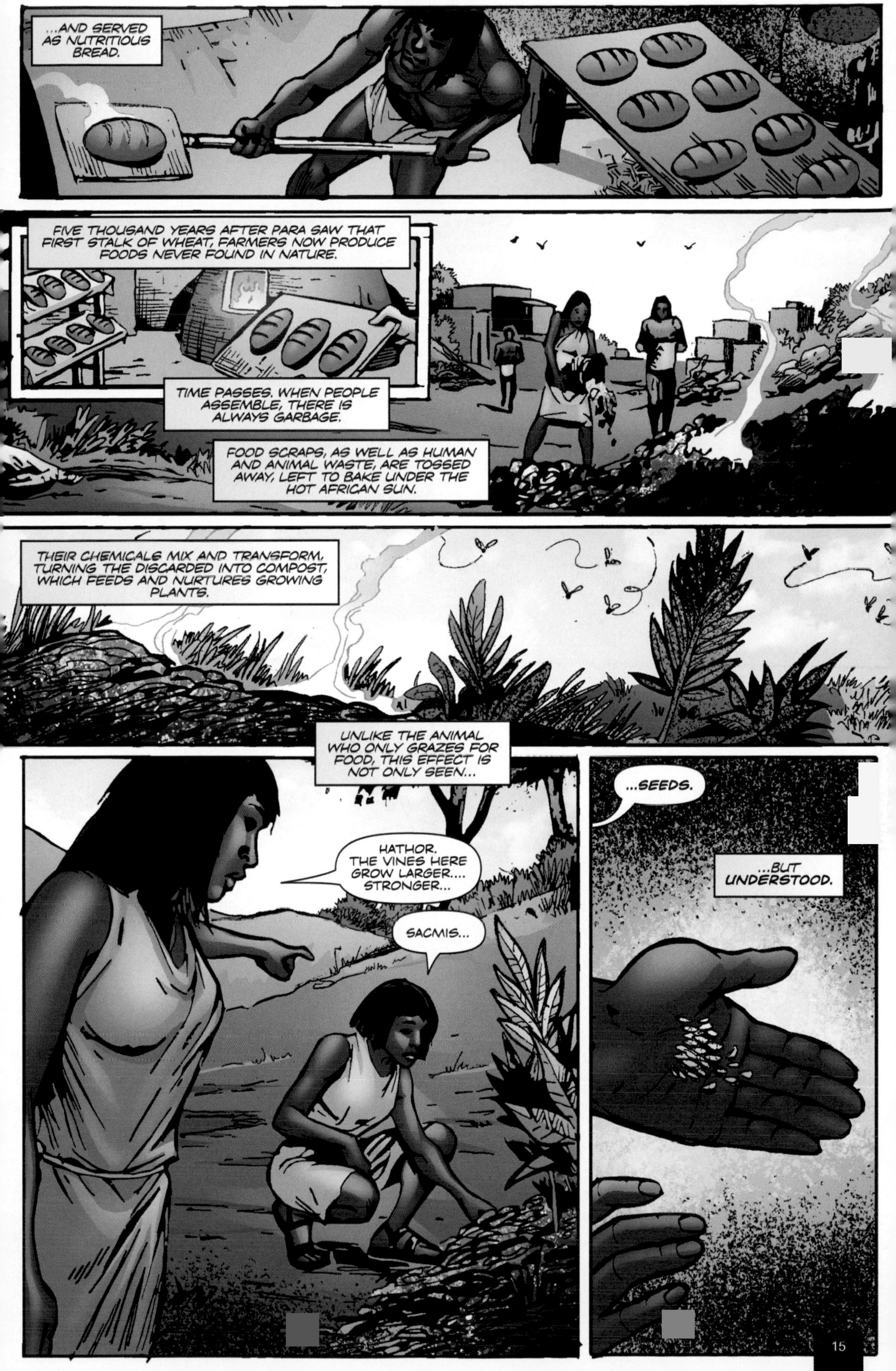
...AND SERVED AS NUTRITIOUS BREAD.
FIVE THOUSAND YEARS AFTER PARA SAW THAT FIRST STALK OF WHEAT, FARMERS NOW PRODUCE FOODS NEVER FOUND IN NATURE.
TIME PASSES. WHEN PEOPLE ASSEMBLE, THERE IS ALWAYS GARBAGE.
FOOD SCRAPS, AS WELL AS HUMAN AND ANIMAL WASTE, ARE TOSSED AWAY, LEFT TO BAKE UNDER THE HOT AFRICAN SUN.
THEIR CHEMICALS MIX AND TRANSFORM, TURNING THE DISCARDED INTO COMPOST, WHICH FEEDS AND NURTURES GROWING PLANTS.
UNLIKE THE ANIMAL WHO ONLY GRAZES FOR FOOD, THIS EFFECT IS NOT ONLY SEEN...
HATHOR. THE VINES HERE GROW LARGER.... STRONGER...
SACMIS...
...SEEDS.
...BUT UNDERSTOOD.

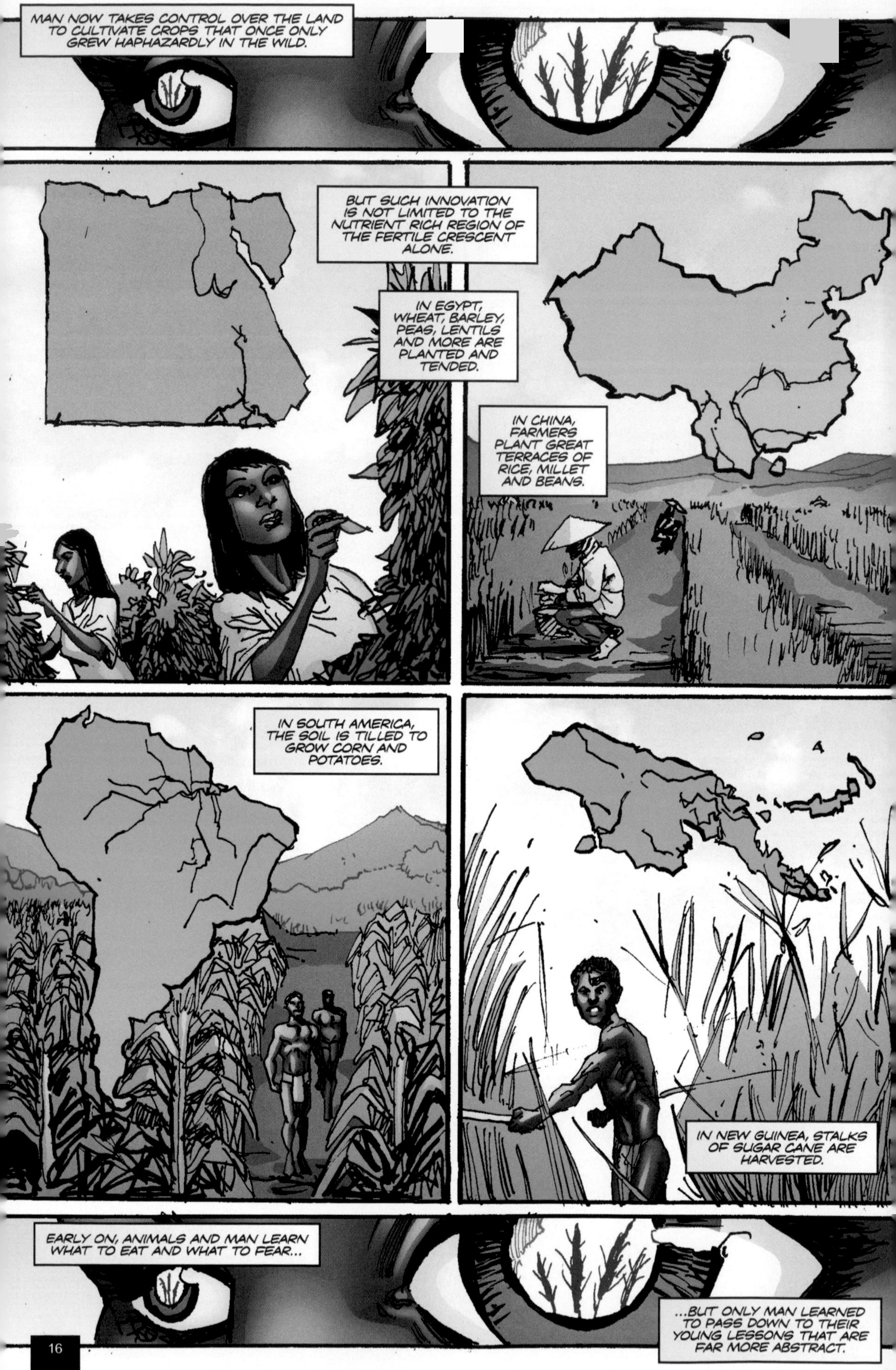
MAN NOW TAKES CONTROL OVER THE LAND TO CULTIVATE CROPS THAT ONCE ONLY GREW HAPHAZARDLY IN THE WILD.
BUT SUCH INNOVATION IS NOT LIMITED TO THE NUTRIENT RICH REGION OF THE FERTILE CRESCENT ALONE.
IN EGYPT, WHEAT, BARLEY, PEAS, LENTILS AND MORE ARE PLANTED AND TENDED.
IN CHINA, FARMERS PLANT GREAT TERRACES OF RICE, MILLET AND BEANS.
IN SOUTH AMERICA, THE SOIL IS TILLED TO GROW CORN AND POTATOES.
IN NEW GUINEA, STALKS OF SUGAR CANE ARE HARVESTED.
EARLY ON, ANIMALS AND MAN LEARN WHAT TO EAT AND WHAT TO FEAR...
...BUT ONLY MAN LEARNED TO PASS DOWN TO THEIR YOUNG LESSONS THAT ARE FAR MORE ABSTRACT.

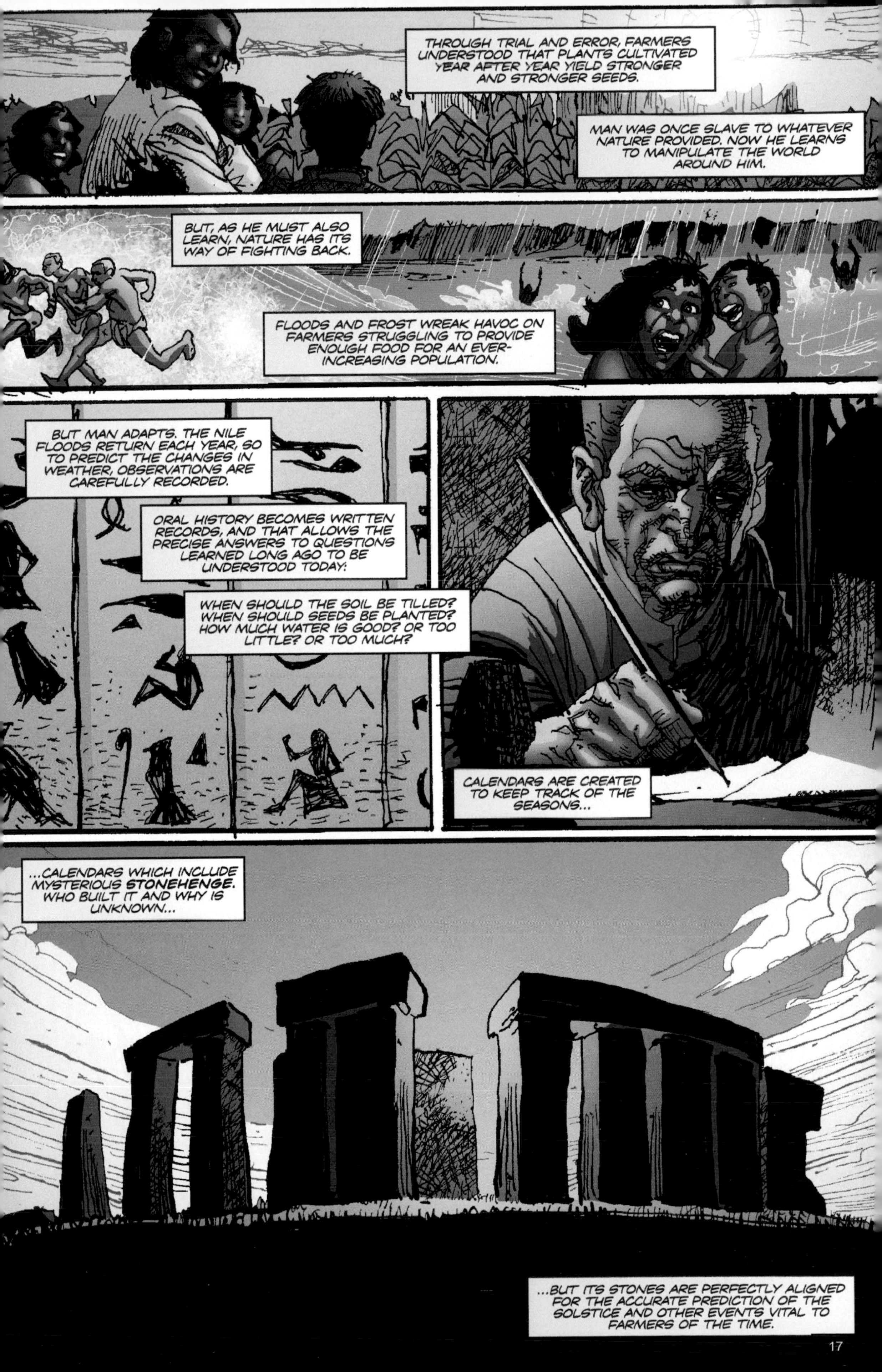
THROUGH TRIAL AND ERROR, FARMERS UNDERSTOOD THAT PLANTS CULTIVATED YEAR AFTER YEAR YIELD STRONGER AND STRONGER SEEDS.
MAN WAS ONCE SLAVE TO WHATEVER NATURE PROVIDED. NOW HE LEARNS TO MANIPULATE THE WORLD AROUND HIM.
BUT, AS HE MUST ALSO LEARN, NATURE HAS ITS WAY OF FIGHTING BACK.
FLOODS AND FROST WREAK HAVOC ON FARMERS STRUGGLING TO PROVIDE ENOUGH FOOD FOR AN EVER-INCREASING POPULATION.
BUT MAN ADAPTS. THE NILE FLOODS RETURN EACH YEAR, SO TO PREDICT THE CHANGES IN WEATHER, OBSERVATIONS ARE CAREFULLY RECORDED.
ORAL HISTORY BECOMES WRITTEN RECORDS, AND THAT ALLOWS THE PRECISE ANSWERS TO QUESTIONS LEARNED LONG AGO TO BE UNDERSTOOD TODAY:
WHEN SHOULD THE SOIL BE TILLED? WHEN SHOULD SEEDS BE PLANTED? HOW MUCH WATER IS GOOD? OR TOO LITTLE? OR TOO MUCH?
CALENDARS ARE CREATED TO KEEP TRACK OF THE SEASONS...
...CALENDARS WHICH INCLUDE MYSTERIOUS STONEHENGE. WHO BUILT IT AND WHY IS UNKNOWN...
...BUT ITS STONES ARE PERFECTLY ALIGNED FOR THE ACCURATE PREDICTION OF THE SOLSTICE AND OTHER EVENTS VITAL TO FARMERS OF THE TIME.

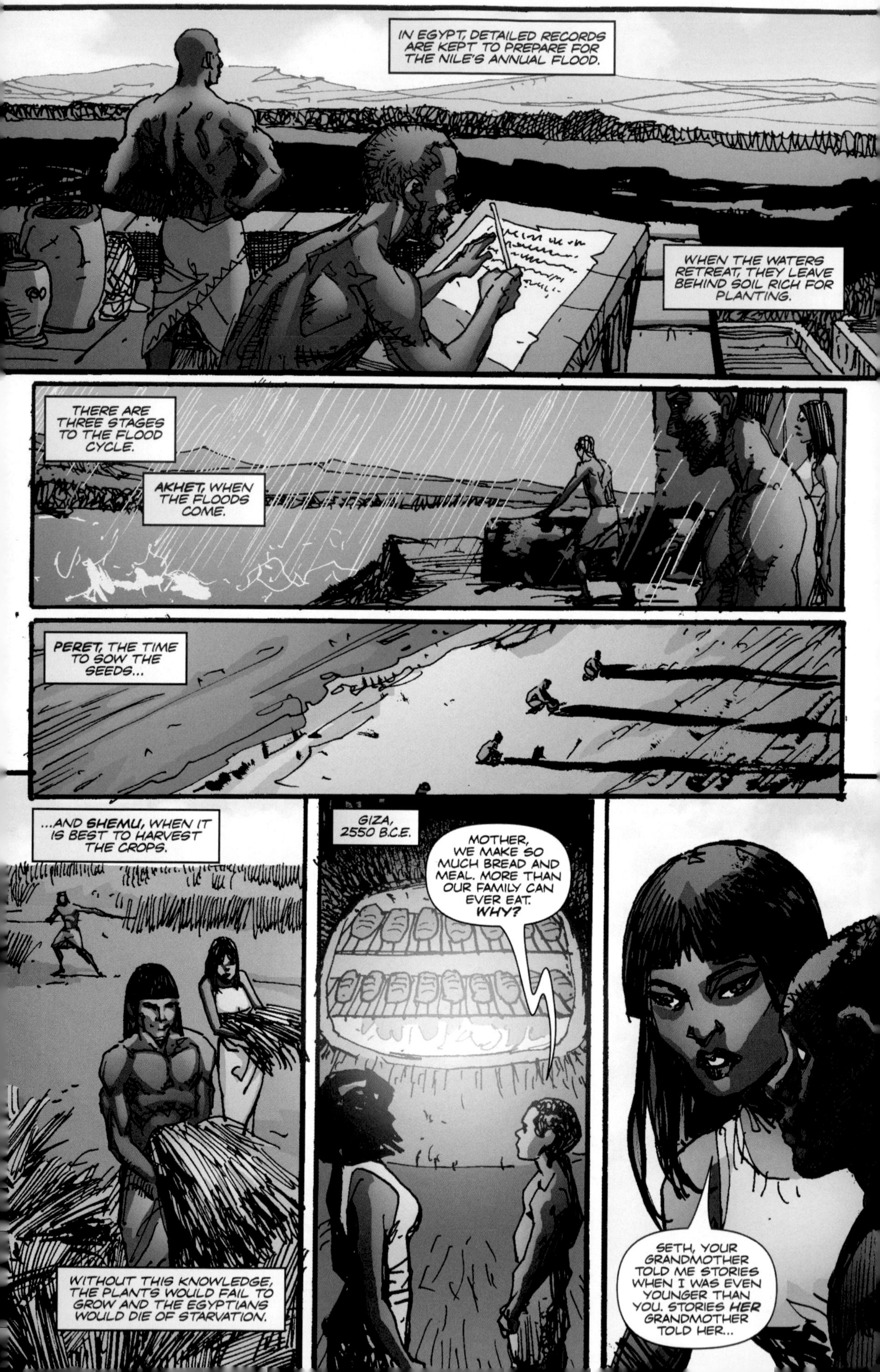
IN EGYPT, DETAILED RECORDS ARE KEPT TO PREPARE FOR THE NILE'S ANNUAL FLOOD.
WHEN THE WATERS RETREAT, THEY LEAVE BEHIND SOIL RICH FOR PLANTING.
THERE ARE THREE STAGES TO THE FLOOD CYCLE.
AKHET, WHEN THE FLOODS COME.
PERET, THE TIME TO SOW THE SEEDS...
...AND SHEMU, WHEN IT IS BEST TO HARVEST THE CROPS.
WITHOUT THIS KNOWLEDGE, THE PLANTS WOULD FAIL TO GROW AND THE EGYPTIANS WOULD DIE OF STARVATION.
GIZA, 2550 B.C.E.
MOTHER, WE MAKE SO MUCH BREAD AND MEAL. MORE THAN OUR FAMILY CAN EVER EAT. WHY?
SETH, YOUR GRANDMOTHER TOLD ME STORIES WHEN I WAS EVEN YOUNGER THAN YOU. STORIES HER GRANDMOTHER TOLD HER...

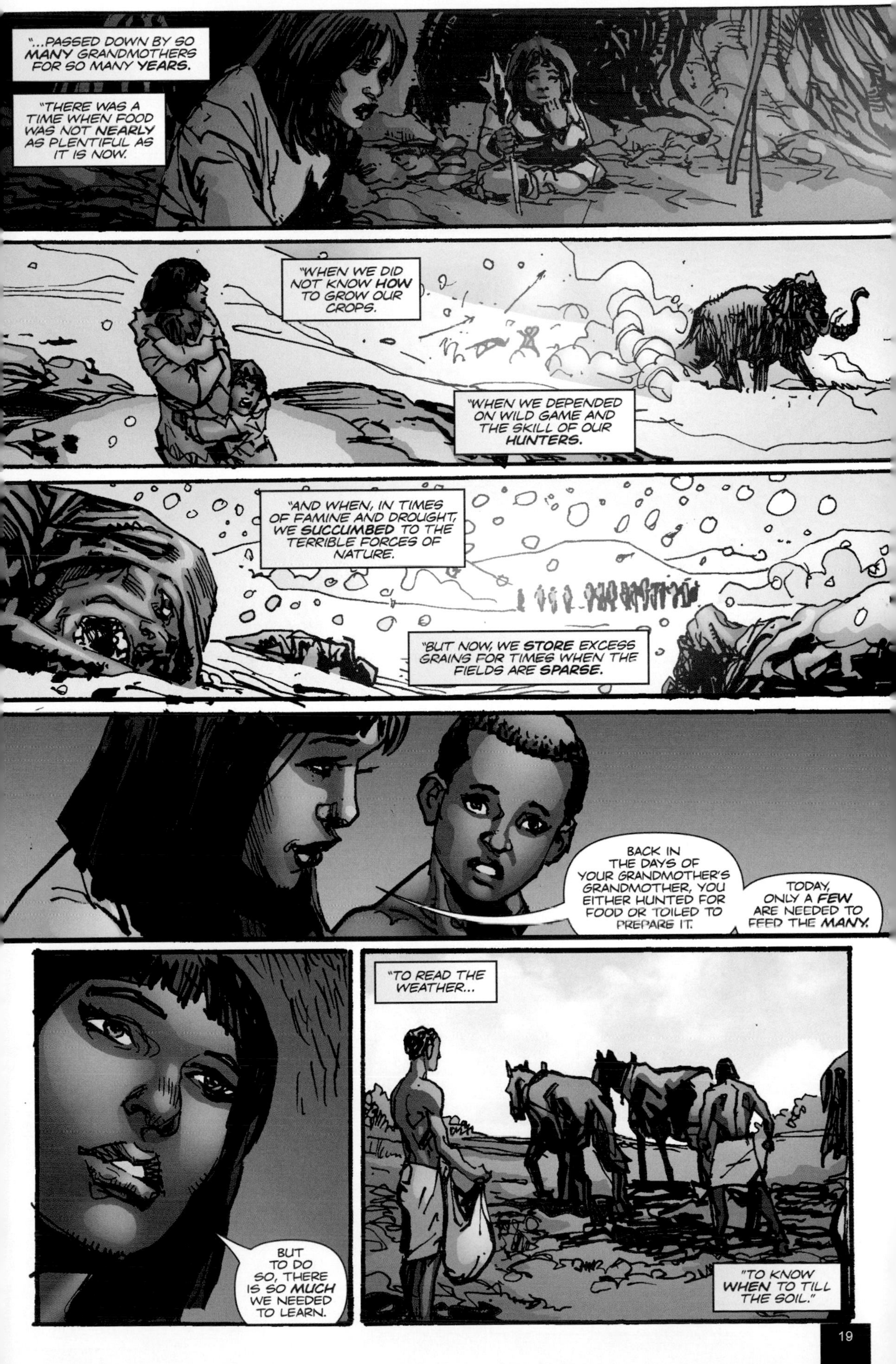
"...PASSED DOWN BY SO MANY GRANDMOTHERS FOR SO MANY YEARS.
"THERE WAS A TIME WHEN FOOD WAS NOT NEARLY AS PLENTIFUL AS IT IS NOW.
"WHEN WE DID NOT KNOW HOW TO GROW OUR CROPS.
"WHEN WE DEPENDED ON WILD GAME AND THE SKILL OF OUR HUNTERS.
"AND WHEN, IN TIMES OF FAMINE AND DROUGHT, WE SUCCUMBED TO THE TERRIBLE FORCES OF NATURE.
"BUT NOW, WE STORE EXCESS GRAINS FOR TIMES WHEN THE FIELDS ARE SPARSE.
BACK IN THE DAYS OF YOUR GRANDMOTHER'S GRANDMOTHER, YOU EITHER HUNTED FOR FOOD OR TOILED TO PREPARE IT.
TODAY, ONLY A FEW ARE NEEDED TO FEED THE MANY.
BUT TO DO SO, THERE IS SO MUCH WE NEEDED TO LEARN.
"TO READ THE WEATHER...
"TO KNOW WHEN TO TILL THE SOIL."

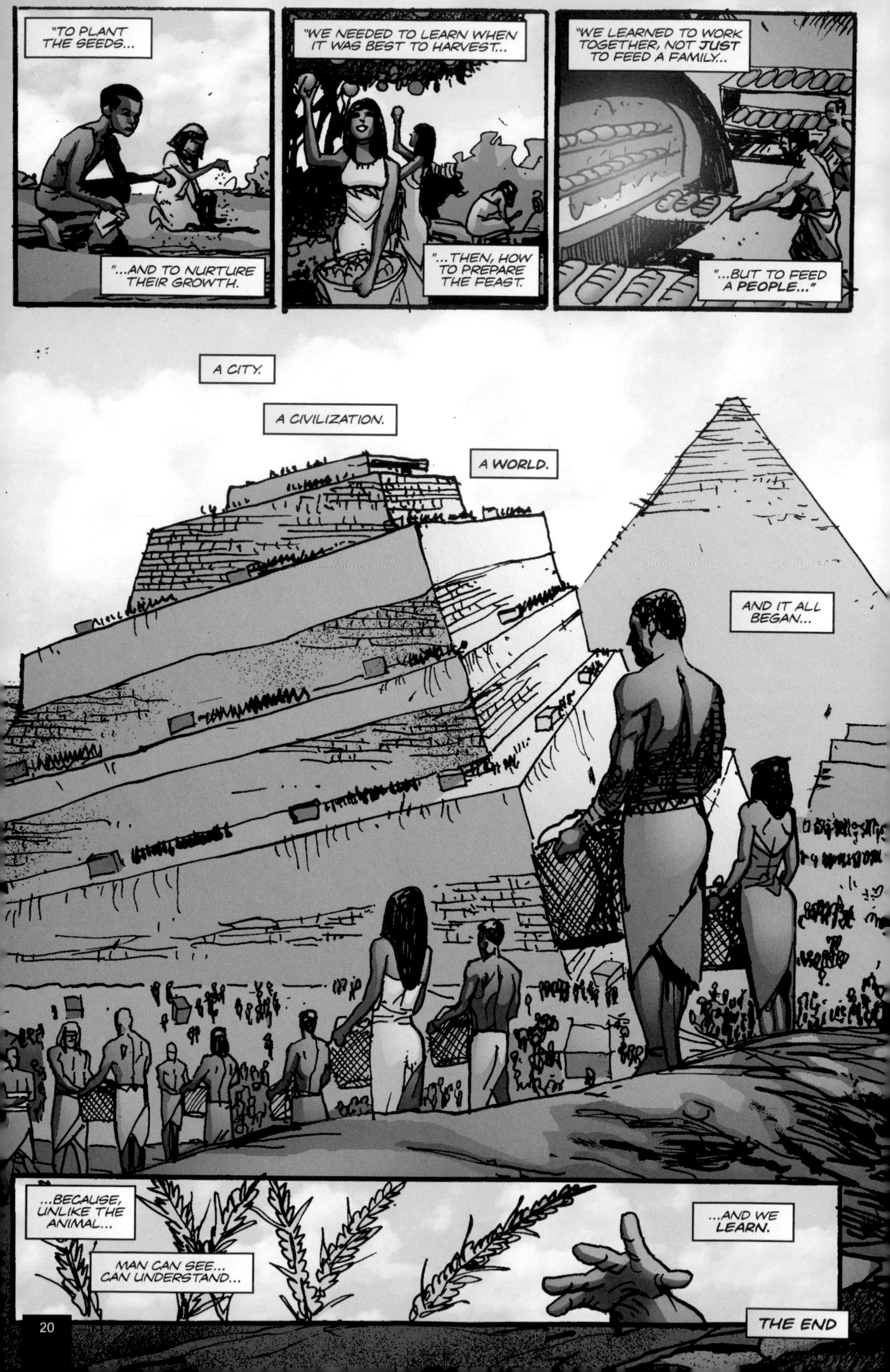
"TO PLANT THE SEEDS...
"...AND TO NURTURE THEIR GROWTH.
"WE NEEDED TO LEARN WHEN IT WAS BEST TO HARVEST...
"...THEN, HOW TO PREPARE THE FEAST.
"WE LEARNED TO WORK TOGETHER, NOT JUST TO FEED A FAMILY...
"...BUT TO FEED A PEOPLE..."
A CITY.
A CIVILIZATION.
A WORLD.
AND IT ALL BEGAN...
...BECAUSE, UNLIKE THE ANIMAL...
MAN CAN SEE... CAN UNDERSTAND...
...AND WE LEARN.
THE END

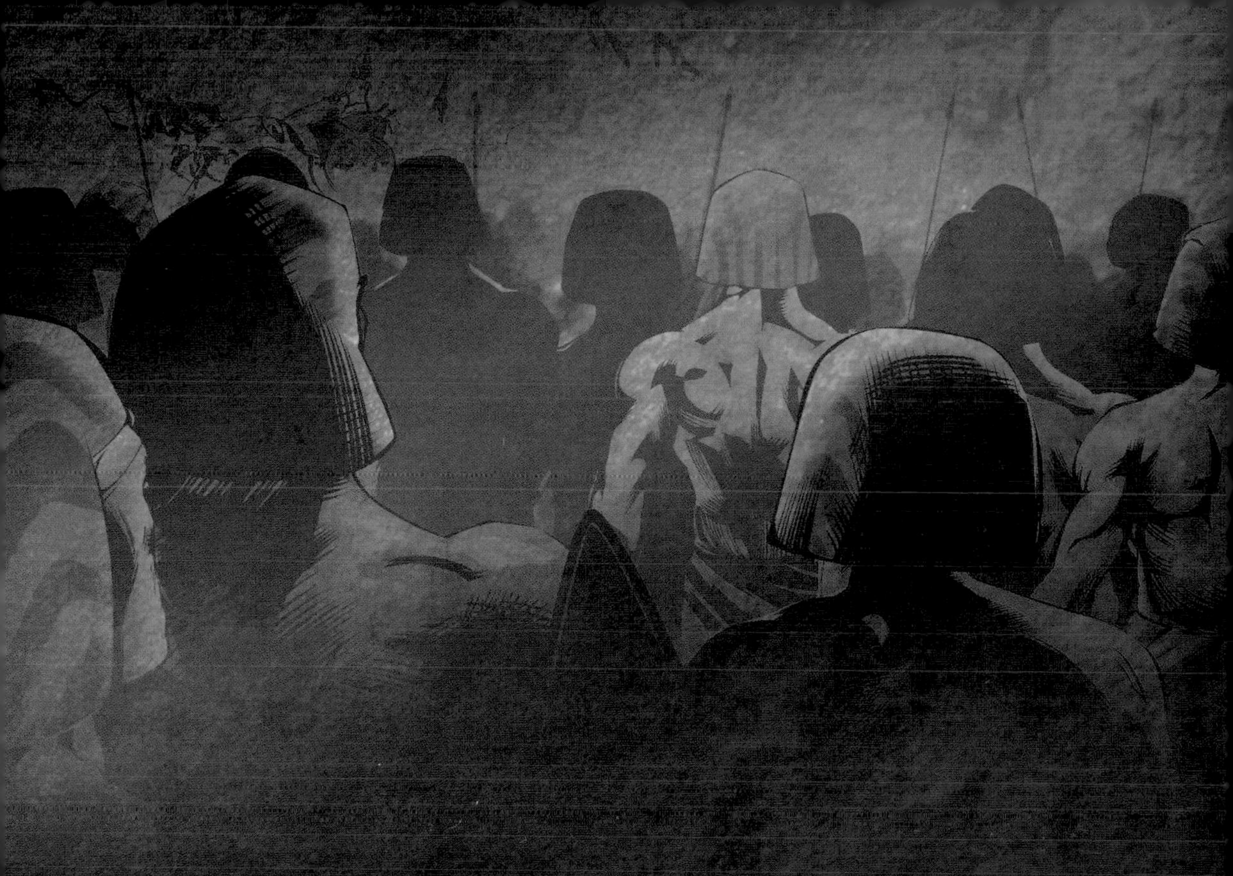

PYRAMID OF MAN

WRITTEN BY
NATHAN EDMONDSON

ART BY
DENNIS CALERO

LETTERS BY
JIM CAMPBELL

A YOUNG BRONZESMITH SEES THE EVOLUTION OF HIS TRADE'S TOOLS AT THE WORLD'S FIRST RECORDED BATTLE

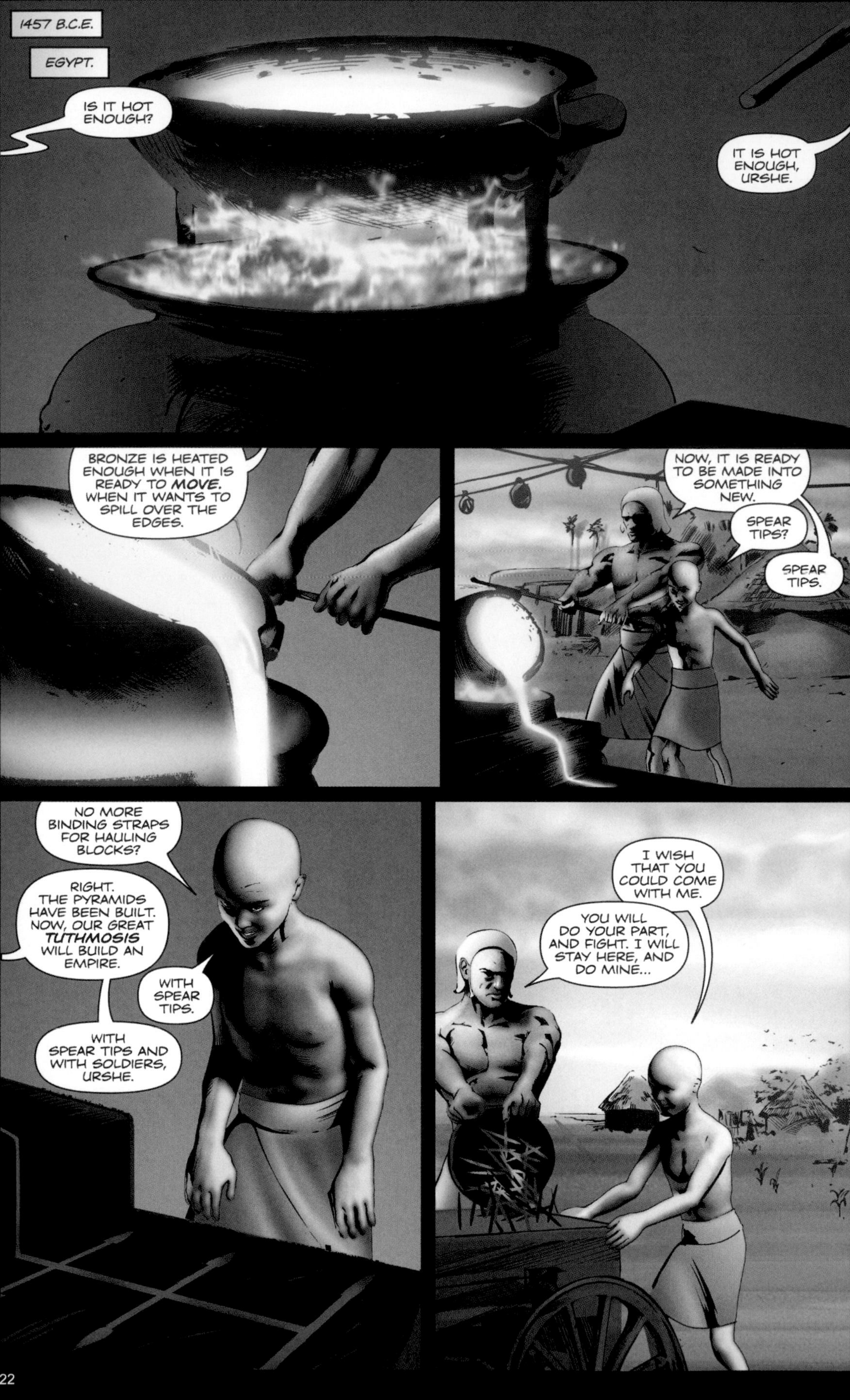
1457 B.C.E.
EGYPT.
IS IT HOT ENOUGH?
IT IS HOT ENOUGH, URSHE.
BRONZE IS HEATED ENOUGH WHEN IT IS READY TO MOVE. WHEN IT WANTS TO SPILL OVER THE EDGES.
NOW, IT IS READY TO BE MADE INTO SOMETHING NEW.
SPEAR TIPS?
SPEAR TIPS.
NO MORE BINDING STRAPS FOR HAULING BLOCKS?
RIGHT. THE PYRAMIDS HAVE BEEN BUILT. NOW, OUR GREAT TUTHMOSIS WILL BUILD AN EMPIRE.
WITH SPEAR TIPS.
WITH SPEAR TIPS AND WITH SOLDIERS, URSHE.
I WISH THAT YOU COULD COME WITH ME.
YOU WILL DO YOUR PART, AND FIGHT. I WILL STAY HERE, AND DO MINE...

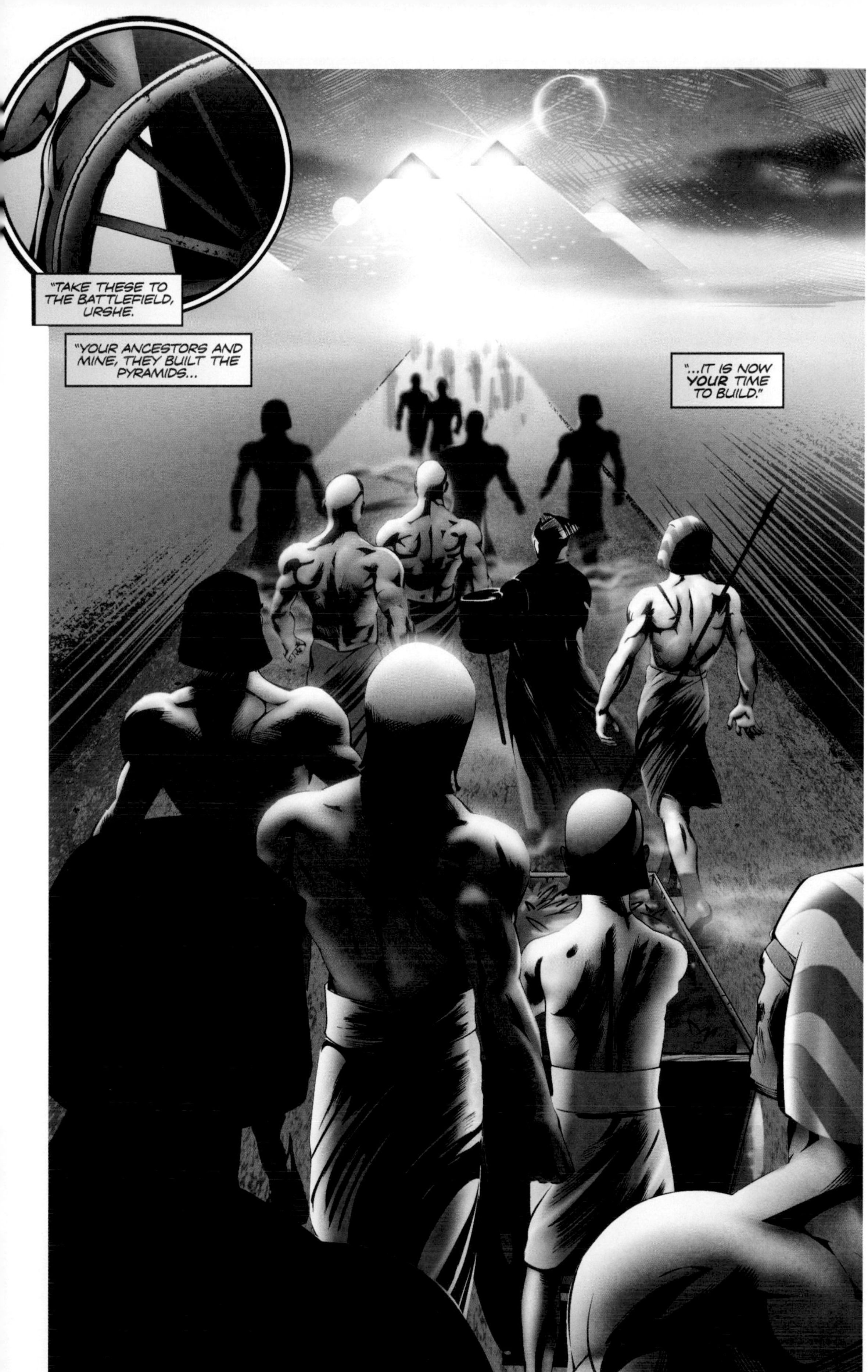
"TAKE THESE TO THE BATTLEFIELD, URSHE.
"YOUR ANCESTORS AND MINE, THEY BUILT THE PYRAMIDS...
"...IT IS NOW YOUR TIME TO BUILD."

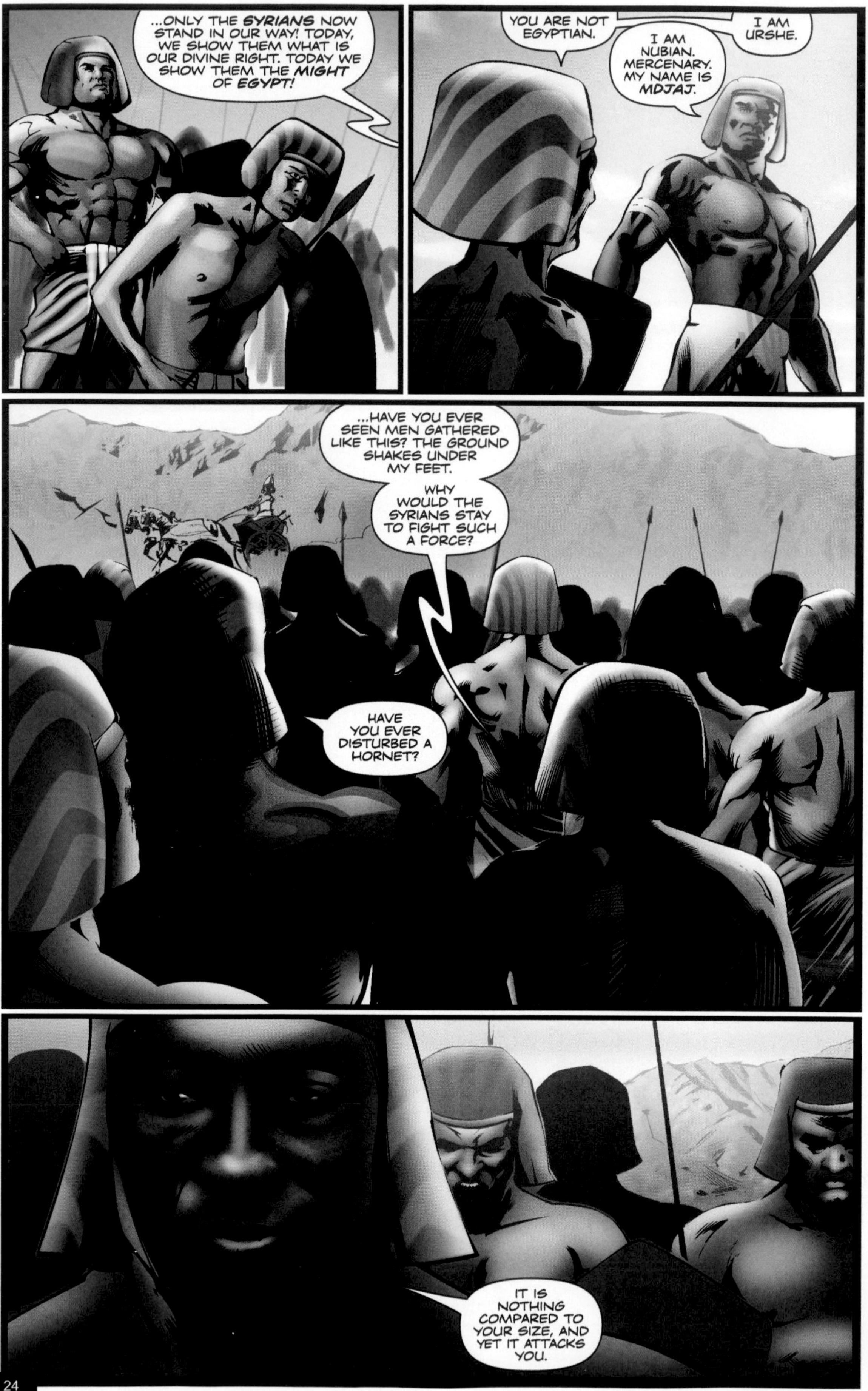
...ONLY THE SYRIANS NOW STAND IN OUR WAY! TODAY, WE SHOW THEM WHAT IS OUR DIVINE RIGHT. TODAY WE SHOW THEM THE MIGHT OF EGYPT!
YOU ARE NOT EGYPTIAN.
I AM NUBIAN. MERCENARY. MY NAME IS MDJAJ.
I AM URSHE.
...HAVE YOU EVER SEEN MEN GATHERED LIKE THIS? THE GROUND SHAKES UNDER MY FEET.
WHY WOULD THE SYRIANS STAY TO FIGHT SUCH A FORCE?
HAVE YOU EVER DISTURBED A HORNET?
IT IS NOTHING COMPARED TO YOUR SIZE, AND YET IT ATTACKS YOU.

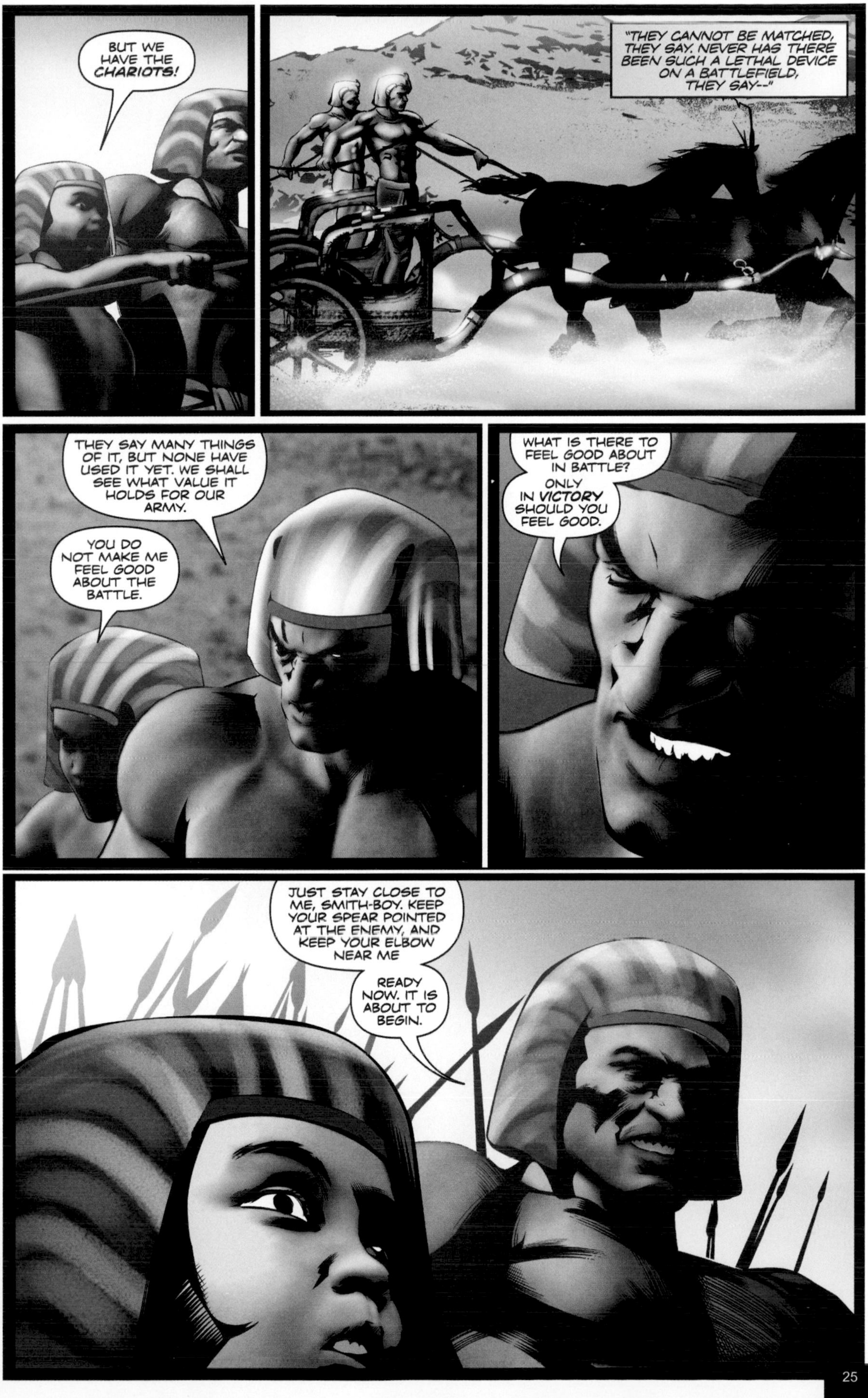
BUT WE HAVE THE CHARIOTS!
"THEY CANNOT BE MATCHED, THEY SAY. NEVER HAS THERE BEEN SUCH A LETHAL DEVICE ON A BATTLEFIELD, THEY SAY--"
THEY SAY MANY THINGS OF IT, BUT NONE HAVE USED IT YET. WE SHALL SEE WHAT VALUE IT HOLDS FOR OUR ARMY.
YOU DO NOT MAKE ME FEEL GOOD ABOUT THE BATTLE.
WHAT IS THERE TO FEEL GOOD ABOUT IN BATTLE?
ONLY IN VICTORY SHOULD YOU FEEL GOOD.
JUST STAY CLOSE TO ME, SMITH-BOY. KEEP YOUR SPEAR POINTED AT THE ENEMY, AND KEEP YOUR ELBOW NEAR ME
READY NOW. IT IS ABOUT TO BEGIN.

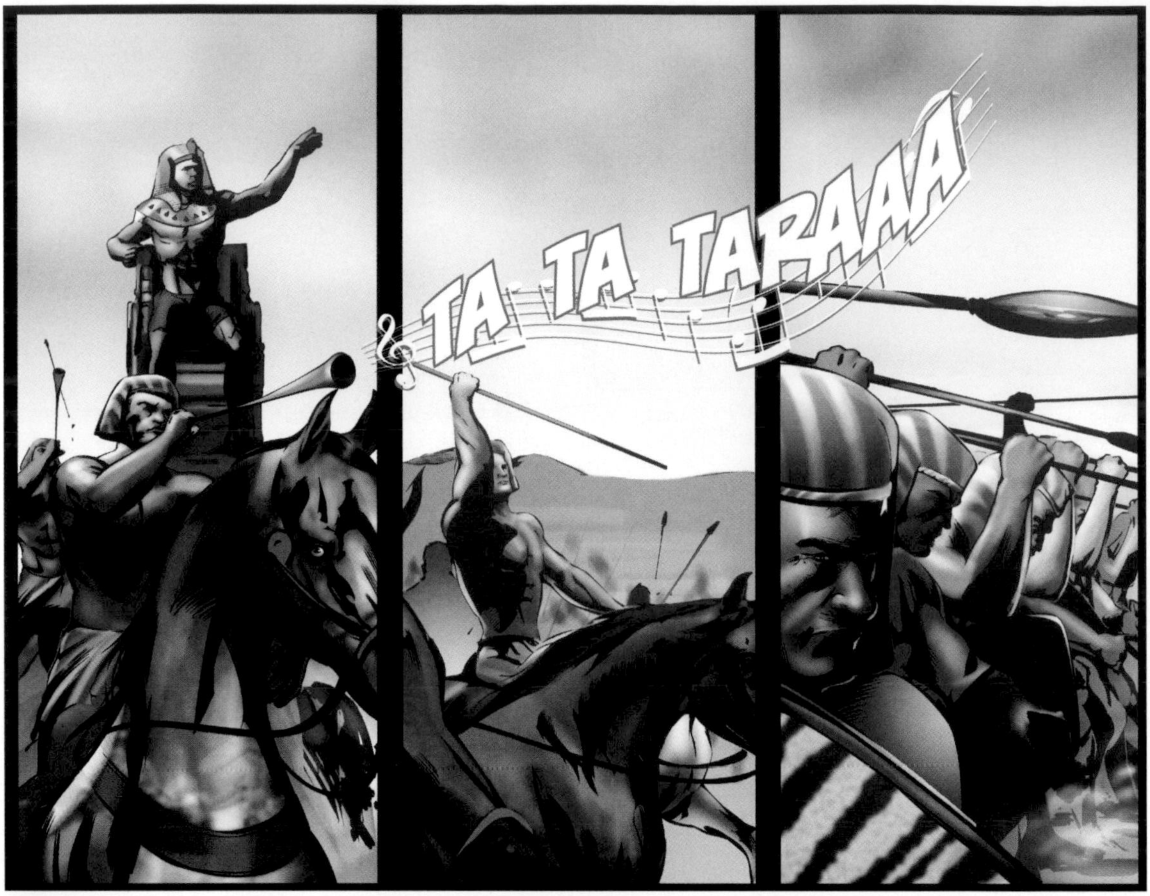
TA TA TARAAA

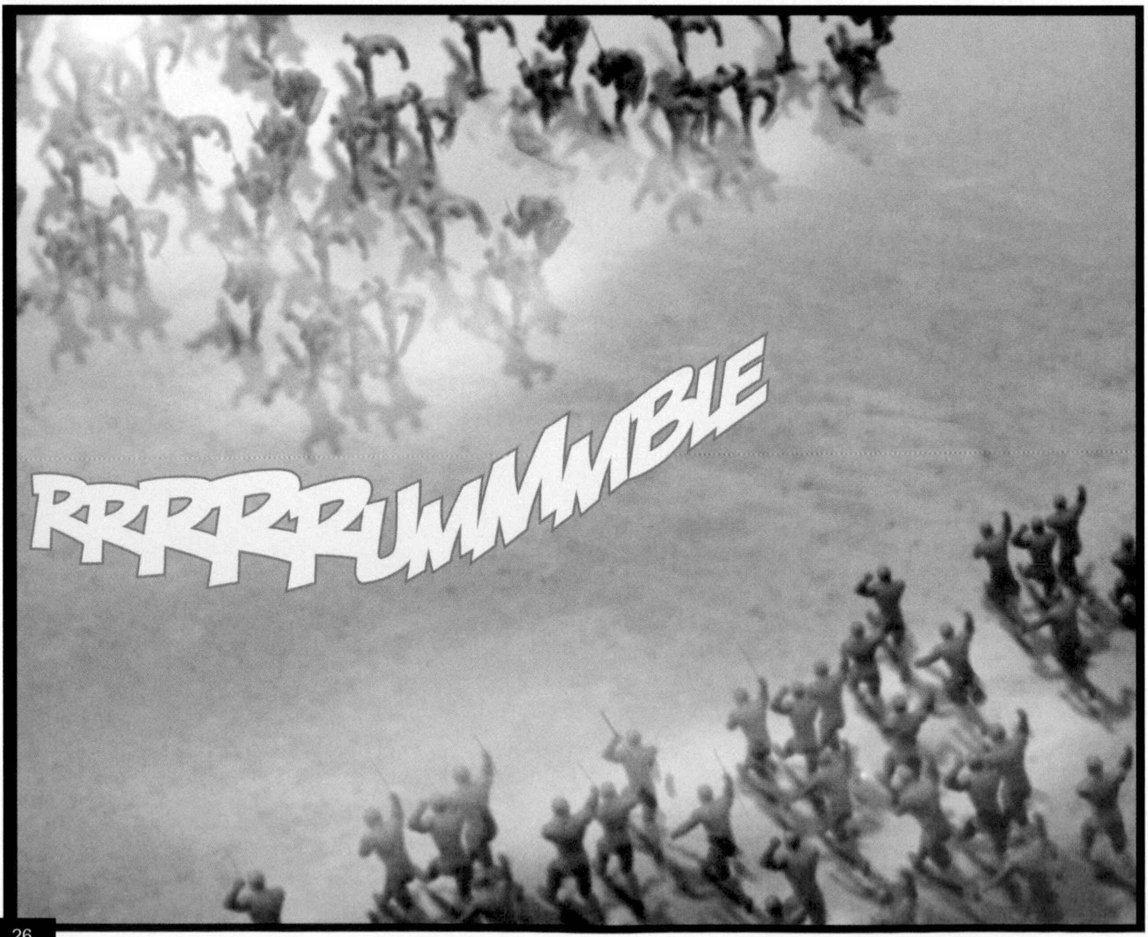
RRRRRUMMMBLE

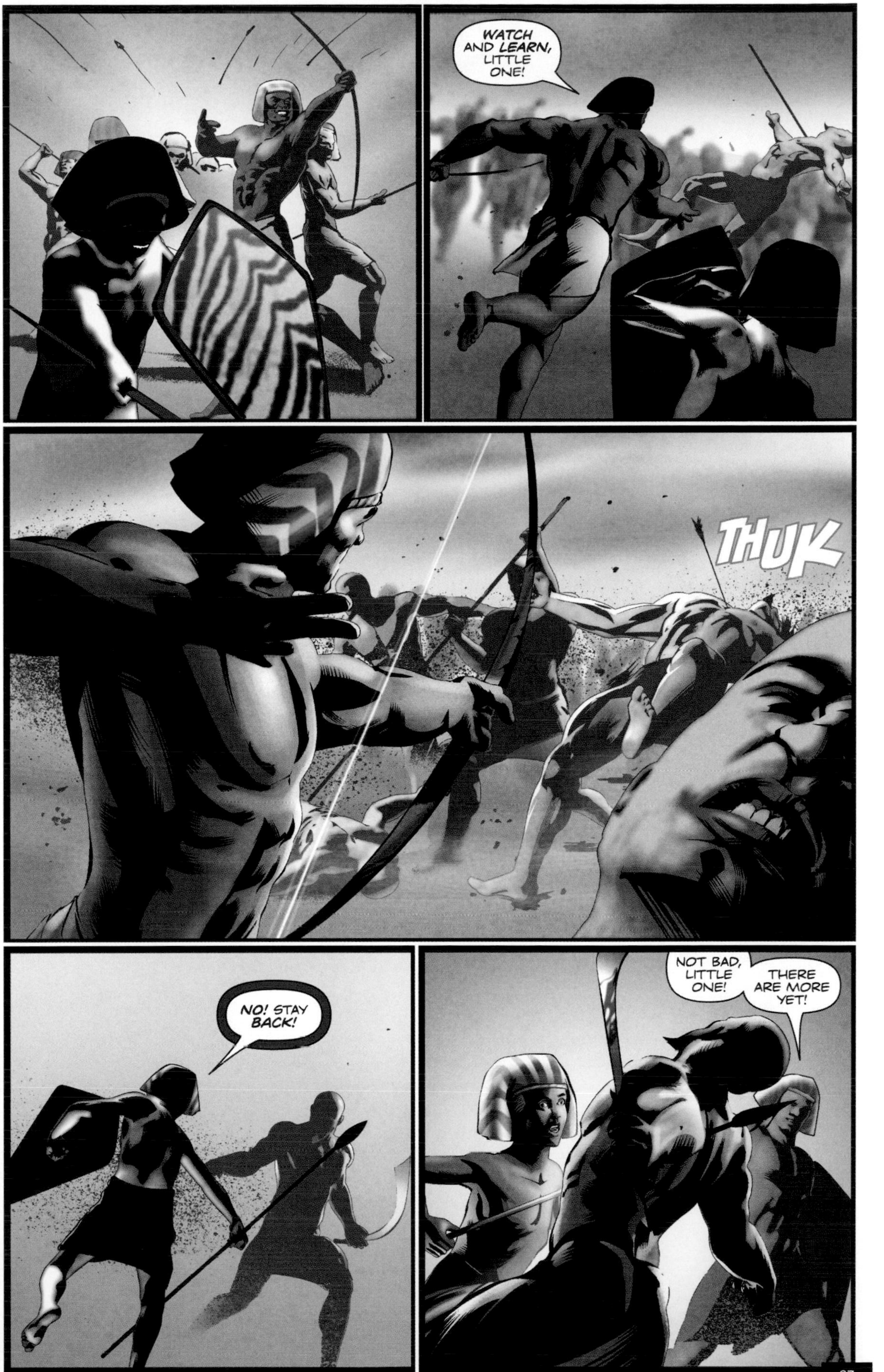

WATCH AND LEARN, LITTLE ONE!
THUK
NO! STAY BACK!
NOT BAD, LITTLE ONE!
THERE ARE MORE YET!

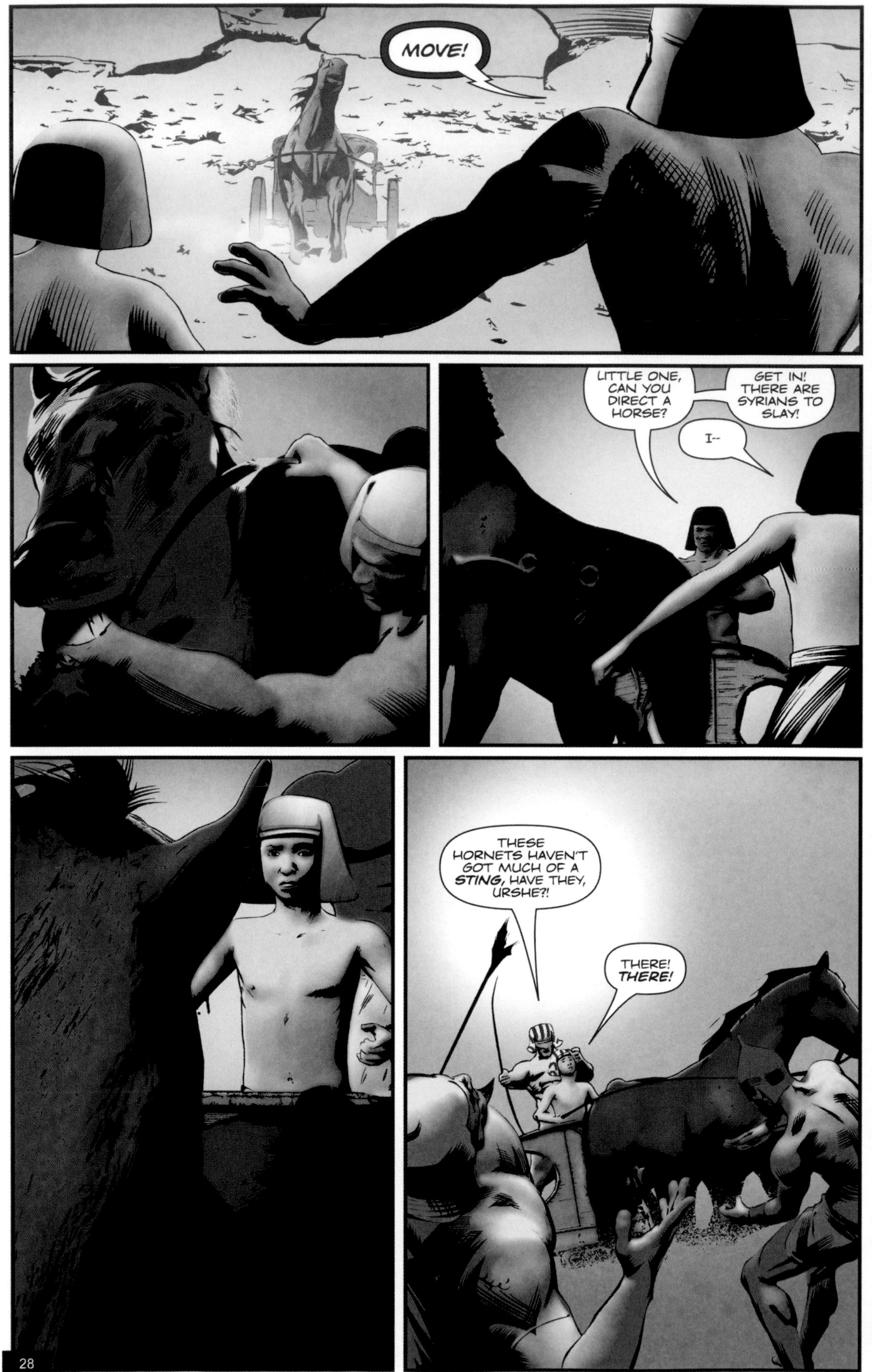
MOVE!
LITTLE ONE, CAN YOU DIRECT A HORSE?
GET IN! THERE ARE SYRIANS TO SLAY!
I--
THESE HORNETS HAVEN'T GOT MUCH OF A STING, HAVE THEY, URSHE?!
THERE! THERE!

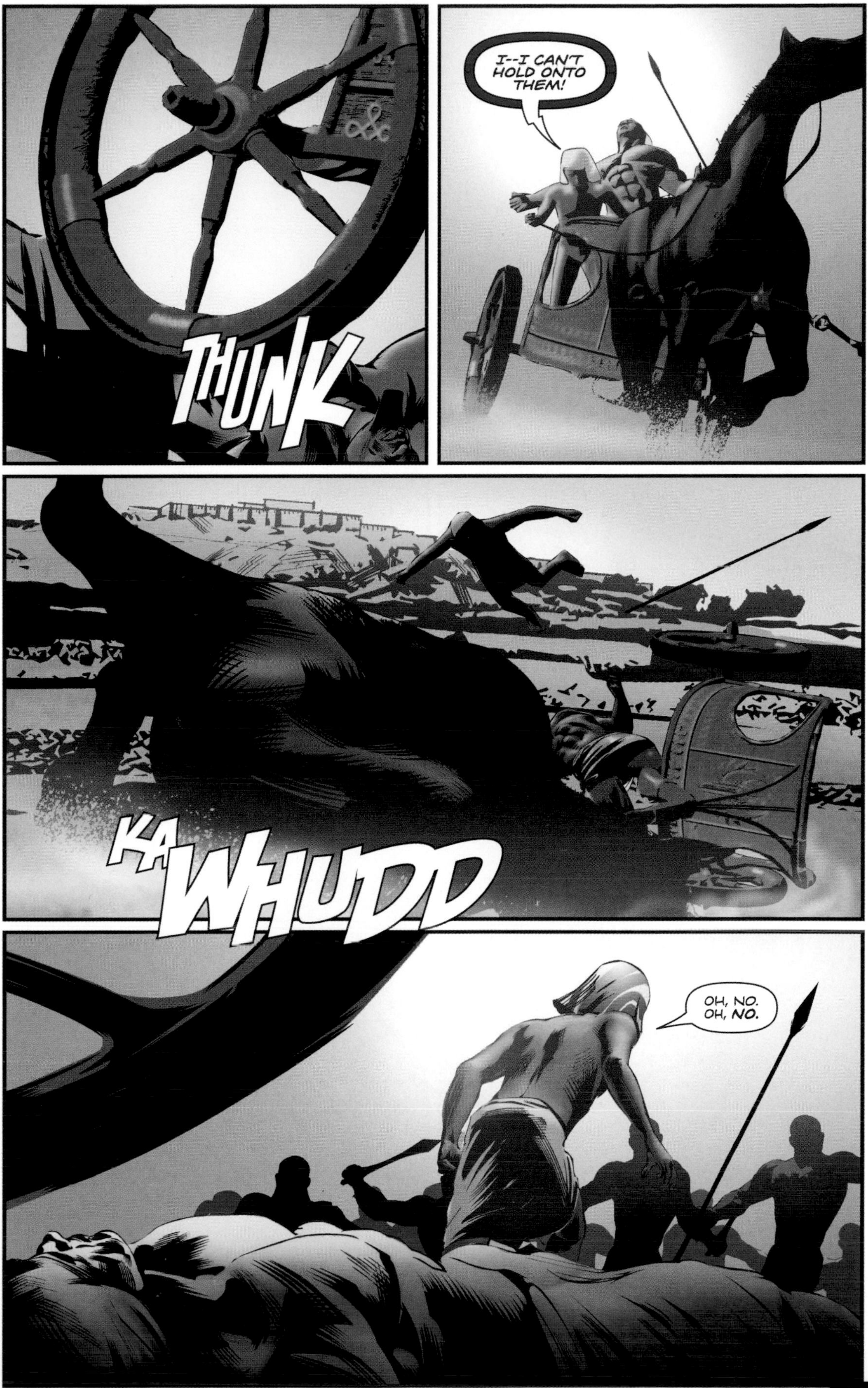
THUNK
I--I CAN'T HOLD ONTO THEM!
KA WHUDD
OH, NO. OH, **NO.**

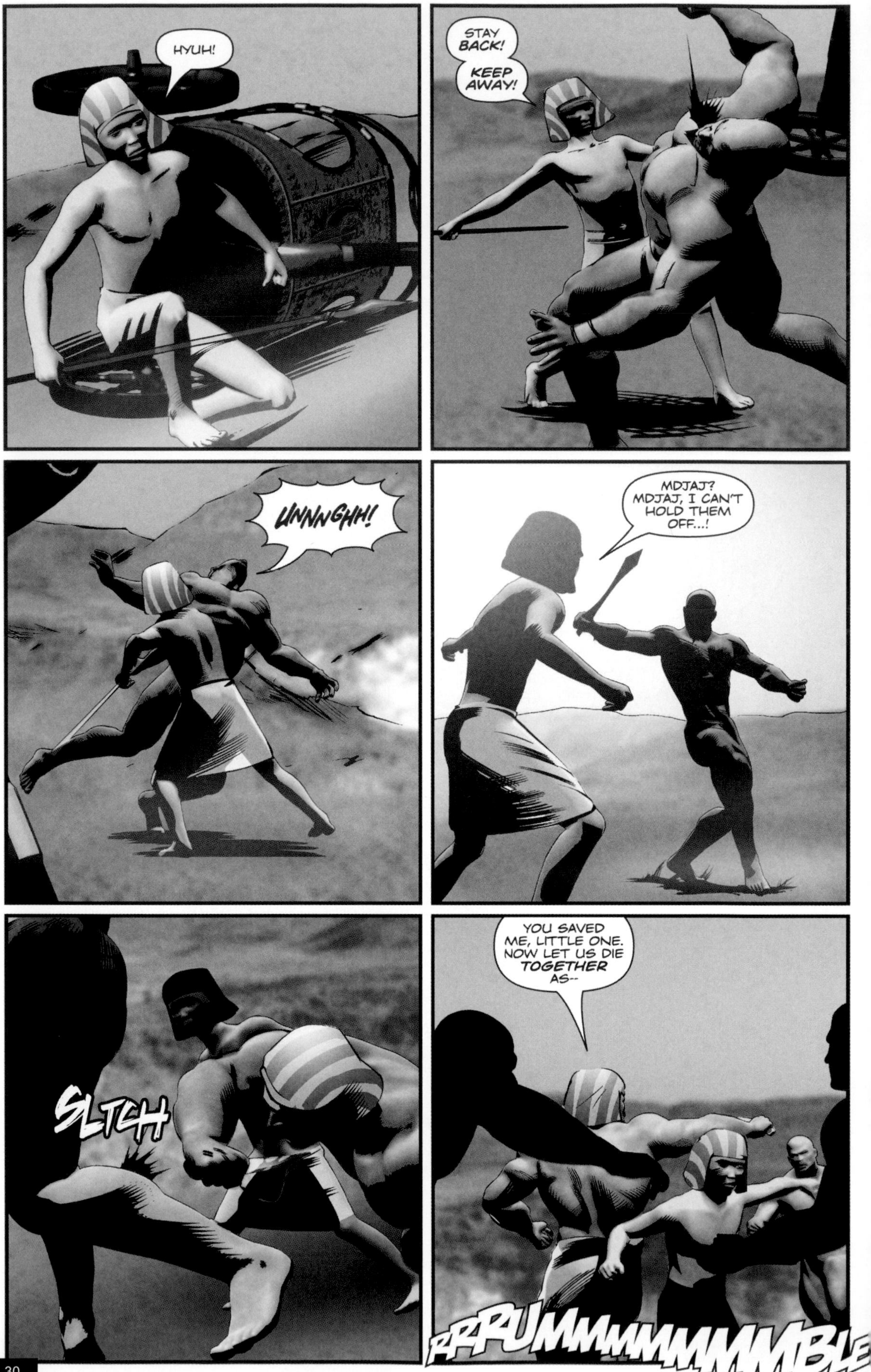
HYUH!
STAY BACK!
KEEP AWAY!
UNNNGHH!
MDJAJ? MDJAJ, I CAN'T HOLD THEM OFF...!
SLTCH
YOU SAVED ME, LITTLE ONE. NOW LET US DIE TOGETHER AS--
RRRUMMMMMMMMBLE

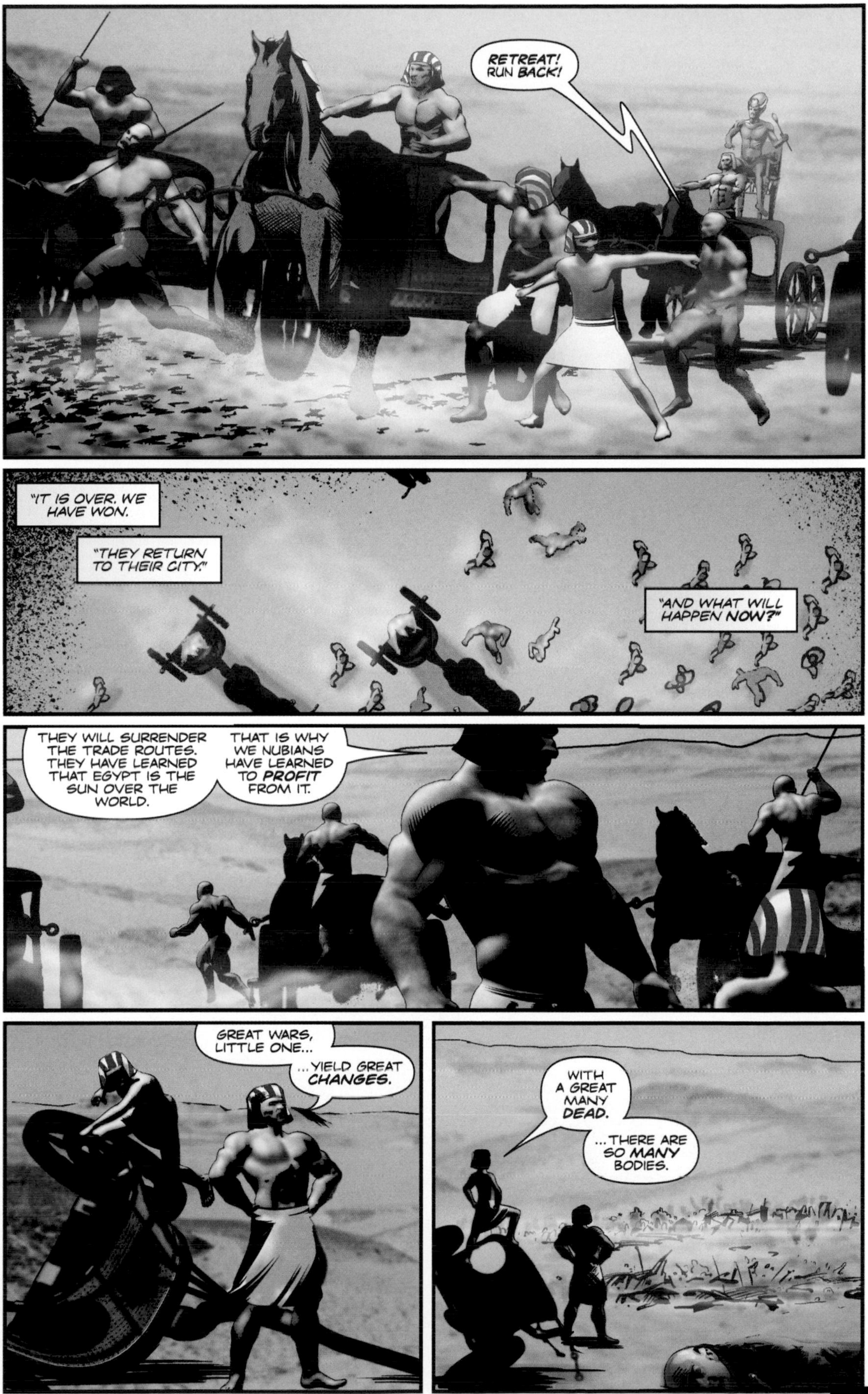
RETREAT! RUN BACK!
"IT IS OVER. WE HAVE WON.
"THEY RETURN TO THEIR CITY."
"AND WHAT WILL HAPPEN NOW?"
THEY WILL SURRENDER THE TRADE ROUTES. THEY HAVE LEARNED THAT EGYPT IS THE SUN OVER THE WORLD.
THAT IS WHY WE NUBIANS HAVE LEARNED TO PROFIT FROM IT.
GREAT WARS, LITTLE ONE...
...YIELD GREAT CHANGES.
WITH A GREAT MANY DEAD.
...THERE ARE SO MANY BODIES.

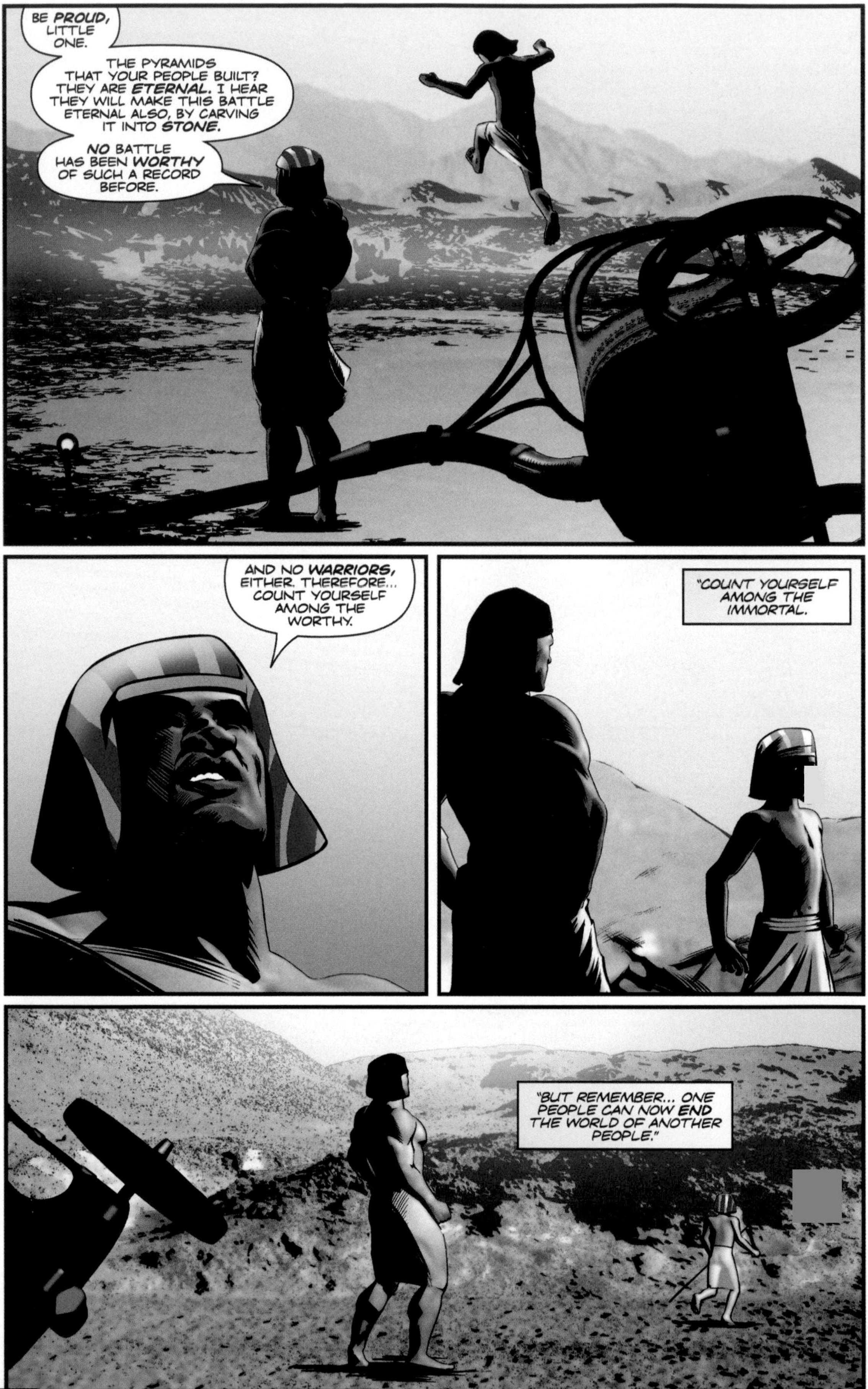
BE PROUD, LITTLE ONE.
THE PYRAMIDS THAT YOUR PEOPLE BUILT? THEY ARE ETERNAL. I HEAR THEY WILL MAKE THIS BATTLE ETERNAL ALSO, BY CARVING IT INTO STONE.
NO BATTLE HAS BEEN WORTHY OF SUCH A RECORD BEFORE.
AND NO WARRIORS, EITHER. THEREFORE... COUNT YOURSELF AMONG THE WORTHY.
"COUNT YOURSELF AMONG THE IMMORTAL.
"BUT REMEMBER... ONE PEOPLE CAN NOW END THE WORLD OF ANOTHER PEOPLE."

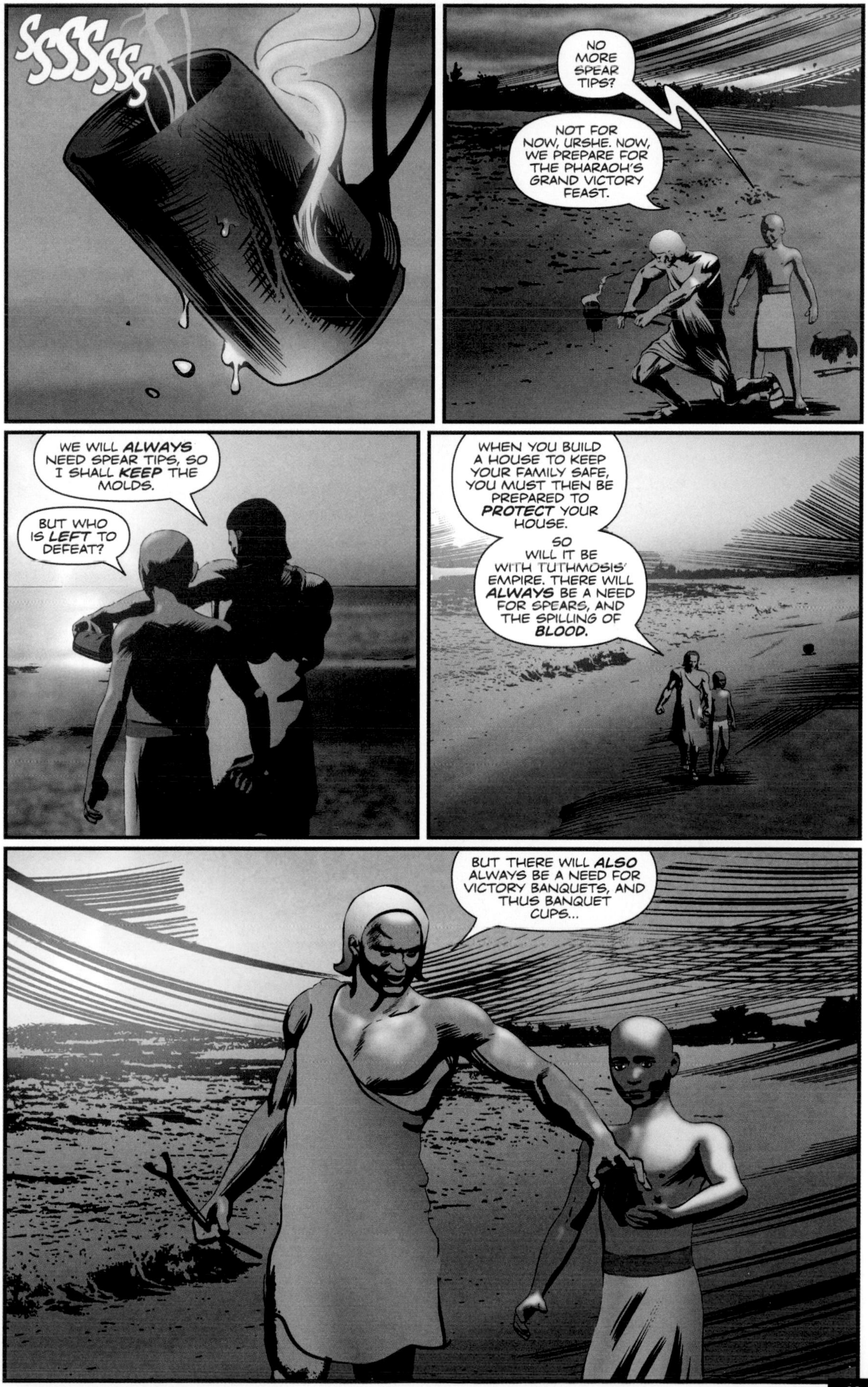
SSSSSSS
NO MORE SPEAR TIPS?
NOT FOR NOW, URSHE. NOW, WE PREPARE FOR THE PHARAOH'S GRAND VICTORY FEAST.
WE WILL ALWAYS NEED SPEAR TIPS, SO I SHALL KEEP THE MOLDS.
BUT WHO IS LEFT TO DEFEAT?
WHEN YOU BUILD A HOUSE TO KEEP YOUR FAMILY SAFE, YOU MUST THEN BE PREPARED TO PROTECT YOUR HOUSE.
SO WILL IT BE WITH TUTHMOSIS' EMPIRE. THERE WILL ALWAYS BE A NEED FOR SPEARS, AND THE SPILLING OF BLOOD.
BUT THERE WILL ALSO ALWAYS BE A NEED FOR VICTORY BANQUETS, AND THUS BANQUET CUPS...

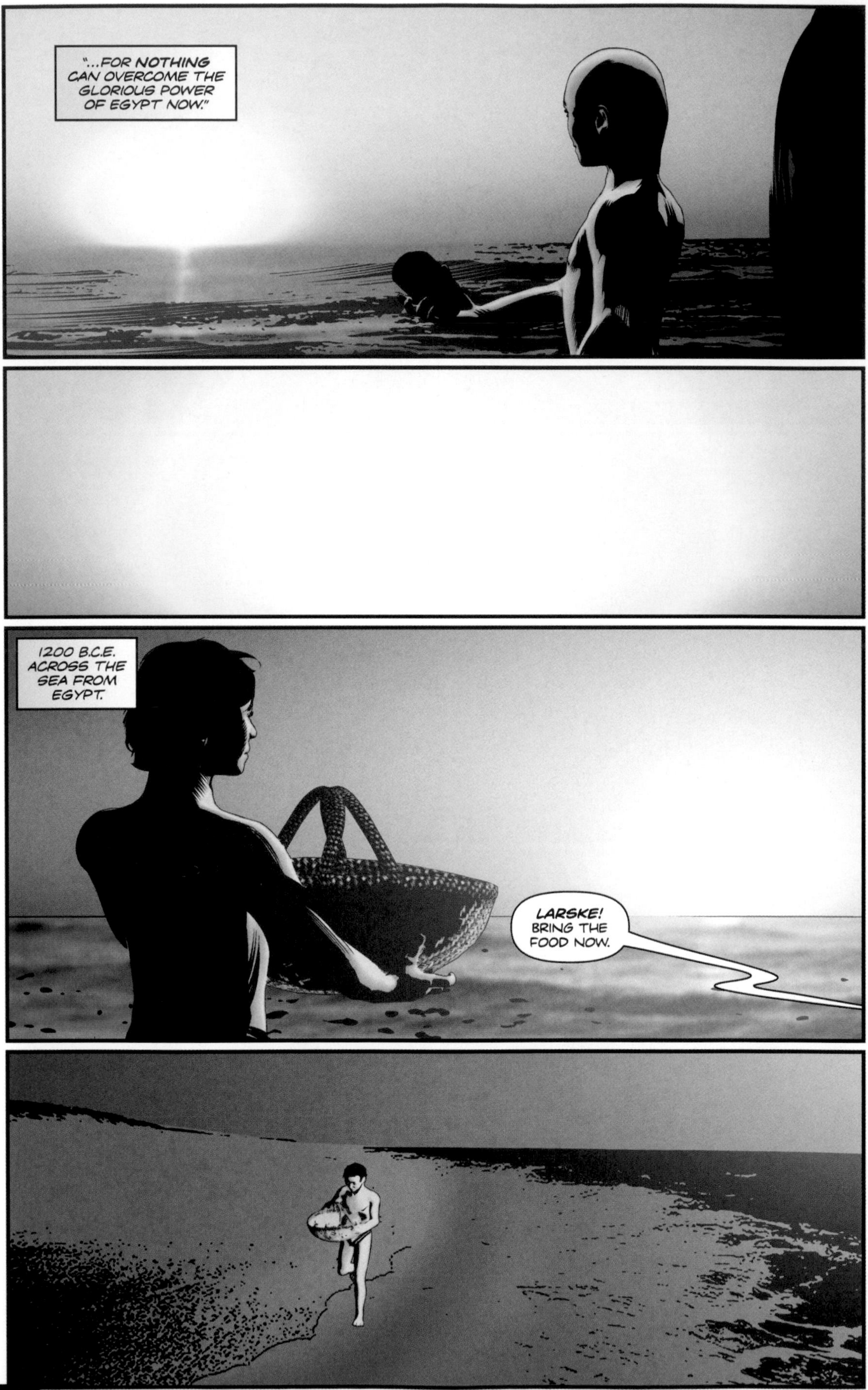
"...FOR NOTHING CAN OVERCOME THE GLORIOUS POWER OF EGYPT NOW."
1200 B.C.E. ACROSS THE SEA FROM EGYPT.
LARSKE! BRING THE FOOD NOW.

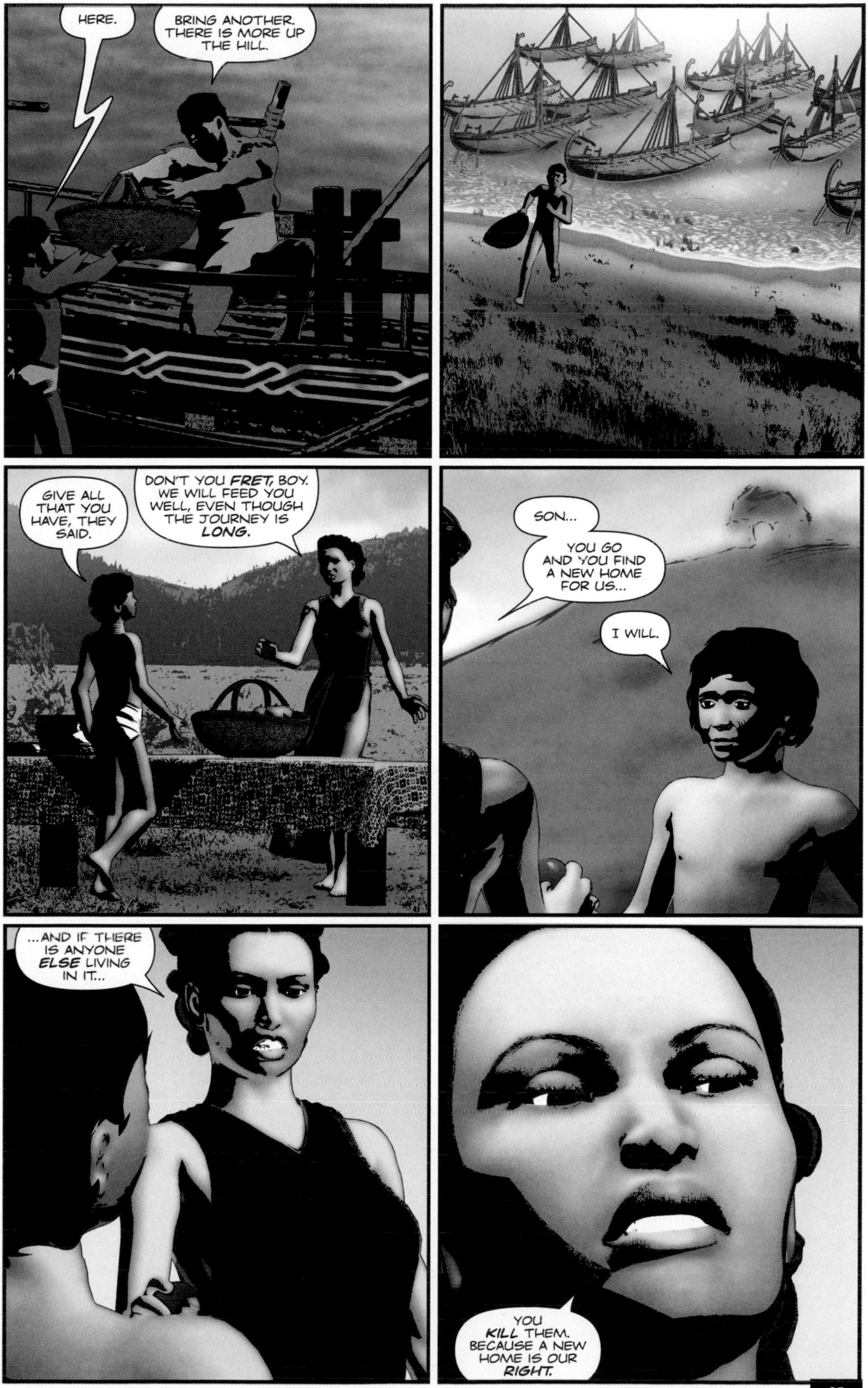
HERE.
BRING ANOTHER. THERE IS MORE UP THE HILL.
GIVE ALL THAT YOU HAVE, THEY SAID.
DON'T YOU FRET, BOY. WE WILL FEED YOU WELL, EVEN THOUGH THE JOURNEY IS LONG.
SON...
YOU GO AND YOU FIND A NEW HOME FOR US...
I WILL.
...AND IF THERE IS ANYONE ELSE LIVING IN IT...
YOU KILL THEM. BECAUSE A NEW HOME IS OUR RIGHT.

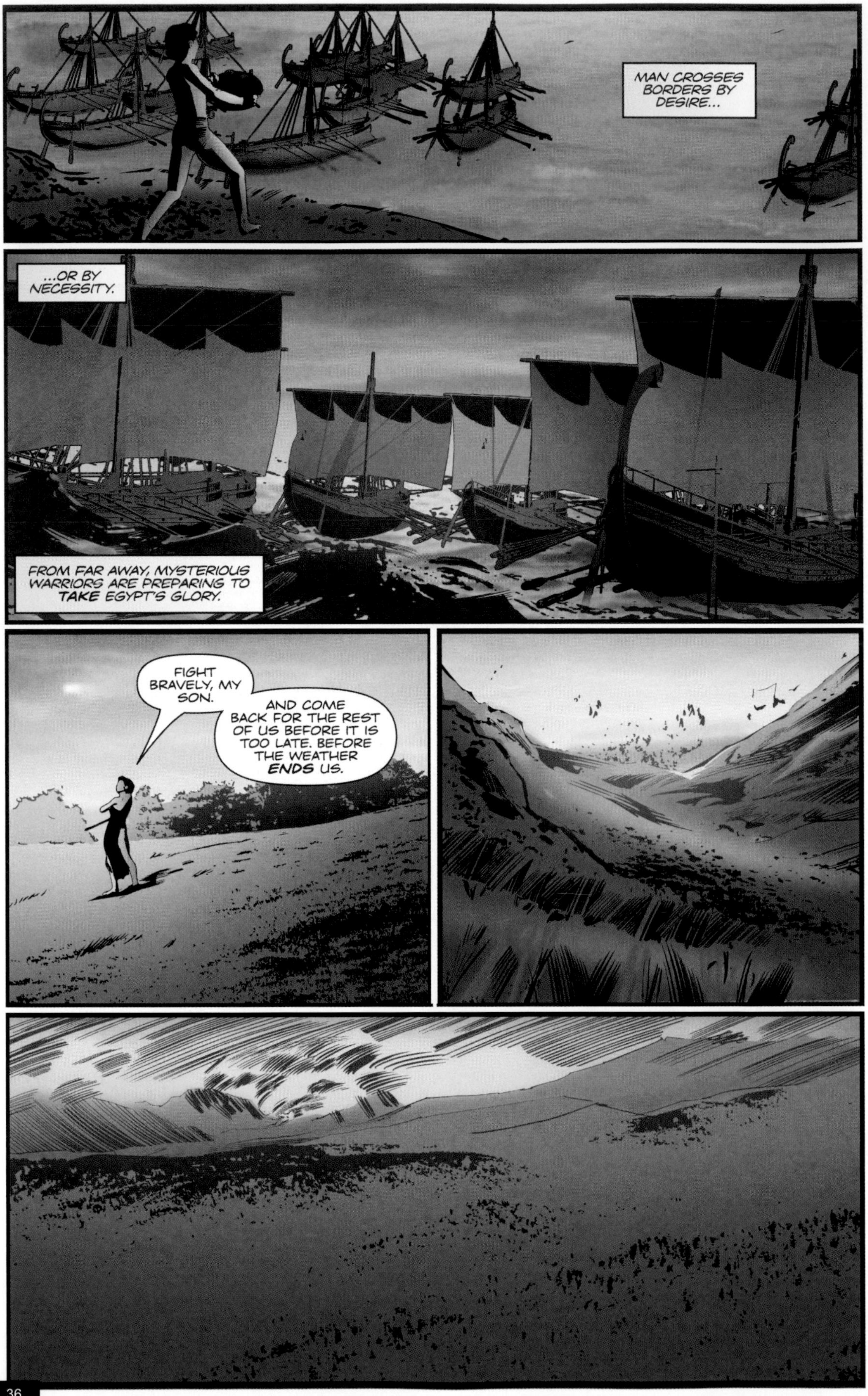
MAN CROSSES BORDERS BY DESIRE...
...OR BY NECESSITY.
FROM FAR AWAY, MYSTERIOUS WARRIORS ARE PREPARING TO **TAKE** EGYPT'S GLORY.
FIGHT BRAVELY, MY SON.
AND COME BACK FOR THE REST OF US BEFORE IT IS TOO LATE. BEFORE THE WEATHER **ENDS** US.

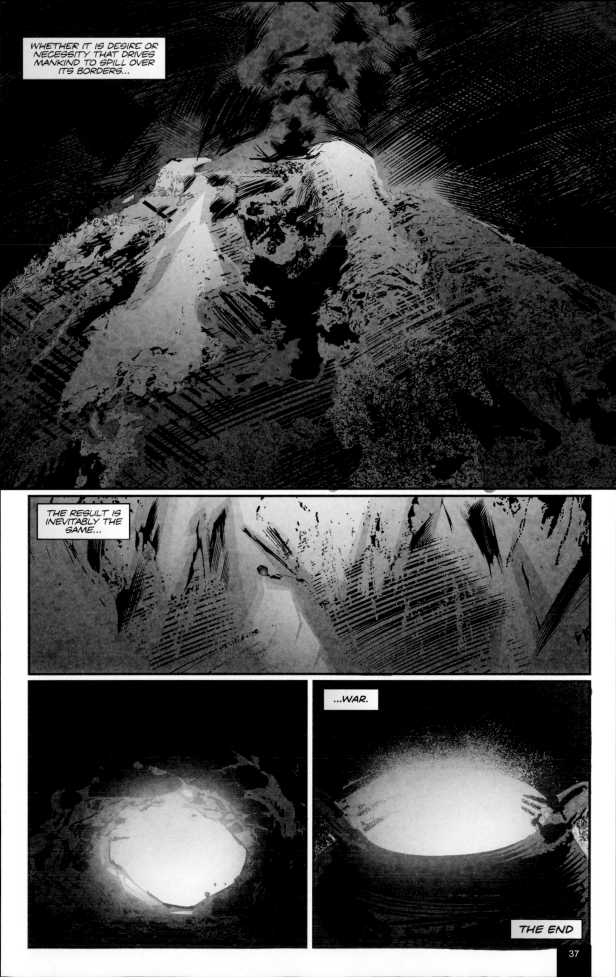

WHETHER IT IS DESIRE OR NECESSITY THAT DRIVES MANKIND TO SPILL OVER ITS BORDERS...

THE RESULT IS INEVITABLY THE SAME...

...WAR.

THE END

MANKIND DECODED

In *Pyramid of Man*, Urshe experiences one of the most vibrant eras in ancient Egypt.

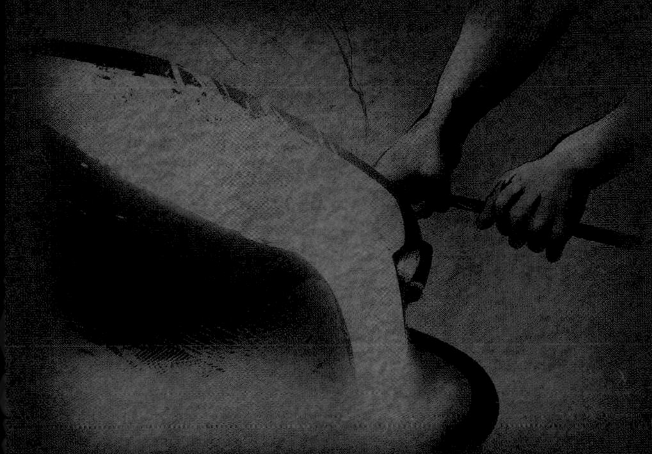

Urshe's father uses **fire** to heat and better refine a key material in the story of humanity – **bronze**. Egyptians refined the use of bronze in making weapons and armor. These refinements helped the empire of Egypt expand and conquer vast areas, including the regions that are known today as Syria, Lebanon, Israel, and Palestine. Tuthmosis III is often described as the "Napoleon of Egypt" because of the expansion of the Egyptian empire under his rule.

In addition to conquest and political growth, Tuthmosis III built many temples and monuments. Like the construction of the pyramids in previous centuries, communicating complex architectural plans to thousands of craftsmen, supervisors, and laborers was only possible with the fundamental human tool of **writing.**

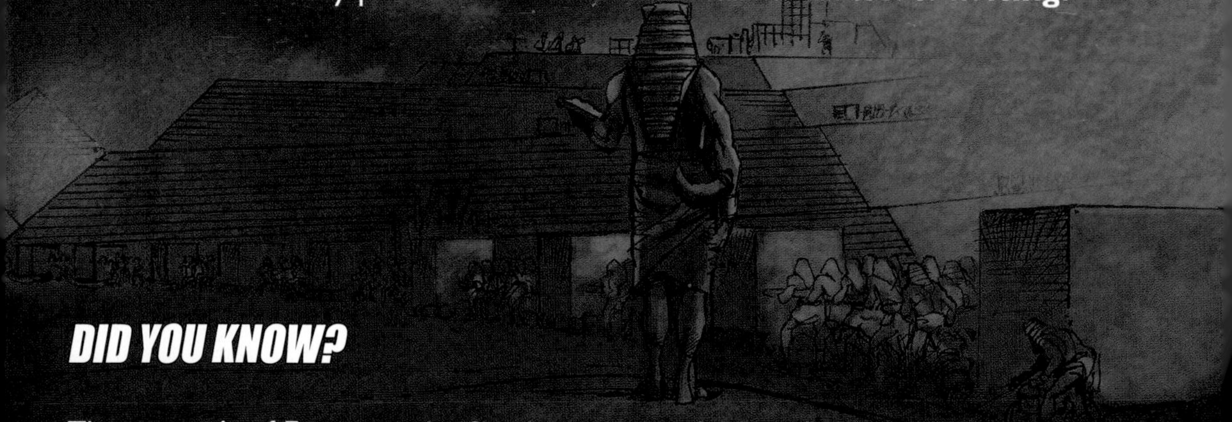

DID YOU KNOW?

The pyramids of Egypt are the first known use of dressed masonry in human history — the use of similar, rectangular cut, and sculpted stone blocks were assembled in measured, parallel courses to create smooth faces and sharp edges. Prior to this, only rough, irregular shaped stones were used.

Commissioned by the pharaoh Khufu, the Great Pyramid of Giza was built around 2500 B.C.E. Although construction began earlier, Stonehenge in England was also being built during this same period. Both monuments are excellent examples of architectural grandeur and human innovation.

THE RUNNER

WRITTEN BY
SHAWN BROCK

ART BY
GIOVANNI TIMPANO

COLORS BY
FALK

LETTERS BY
JIM CAMPBELL

A LONELY FIGURE RUNS AN IMPOSSIBLE TRAJECTORY ALONG A SET COURSE, DESTINED TO MAKE HISTORY.

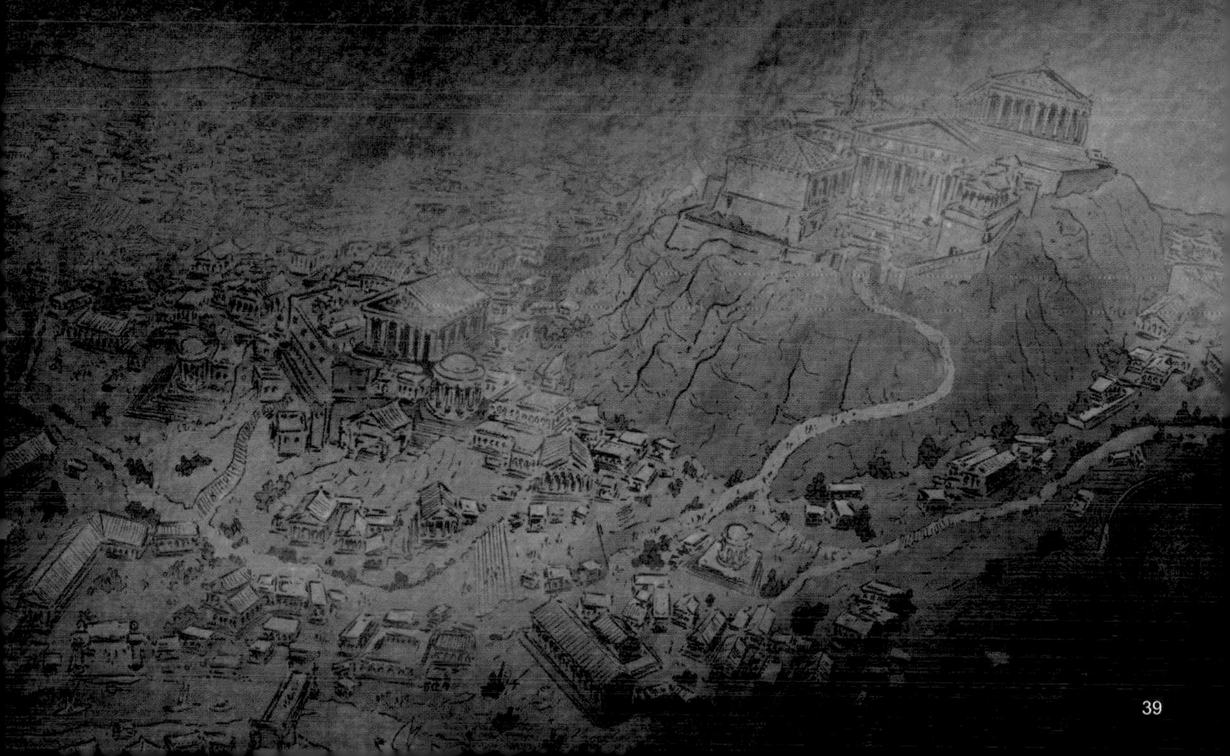

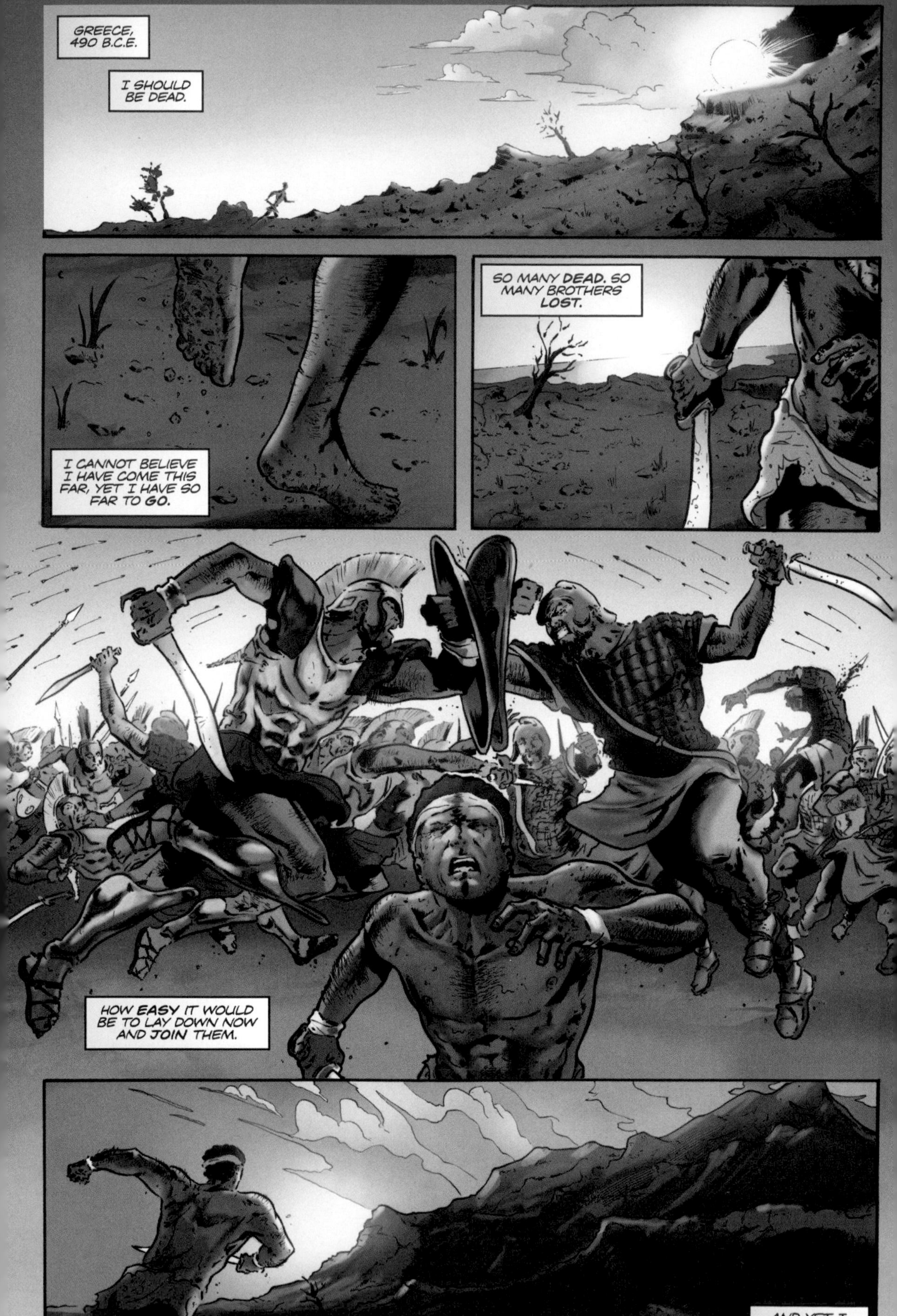
GREECE, 490 B.C.E.
I SHOULD BE DEAD.
I CANNOT BELIEVE I HAVE COME THIS FAR, YET I HAVE SO FAR TO GO.
SO MANY DEAD. SO MANY BROTHERS LOST.
HOW EASY IT WOULD BE TO LAY DOWN NOW AND JOIN THEM.
AND YET I MUST GO ON.

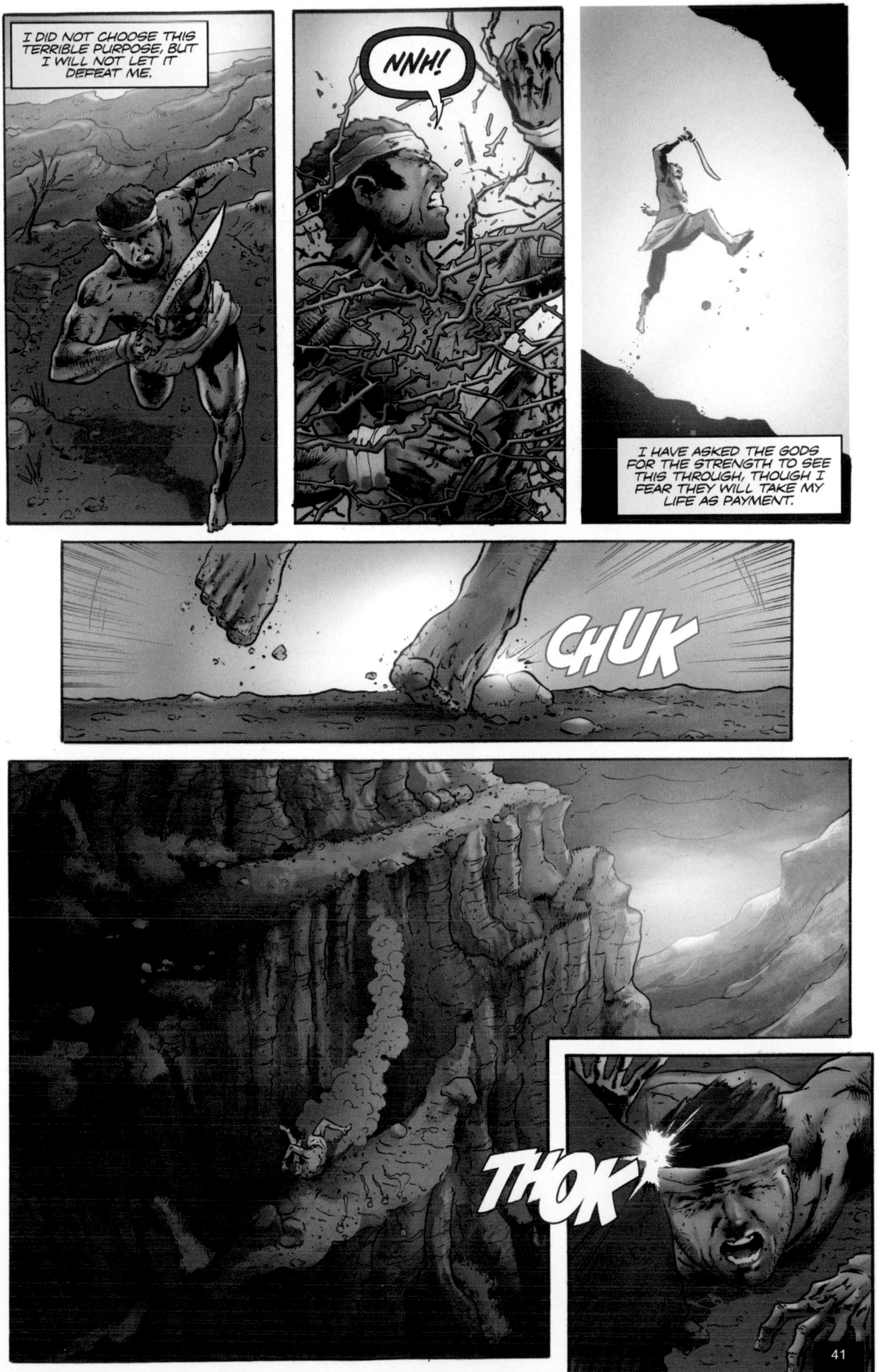
I DID NOT CHOOSE THIS TERRIBLE PURPOSE, BUT I WILL NOT LET IT DEFEAT ME.
NNH!
I HAVE ASKED THE GODS FOR THE STRENGTH TO SEE THIS THROUGH, THOUGH I FEAR THEY WILL TAKE MY LIFE AS PAYMENT.
CHUK
THOK

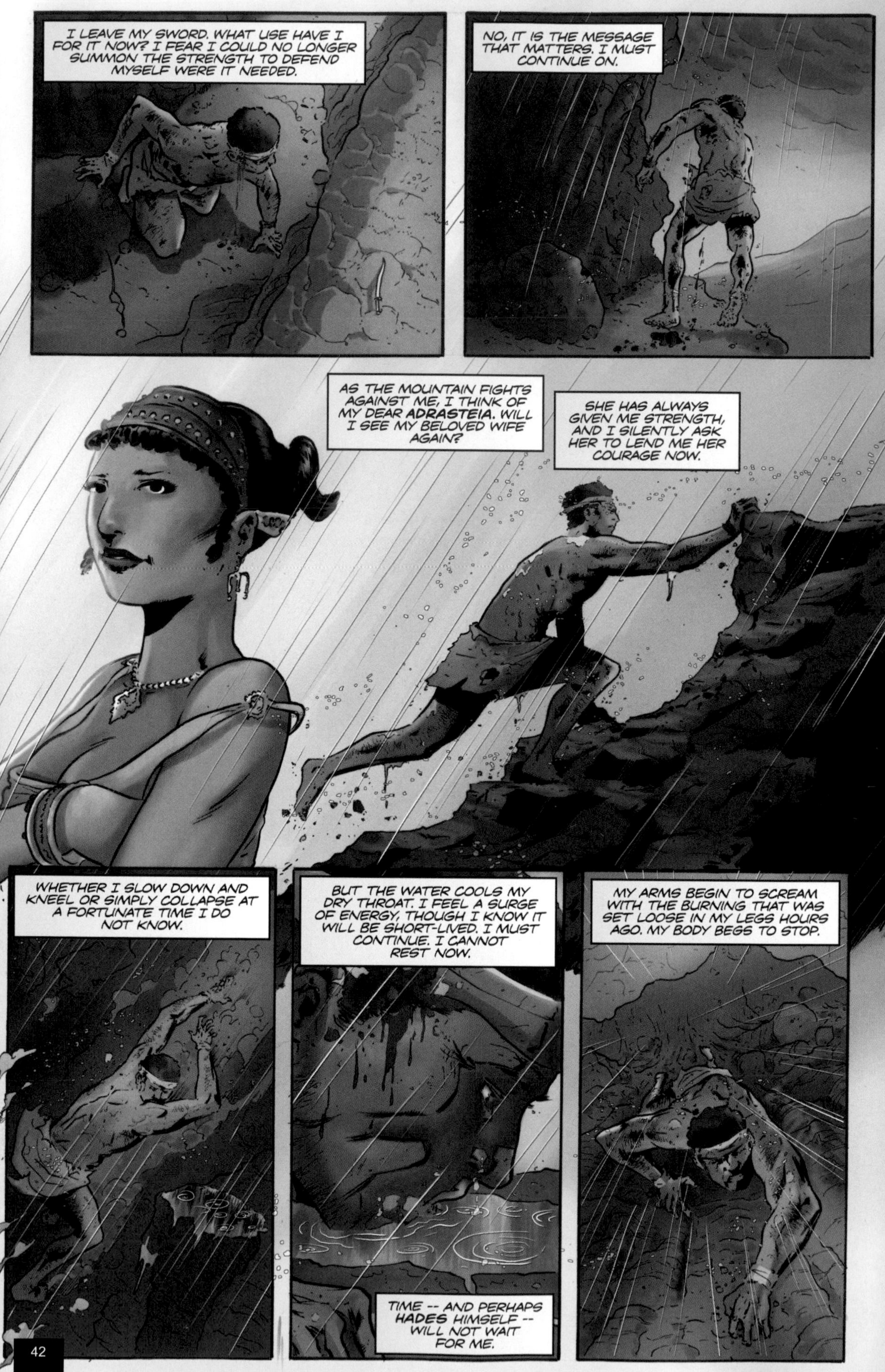
I LEAVE MY SWORD. WHAT USE HAVE I FOR IT NOW? I FEAR I COULD NO LONGER SUMMON THE STRENGTH TO DEFEND MYSELF WERE IT NEEDED.
NO, IT IS THE MESSAGE THAT MATTERS. I MUST CONTINUE ON.
AS THE MOUNTAIN FIGHTS AGAINST ME, I THINK OF MY DEAR ADRASTEIA. WILL I SEE MY BELOVED WIFE AGAIN?
SHE HAS ALWAYS GIVEN ME STRENGTH, AND I SILENTLY ASK HER TO LEND ME HER COURAGE NOW.
WHETHER I SLOW DOWN AND KNEEL OR SIMPLY COLLAPSE AT A FORTUNATE TIME I DO NOT KNOW.
BUT THE WATER COOLS MY DRY THROAT. I FEEL A SURGE OF ENERGY, THOUGH I KNOW IT WILL BE SHORT-LIVED. I MUST CONTINUE. I CANNOT REST NOW.
TIME -- AND PERHAPS HADES HIMSELF -- WILL NOT WAIT FOR ME.
MY ARMS BEGIN TO SCREAM WITH THE BURNING THAT WAS SET LOOSE IN MY LEGS HOURS AGO. MY BODY BEGS TO STOP.

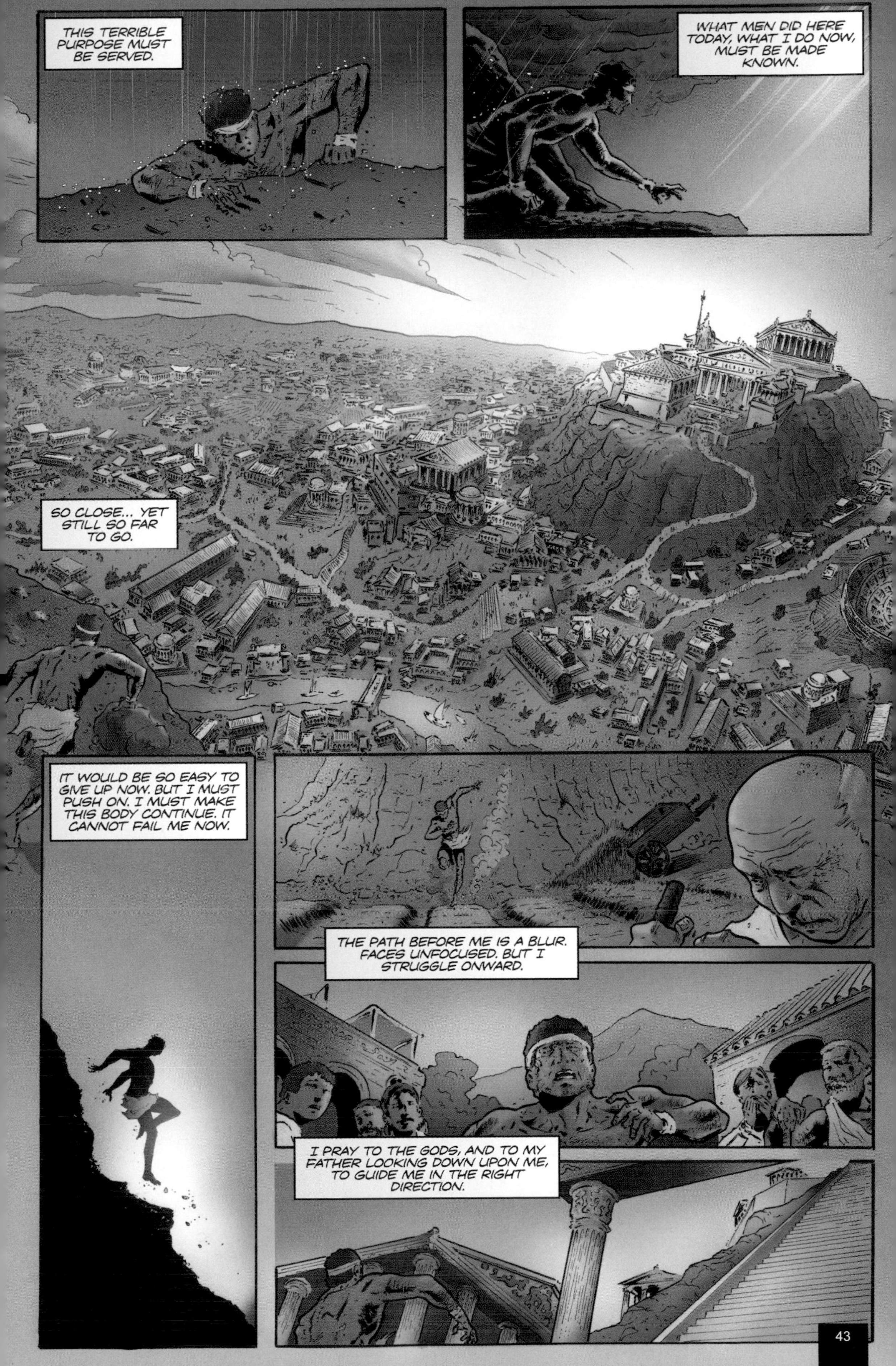
THIS TERRIBLE PURPOSE MUST BE SERVED.
WHAT MEN DID HERE TODAY, WHAT I DO NOW, MUST BE MADE KNOWN.
SO CLOSE... YET STILL SO FAR TO GO.
IT WOULD BE SO EASY TO GIVE UP NOW. BUT I MUST PUSH ON. I MUST MAKE THIS BODY CONTINUE. IT CANNOT FAIL ME NOW.
THE PATH BEFORE ME IS A BLUR. FACES UNFOCUSED. BUT I STRUGGLE ONWARD.
I PRAY TO THE GODS, AND TO MY FATHER LOOKING DOWN UPON ME, TO GUIDE ME IN THE RIGHT DIRECTION.

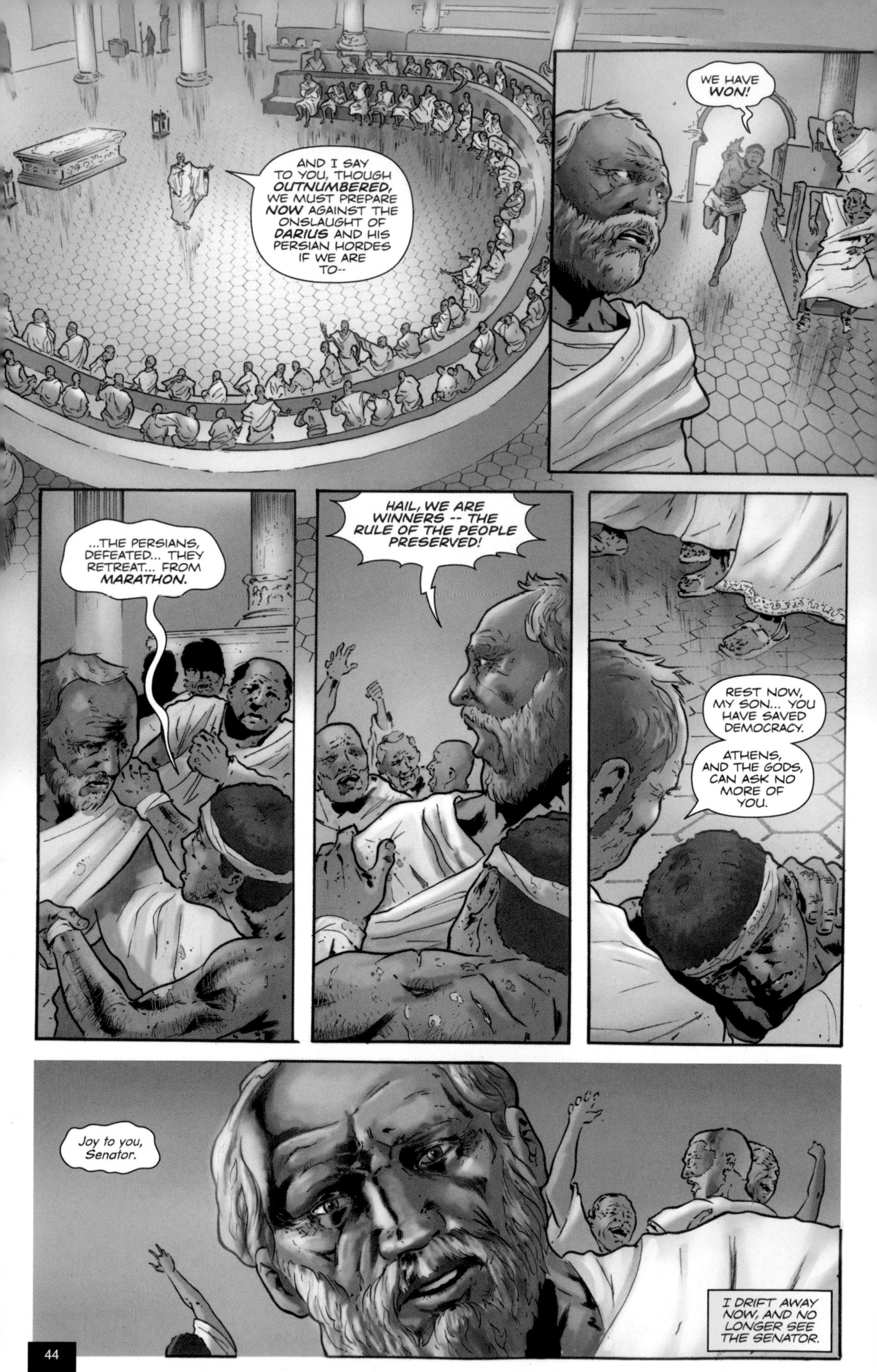
AND I SAY TO YOU, THOUGH OUTNUMBERED, WE MUST PREPARE NOW AGAINST THE ONSLAUGHT OF DARIUS AND HIS PERSIAN HORDES IF WE ARE TO--
WE HAVE WON!
...THE PERSIANS, DEFEATED... THEY RETREAT... FROM MARATHON.
HAIL, WE ARE WINNERS -- THE RULE OF THE PEOPLE PRESERVED!
REST NOW, MY SON... YOU HAVE SAVED DEMOCRACY.
ATHENS, AND THE GODS, CAN ASK NO MORE OF YOU.
Joy to you, Senator.
I DRIFT AWAY NOW, AND NO LONGER SEE THE SENATOR.

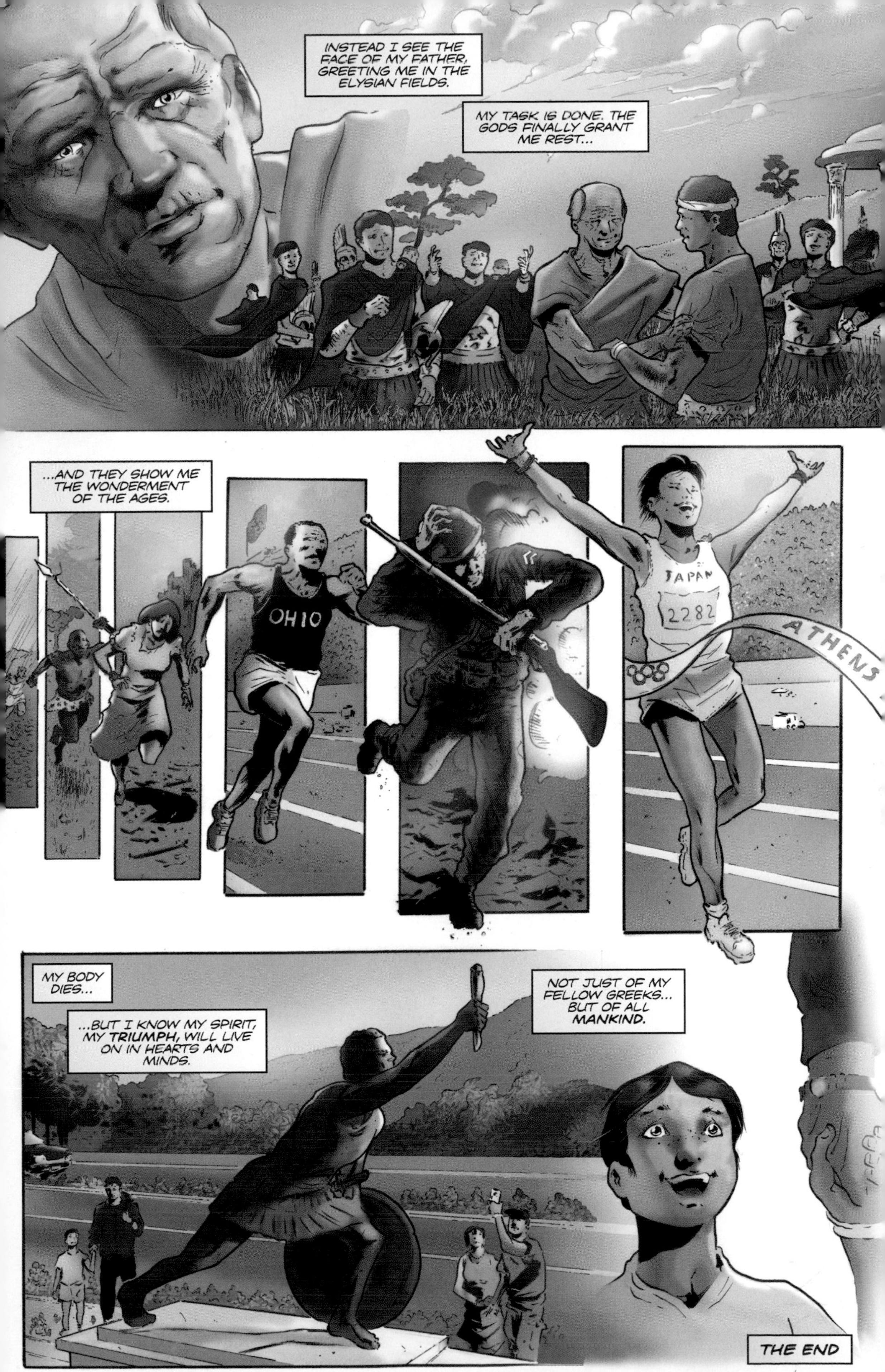
INSTEAD I SEE THE FACE OF MY FATHER, GREETING ME IN THE ELYSIAN FIELDS.
MY TASK IS DONE. THE GODS FINALLY GRANT ME REST...
...AND THEY SHOW ME THE WONDERMENT OF THE AGES.
OHIO
JAPAN
2282
ATHENS
MY BODY DIES...
...BUT I KNOW MY SPIRIT, MY **TRIUMPH**, WILL LIVE ON IN HEARTS AND MINDS.
NOT JUST OF MY FELLOW GREEKS... BUT OF ALL **MANKIND**.
THE END

MANKIND DECODED

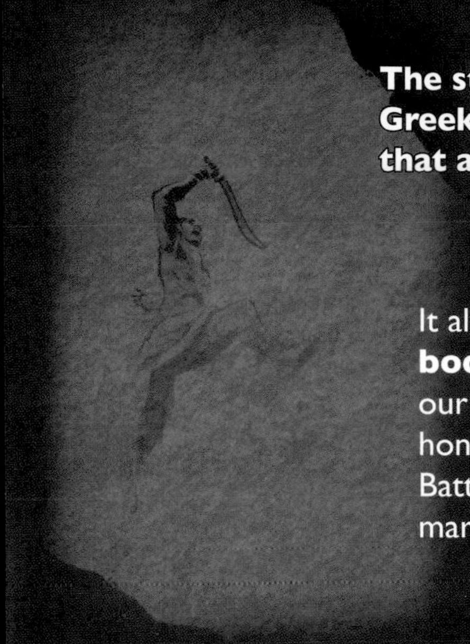

The story of *The Runner* illustrates the legend of a Greek messenger who fought, and ultimately died, so that a new idea called "democracy" could survive.

It also demonstrates mankind's ability to push the **human body** beyond its limits to overcome obstacles and achieve our goals. This heroic journey is still celebrated and honored today — the 26 mile run to Athens following the Battle of Marathon is where our modern sport of running marathons comes from.

Democratic rule was first pioneered by the Greeks, and it continues to shape our world today. The word "democracy" comes from the Greek word Demokratia, which literally means "people power."

The idea of democracy has continued to evolve throughout the centuries, expanding to include more groups, becoming more representative, and also integrating with other forms of government such as monarchies.

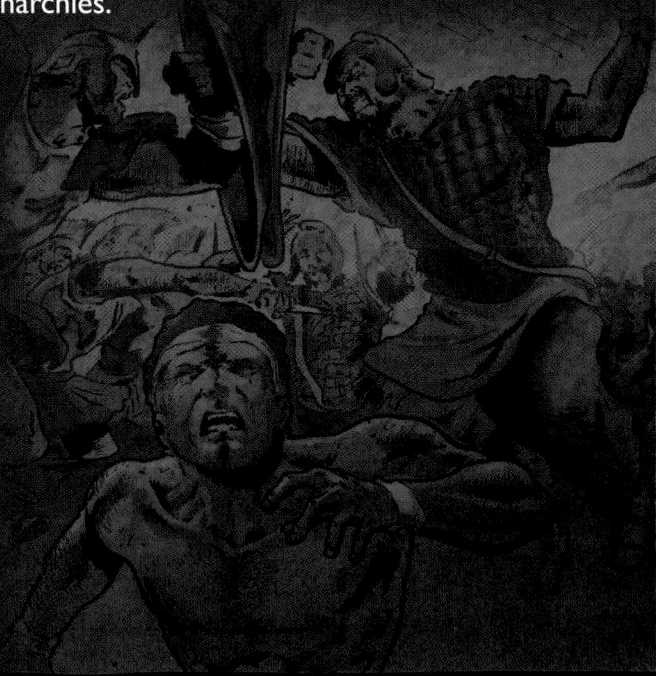

Democracy, in one form or another, is the most common form of government in the world today.

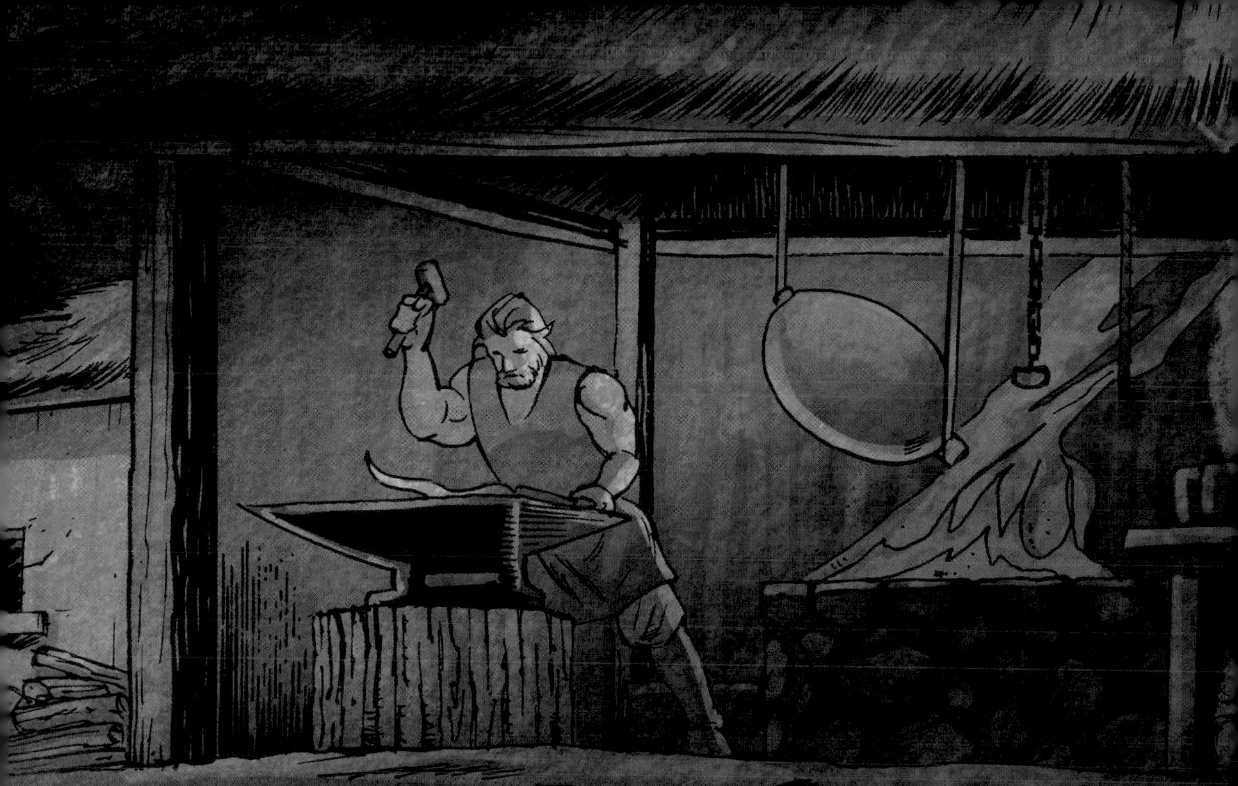

WILL OF IRON

WRITTEN BY
NEO EDMUND

ART BY
LARA BARON

COLORS BY
STEPHEN DOWNER

LETTERS BY
JIM CAMPBELL

FROM ITS ORIGIN AT THE EARTH'S CORE, THROUGH BATTLEFIELDS AND
BUILDINGS, IRON CHANGES THE COURSE OF MANKIND

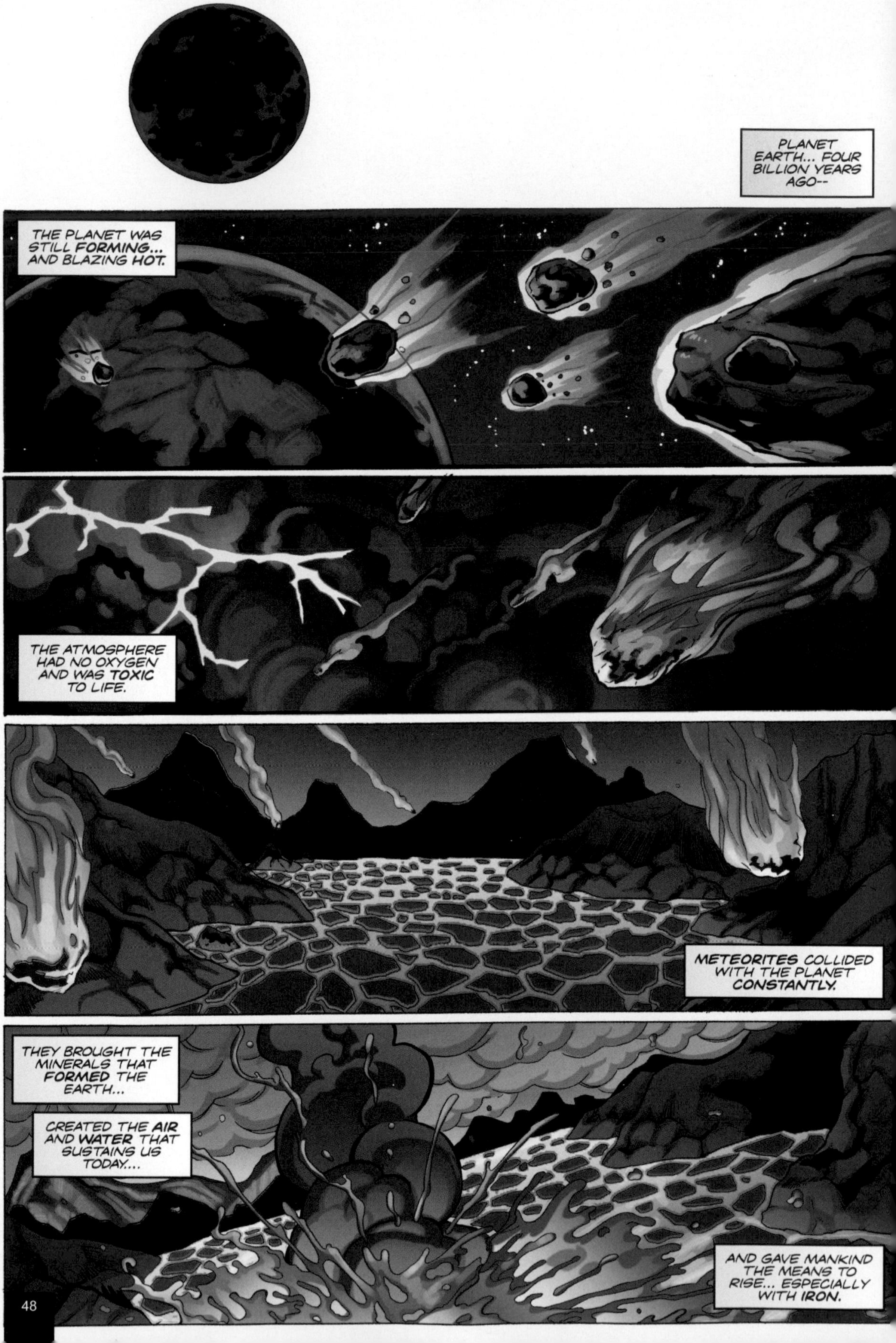
PLANET EARTH... FOUR BILLION YEARS AGO--
THE PLANET WAS STILL FORMING... AND BLAZING HOT.
THE ATMOSPHERE HAD NO OXYGEN AND WAS TOXIC TO LIFE.
METEORITES COLLIDED WITH THE PLANET CONSTANTLY.
THEY BROUGHT THE MINERALS THAT FORMED THE EARTH...
CREATED THE AIR AND WATER THAT SUSTAINS US TODAY....
AND GAVE MANKIND THE MEANS TO RISE... ESPECIALLY WITH IRON.

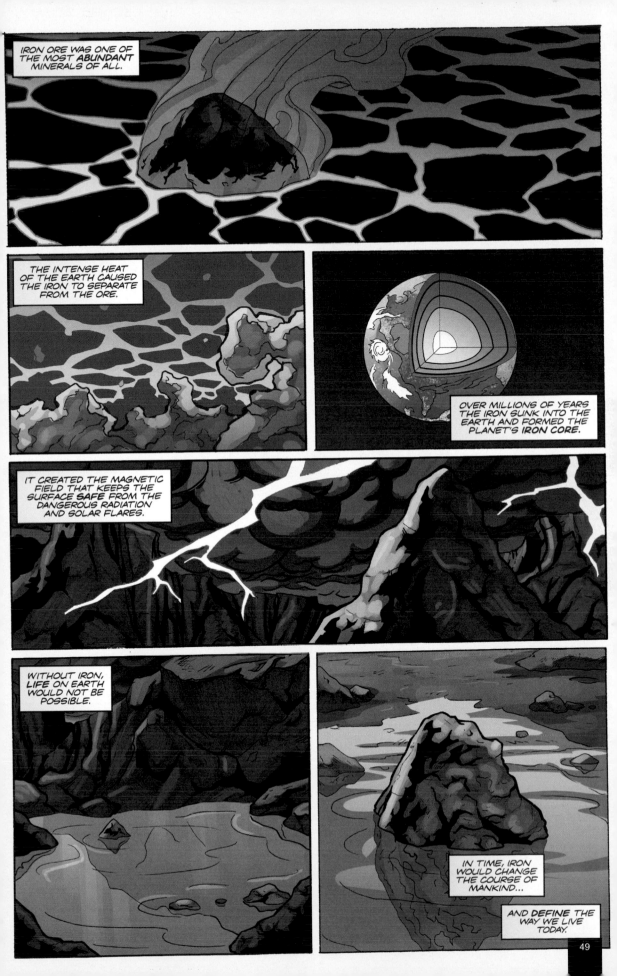

IRON ORE WAS ONE OF THE MOST **ABUNDANT** MINERALS OF ALL.

THE INTENSE HEAT OF THE EARTH CAUSED THE IRON TO SEPARATE FROM THE ORE.

OVER MILLIONS OF YEARS THE IRON SUNK INTO THE EARTH AND FORMED THE PLANET'S **IRON CORE.**

IT CREATED THE MAGNETIC FIELD THAT KEEPS THE SURFACE **SAFE** FROM THE DANGEROUS RADIATION AND SOLAR FLARES.

WITHOUT IRON, **LIFE ON EARTH** WOULD NOT BE POSSIBLE.

IN TIME, IRON WOULD CHANGE THE COURSE OF MANKIND...

AND DEFINE THE WAY WE LIVE TODAY.

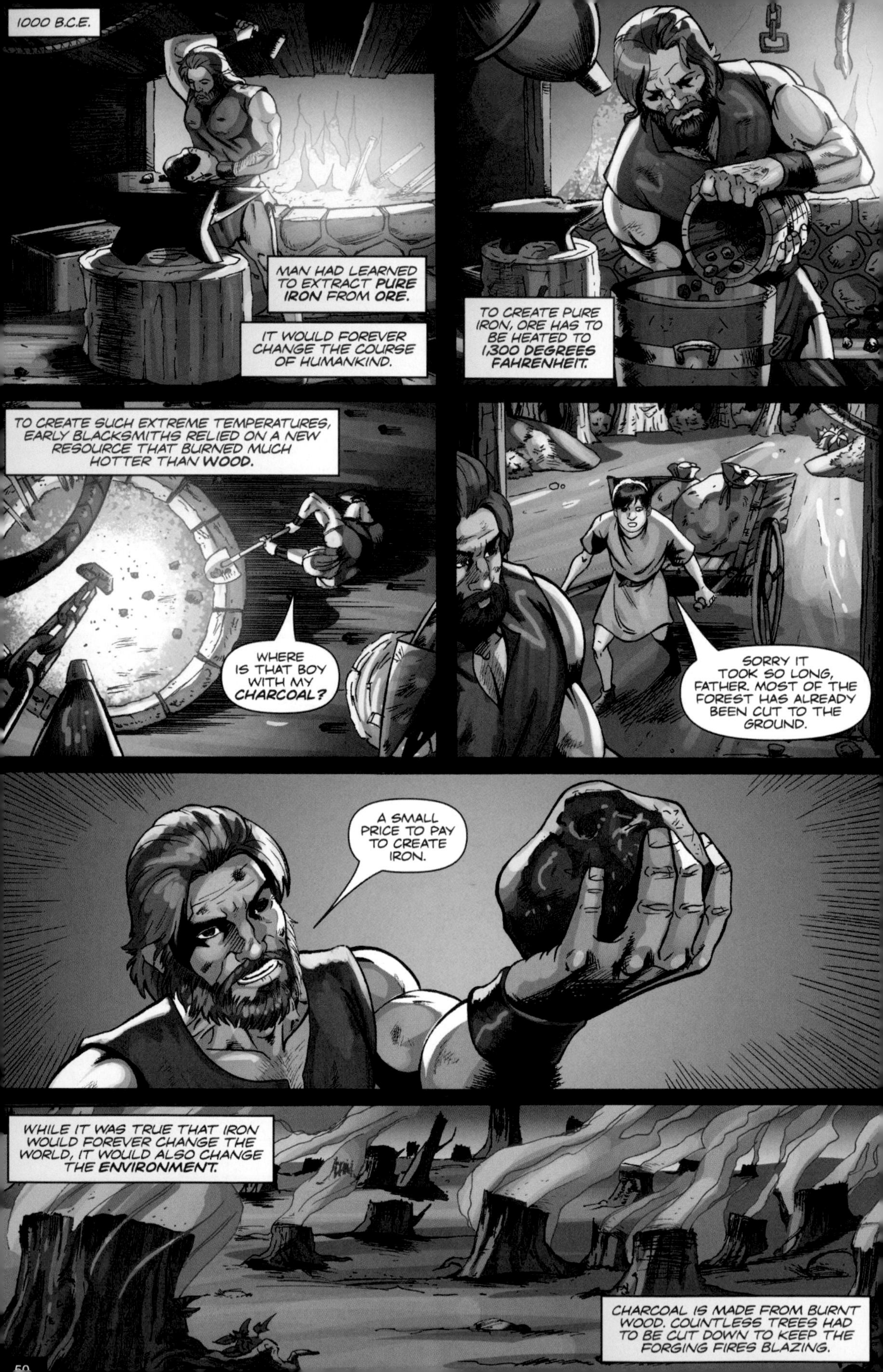
1000 B.C.E.
MAN HAD LEARNED TO EXTRACT PURE IRON FROM ORE.
IT WOULD FOREVER CHANGE THE COURSE OF HUMANKIND.
TO CREATE PURE IRON, ORE HAS TO BE HEATED TO 1,300 DEGREES FAHRENHEIT.
TO CREATE SUCH EXTREME TEMPERATURES, EARLY BLACKSMITHS RELIED ON A NEW RESOURCE THAT BURNED MUCH HOTTER THAN WOOD.
WHERE IS THAT BOY WITH MY CHARCOAL?
SORRY IT TOOK SO LONG, FATHER. MOST OF THE FOREST HAS ALREADY BEEN CUT TO THE GROUND.
A SMALL PRICE TO PAY TO CREATE IRON.
WHILE IT WAS TRUE THAT IRON WOULD FOREVER CHANGE THE WORLD, IT WOULD ALSO CHANGE THE ENVIRONMENT.
CHARCOAL IS MADE FROM BURNT WOOD. COUNTLESS TREES HAD TO BE CUT DOWN TO KEEP THE FORGING FIRES BLAZING.

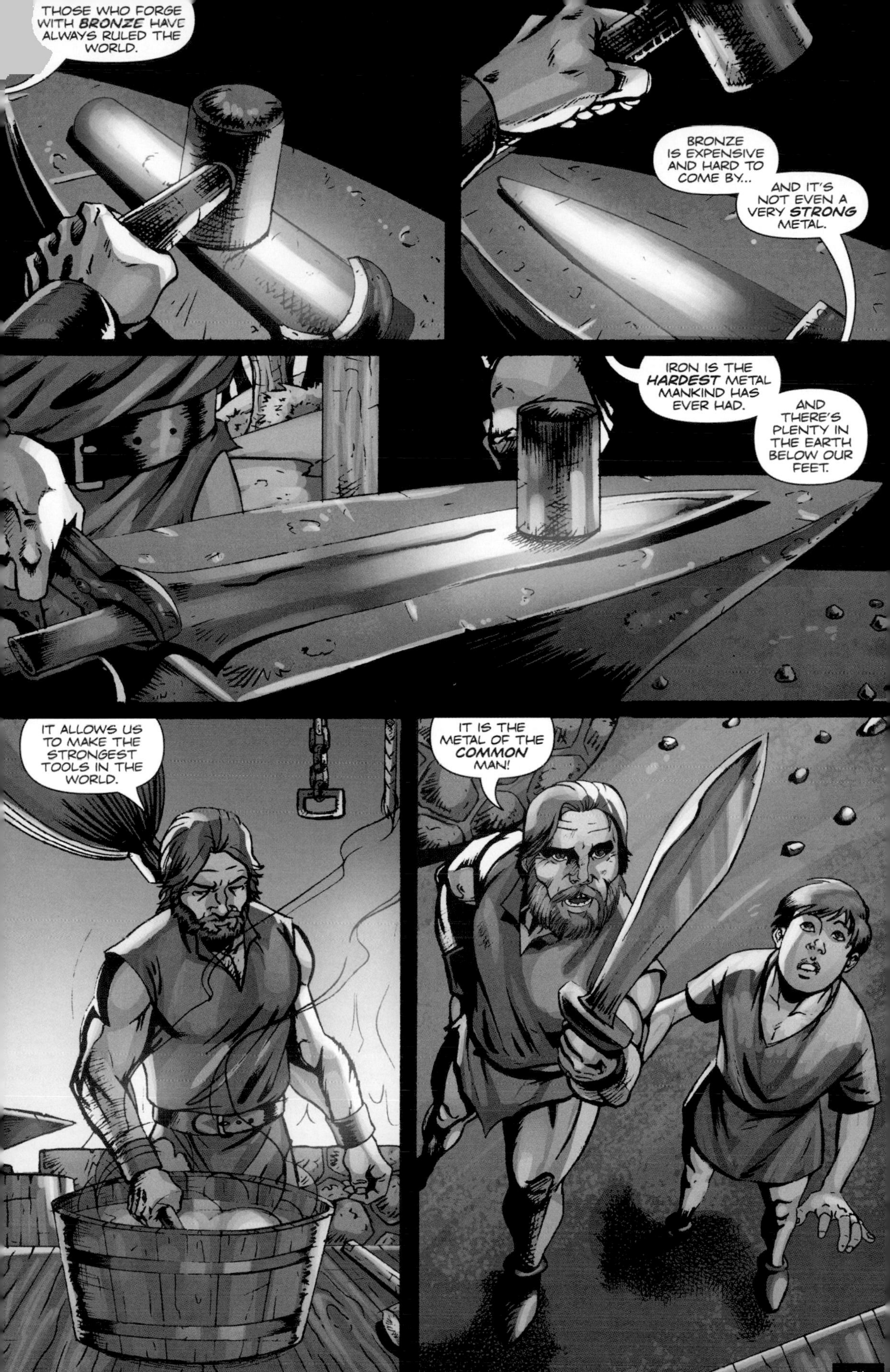
THOSE WHO FORGE WITH BRONZE HAVE ALWAYS RULED THE WORLD.
BRONZE IS EXPENSIVE AND HARD TO COME BY...
AND IT'S NOT EVEN A VERY STRONG METAL.
IRON IS THE HARDEST METAL MANKIND HAS EVER HAD.
AND THERE'S PLENTY IN THE EARTH BELOW OUR FEET.
IT ALLOWS US TO MAKE THE STRONGEST TOOLS IN THE WORLD.
IT IS THE METAL OF THE COMMON MAN!

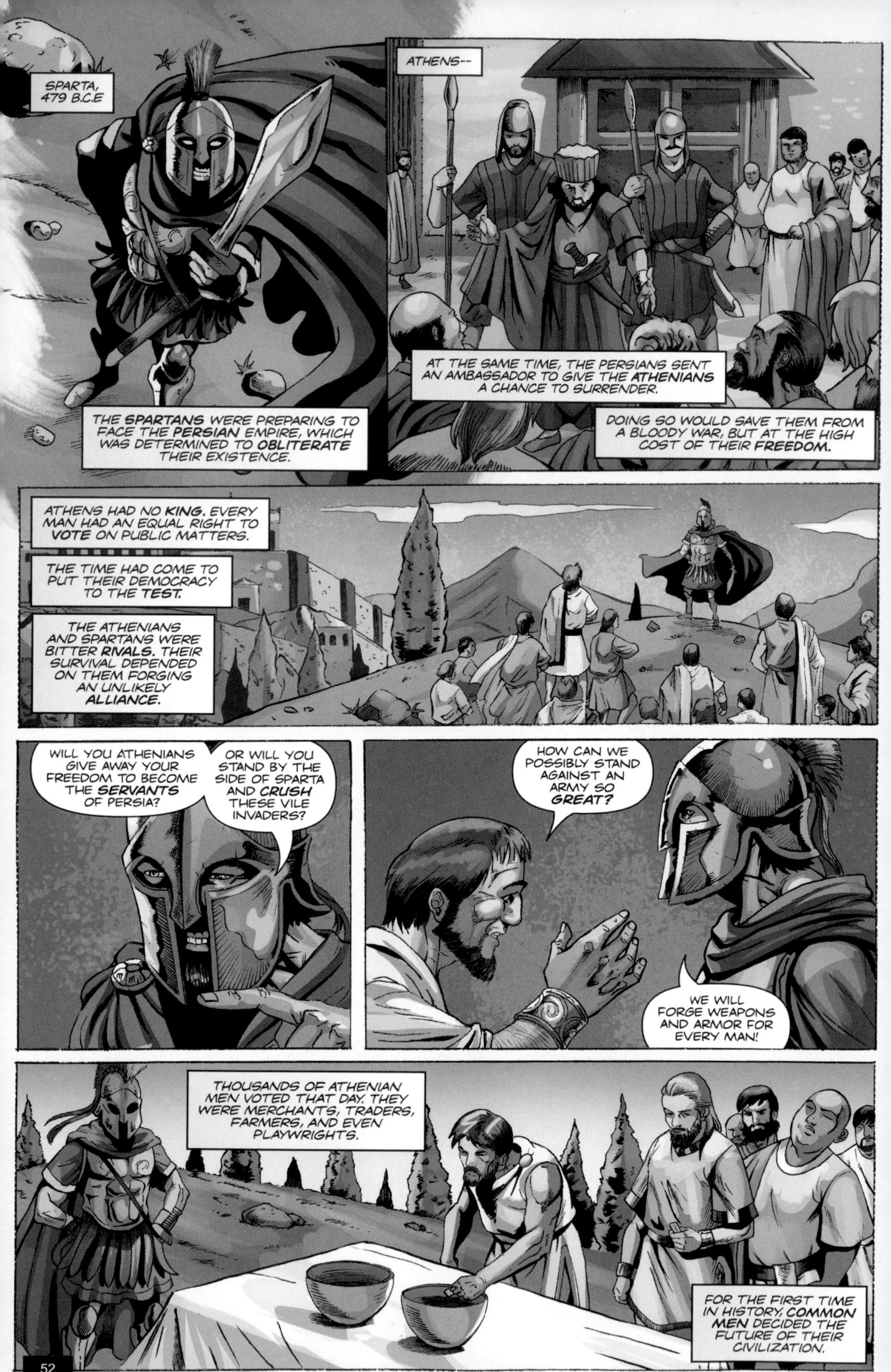
SPARTA, 479 B.C.E
THE SPARTANS WERE PREPARING TO FACE THE PERSIAN EMPIRE, WHICH WAS DETERMINED TO OBLITERATE THEIR EXISTENCE.
ATHENS--
AT THE SAME TIME, THE PERSIANS SENT AN AMBASSADOR TO GIVE THE ATHENIANS A CHANCE TO SURRENDER.
DOING SO WOULD SAVE THEM FROM A BLOODY WAR, BUT AT THE HIGH COST OF THEIR FREEDOM.
ATHENS HAD NO KING. EVERY MAN HAD AN EQUAL RIGHT TO VOTE ON PUBLIC MATTERS.
THE TIME HAD COME TO PUT THEIR DEMOCRACY TO THE TEST.
THE ATHENIANS AND SPARTANS WERE BITTER RIVALS. THEIR SURVIVAL DEPENDED ON THEM FORGING AN UNLIKELY ALLIANCE.
WILL YOU ATHENIANS GIVE AWAY YOUR FREEDOM TO BECOME THE SERVANTS OF PERSIA?
OR WILL YOU STAND BY THE SIDE OF SPARTA AND CRUSH THESE VILE INVADERS?
HOW CAN WE POSSIBLY STAND AGAINST AN ARMY SO GREAT?
WE WILL FORGE WEAPONS AND ARMOR FOR EVERY MAN!
THOUSANDS OF ATHENIAN MEN VOTED THAT DAY. THEY WERE MERCHANTS, TRADERS, FARMERS, AND EVEN PLAYWRIGHTS.
FOR THE FIRST TIME IN HISTORY, COMMON MEN DECIDED THE FUTURE OF THEIR CIVILIZATION.

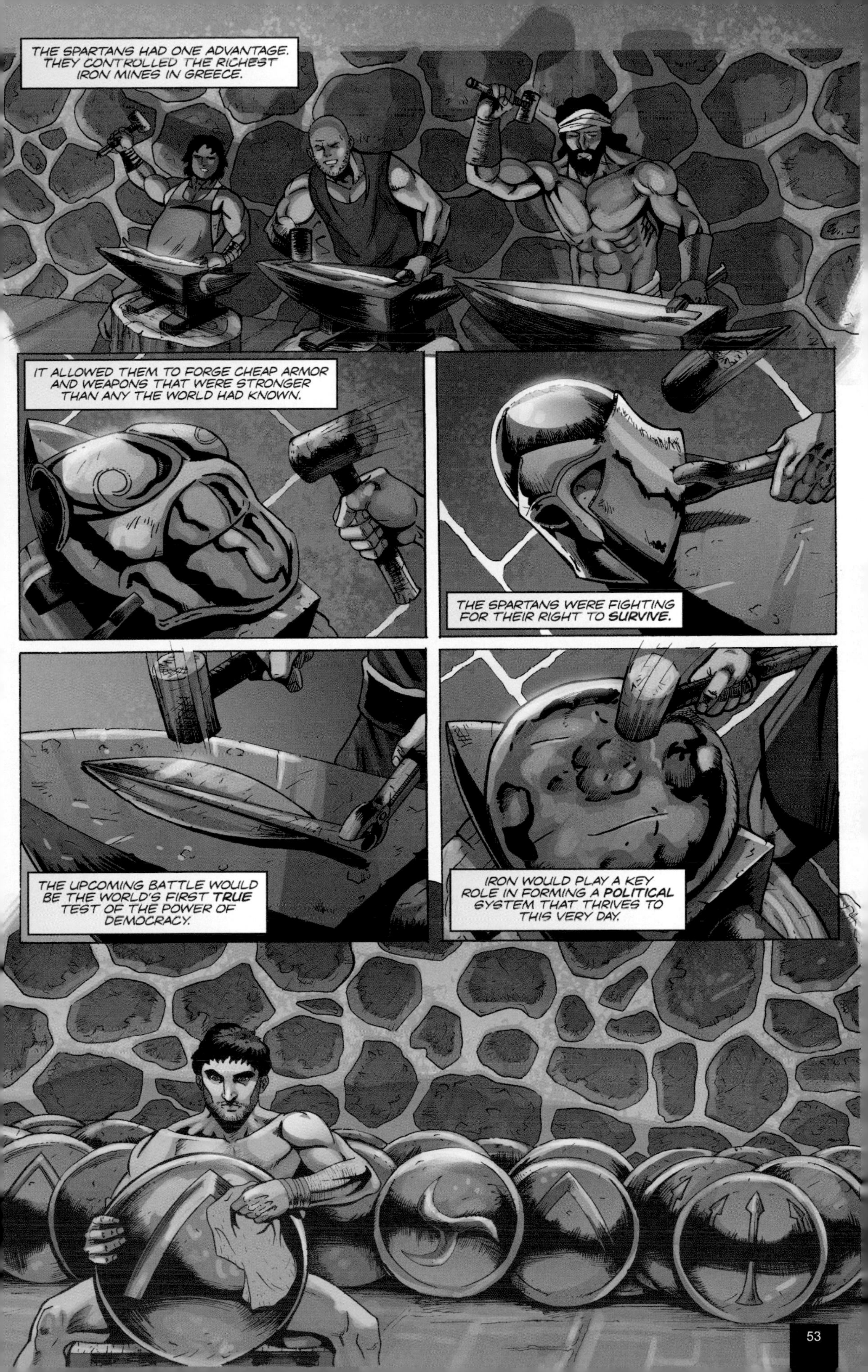
THE SPARTANS HAD ONE ADVANTAGE. THEY CONTROLLED THE RICHEST IRON MINES IN GREECE.
IT ALLOWED THEM TO FORGE CHEAP ARMOR AND WEAPONS THAT WERE STRONGER THAN ANY THE WORLD HAD KNOWN.
THE SPARTANS WERE FIGHTING FOR THEIR RIGHT TO **SURVIVE**.
THE UPCOMING BATTLE WOULD BE THE WORLD'S FIRST **TRUE** TEST OF THE POWER OF DEMOCRACY.
IRON WOULD PLAY A KEY ROLE IN FORMING A **POLITICAL** SYSTEM THAT THRIVES TO THIS VERY DAY.

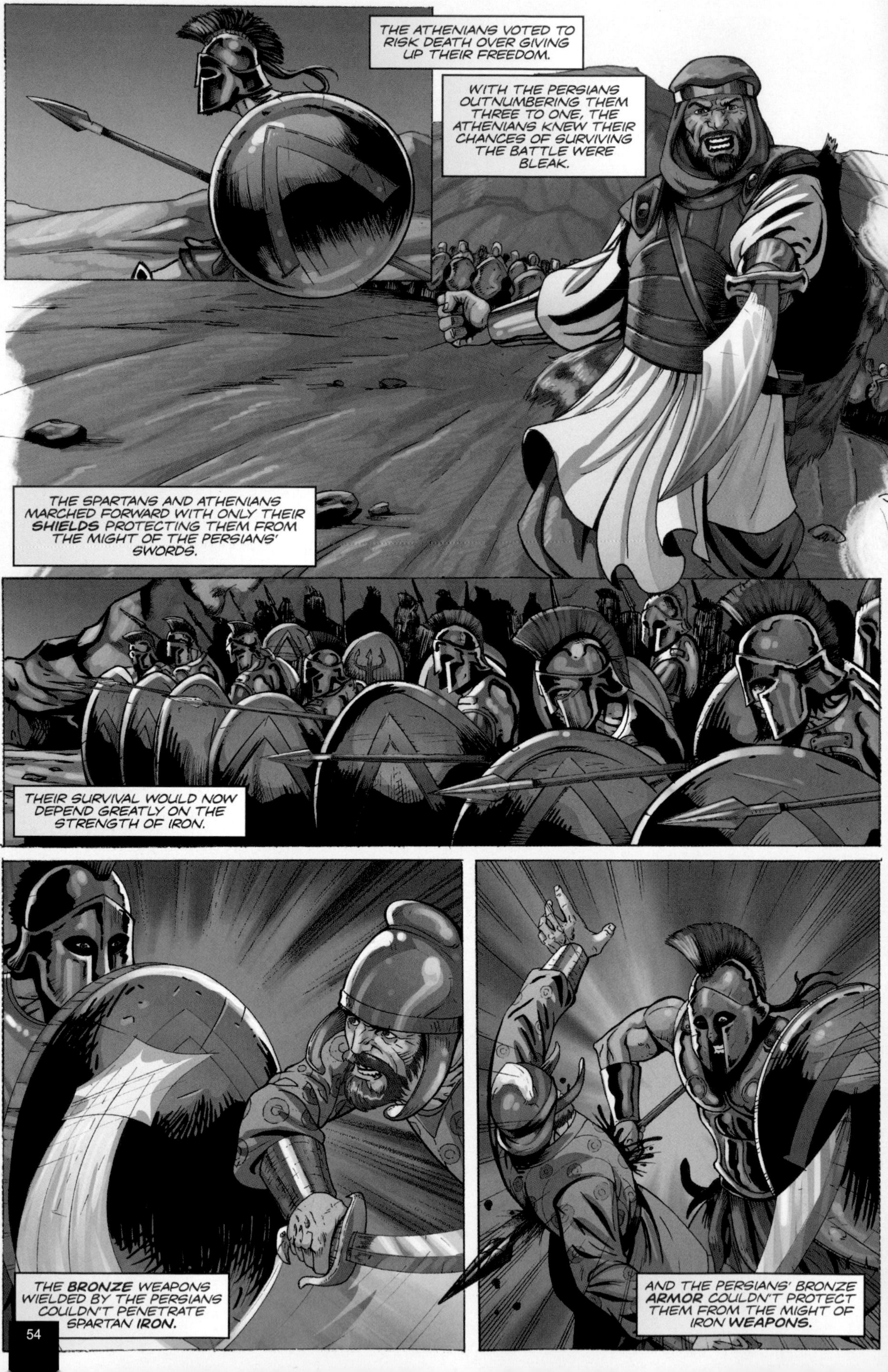
THE ATHENIANS VOTED TO RISK DEATH OVER GIVING UP THEIR FREEDOM.
WITH THE PERSIANS OUTNUMBERING THEM THREE TO ONE, THE ATHENIANS KNEW THEIR CHANCES OF SURVIVING THE BATTLE WERE BLEAK.
THE SPARTANS AND ATHENIANS MARCHED FORWARD WITH ONLY THEIR **SHIELDS** PROTECTING THEM FROM THE MIGHT OF THE PERSIANS' SWORDS.
THEIR SURVIVAL WOULD NOW DEPEND GREATLY ON THE STRENGTH OF IRON.
THE **BRONZE** WEAPONS WIELDED BY THE PERSIANS COULDN'T PENETRATE SPARTAN **IRON.**
AND THE PERSIANS' BRONZE **ARMOR** COULDN'T PROTECT THEM FROM THE MIGHT OF IRON **WEAPONS.**

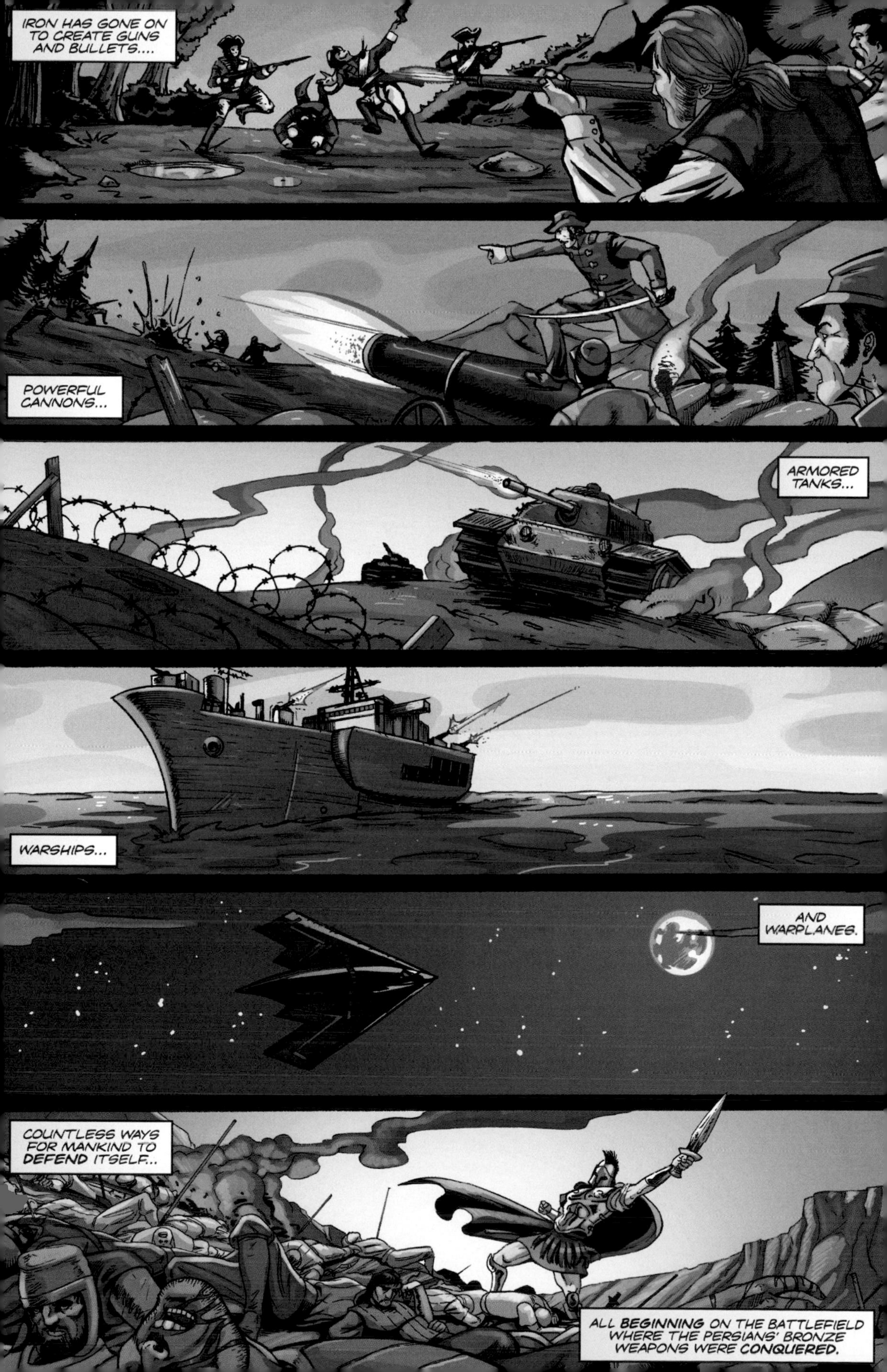
IRON HAS GONE ON TO CREATE GUNS AND BULLETS....
POWERFUL CANNONS...
ARMORED TANKS...
WARSHIPS...
AND WARPLANES.
COUNTLESS WAYS FOR MANKIND TO **DEFEND** ITSELF...
ALL **BEGINNING** ON THE BATTLEFIELD WHERE THE PERSIANS' BRONZE WEAPONS WERE **CONQUERED**.

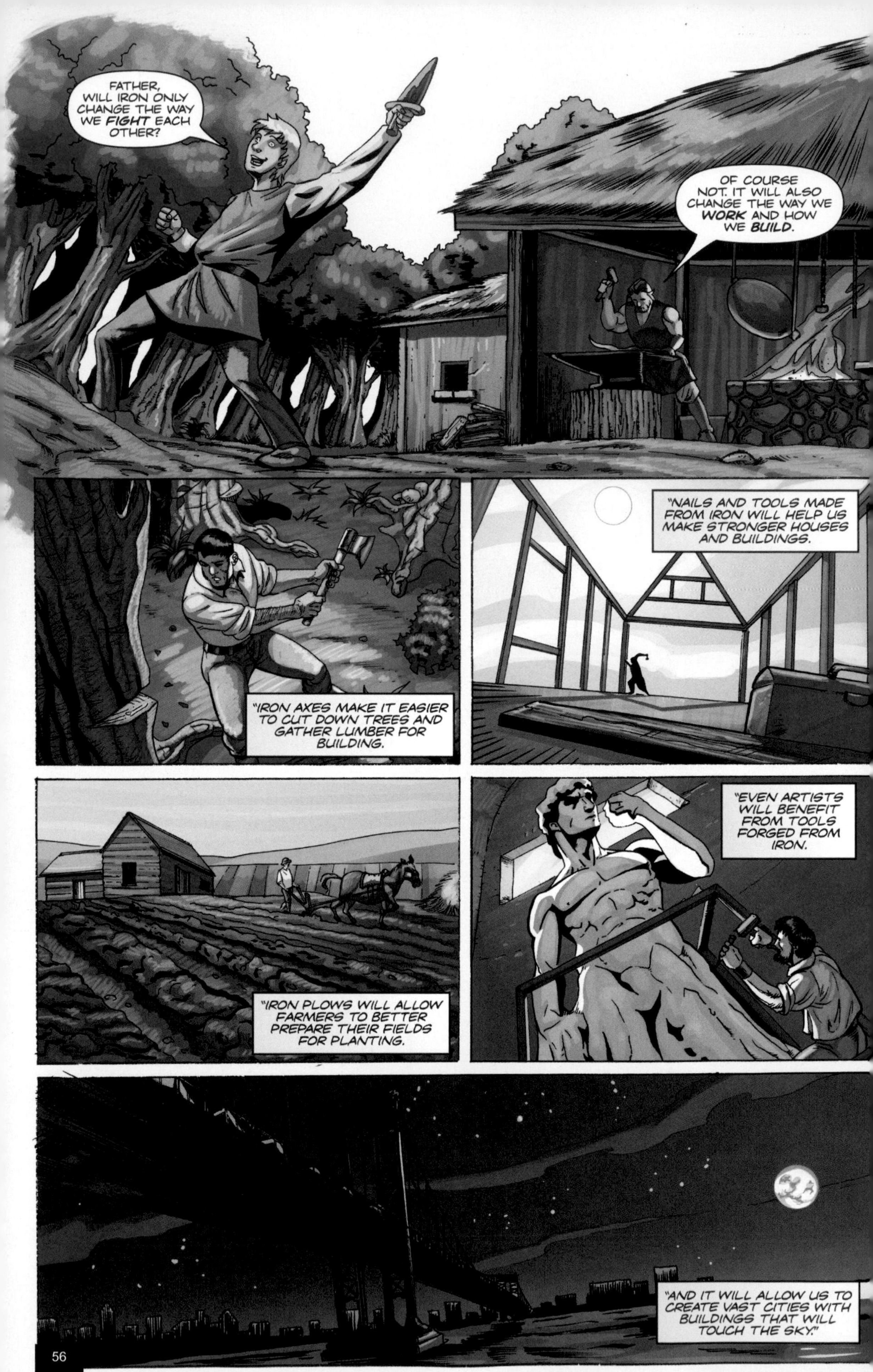
FATHER, WILL IRON ONLY CHANGE THE WAY WE FIGHT EACH OTHER?
OF COURSE NOT. IT WILL ALSO CHANGE THE WAY WE WORK AND HOW WE BUILD.
"IRON AXES MAKE IT EASIER TO CUT DOWN TREES AND GATHER LUMBER FOR BUILDING.
"NAILS AND TOOLS MADE FROM IRON WILL HELP US MAKE STRONGER HOUSES AND BUILDINGS.
"IRON PLOWS WILL ALLOW FARMERS TO BETTER PREPARE THEIR FIELDS FOR PLANTING.
"EVEN ARTISTS WILL BENEFIT FROM TOOLS FORGED FROM IRON.
"AND IT WILL ALLOW US TO CREATE VAST CITIES WITH BUILDINGS THAT WILL TOUCH THE SKY."

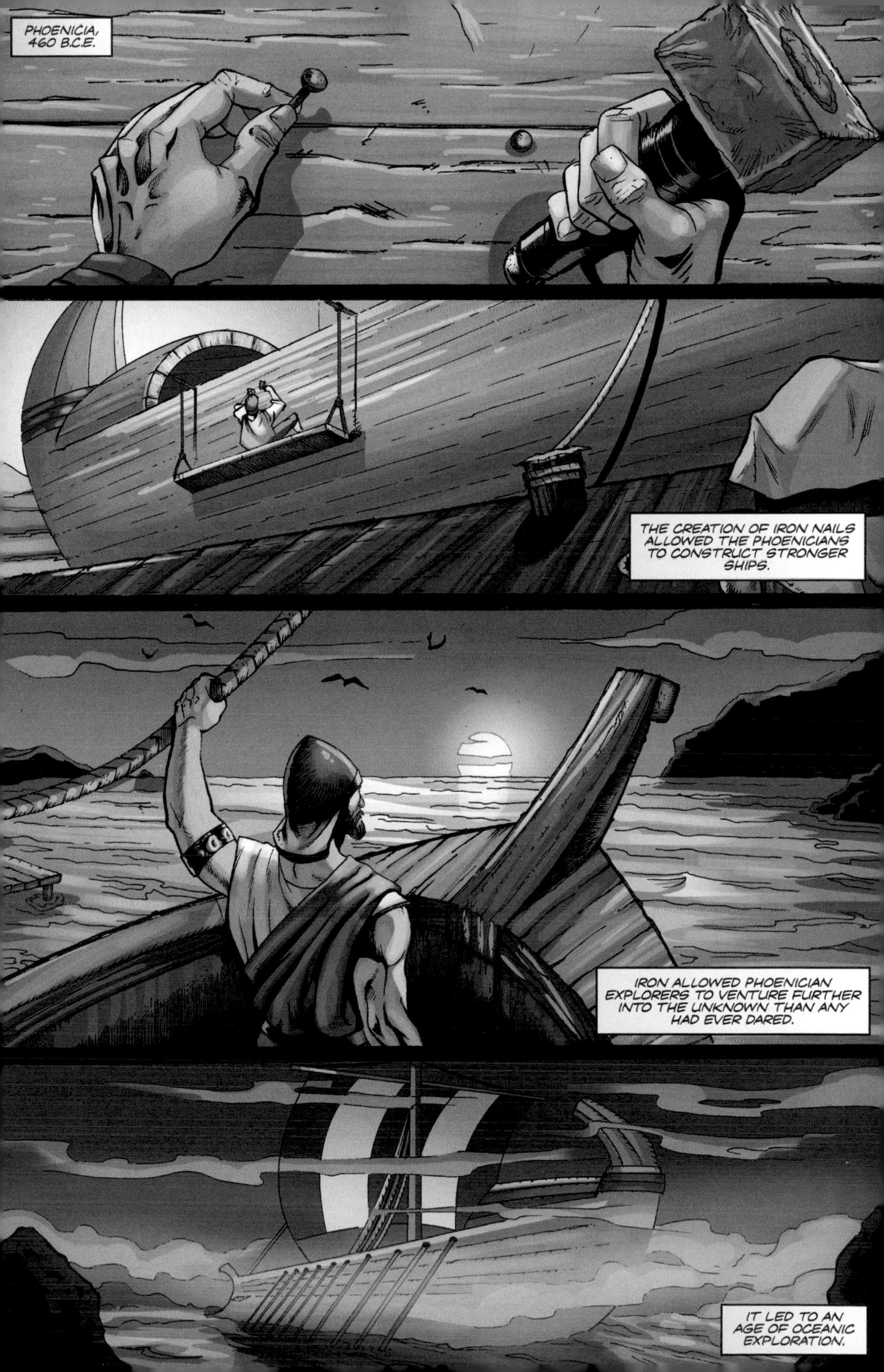
PHOENICIA, 460 B.C.E.
THE CREATION OF IRON NAILS ALLOWED THE PHOENICIANS TO CONSTRUCT STRONGER SHIPS.
IRON ALLOWED PHOENICIAN EXPLORERS TO VENTURE FURTHER INTO THE UNKNOWN THAN ANY HAD EVER DARED.
IT LED TO AN AGE OF OCEANIC EXPLORATION.

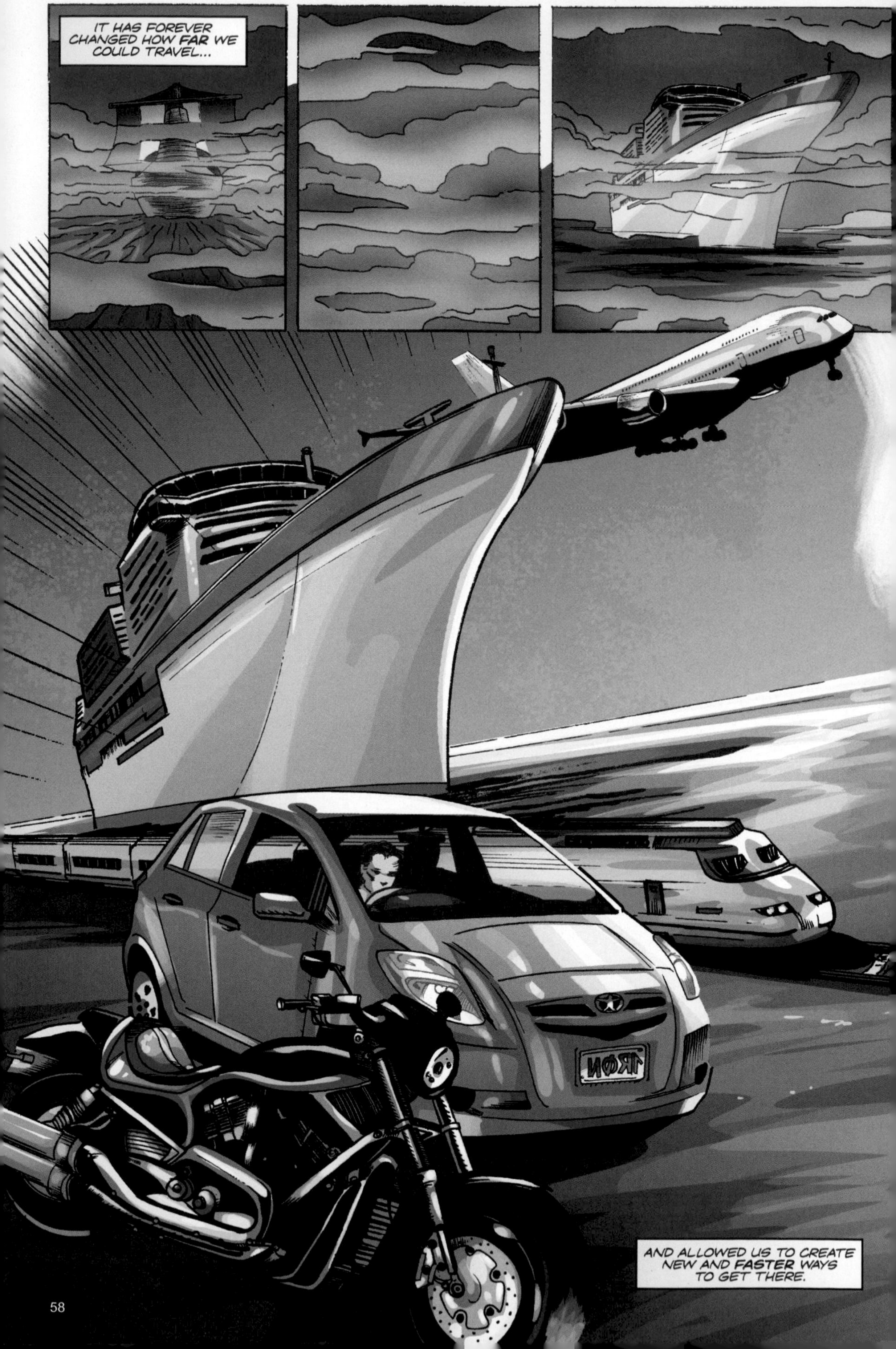
IT HAS FOREVER CHANGED HOW FAR WE COULD TRAVEL...
AND ALLOWED US TO CREATE NEW AND FASTER WAYS TO GET THERE.

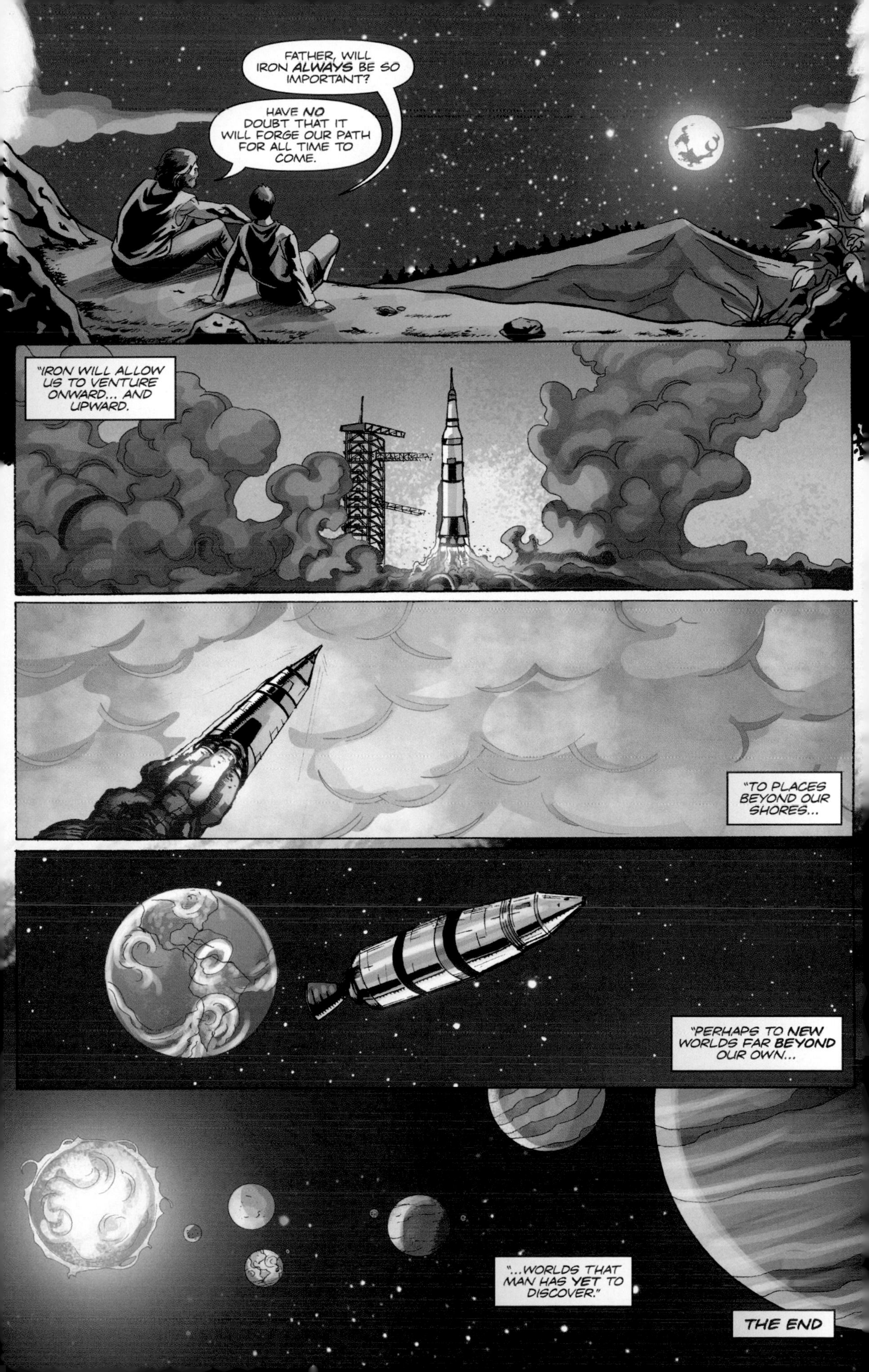
FATHER, WILL IRON ALWAYS BE SO IMPORTANT?
HAVE NO DOUBT THAT IT WILL FORGE OUR PATH FOR ALL TIME TO COME.
"IRON WILL ALLOW US TO VENTURE ONWARD... AND UPWARD.
"TO PLACES BEYOND OUR SHORES...
"PERHAPS TO NEW WORLDS FAR BEYOND OUR OWN...
"...WORLDS THAT MAN HAS YET TO DISCOVER."
THE END

MANKIND
DECODED

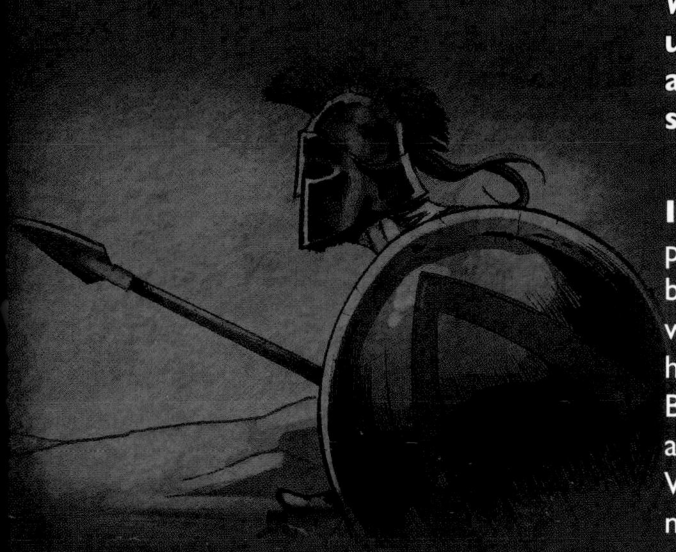

***Will of Iron* illustrates the many uses of iron in human history as an essential key to Mankind's survival.**

Iron makes ordinary humans more powerful and also allows us to make better tools, which in turn makes hard work much easier and faster to finish. It has been actively used as early as 1800 B.C.E. and remains the most common and important metal used today. Without iron, life as we know it would not exist.

The core of our planet is made up of white-hot iron, which creates a magnetic field that surrounds and protects the Earth from devastating solar winds and radiation. This magnetic iron core also makes air and sea navigation possible.

Iron is used not just on Earth, but also within our bodies. Microscopic iron proteins are found in every living organism on the planet. It is essential to the **human body** in transporting oxygen throughout the bloodstream, helping fight off infection and disease, as well as maintaining other critical functions.

Iron is used to make steel by extracting various impurities and adding other alloys. Without iron and steel, we would not be able to build the skyscrapers and bridges we use today.

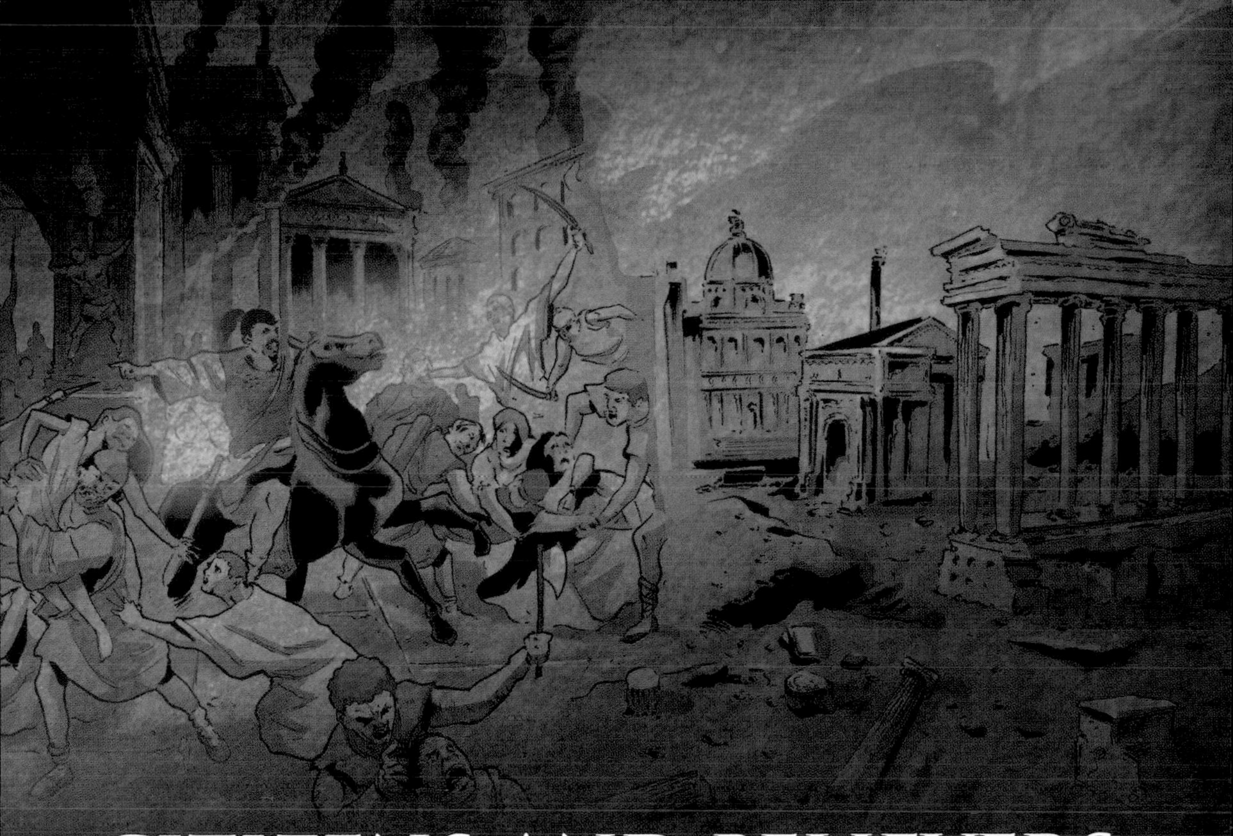

CITIZENS AND BELIEVERS

WRITTEN BY
NEO EDMUND

ART BY
GIOVANNI TIMPANO

COLORS BY
STEPHEN DOWNER

LETTERS BY
JIM CAMPBELL

AS ROMAN EMPERORS VIE TO BUILD THEIR LEGACIES OUT OF PLUNDER AND SILVER, ONE MAN IN JERUSALEM BUILDS HIS LEGACY OUT OF BELIEF AND FAITH.

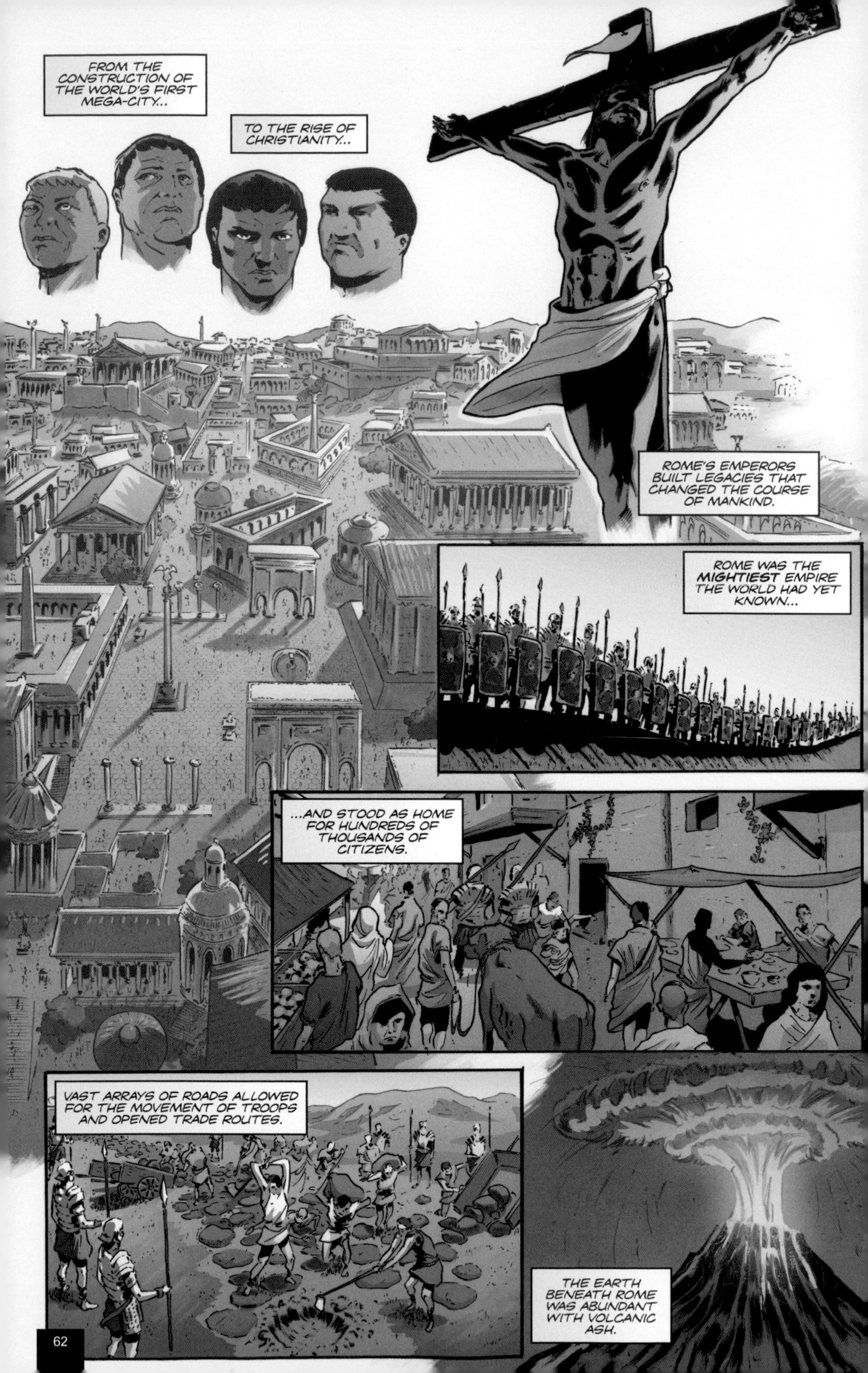
FROM THE CONSTRUCTION OF THE WORLD'S FIRST MEGA-CITY...
TO THE RISE OF CHRISTIANITY...
ROME'S EMPERORS BUILT LEGACIES THAT CHANGED THE COURSE OF MANKIND.
ROME WAS THE MIGHTIEST EMPIRE THE WORLD HAD YET KNOWN...
...AND STOOD AS HOME FOR HUNDREDS OF THOUSANDS OF CITIZENS.
VAST ARRAYS OF ROADS ALLOWED FOR THE MOVEMENT OF TROOPS AND OPENED TRADE ROUTES.
THE EARTH BENEATH ROME WAS ABUNDANT WITH VOLCANIC ASH.

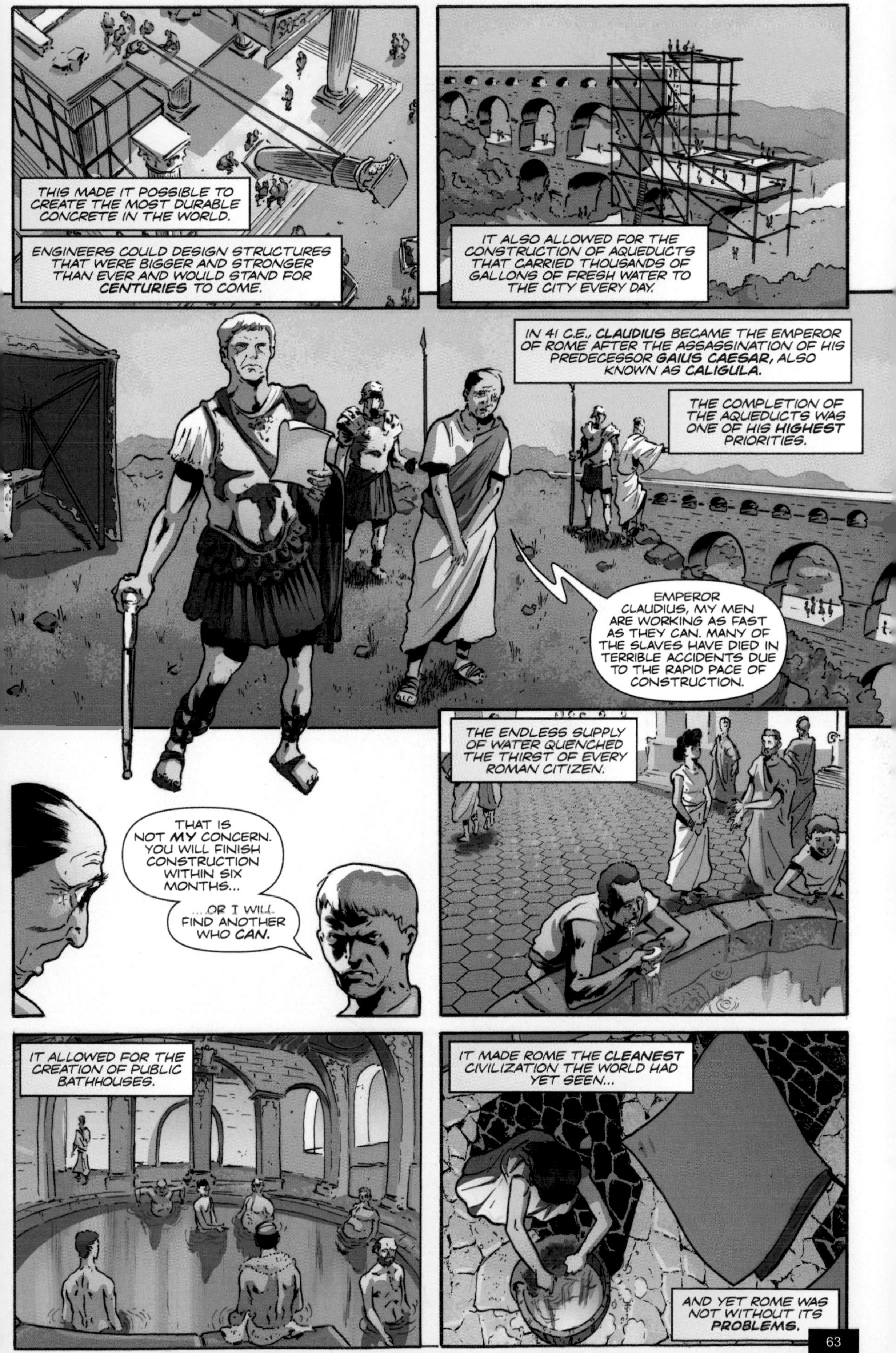

THIS MADE IT POSSIBLE TO CREATE THE MOST DURABLE CONCRETE IN THE WORLD.
ENGINEERS COULD DESIGN STRUCTURES THAT WERE BIGGER AND STRONGER THAN EVER AND WOULD STAND FOR **CENTURIES** TO COME.
IT ALSO ALLOWED FOR THE CONSTRUCTION OF AQUEDUCTS THAT CARRIED THOUSANDS OF GALLONS OF FRESH WATER TO THE CITY EVERY DAY.
IN 41 C.E., **CLAUDIUS** BECAME THE EMPEROR OF ROME AFTER THE ASSASSINATION OF HIS PREDECESSOR **GAIUS CAESAR,** ALSO KNOWN AS **CALIGULA.**
THE COMPLETION OF THE AQUEDUCTS WAS ONE OF HIS **HIGHEST** PRIORITIES.
EMPEROR CLAUDIUS, MY MEN ARE WORKING AS FAST AS THEY CAN. MANY OF THE SLAVES HAVE DIED IN TERRIBLE ACCIDENTS DUE TO THE RAPID PACE OF CONSTRUCTION.
THAT IS NOT **MY** CONCERN. YOU WILL FINISH CONSTRUCTION WITHIN SIX MONTHS...
...OR I WILL FIND ANOTHER WHO **CAN.**
THE ENDLESS SUPPLY OF WATER QUENCHED THE THIRST OF EVERY ROMAN CITIZEN.
IT ALLOWED FOR THE CREATION OF PUBLIC BATHHOUSES.
IT MADE ROME THE **CLEANEST** CIVILIZATION THE WORLD HAD YET SEEN...
AND YET ROME WAS NOT WITHOUT ITS **PROBLEMS.**

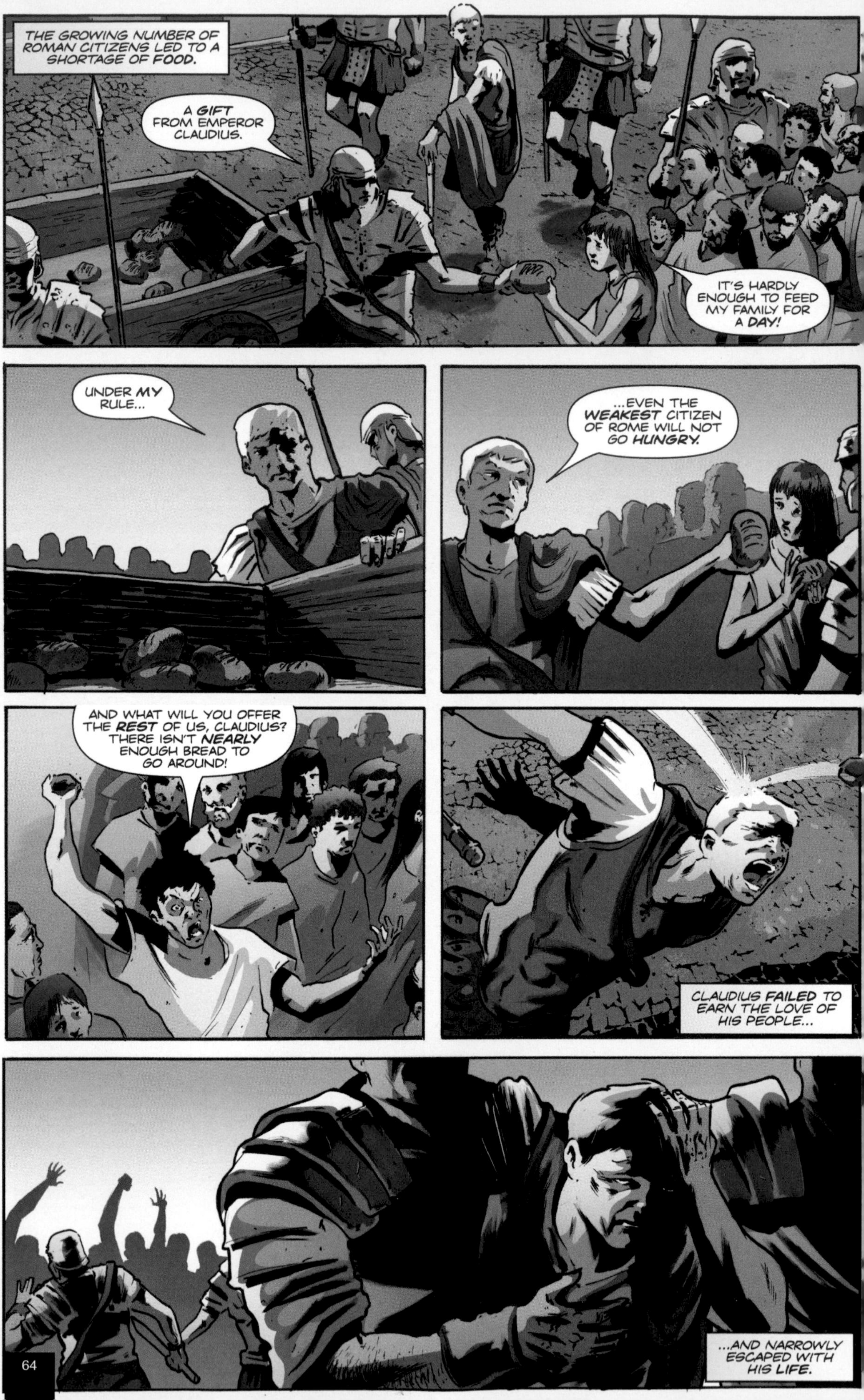
THE GROWING NUMBER OF ROMAN CITIZENS LED TO A SHORTAGE OF FOOD.
A GIFT FROM EMPEROR CLAUDIUS.
IT'S HARDLY ENOUGH TO FEED MY FAMILY FOR A DAY!
UNDER MY RULE...
...EVEN THE WEAKEST CITIZEN OF ROME WILL NOT GO HUNGRY.
AND WHAT WILL YOU OFFER THE REST OF US, CLAUDIUS? THERE ISN'T NEARLY ENOUGH BREAD TO GO AROUND!
CLAUDIUS FAILED TO EARN THE LOVE OF HIS PEOPLE...
...AND NARROWLY ESCAPED WITH HIS LIFE.

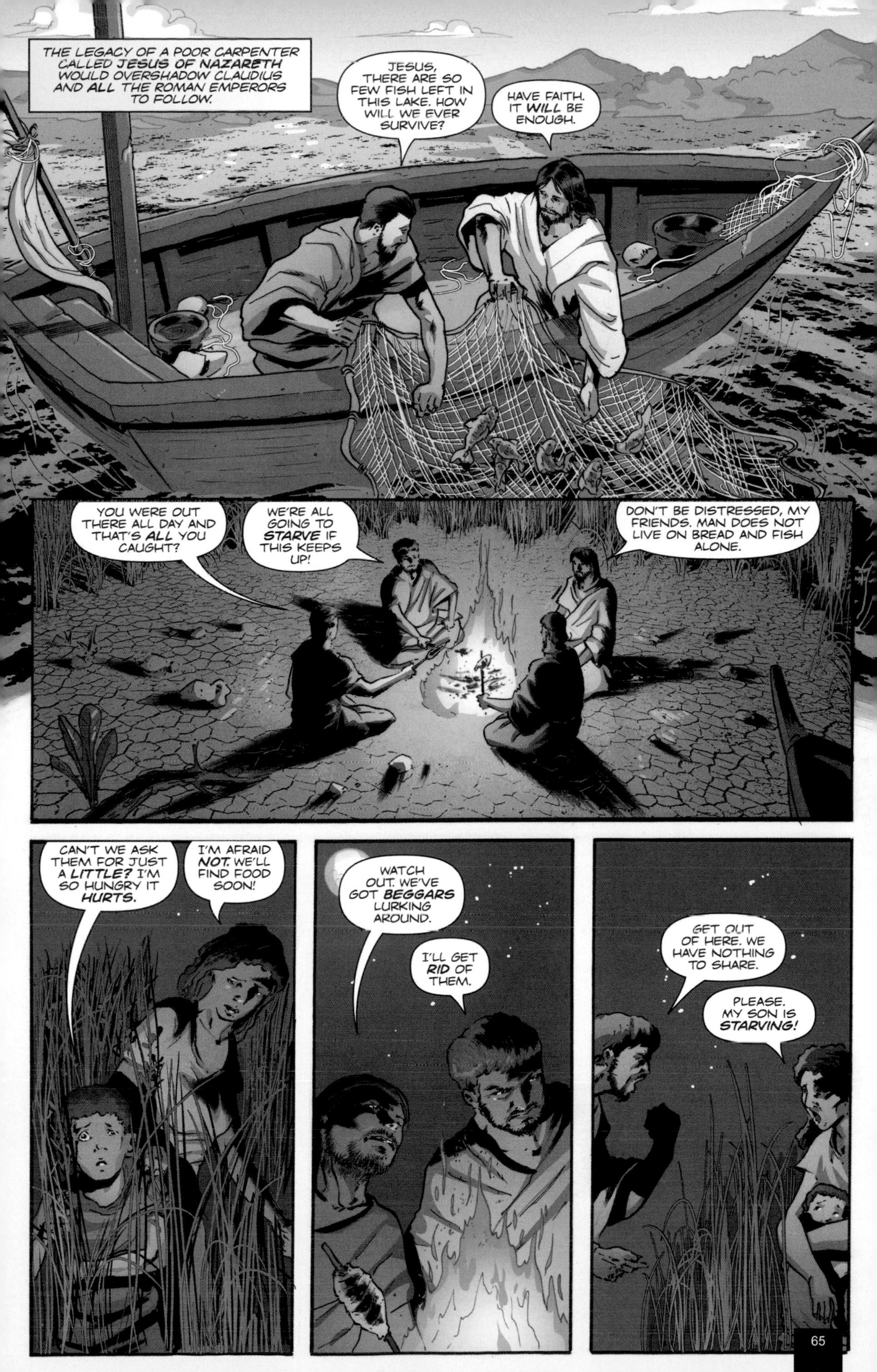
THE LEGACY OF A POOR CARPENTER CALLED JESUS OF NAZARETH WOULD OVERSHADOW CLAUDIUS AND ALL THE ROMAN EMPERORS TO FOLLOW.
JESUS, THERE ARE SO FEW FISH LEFT IN THIS LAKE. HOW WILL WE EVER SURVIVE?
HAVE FAITH. IT WILL BE ENOUGH.
YOU WERE OUT THERE ALL DAY AND THAT'S ALL YOU CAUGHT?
WE'RE ALL GOING TO STARVE IF THIS KEEPS UP!
DON'T BE DISTRESSED, MY FRIENDS. MAN DOES NOT LIVE ON BREAD AND FISH ALONE.
CAN'T WE ASK THEM FOR JUST A LITTLE? I'M SO HUNGRY IT HURTS.
I'M AFRAID NOT. WE'LL FIND FOOD SOON!
WATCH OUT. WE'VE GOT BEGGARS LURKING AROUND.
I'LL GET RID OF THEM.
GET OUT OF HERE. WE HAVE NOTHING TO SHARE.
PLEASE. MY SON IS STARVING!

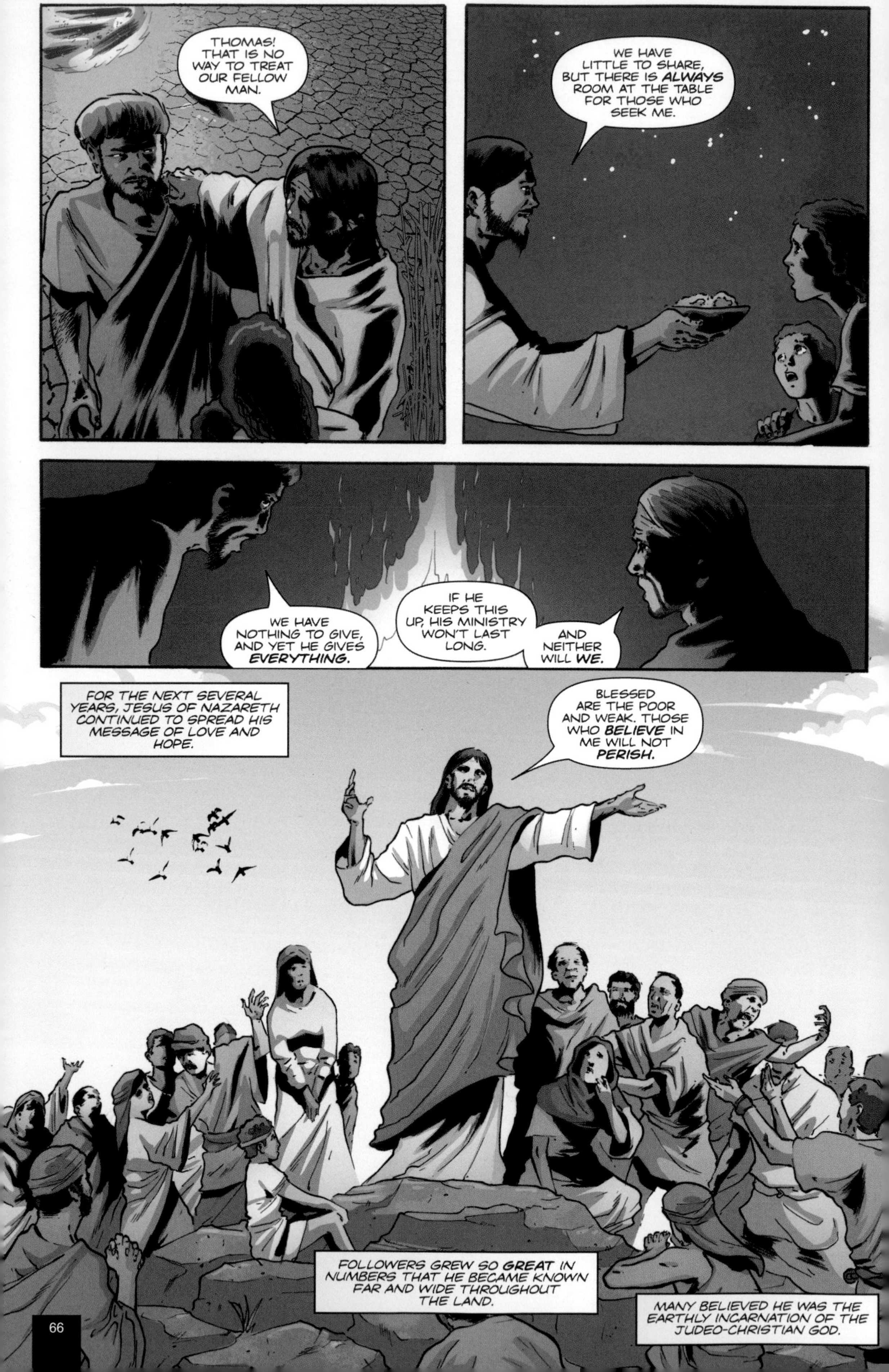

THOMAS! THAT IS NO WAY TO TREAT OUR FELLOW MAN.
WE HAVE LITTLE TO SHARE, BUT THERE IS ALWAYS ROOM AT THE TABLE FOR THOSE WHO SEEK ME.
WE HAVE NOTHING TO GIVE, AND YET HE GIVES EVERYTHING.
IF HE KEEPS THIS UP, HIS MINISTRY WON'T LAST LONG.
AND NEITHER WILL WE.
FOR THE NEXT SEVERAL YEARS, JESUS OF NAZARETH CONTINUED TO SPREAD HIS MESSAGE OF LOVE AND HOPE.
BLESSED ARE THE POOR AND WEAK. THOSE WHO BELIEVE IN ME WILL NOT PERISH.
FOLLOWERS GREW SO GREAT IN NUMBERS THAT HE BECAME KNOWN FAR AND WIDE THROUGHOUT THE LAND.
MANY BELIEVED HE WAS THE EARTHLY INCARNATION OF THE JUDEO-CHRISTIAN GOD.

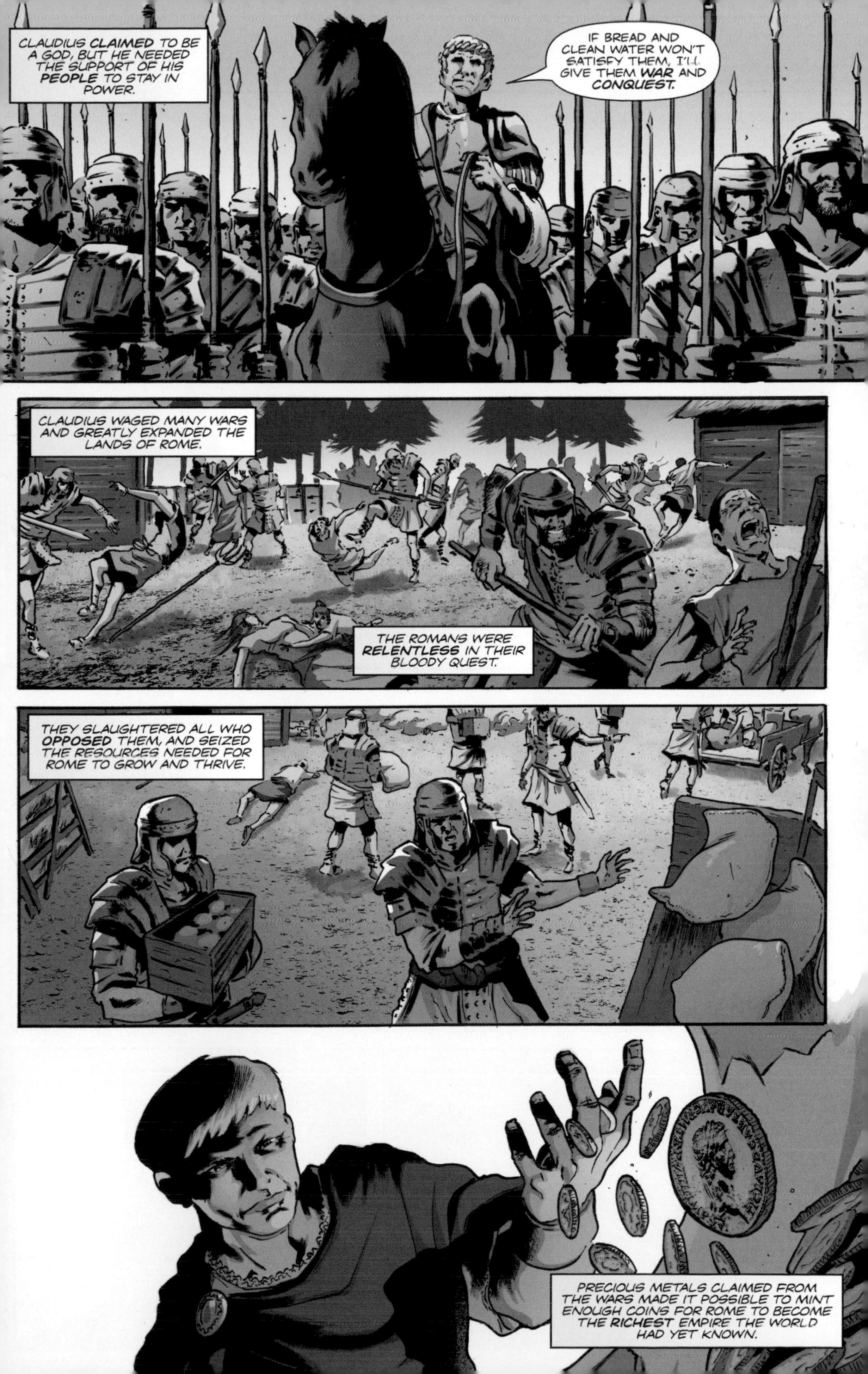
CLAUDIUS CLAIMED TO BE A GOD, BUT HE NEEDED THE SUPPORT OF HIS PEOPLE TO STAY IN POWER.
IF BREAD AND CLEAN WATER WON'T SATISFY THEM, I'LL GIVE THEM WAR AND CONQUEST.
CLAUDIUS WAGED MANY WARS AND GREATLY EXPANDED THE LANDS OF ROME.
THE ROMANS WERE RELENTLESS IN THEIR BLOODY QUEST.
THEY SLAUGHTERED ALL WHO OPPOSED THEM, AND SEIZED THE RESOURCES NEEDED FOR ROME TO GROW AND THRIVE.
PRECIOUS METALS CLAIMED FROM THE WARS MADE IT POSSIBLE TO MINT ENOUGH COINS FOR ROME TO BECOME THE RICHEST EMPIRE THE WORLD HAD YET KNOWN.

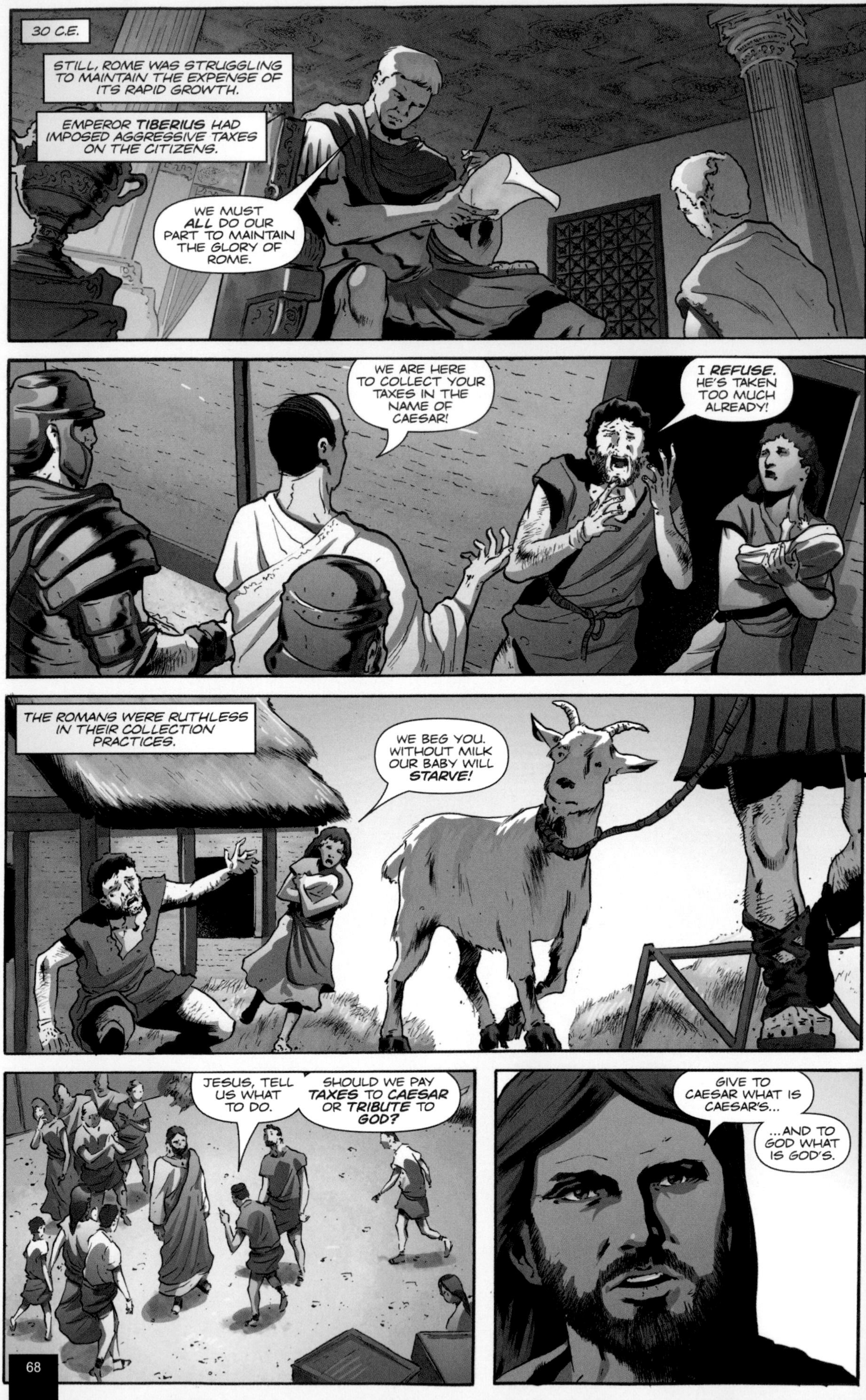
30 C.E.
STILL, ROME WAS STRUGGLING TO MAINTAIN THE EXPENSE OF ITS RAPID GROWTH.
EMPEROR TIBERIUS HAD IMPOSED AGGRESSIVE TAXES ON THE CITIZENS.
WE MUST ALL DO OUR PART TO MAINTAIN THE GLORY OF ROME.
WE ARE HERE TO COLLECT YOUR TAXES IN THE NAME OF CAESAR!
I REFUSE. HE'S TAKEN TOO MUCH ALREADY!
THE ROMANS WERE RUTHLESS IN THEIR COLLECTION PRACTICES.
WE BEG YOU. WITHOUT MILK OUR BABY WILL STARVE!
JESUS, TELL US WHAT TO DO.
SHOULD WE PAY TAXES TO CAESAR OR TRIBUTE TO GOD?
GIVE TO CAESAR WHAT IS CAESAR'S...
...AND TO GOD WHAT IS GOD'S.

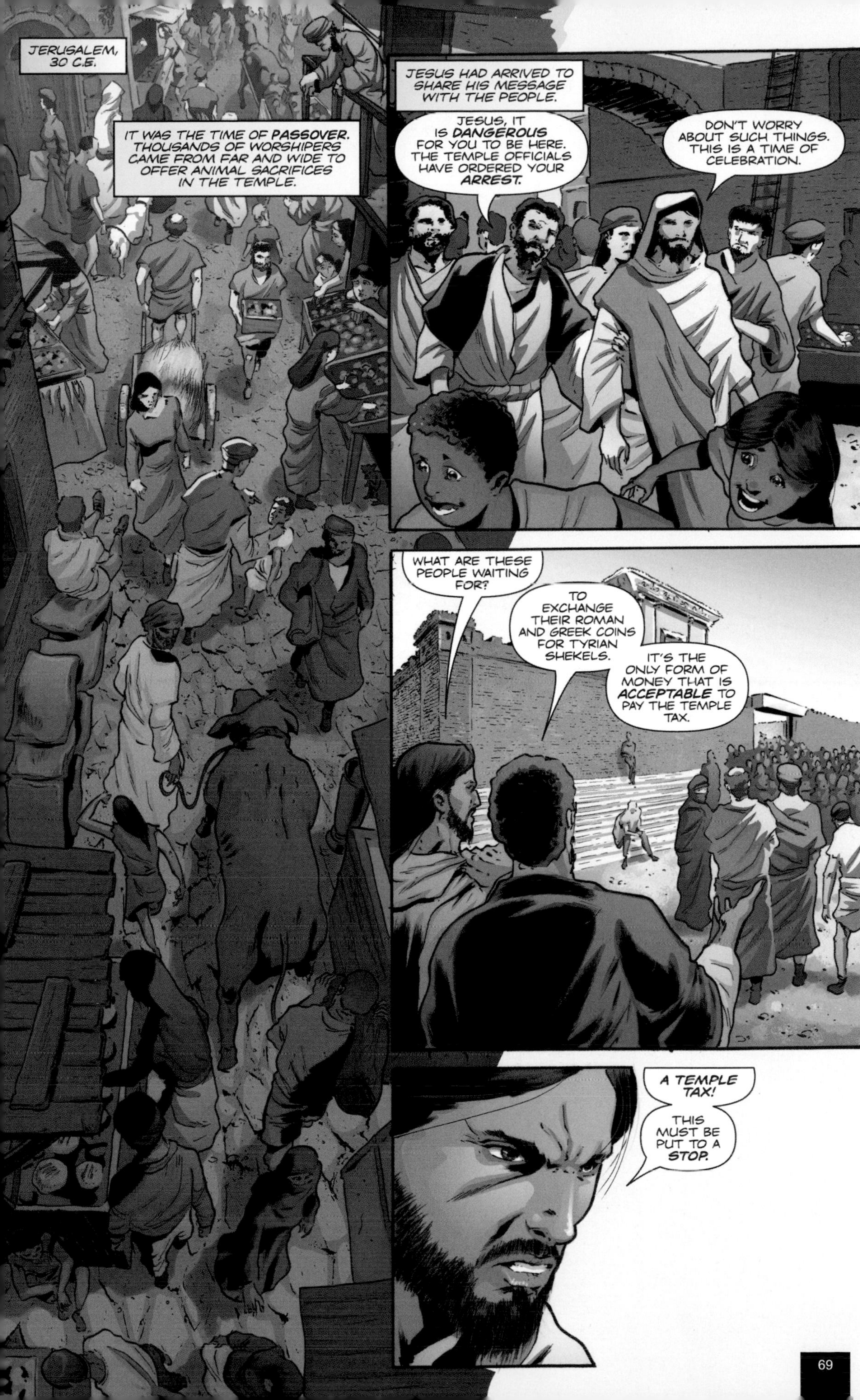
JERUSALEM, 30 C.E.
IT WAS THE TIME OF PASSOVER. THOUSANDS OF WORSHIPERS CAME FROM FAR AND WIDE TO OFFER ANIMAL SACRIFICES IN THE TEMPLE.
JESUS HAD ARRIVED TO SHARE HIS MESSAGE WITH THE PEOPLE.
JESUS, IT IS DANGEROUS FOR YOU TO BE HERE. THE TEMPLE OFFICIALS HAVE ORDERED YOUR ARREST.
DON'T WORRY ABOUT SUCH THINGS. THIS IS A TIME OF CELEBRATION.
WHAT ARE THESE PEOPLE WAITING FOR?
TO EXCHANGE THEIR ROMAN AND GREEK COINS FOR TYRIAN SHEKELS.
IT'S THE ONLY FORM OF MONEY THAT IS ACCEPTABLE TO PAY THE TEMPLE TAX.
A TEMPLE TAX!
THIS MUST BE PUT TO A STOP.

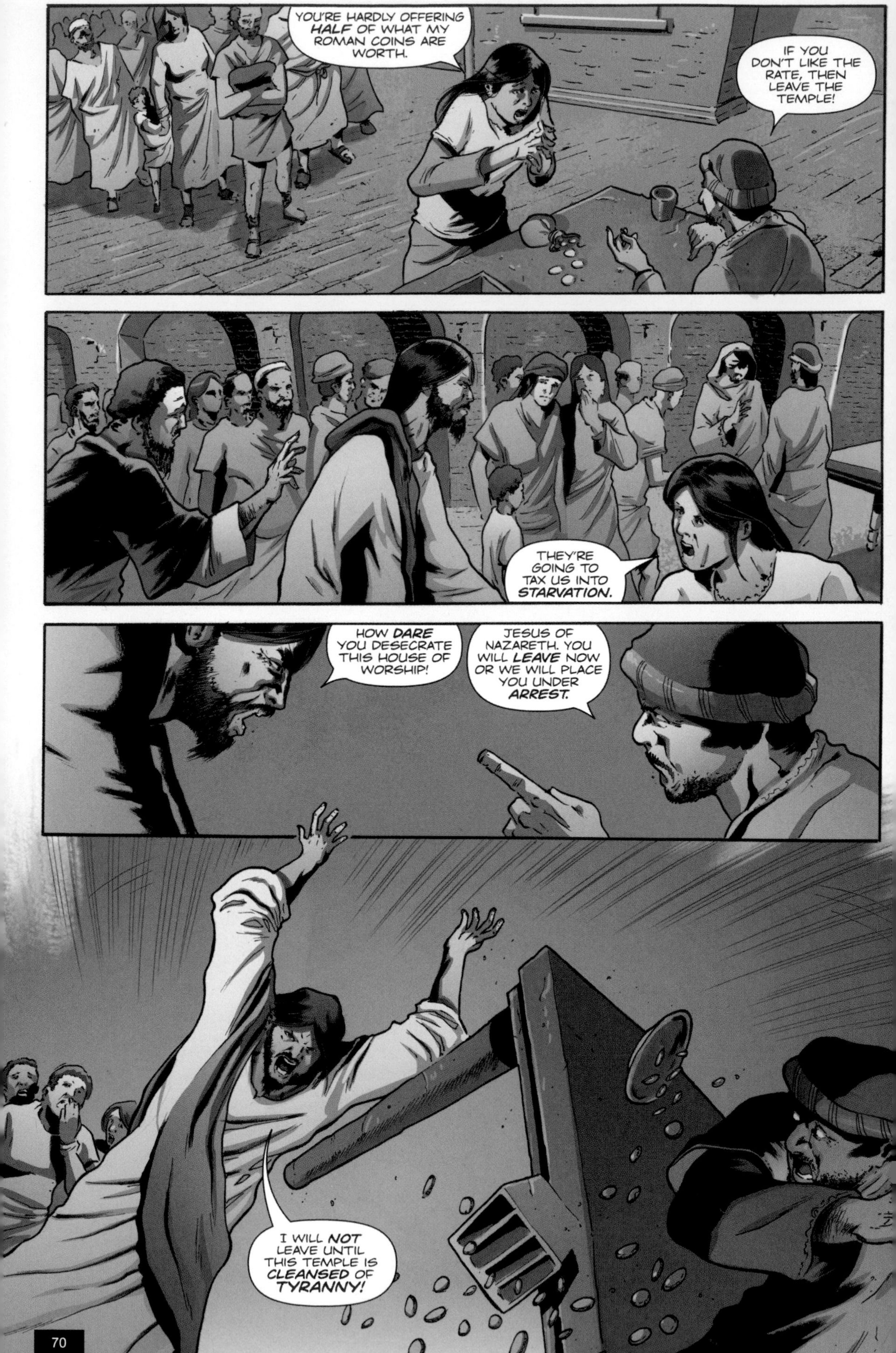
YOU'RE HARDLY OFFERING **HALF** OF WHAT MY ROMAN COINS ARE WORTH.
IF YOU DON'T LIKE THE RATE, THEN LEAVE THE TEMPLE!
THEY'RE GOING TO TAX US INTO **STARVATION.**
HOW **DARE** YOU DESECRATE THIS HOUSE OF WORSHIP!
JESUS OF NAZARETH. YOU WILL **LEAVE** NOW OR WE WILL PLACE YOU UNDER **ARREST.**
I WILL **NOT** LEAVE UNTIL THIS TEMPLE IS **CLEANSED** OF **TYRANNY!**

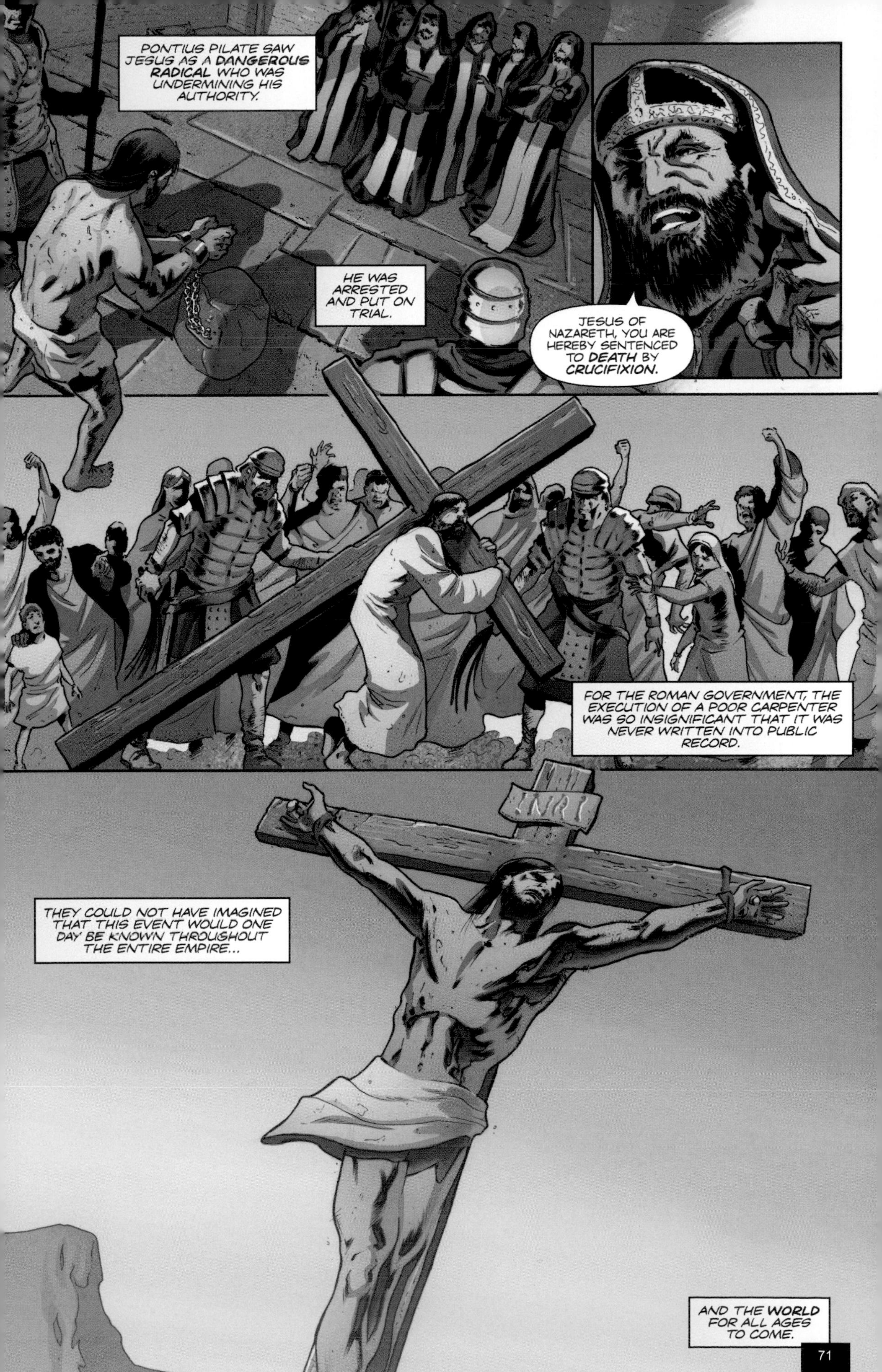
PONTIUS PILATE SAW JESUS AS A DANGEROUS RADICAL WHO WAS UNDERMINING HIS AUTHORITY.
HE WAS ARRESTED AND PUT ON TRIAL.
JESUS OF NAZARETH, YOU ARE HEREBY SENTENCED TO DEATH BY CRUCIFIXION.
FOR THE ROMAN GOVERNMENT, THE EXECUTION OF A POOR CARPENTER WAS SO INSIGNIFICANT THAT IT WAS NEVER WRITTEN INTO PUBLIC RECORD.
INRI
THEY COULD NOT HAVE IMAGINED THAT THIS EVENT WOULD ONE DAY BE KNOWN THROUGHOUT THE ENTIRE EMPIRE...
AND THE WORLD FOR ALL AGES TO COME.

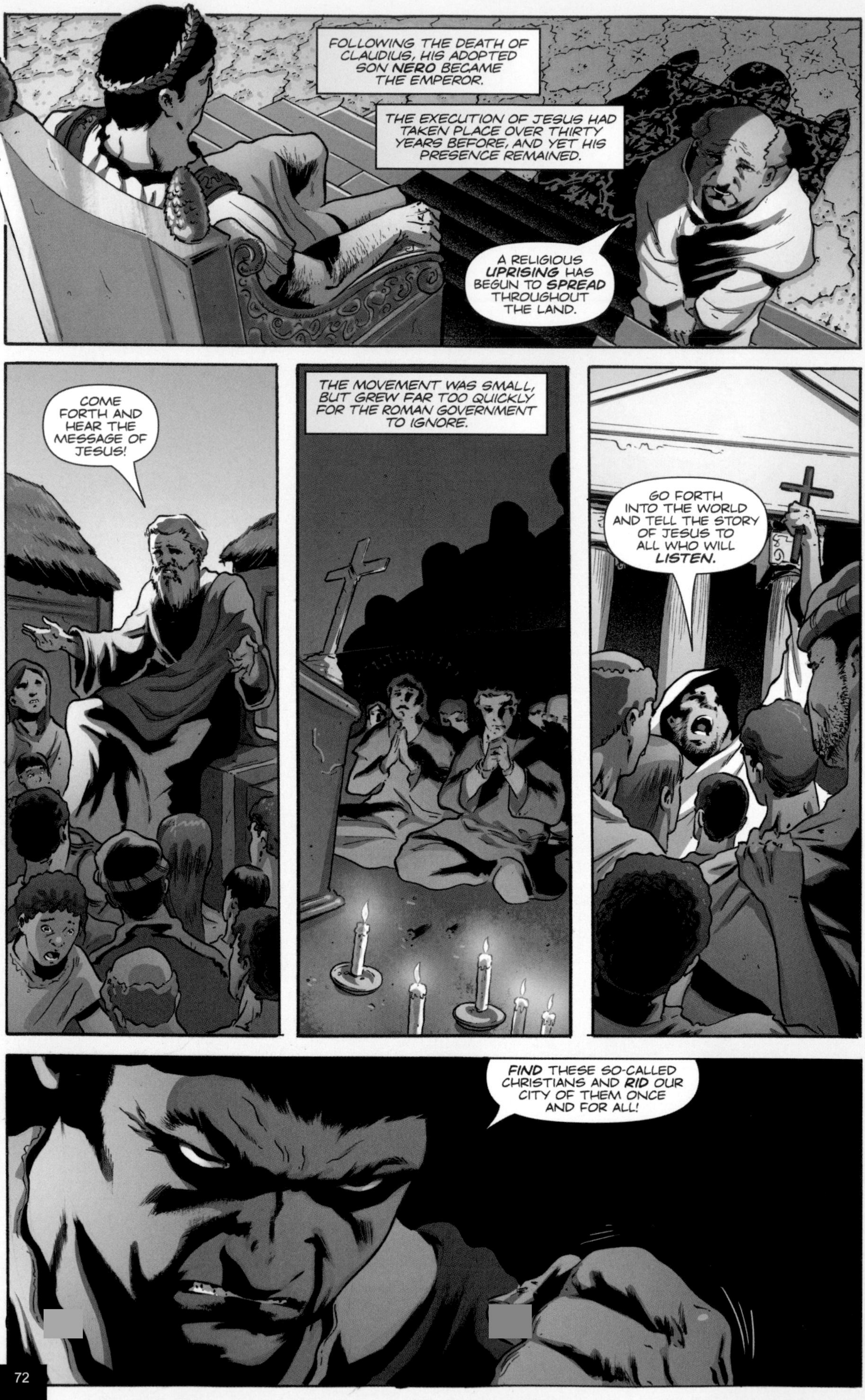
FOLLOWING THE DEATH OF CLAUDIUS, HIS ADOPTED SON NERO BECAME THE EMPEROR.
THE EXECUTION OF JESUS HAD TAKEN PLACE OVER THIRTY YEARS BEFORE, AND YET HIS PRESENCE REMAINED.
A RELIGIOUS UPRISING HAS BEGUN TO SPREAD THROUGHOUT THE LAND.
COME FORTH AND HEAR THE MESSAGE OF JESUS!
THE MOVEMENT WAS SMALL, BUT GREW FAR TOO QUICKLY FOR THE ROMAN GOVERNMENT TO IGNORE.
GO FORTH INTO THE WORLD AND TELL THE STORY OF JESUS TO ALL WHO WILL LISTEN.
FIND THESE SO-CALLED CHRISTIANS AND RID OUR CITY OF THEM ONCE AND FOR ALL!

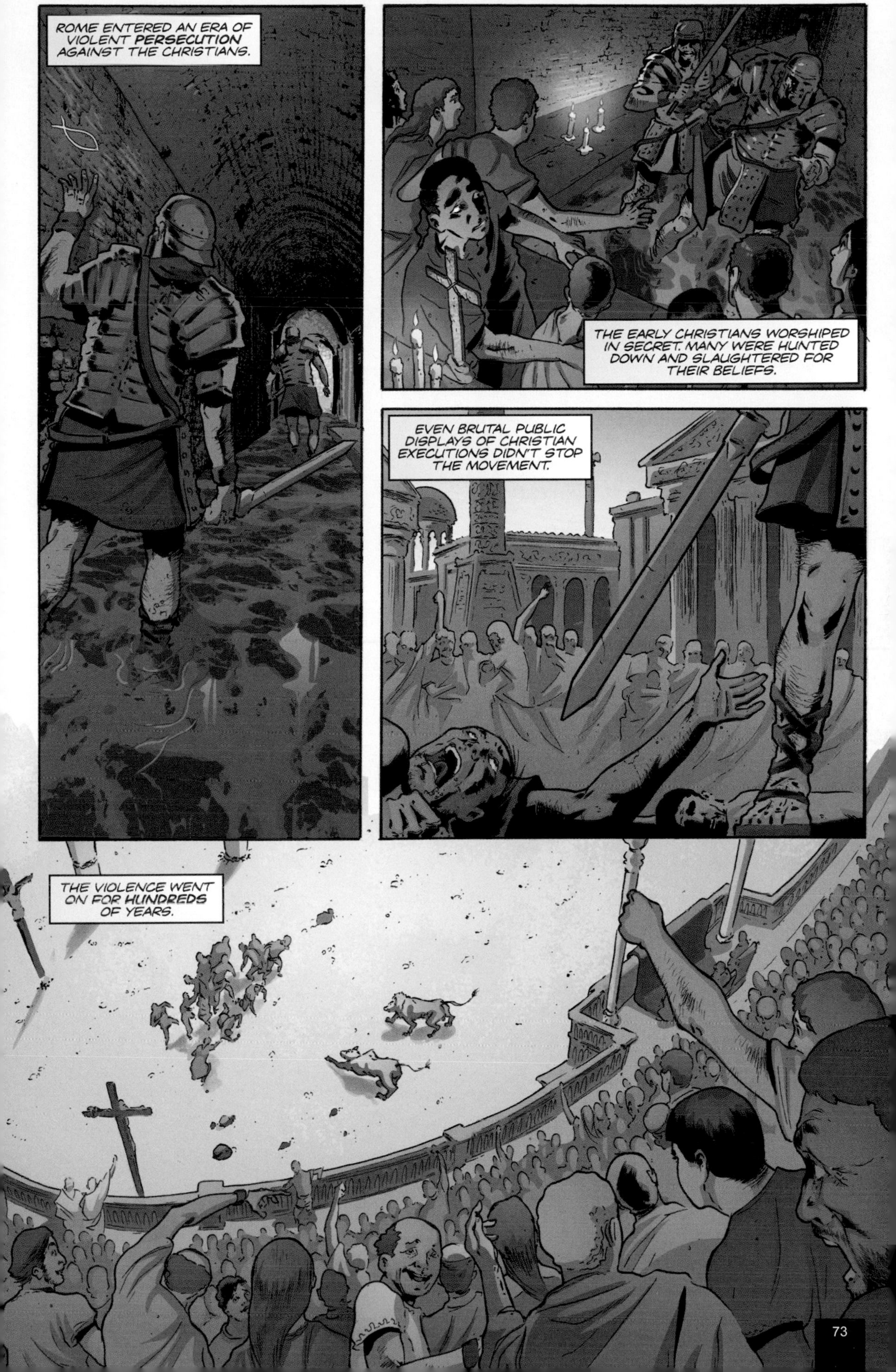
ROME ENTERED AN ERA OF VIOLENT PERSECUTION AGAINST THE CHRISTIANS.
THE EARLY CHRISTIANS WORSHIPED IN SECRET. MANY WERE HUNTED DOWN AND SLAUGHTERED FOR THEIR BELIEFS.
EVEN BRUTAL PUBLIC DISPLAYS OF CHRISTIAN EXECUTIONS DIDN'T STOP THE MOVEMENT.
THE VIOLENCE WENT ON FOR HUNDREDS OF YEARS.

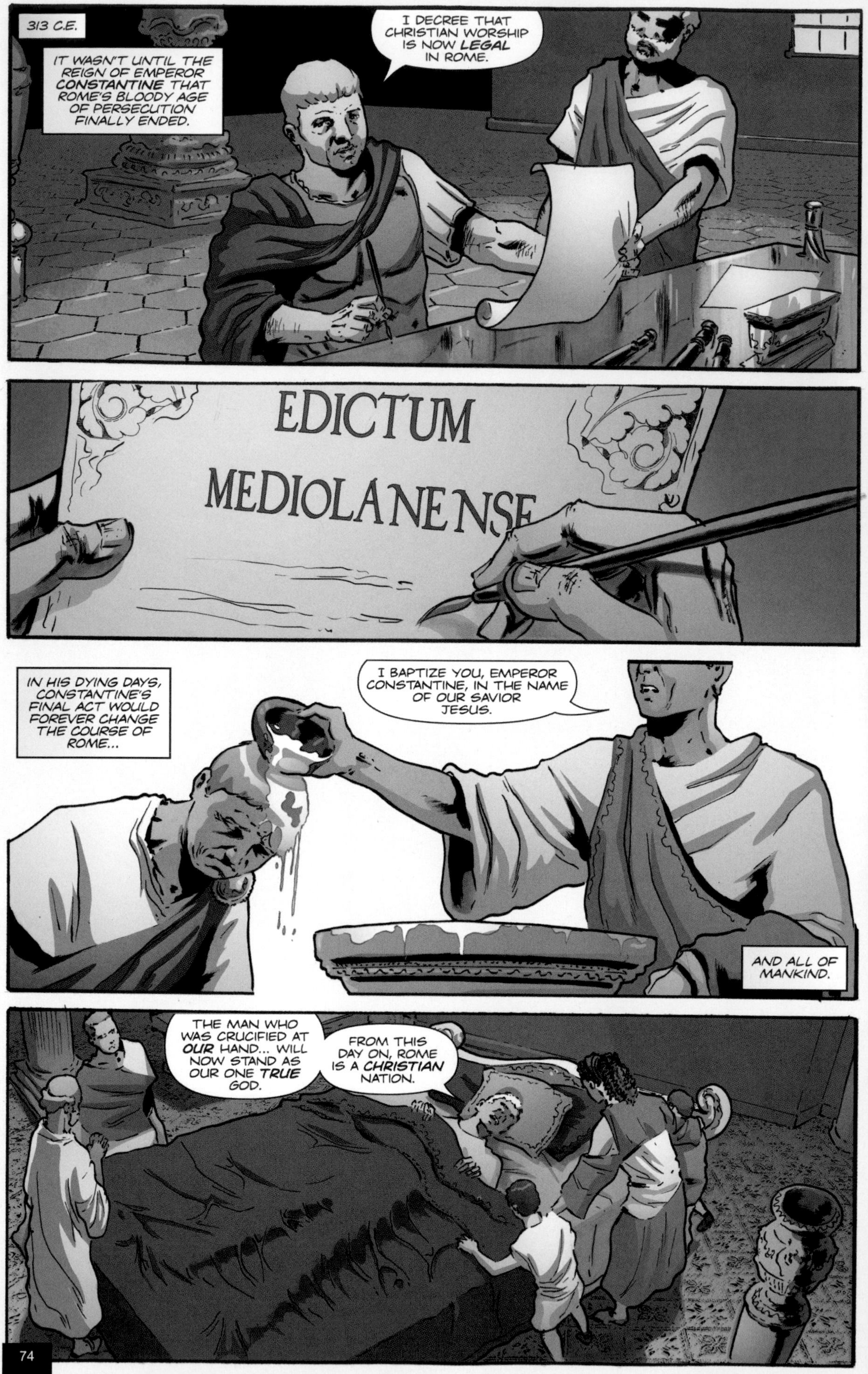

313 C.E.
IT WASN'T UNTIL THE REIGN OF EMPEROR CONSTANTINE THAT ROME'S BLOODY AGE OF PERSECUTION FINALLY ENDED.
I DECREE THAT CHRISTIAN WORSHIP IS NOW LEGAL IN ROME.
EDICTUM MEDIOLANENSE
IN HIS DYING DAYS, CONSTANTINE'S FINAL ACT WOULD FOREVER CHANGE THE COURSE OF ROME...
I BAPTIZE YOU, EMPEROR CONSTANTINE, IN THE NAME OF OUR SAVIOR JESUS.
AND ALL OF MANKIND.
THE MAN WHO WAS CRUCIFIED AT OUR HAND... WILL NOW STAND AS OUR ONE TRUE GOD.
FROM THIS DAY ON, ROME IS A CHRISTIAN NATION.

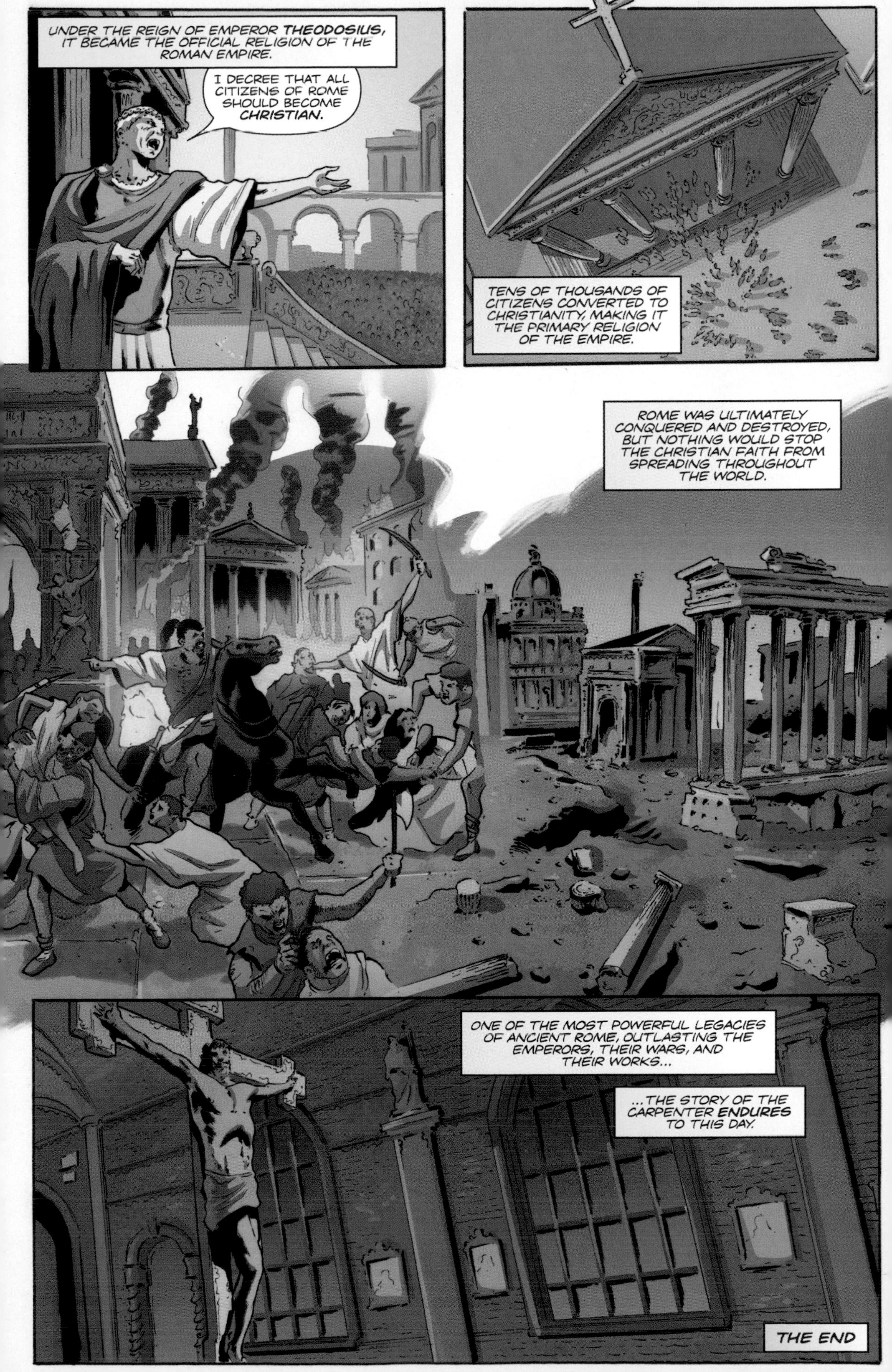

UNDER THE REIGN OF EMPEROR THEODOSIUS, IT BECAME THE OFFICIAL RELIGION OF THE ROMAN EMPIRE.
I DECREE THAT ALL CITIZENS OF ROME SHOULD BECOME CHRISTIAN.
TENS OF THOUSANDS OF CITIZENS CONVERTED TO CHRISTIANITY, MAKING IT THE PRIMARY RELIGION OF THE EMPIRE.
ROME WAS ULTIMATELY CONQUERED AND DESTROYED, BUT NOTHING WOULD STOP THE CHRISTIAN FAITH FROM SPREADING THROUGHOUT THE WORLD.
ONE OF THE MOST POWERFUL LEGACIES OF ANCIENT ROME, OUTLASTING THE EMPERORS, THEIR WARS, AND THEIR WORKS...
...THE STORY OF THE CARPENTER ENDURES TO THIS DAY.
THE END

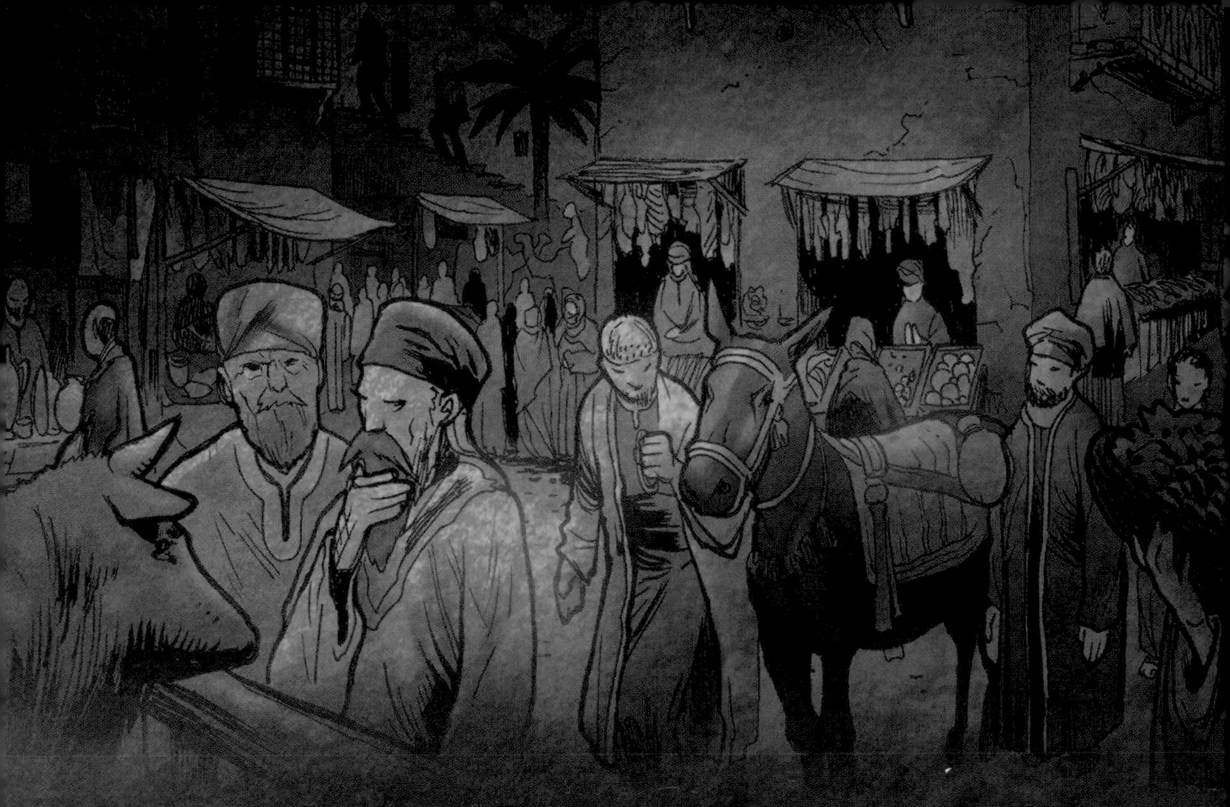

BLOOD AND SILK

WRITTEN BY
DEVIN GRAYSON

ART BY
JAVIER ARANDA

COLORS BY
FALK

LETTERS BY
JIM CAMPBELL

A YOUNG TRADER EXCEEDS HIS FAMILY'S WILDEST HOPES AS THE SILK ROAD UNLOCKS EASTERN LUXURIES.

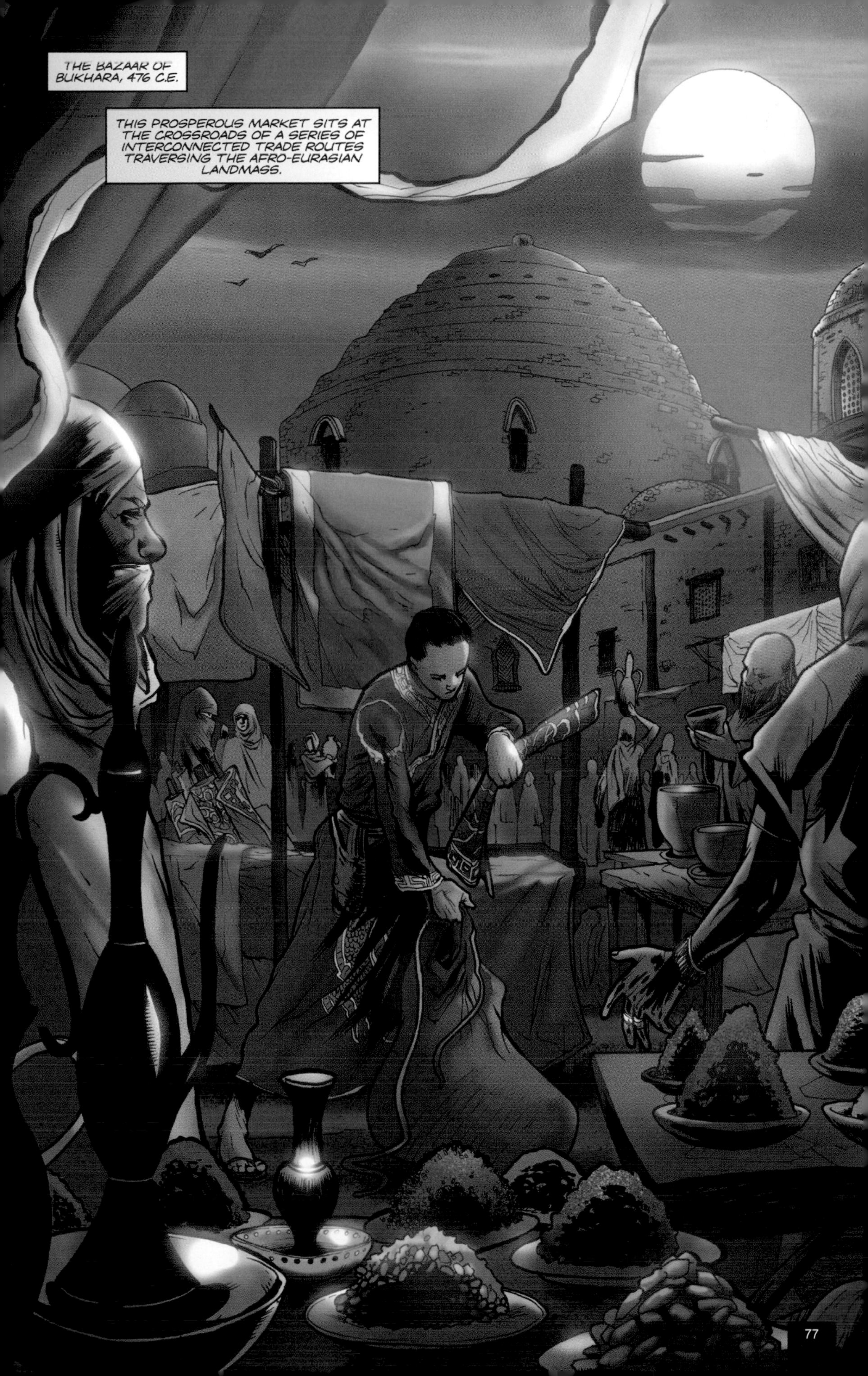

THE BAZAAR OF BUKHARA, 476 C.E.
THIS PROSPEROUS MARKET SITS AT THE CROSSROADS OF A SERIES OF INTERCONNECTED TRADE ROUTES TRAVERSING THE AFRO-EURASIAN LANDMASS.

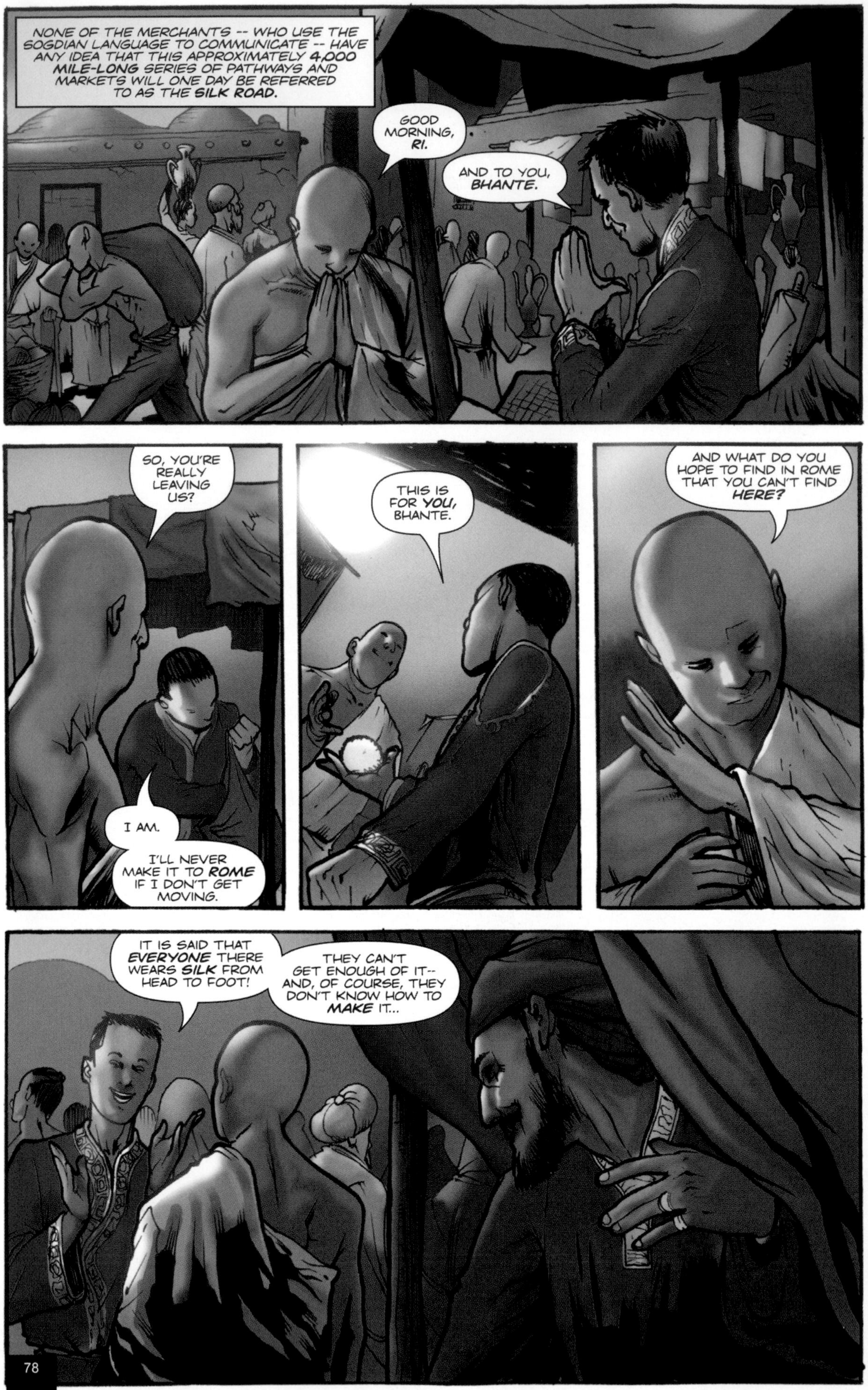
NONE OF THE MERCHANTS -- WHO USE THE SOGDIAN LANGUAGE TO COMMUNICATE -- HAVE ANY IDEA THAT THIS APPROXIMATELY 4,000 MILE-LONG SERIES OF PATHWAYS AND MARKETS WILL ONE DAY BE REFERRED TO AS THE SILK ROAD.
GOOD MORNING, RI.
AND TO YOU, BHANTE.
SO, YOU'RE REALLY LEAVING US?
I AM.
I'LL NEVER MAKE IT TO ROME IF I DON'T GET MOVING.
THIS IS FOR YOU, BHANTE.
AND WHAT DO YOU HOPE TO FIND IN ROME THAT YOU CAN'T FIND HERE?
IT IS SAID THAT EVERYONE THERE WEARS SILK FROM HEAD TO FOOT!
THEY CAN'T GET ENOUGH OF IT-- AND, OF COURSE, THEY DON'T KNOW HOW TO MAKE IT...

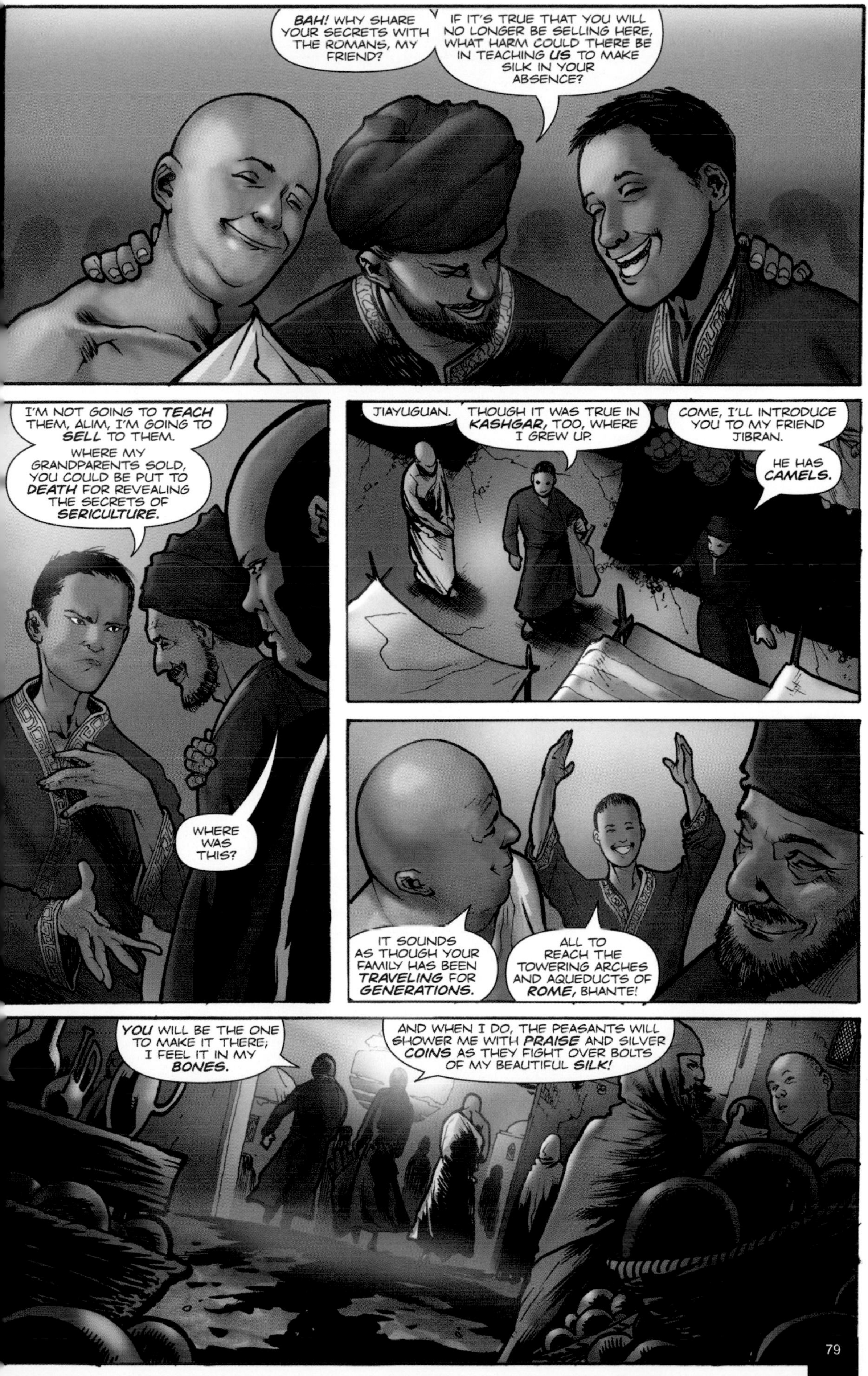
BAH! WHY SHARE YOUR SECRETS WITH THE ROMANS, MY FRIEND?
IF IT'S TRUE THAT YOU WILL NO LONGER BE SELLING HERE, WHAT HARM COULD THERE BE IN TEACHING US TO MAKE SILK IN YOUR ABSENCE?
I'M NOT GOING TO TEACH THEM, ALIM, I'M GOING TO SELL TO THEM.
WHERE MY GRANDPARENTS SOLD, YOU COULD BE PUT TO DEATH FOR REVEALING THE SECRETS OF SERICULTURE.
WHERE WAS THIS?
JIAYUGUAN.
THOUGH IT WAS TRUE IN KASHGAR, TOO, WHERE I GREW UP.
COME, I'LL INTRODUCE YOU TO MY FRIEND JIBRAN.
HE HAS CAMELS.
IT SOUNDS AS THOUGH YOUR FAMILY HAS BEEN TRAVELING FOR GENERATIONS.
ALL TO REACH THE TOWERING ARCHES AND AQUEDUCTS OF ROME, BHANTE!
YOU WILL BE THE ONE TO MAKE IT THERE; I FEEL IT IN MY BONES.
AND WHEN I DO, THE PEASANTS WILL SHOWER ME WITH PRAISE AND SILVER COINS AS THEY FIGHT OVER BOLTS OF MY BEAUTIFUL SILK!

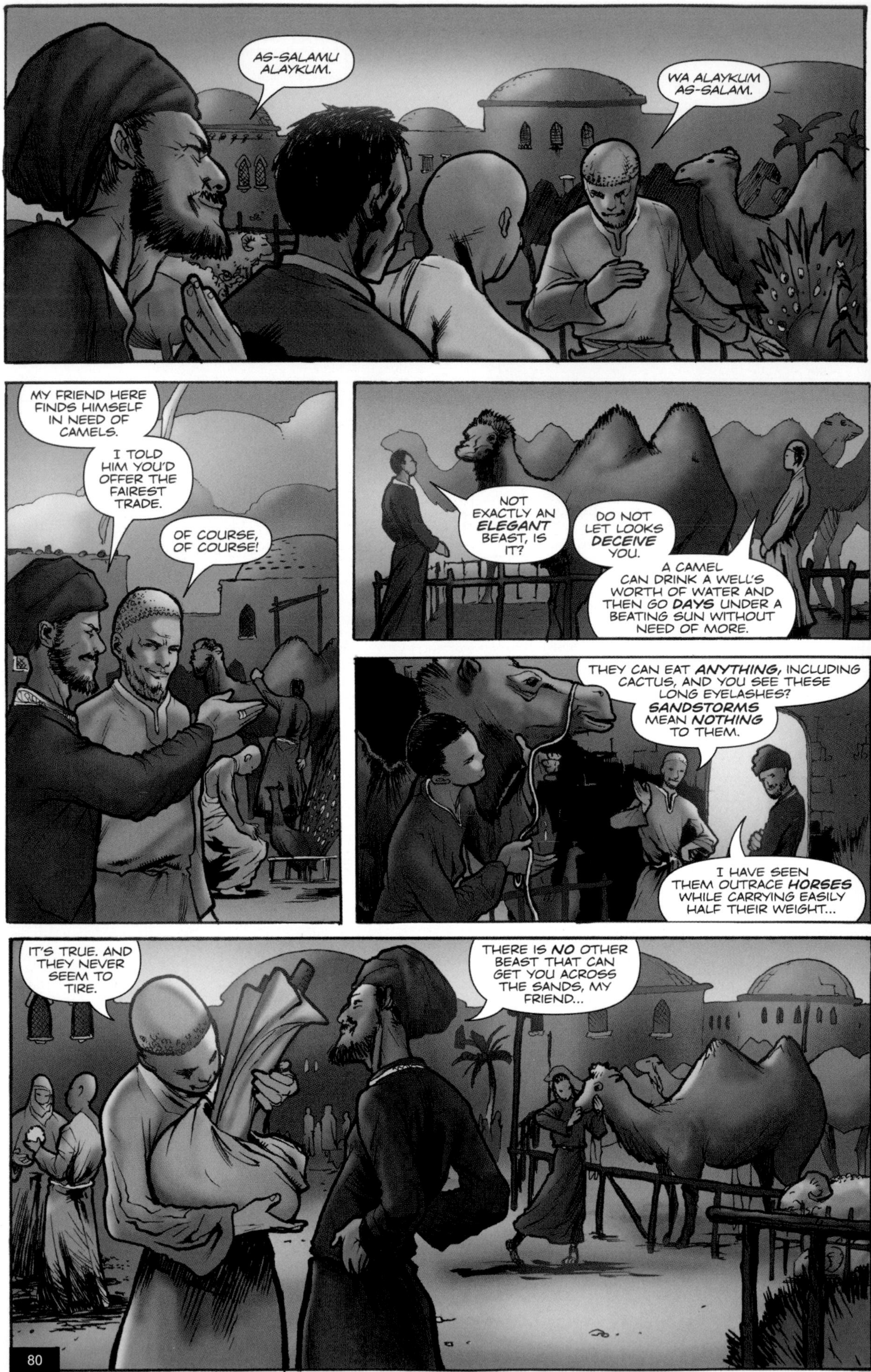
AS-SALAMU ALAYKUM.
WA ALAYKUM AS-SALAM.
MY FRIEND HERE FINDS HIMSELF IN NEED OF CAMELS.
I TOLD HIM YOU'D OFFER THE FAIREST TRADE.
OF COURSE, OF COURSE!
NOT EXACTLY AN ELEGANT BEAST, IS IT?
DO NOT LET LOOKS DECEIVE YOU.
A CAMEL CAN DRINK A WELL'S WORTH OF WATER AND THEN GO DAYS UNDER A BEATING SUN WITHOUT NEED OF MORE.
THEY CAN EAT ANYTHING, INCLUDING CACTUS, AND YOU SEE THESE LONG EYELASHES? SANDSTORMS MEAN NOTHING TO THEM.
I HAVE SEEN THEM OUTRACE HORSES WHILE CARRYING EASILY HALF THEIR WEIGHT...
IT'S TRUE. AND THEY NEVER SEEM TO TIRE.
THERE IS NO OTHER BEAST THAT CAN GET YOU ACROSS THE SANDS, MY FRIEND...

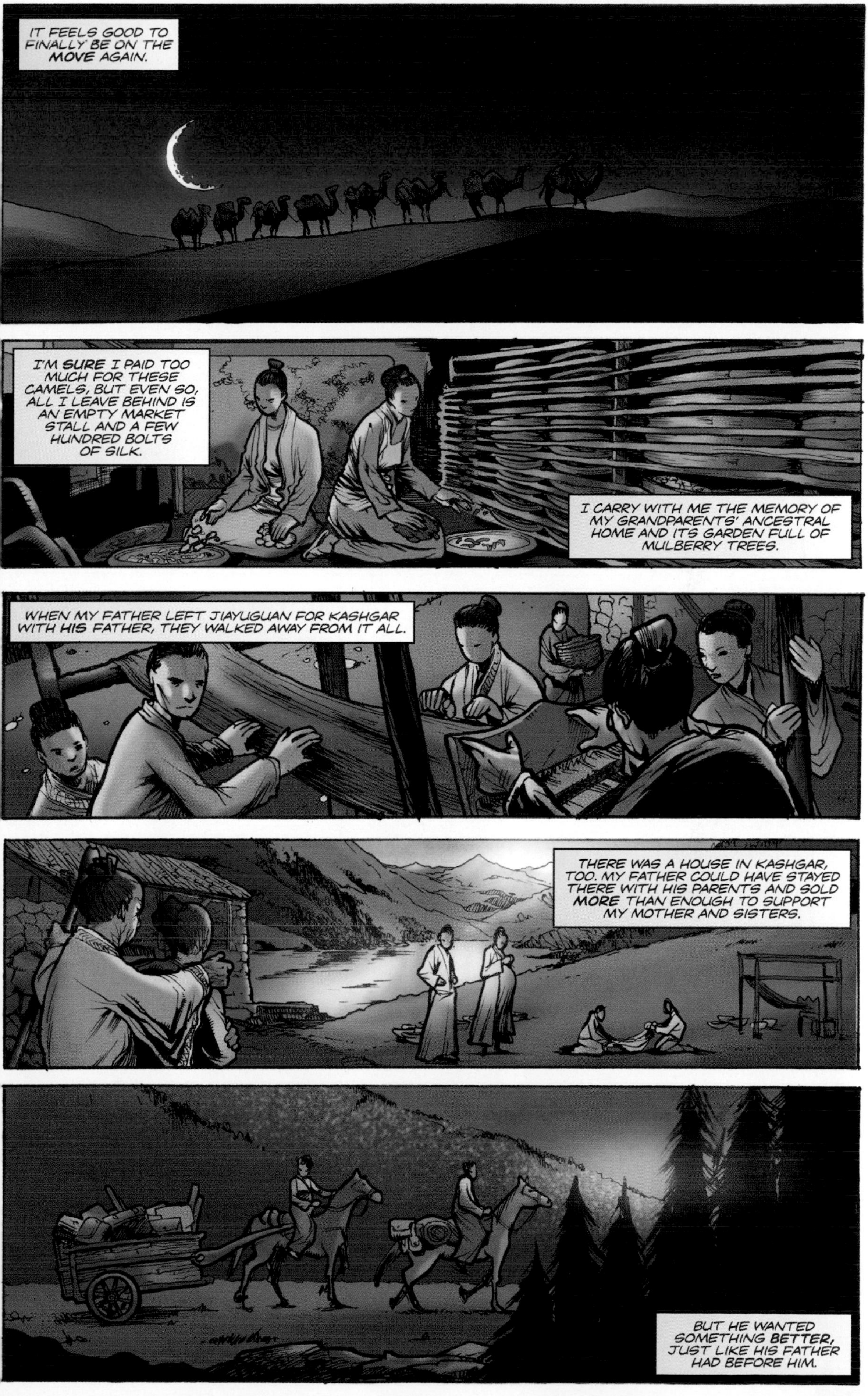
IT FEELS GOOD TO FINALLY BE ON THE MOVE AGAIN.
I'M SURE I PAID TOO MUCH FOR THESE CAMELS, BUT EVEN SO, ALL I LEAVE BEHIND IS AN EMPTY MARKET STALL AND A FEW HUNDRED BOLTS OF SILK.
I CARRY WITH ME THE MEMORY OF MY GRANDPARENTS' ANCESTRAL HOME AND ITS GARDEN FULL OF MULBERRY TREES.
WHEN MY FATHER LEFT JIAYUGUAN FOR KASHGAR WITH HIS FATHER, THEY WALKED AWAY FROM IT ALL.
THERE WAS A HOUSE IN KASHGAR, TOO. MY FATHER COULD HAVE STAYED THERE WITH HIS PARENTS AND SOLD MORE THAN ENOUGH TO SUPPORT MY MOTHER AND SISTERS.
BUT HE WANTED SOMETHING BETTER, JUST LIKE HIS FATHER HAD BEFORE HIM.

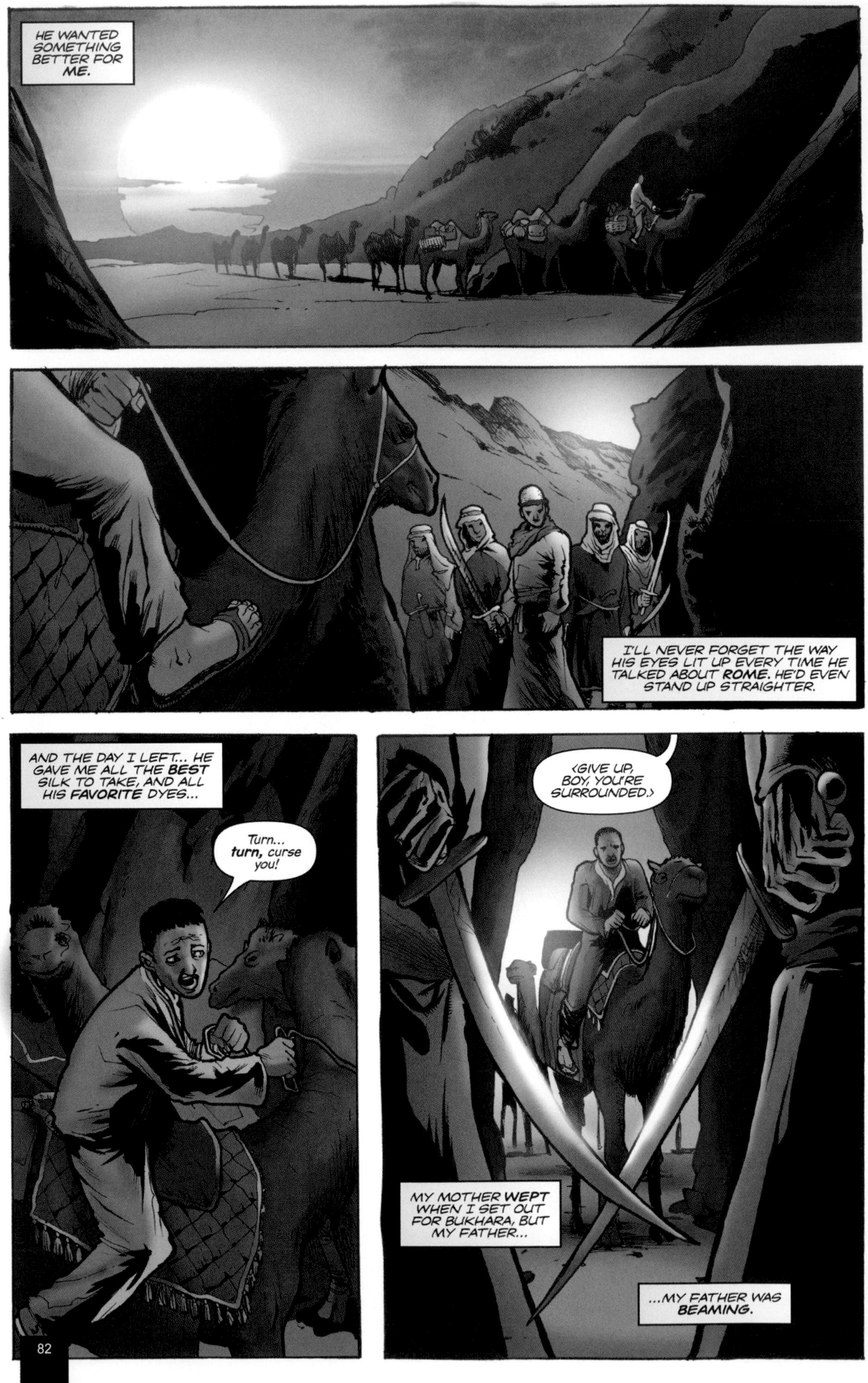
HE WANTED SOMETHING BETTER FOR ME.
I'LL NEVER FORGET THE WAY HIS EYES LIT UP EVERY TIME HE TALKED ABOUT ROME. HE'D EVEN STAND UP STRAIGHTER.
AND THE DAY I LEFT... HE GAVE ME ALL THE BEST SILK TO TAKE, AND ALL HIS FAVORITE DYES...
Turn... turn, curse you!
<GIVE UP, BOY, YOU'RE SURROUNDED.>
MY MOTHER WEPT WHEN I SET OUT FOR BUKHARA, BUT MY FATHER...
...MY FATHER WAS BEAMING.

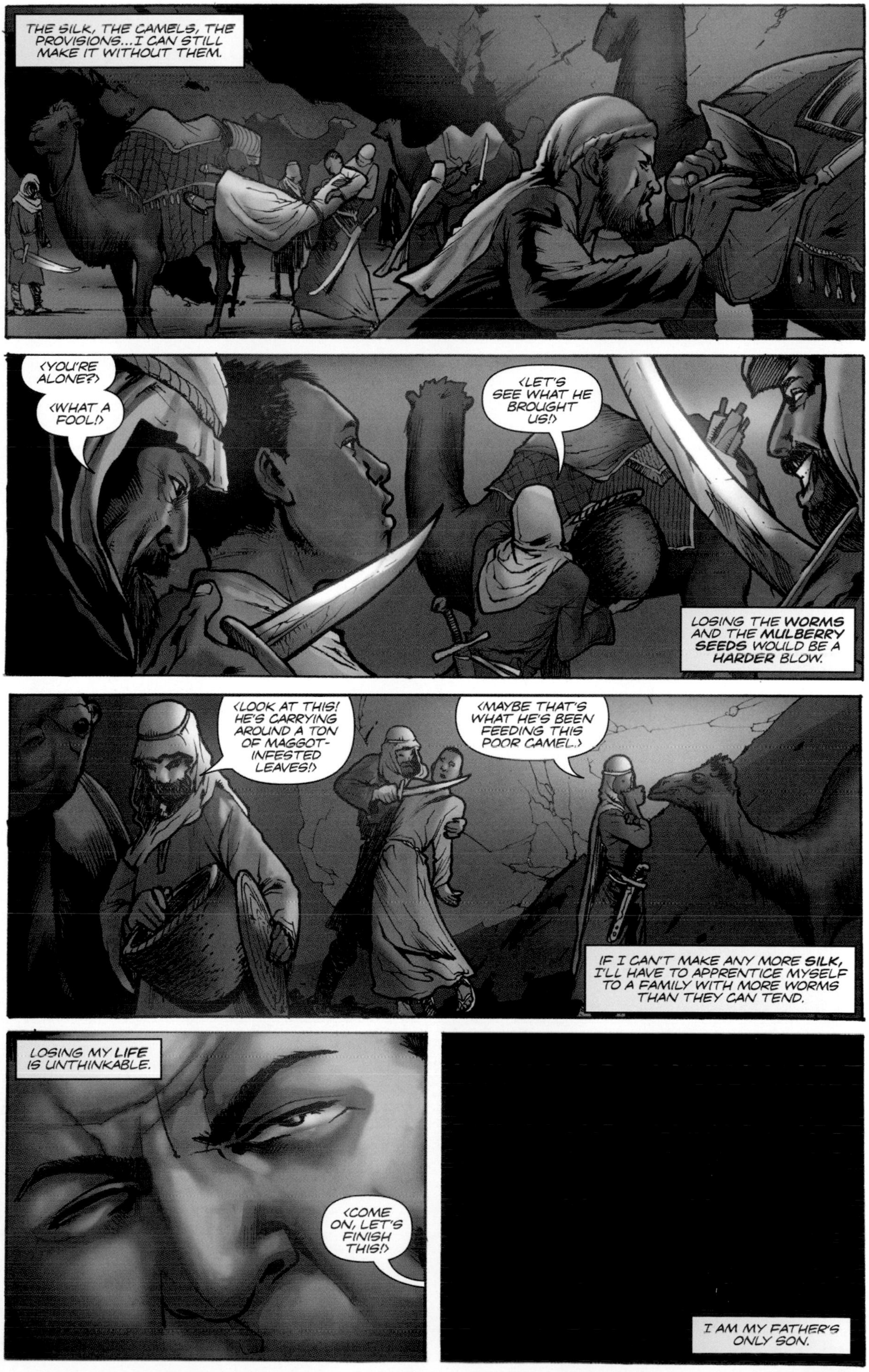
THE SILK, THE CAMELS, THE PROVISIONS...I CAN STILL MAKE IT WITHOUT THEM.
‹YOU'RE ALONE?›
‹WHAT A FOOL!›
‹LET'S SEE WHAT HE BROUGHT US!›
LOSING THE WORMS AND THE MULBERRY SEEDS WOULD BE A HARDER BLOW.
‹LOOK AT THIS! HE'S CARRYING AROUND A TON OF MAGGOT-INFESTED LEAVES!›
‹MAYBE THAT'S WHAT HE'S BEEN FEEDING THIS POOR CAMEL.›
IF I CAN'T MAKE ANY MORE SILK, I'LL HAVE TO APPRENTICE MYSELF TO A FAMILY WITH MORE WORMS THAN THEY CAN TEND.
LOSING MY LIFE IS UNTHINKABLE.
‹COME ON, LET'S FINISH THIS!›
I AM MY FATHER'S ONLY SON.

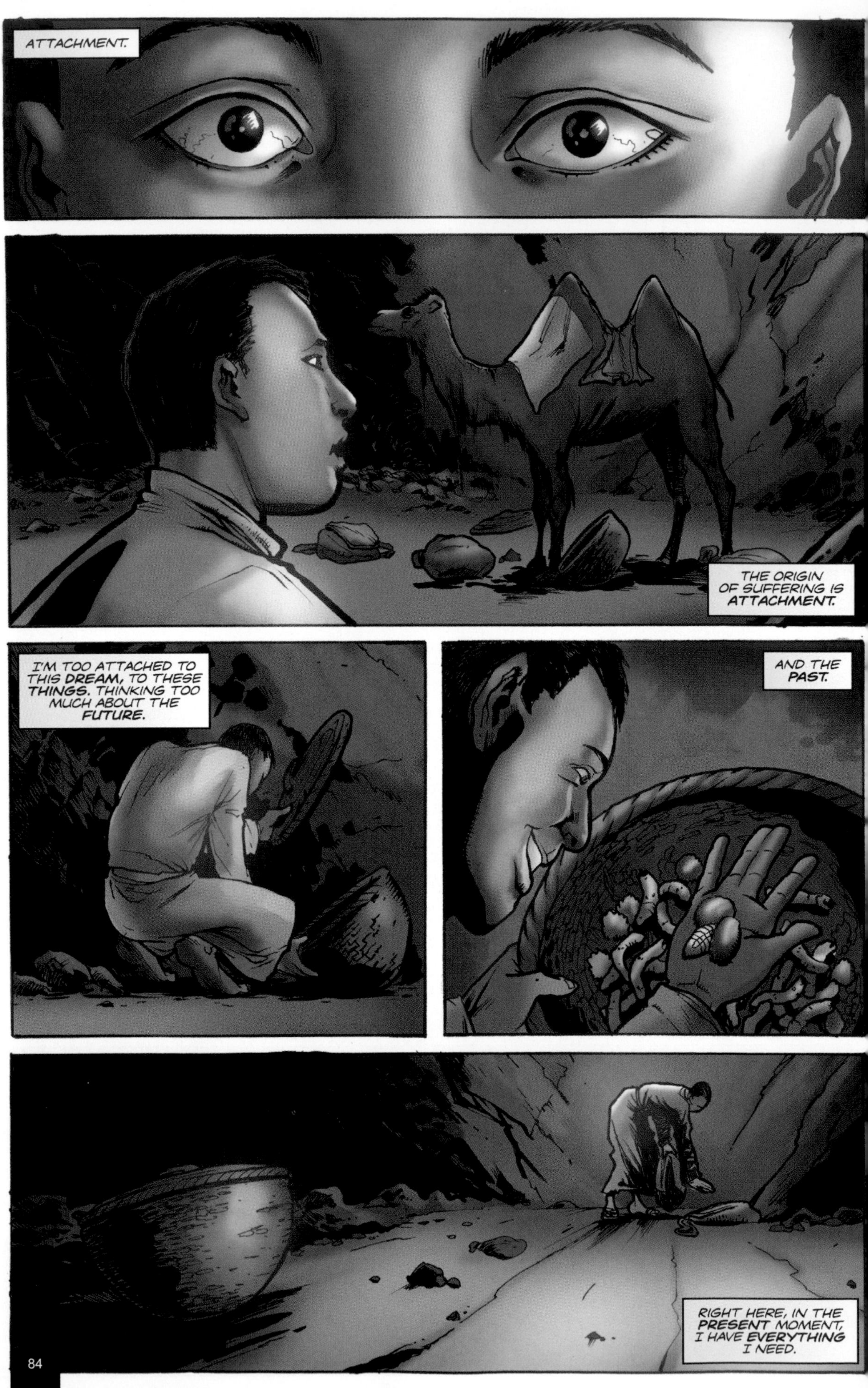
ATTACHMENT.
THE ORIGIN OF SUFFERING IS ATTACHMENT.
I'M TOO ATTACHED TO THIS DREAM, TO THESE THINGS. THINKING TOO MUCH ABOUT THE FUTURE.
AND THE PAST.
RIGHT HERE, IN THE PRESENT MOMENT, I HAVE EVERYTHING I NEED.

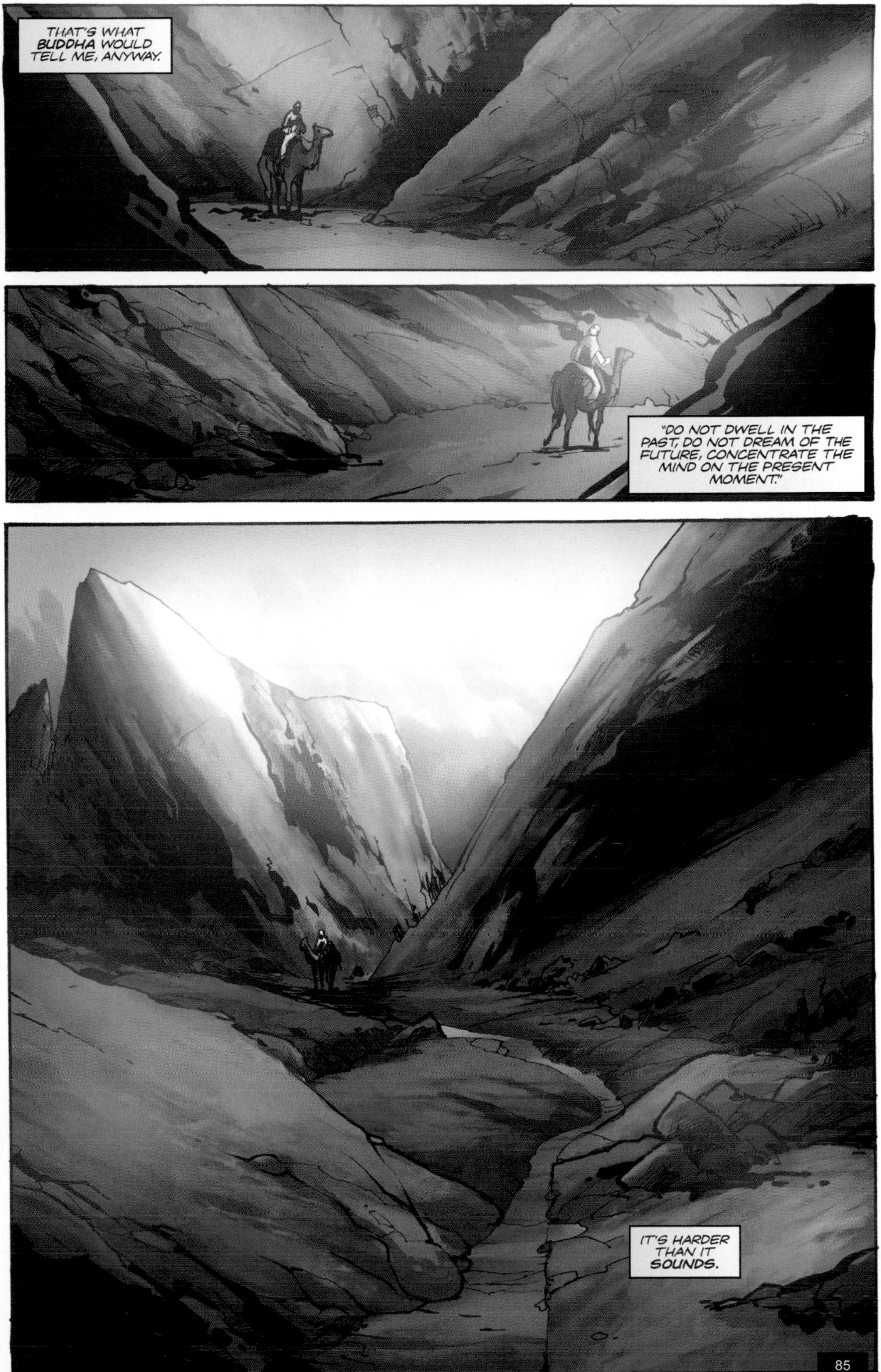
THAT'S WHAT BUDDHA WOULD TELL ME, ANYWAY.
"DO NOT DWELL IN THE PAST, DO NOT DREAM OF THE FUTURE, CONCENTRATE THE MIND ON THE PRESENT MOMENT."
IT'S HARDER THAN IT SOUNDS.

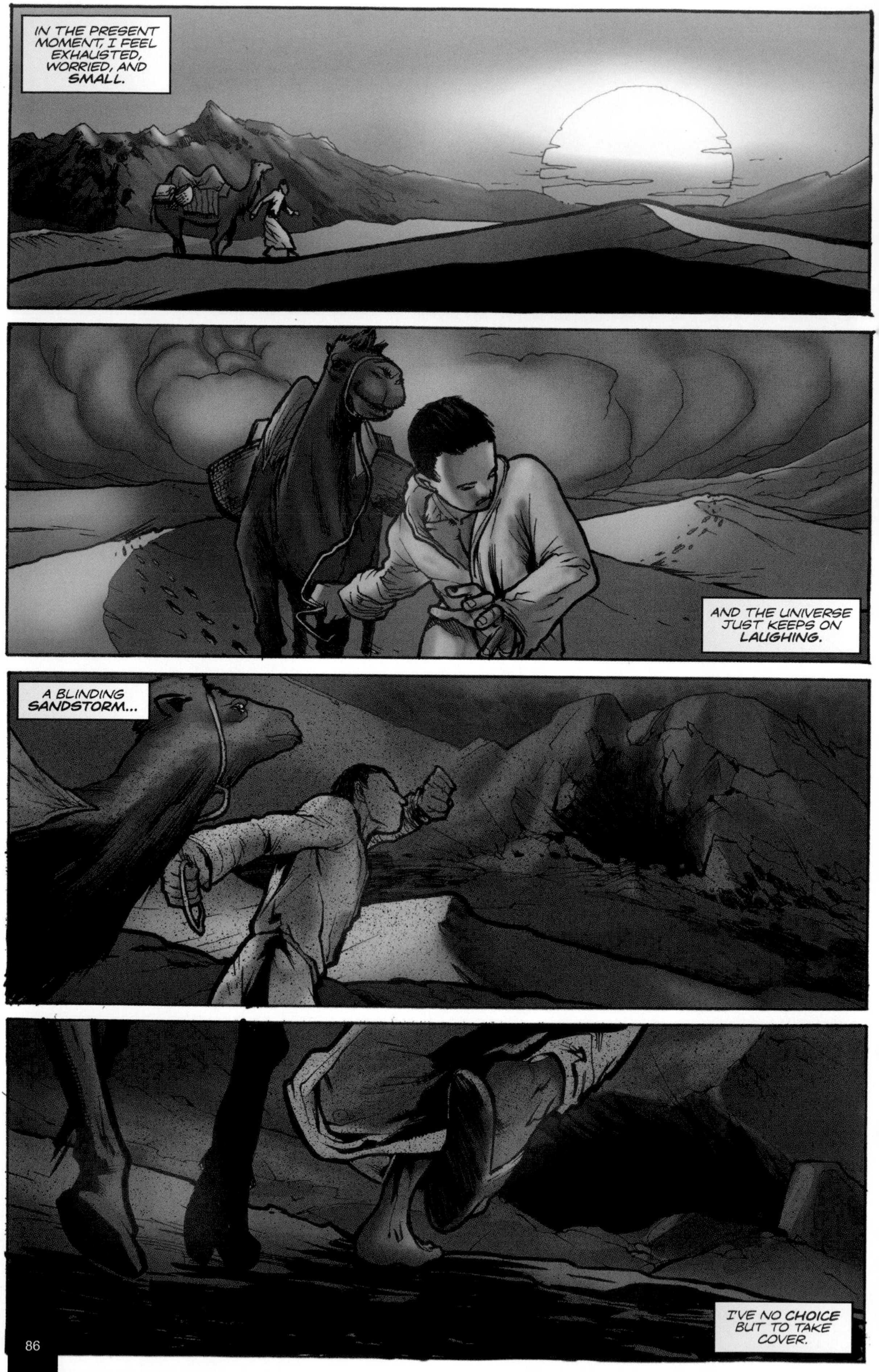
IN THE PRESENT MOMENT, I FEEL EXHAUSTED, WORRIED, AND SMALL.
AND THE UNIVERSE JUST KEEPS ON LAUGHING.
A BLINDING SANDSTORM...
I'VE NO CHOICE BUT TO TAKE COVER.

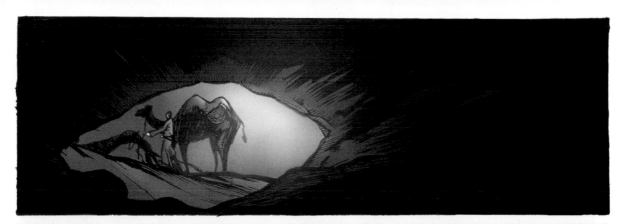

OH! I'M SORRY. I DIDN'T REALIZE--

HOW COULD YOU HAVE KNOWN?

PLEASE, COME IN! JOIN US!

YOU SPEAK SOGDIAN!

TO BRING THE WORD TO ALL OF GOD'S CHILDREN, I HAVE LEARNED **MANY** TONGUES.

PRAISE THE LORD!

YES, **PRAISE** HIM!

THANK YOU, LORD!

FORGIVE THEIR FERVOR.

THESE YOUNG MEN ARE NEWLY SAVED.

87

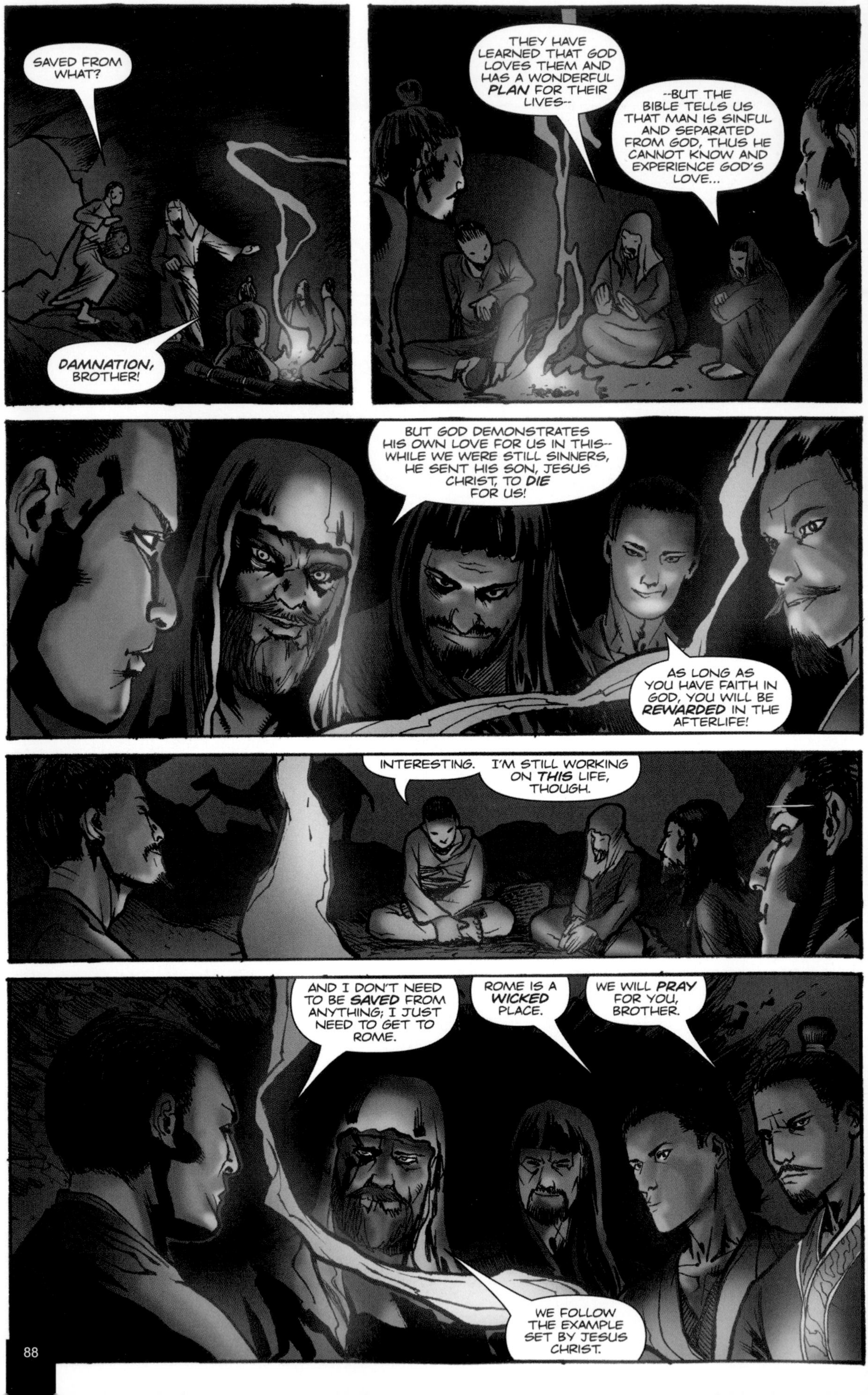
SAVED FROM WHAT?
DAMNATION, BROTHER!
THEY HAVE LEARNED THAT GOD LOVES THEM AND HAS A WONDERFUL PLAN FOR THEIR LIVES--
--BUT THE BIBLE TELLS US THAT MAN IS SINFUL AND SEPARATED FROM GOD, THUS HE CANNOT KNOW AND EXPERIENCE GOD'S LOVE...
BUT GOD DEMONSTRATES HIS OWN LOVE FOR US IN THIS--WHILE WE WERE STILL SINNERS, HE SENT HIS SON, JESUS CHRIST, TO DIE FOR US!
AS LONG AS YOU HAVE FAITH IN GOD, YOU WILL BE REWARDED IN THE AFTERLIFE!
INTERESTING.
I'M STILL WORKING ON THIS LIFE, THOUGH.
AND I DON'T NEED TO BE SAVED FROM ANYTHING; I JUST NEED TO GET TO ROME.
ROME IS A WICKED PLACE.
WE WILL PRAY FOR YOU, BROTHER.
WE FOLLOW THE EXAMPLE SET BY JESUS CHRIST.

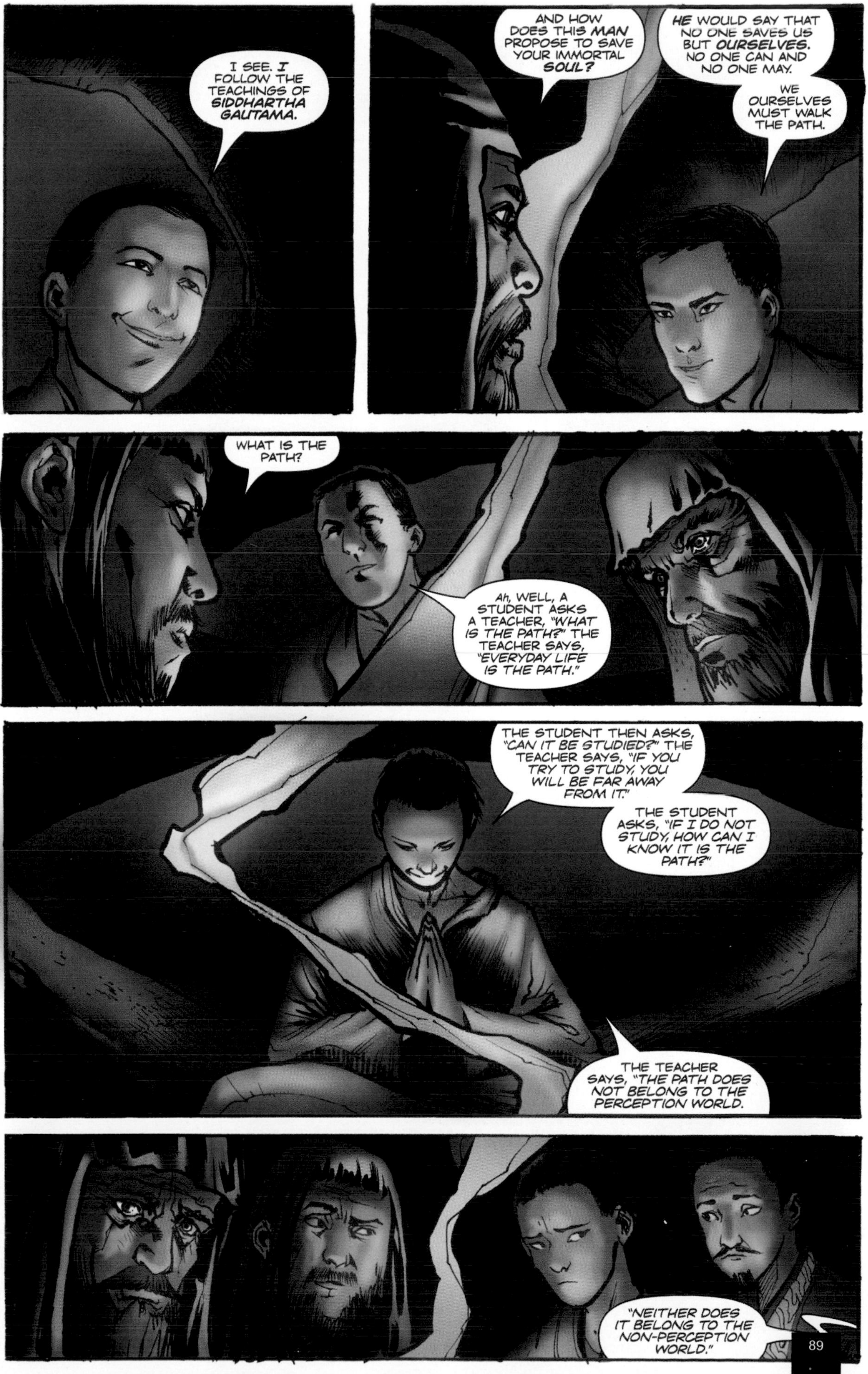
I SEE. *I* FOLLOW THE TEACHINGS OF ***SIDDHARTHA GAUTAMA.***
AND HOW DOES THIS **MAN** PROPOSE TO SAVE YOUR IMMORTAL **SOUL?**
HE WOULD SAY THAT NO ONE SAVES US BUT ***OURSELVES.*** NO ONE CAN AND NO ONE MAY.
WE OURSELVES MUST WALK THE PATH.
WHAT IS THE PATH?
Ah, WELL, A STUDENT ASKS A TEACHER, *"WHAT IS THE PATH?"* THE TEACHER SAYS, *"EVERYDAY LIFE IS THE PATH."*
THE STUDENT THEN ASKS, *"CAN IT BE STUDIED?"* THE TEACHER SAYS, *"IF YOU TRY TO STUDY, YOU WILL BE FAR AWAY FROM IT."*
THE STUDENT ASKS, *"IF I DO NOT STUDY, HOW CAN I KNOW IT IS THE PATH?"*
THE TEACHER SAYS, *"THE PATH DOES NOT BELONG TO THE PERCEPTION WORLD.*
"NEITHER DOES IT BELONG TO THE NON-PERCEPTION WORLD."

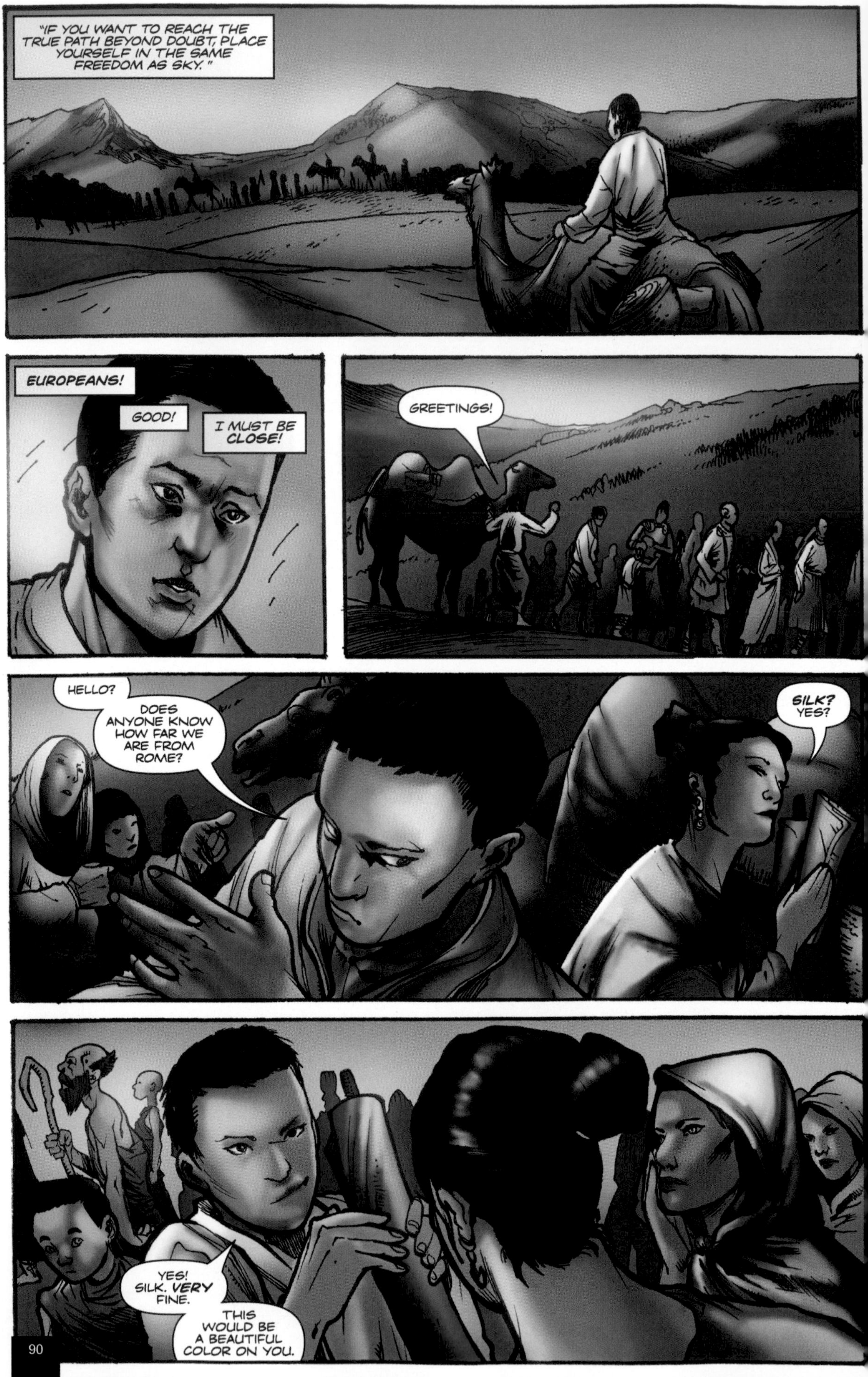
"IF YOU WANT TO REACH THE TRUE PATH BEYOND DOUBT, PLACE YOURSELF IN THE SAME FREEDOM AS SKY."
EUROPEANS!
GOOD!
I MUST BE CLOSE!
GREETINGS!
HELLO?
DOES ANYONE KNOW HOW FAR WE ARE FROM ROME?
SILK? YES?
YES! SILK. VERY FINE.
THIS WOULD BE A BEAUTIFUL COLOR ON YOU.

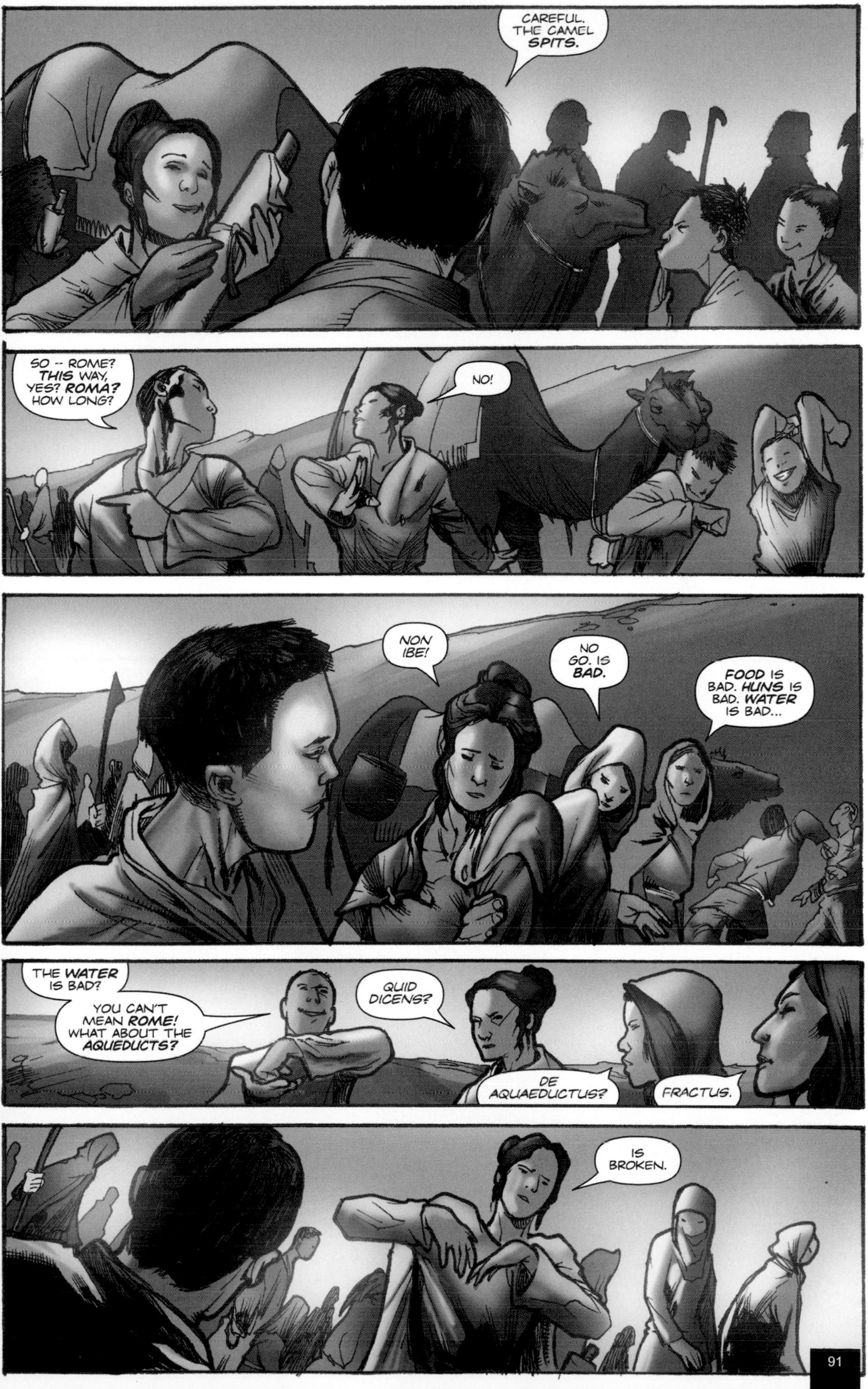
CAREFUL. THE CAMEL SPITS.
SO -- ROME? THIS WAY, YES? ROMA? HOW LONG?
NO!
NON IBE!
NO GO. IS BAD.
FOOD IS BAD. HUNS IS BAD. WATER IS BAD...
THE WATER IS BAD?
YOU CAN'T MEAN ROME! WHAT ABOUT THE AQUEDUCTS?
QUID DICENS?
DE AQUAEDUCTUS?
FRACTUS.
IS BROKEN.

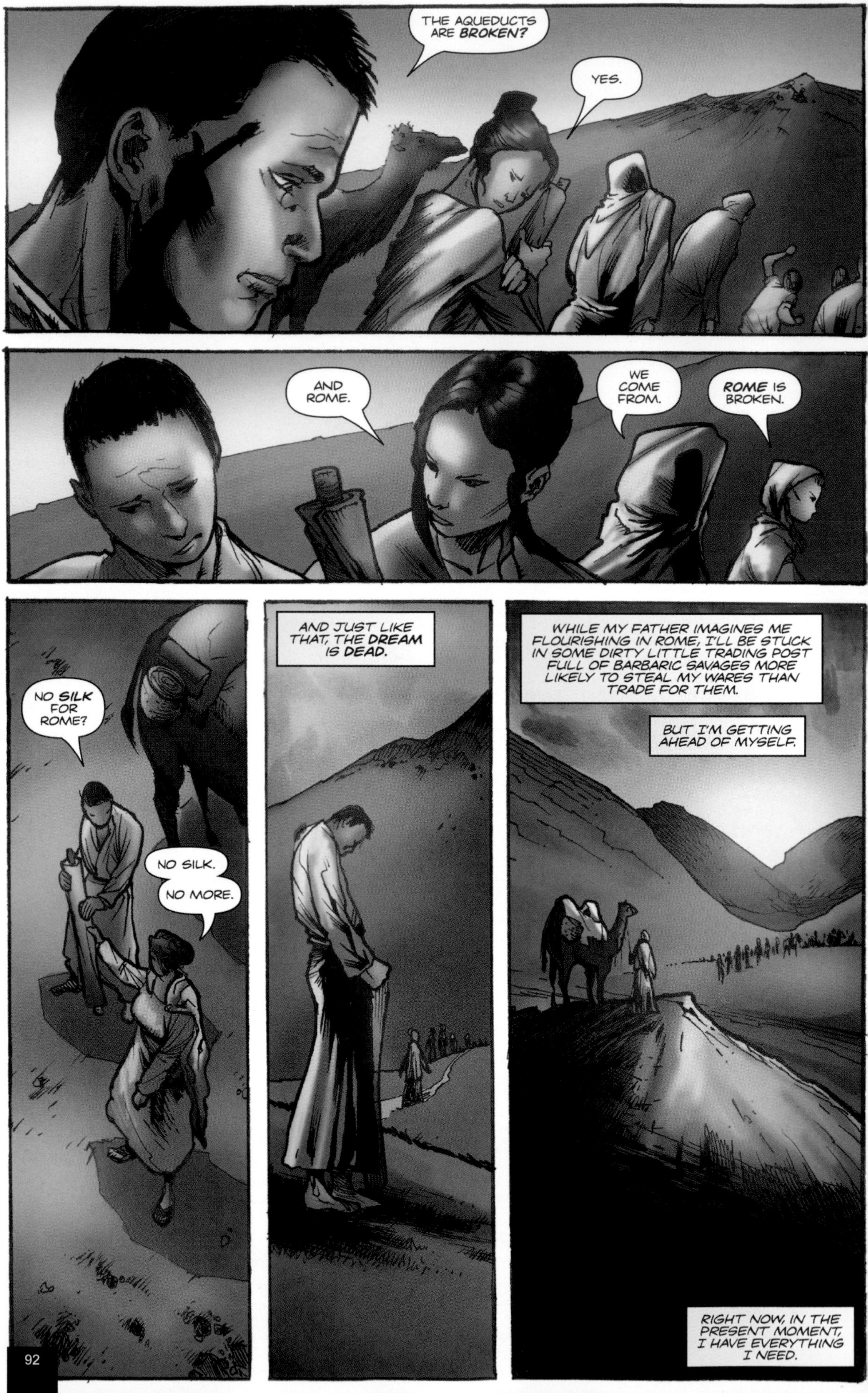

THE AQUEDUCTS ARE **BROKEN?**
YES.
AND ROME.
WE COME FROM.
ROME IS BROKEN.
NO **SILK** FOR ROME?
NO SILK.
NO MORE.
AND JUST LIKE THAT, THE **DREAM** IS **DEAD.**
WHILE MY FATHER IMAGINES ME FLOURISHING IN ROME, I'LL BE STUCK IN SOME DIRTY LITTLE TRADING POST FULL OF BARBARIC SAVAGES MORE LIKELY TO STEAL MY WARES THAN TRADE FOR THEM.
BUT I'M GETTING AHEAD OF MYSELF.
RIGHT NOW, IN THE PRESENT MOMENT, I HAVE EVERYTHING I NEED.

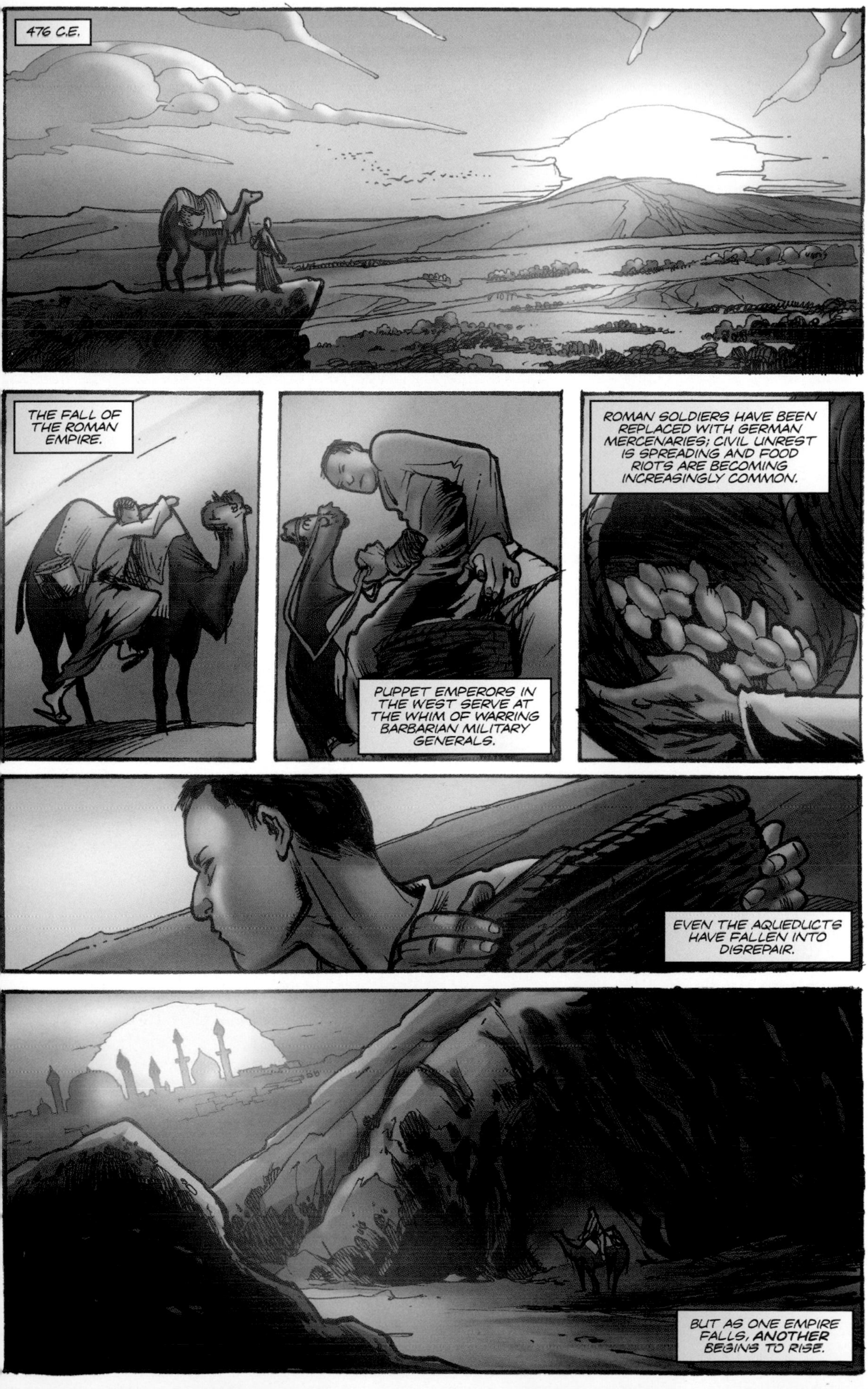
476 C.E.
THE FALL OF THE ROMAN EMPIRE.
PUPPET EMPERORS IN THE WEST SERVE AT THE WHIM OF WARRING BARBARIAN MILITARY GENERALS.
ROMAN SOLDIERS HAVE BEEN REPLACED WITH GERMAN MERCENARIES; CIVIL UNREST IS SPREADING AND FOOD RIOTS ARE BECOMING INCREASINGLY COMMON.
EVEN THE AQUEDUCTS HAVE FALLEN INTO DISREPAIR.
BUT AS ONE EMPIRE FALLS, ANOTHER BEGINS TO RISE.

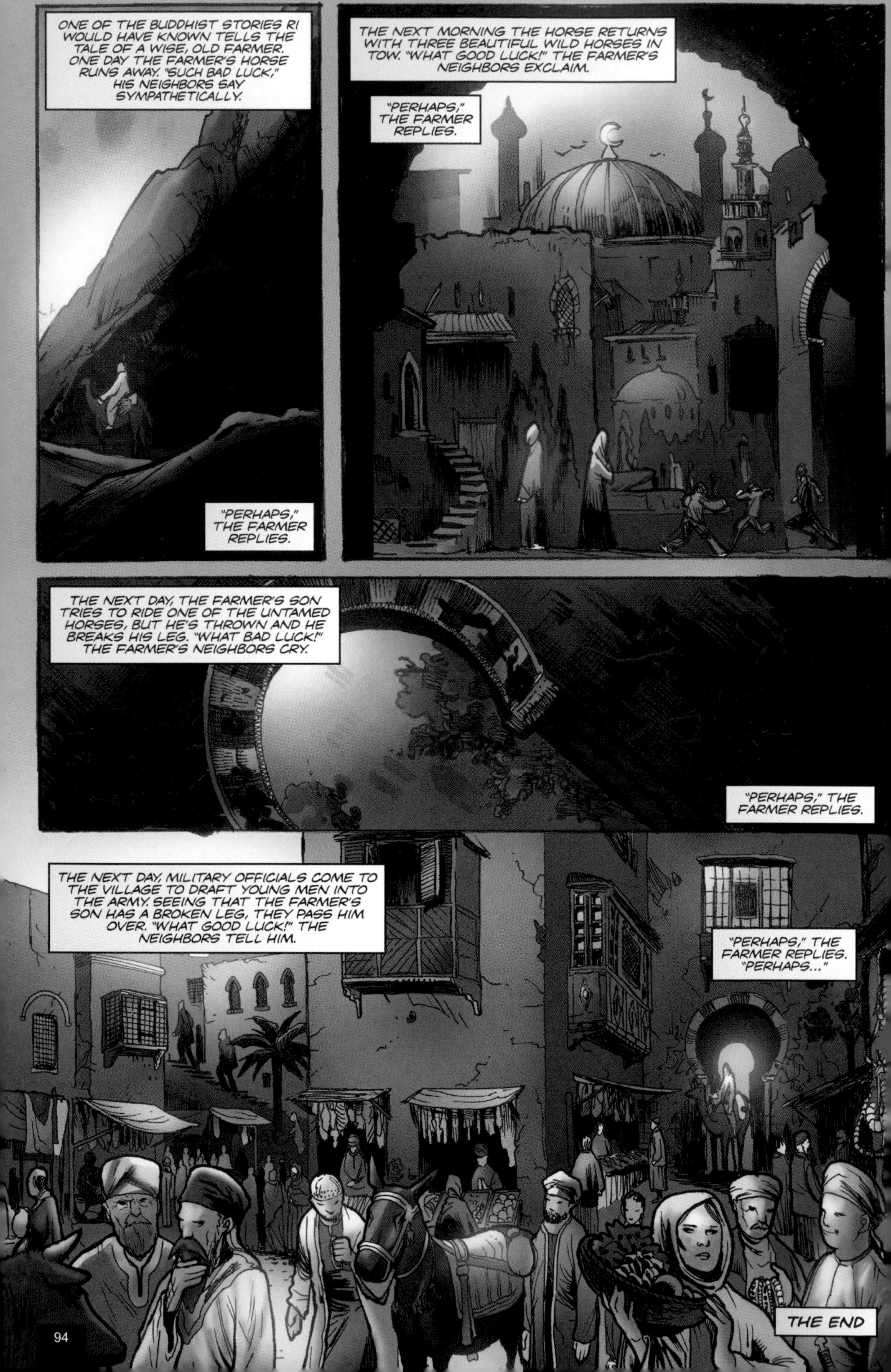
ONE OF THE BUDDHIST STORIES RI WOULD HAVE KNOWN TELLS THE TALE OF A WISE, OLD FARMER. ONE DAY THE FARMER'S HORSE RUNS AWAY. "SUCH BAD LUCK," HIS NEIGHBORS SAY SYMPATHETICALLY.
"PERHAPS," THE FARMER REPLIES.
THE NEXT MORNING THE HORSE RETURNS WITH THREE BEAUTIFUL WILD HORSES IN TOW. "WHAT GOOD LUCK!" THE FARMER'S NEIGHBORS EXCLAIM.
"PERHAPS," THE FARMER REPLIES.
THE NEXT DAY, THE FARMER'S SON TRIES TO RIDE ONE OF THE UNTAMED HORSES, BUT HE'S THROWN AND HE BREAKS HIS LEG. "WHAT BAD LUCK!" THE FARMER'S NEIGHBORS CRY.
"PERHAPS," THE FARMER REPLIES.
THE NEXT DAY, MILITARY OFFICIALS COME TO THE VILLAGE TO DRAFT YOUNG MEN INTO THE ARMY. SEEING THAT THE FARMER'S SON HAS A BROKEN LEG, THEY PASS HIM OVER. "WHAT GOOD LUCK!" THE NEIGHBORS TELL HIM.
"PERHAPS," THE FARMER REPLIES. "PERHAPS..."
THE END

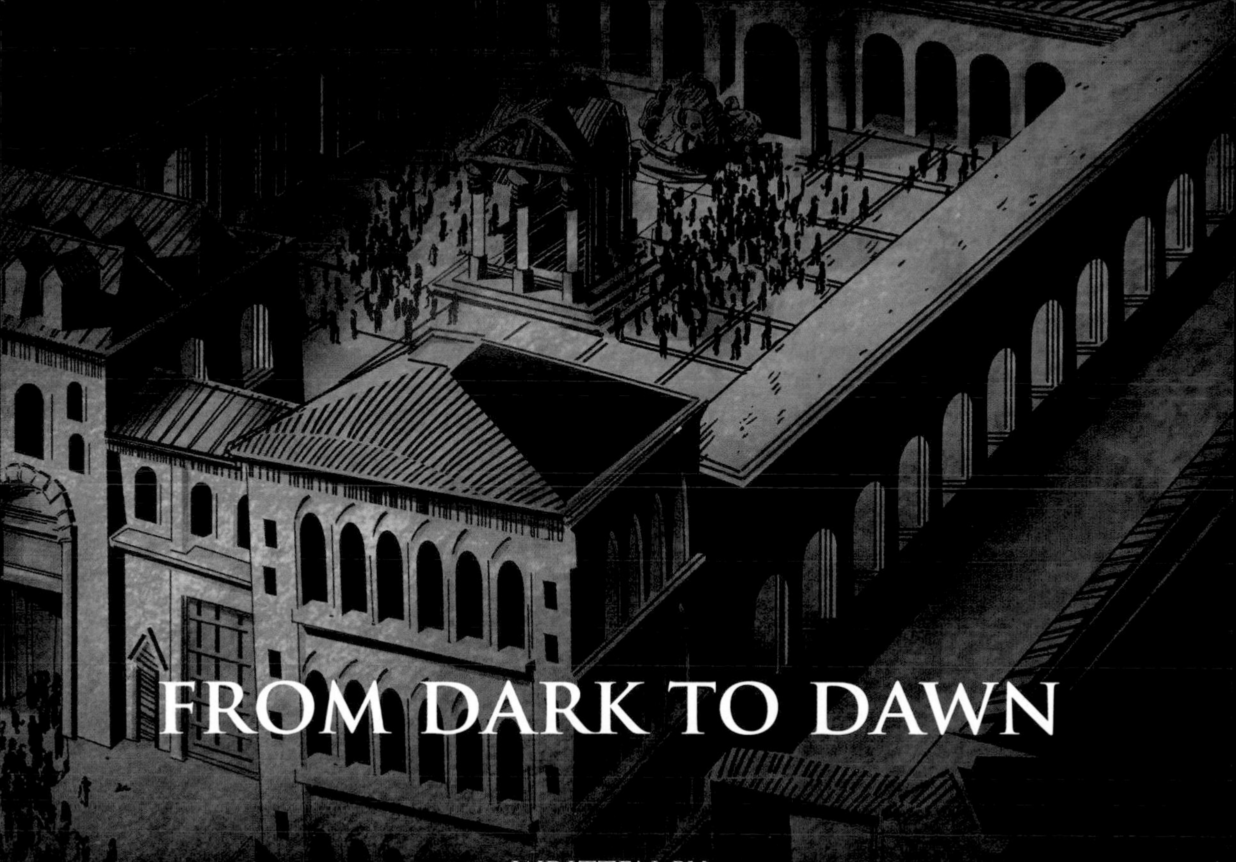

FROM DARK TO DAWN

WRITTEN BY
JOE BRUSHA

ART BY
MATT TRIANO
MIKE DE CARLO
WES HUFFOR

COLORS BY
VANESSA BAÑOS
ALBERTO MURIEL
MARC RUEDA
JOSERA BRAVO

LETTERS BY
JIM CAMPBELL

GOLD BECOMES FUEL FOR THE FIRE IN A CONTINENT-SPANNING CLASH OF CIVILIZATIONS.

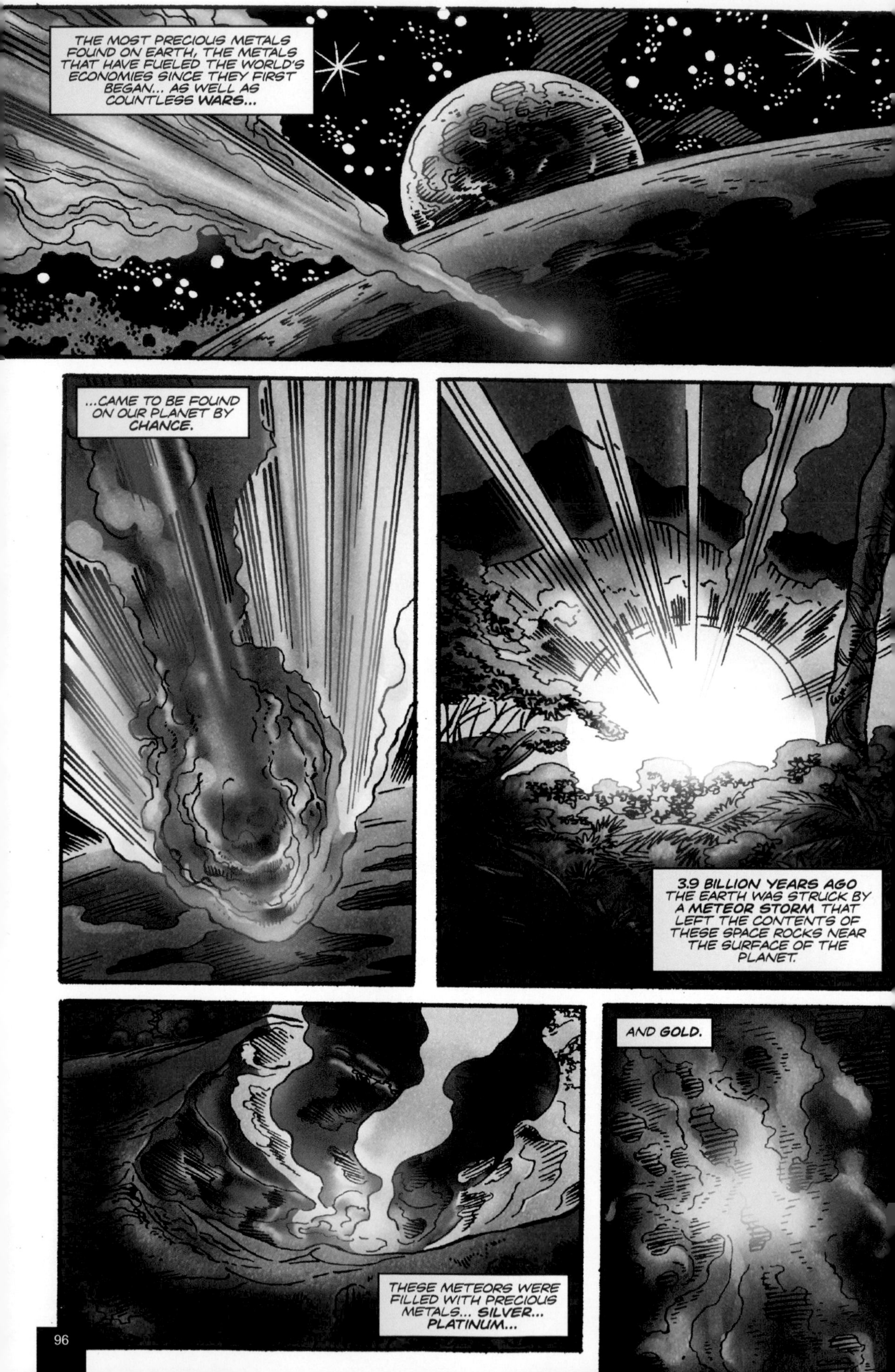
THE MOST PRECIOUS METALS FOUND ON EARTH, THE METALS THAT HAVE FUELED THE WORLD'S ECONOMIES SINCE THEY FIRST BEGAN... AS WELL AS COUNTLESS WARS...
...CAME TO BE FOUND ON OUR PLANET BY CHANCE.
3.9 BILLION YEARS AGO THE EARTH WAS STRUCK BY A METEOR STORM THAT LEFT THE CONTENTS OF THESE SPACE ROCKS NEAR THE SURFACE OF THE PLANET.
THESE METEORS WERE FILLED WITH PRECIOUS METALS... SILVER... PLATINUM...
AND GOLD.

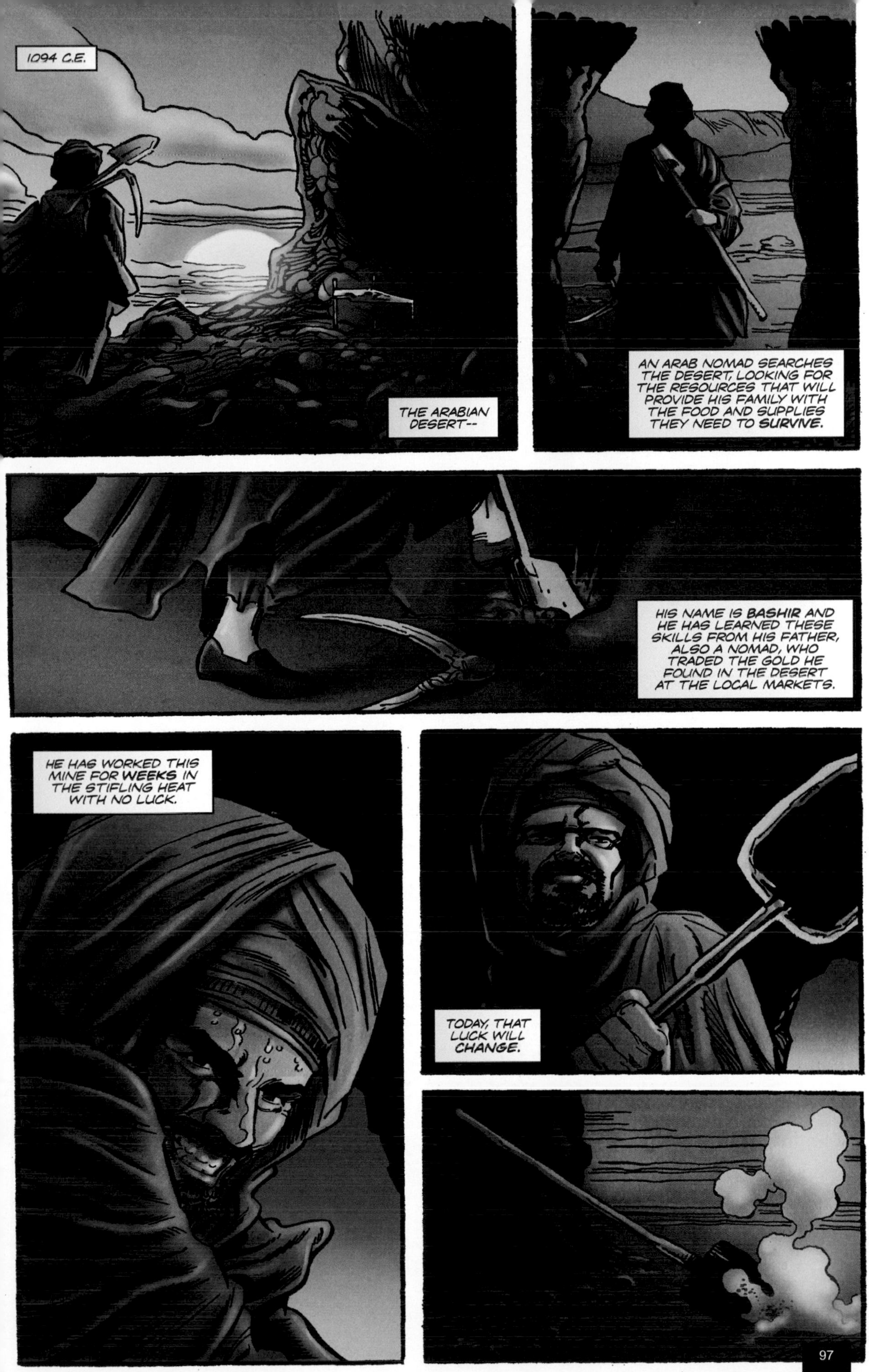
1094 C.E.
THE ARABIAN DESERT--
AN ARAB NOMAD SEARCHES THE DESERT, LOOKING FOR THE RESOURCES THAT WILL PROVIDE HIS FAMILY WITH THE FOOD AND SUPPLIES THEY NEED TO SURVIVE.
HIS NAME IS BASHIR AND HE HAS LEARNED THESE SKILLS FROM HIS FATHER, ALSO A NOMAD, WHO TRADED THE GOLD HE FOUND IN THE DESERT AT THE LOCAL MARKETS.
HE HAS WORKED THIS MINE FOR WEEKS IN THE STIFLING HEAT WITH NO LUCK.
TODAY, THAT LUCK WILL CHANGE.

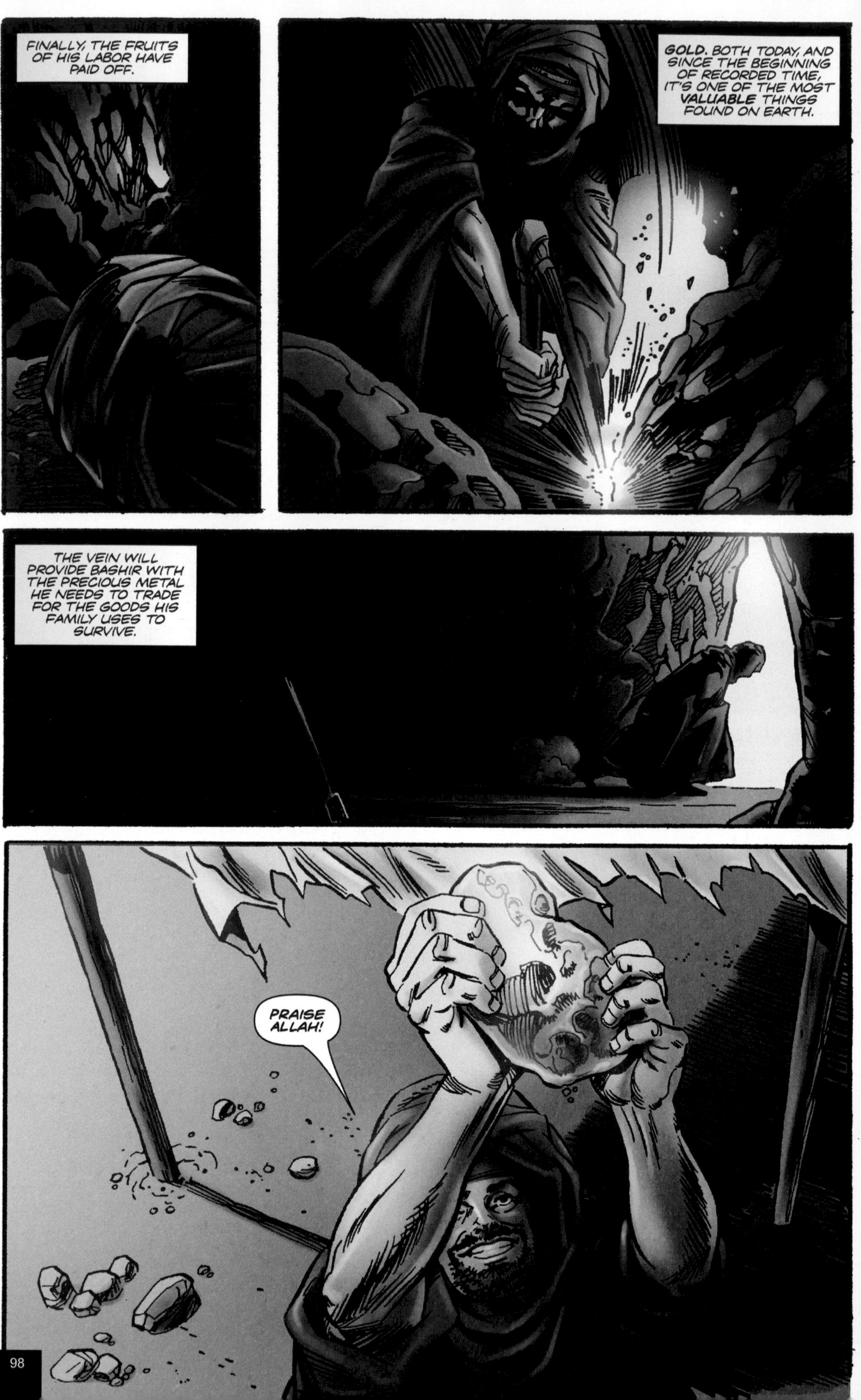
FINALLY, THE FRUITS OF HIS LABOR HAVE PAID OFF.
GOLD. BOTH TODAY, AND SINCE THE BEGINNING OF RECORDED TIME, IT'S ONE OF THE MOST VALUABLE THINGS FOUND ON EARTH.
THE VEIN WILL PROVIDE BASHIR WITH THE PRECIOUS METAL HE NEEDS TO TRADE FOR THE GOODS HIS FAMILY USES TO SURVIVE.
PRAISE ALLAH!

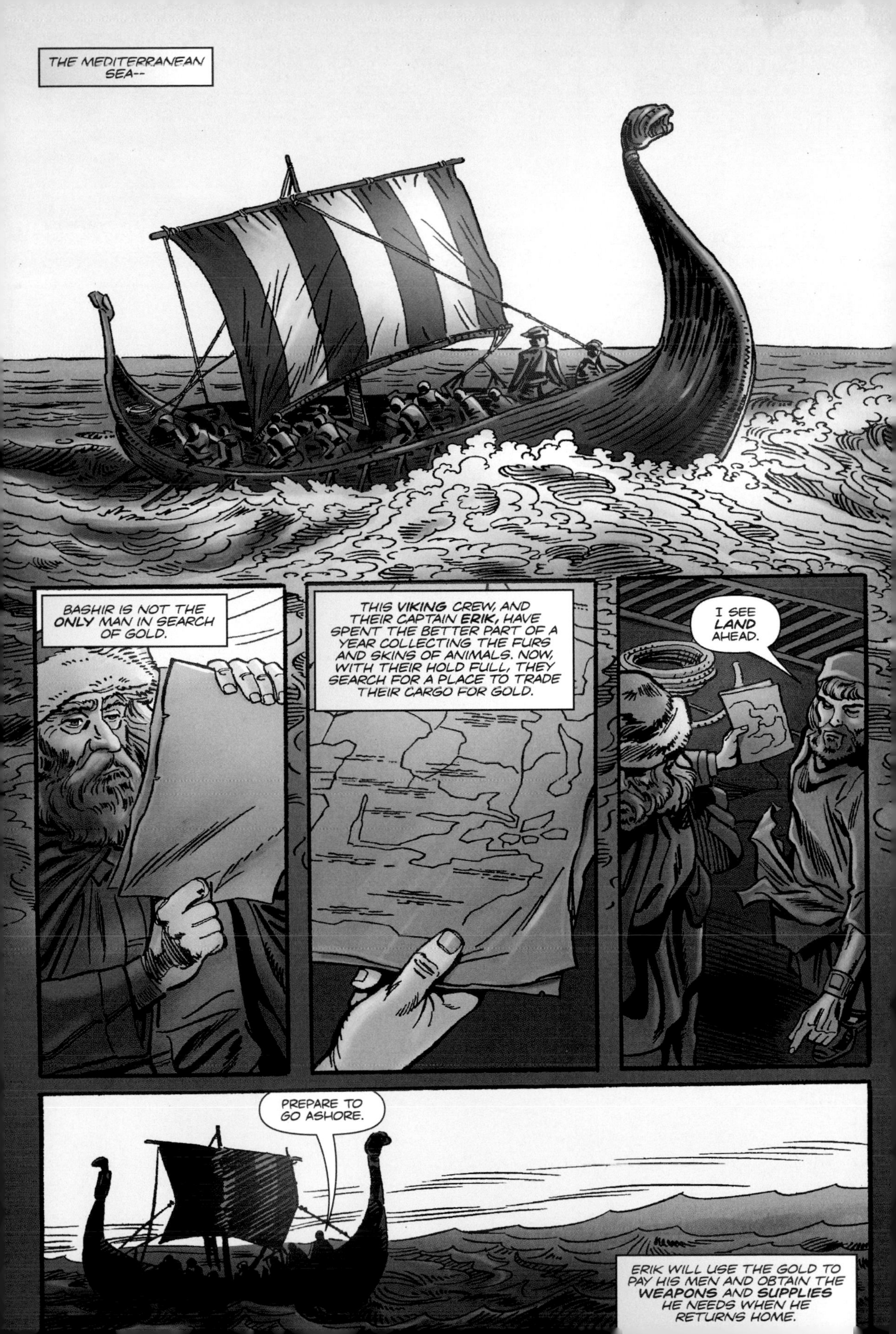
THE MEDITERRANEAN SEA--
BASHIR IS NOT THE ONLY MAN IN SEARCH OF GOLD.
THIS VIKING CREW, AND THEIR CAPTAIN ERIK, HAVE SPENT THE BETTER PART OF A YEAR COLLECTING THE FURS AND SKINS OF ANIMALS. NOW, WITH THEIR HOLD FULL, THEY SEARCH FOR A PLACE TO TRADE THEIR CARGO FOR GOLD.
I SEE LAND AHEAD.
PREPARE TO GO ASHORE.
ERIK WILL USE THE GOLD TO PAY HIS MEN AND OBTAIN THE WEAPONS AND SUPPLIES HE NEEDS WHEN HE RETURNS HOME.

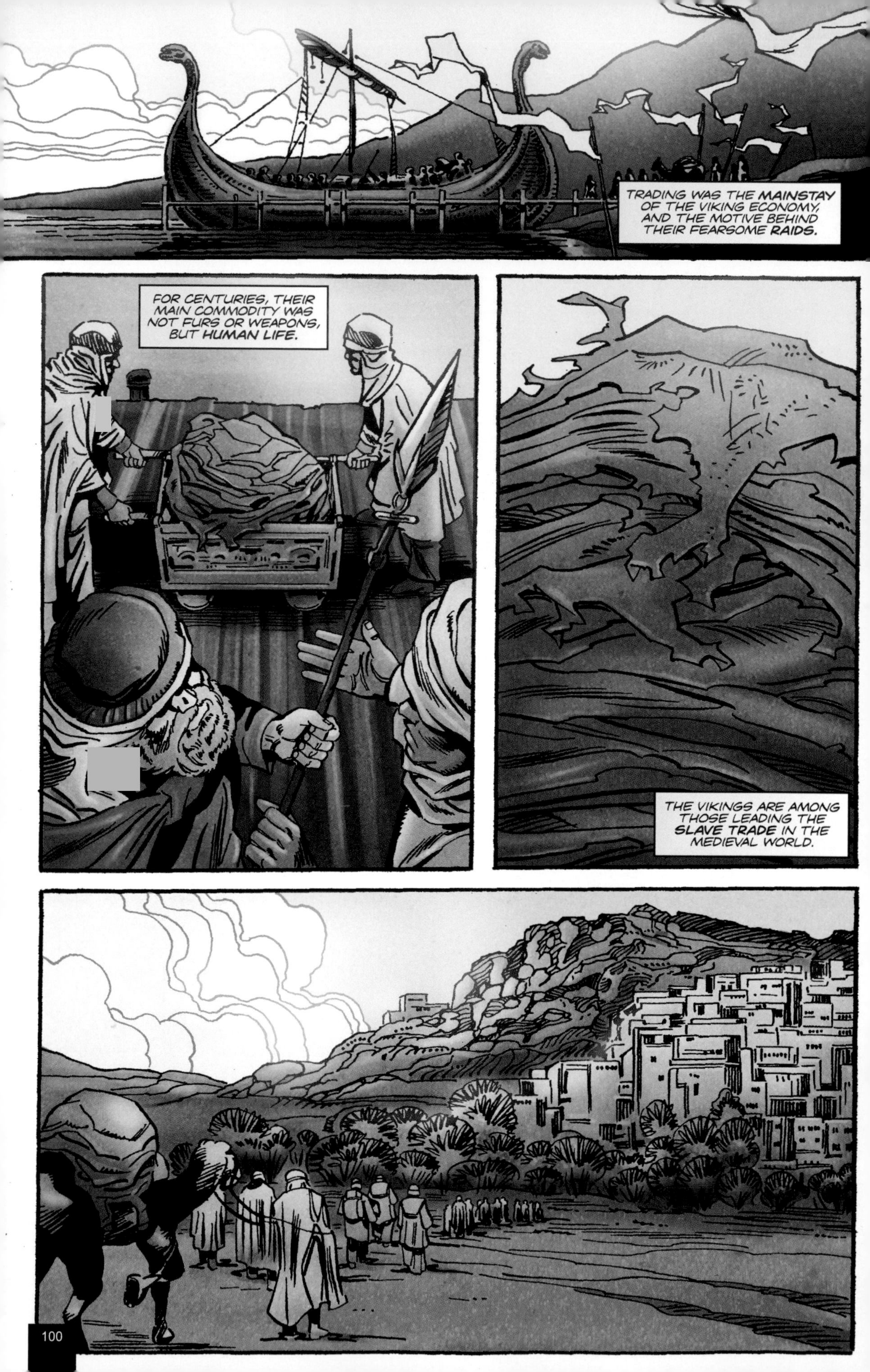
TRADING WAS THE MAINSTAY OF THE VIKING ECONOMY, AND THE MOTIVE BEHIND THEIR FEARSOME RAIDS.
FOR CENTURIES, THEIR MAIN COMMODITY WAS NOT FURS OR WEAPONS, BUT HUMAN LIFE.
THE VIKINGS ARE AMONG THOSE LEADING THE SLAVE TRADE IN THE MEDIEVAL WORLD.

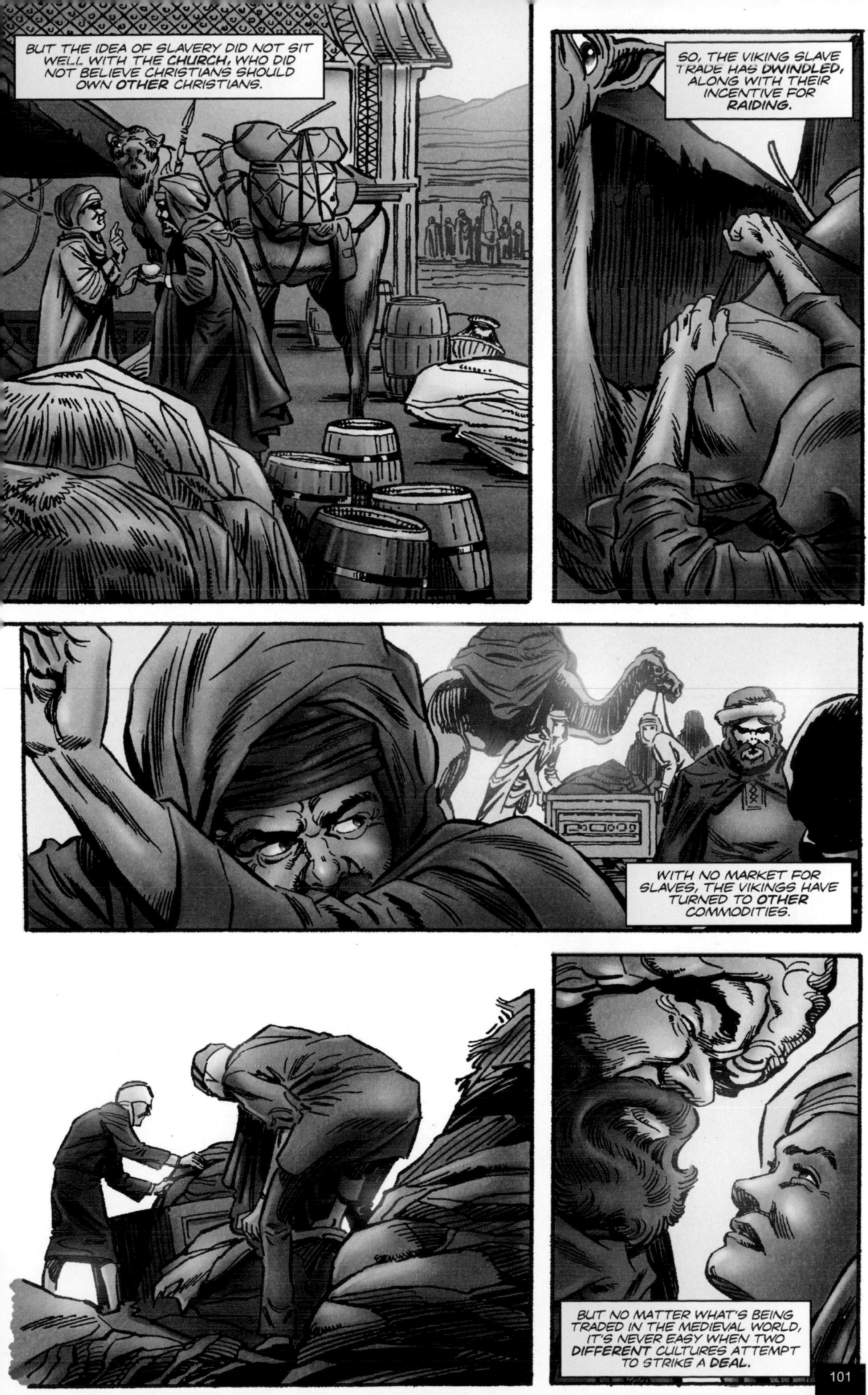
BUT THE IDEA OF SLAVERY DID NOT SIT WELL WITH THE CHURCH, WHO DID NOT BELIEVE CHRISTIANS SHOULD OWN OTHER CHRISTIANS.
SO, THE VIKING SLAVE TRADE HAS DWINDLED, ALONG WITH THEIR INCENTIVE FOR RAIDING.
WITH NO MARKET FOR SLAVES, THE VIKINGS HAVE TURNED TO OTHER COMMODITIES.
BUT NO MATTER WHAT'S BEING TRADED IN THE MEDIEVAL WORLD, IT'S NEVER EASY WHEN TWO DIFFERENT CULTURES ATTEMPT TO STRIKE A DEAL.

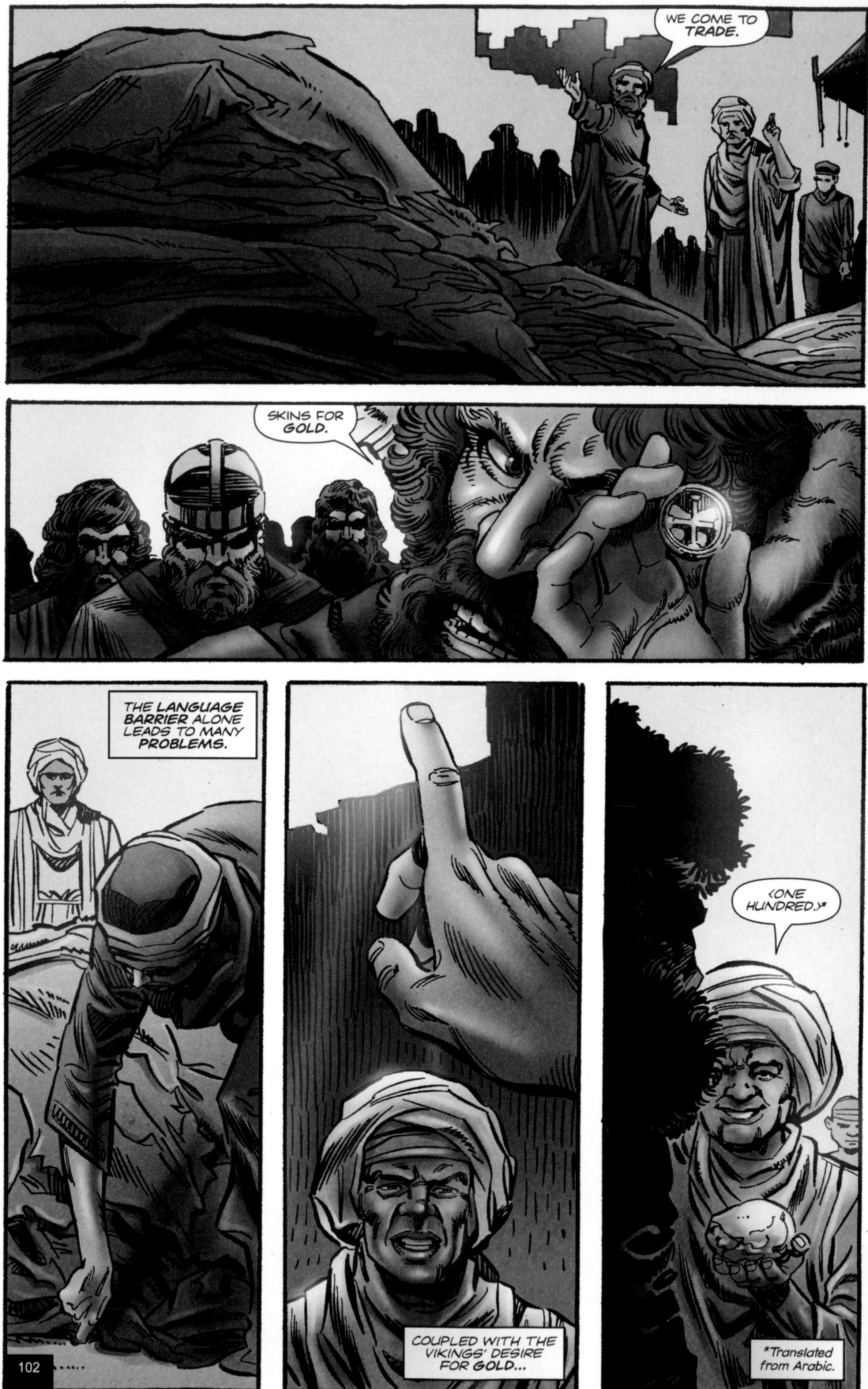
WE COME TO TRADE.
SKINS FOR GOLD.
THE LANGUAGE BARRIER ALONE LEADS TO MANY PROBLEMS.
COUPLED WITH THE VIKINGS' DESIRE FOR GOLD...
<ONE HUNDRED.>*
*Translated from Arabic.

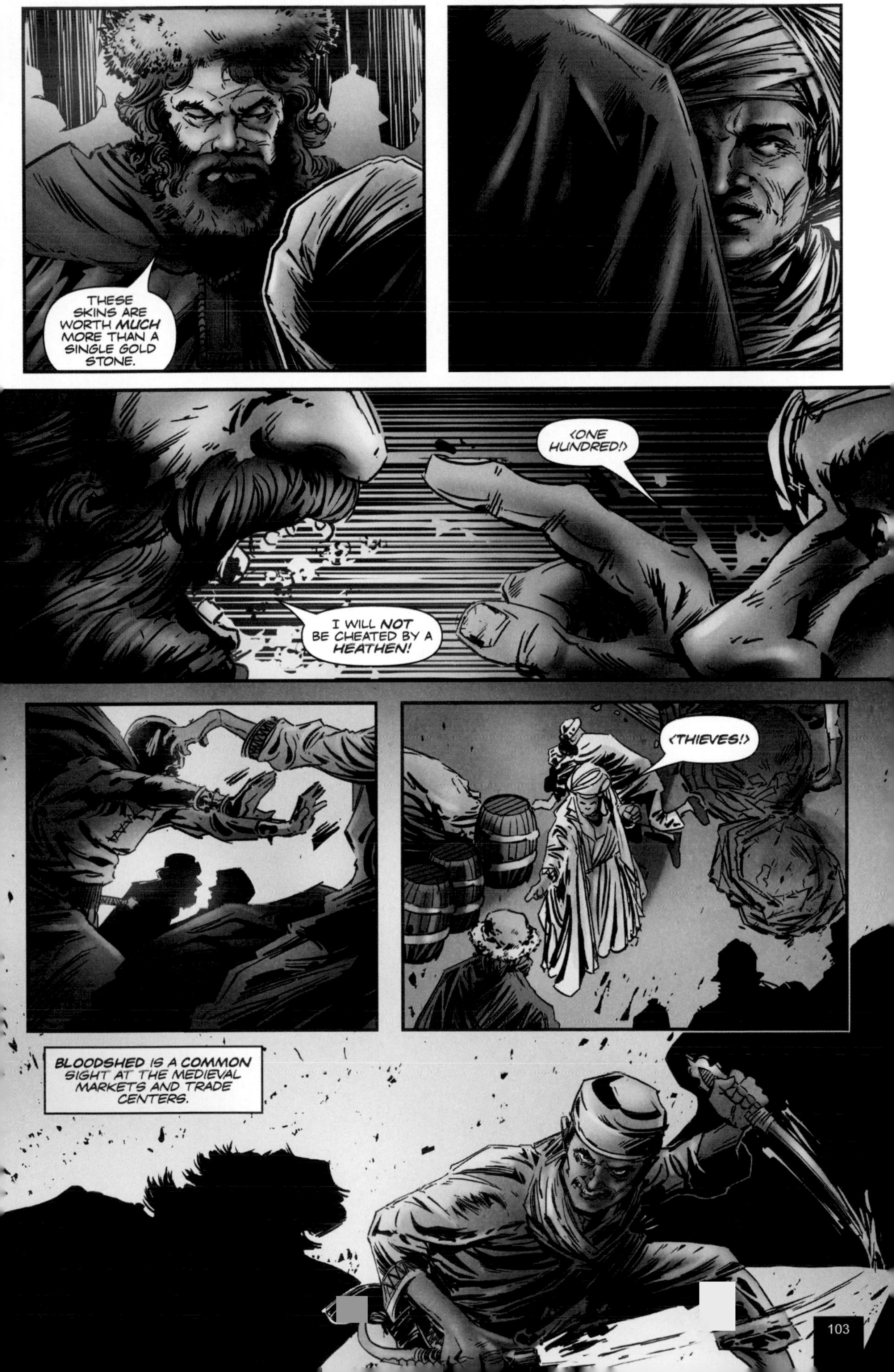
THESE SKINS ARE WORTH MUCH MORE THAN A SINGLE GOLD STONE.
‹ONE HUNDRED!›
I WILL NOT BE CHEATED BY A HEATHEN!
‹THIEVES!›
BLOODSHED IS A COMMON SIGHT AT THE MEDIEVAL MARKETS AND TRADE CENTERS.

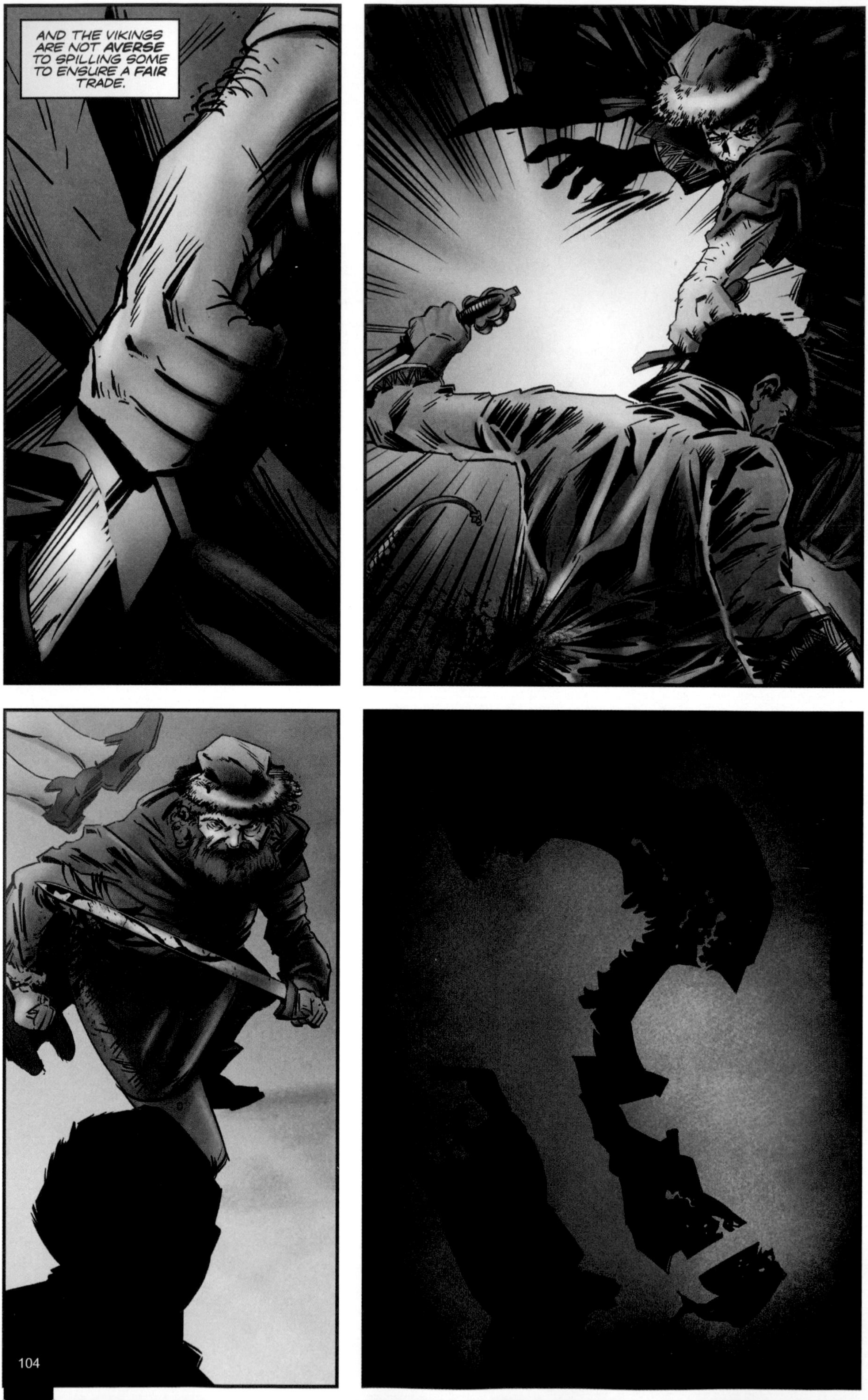
AND THE VIKINGS ARE NOT AVERSE TO SPILLING SOME TO ENSURE A FAIR TRADE.

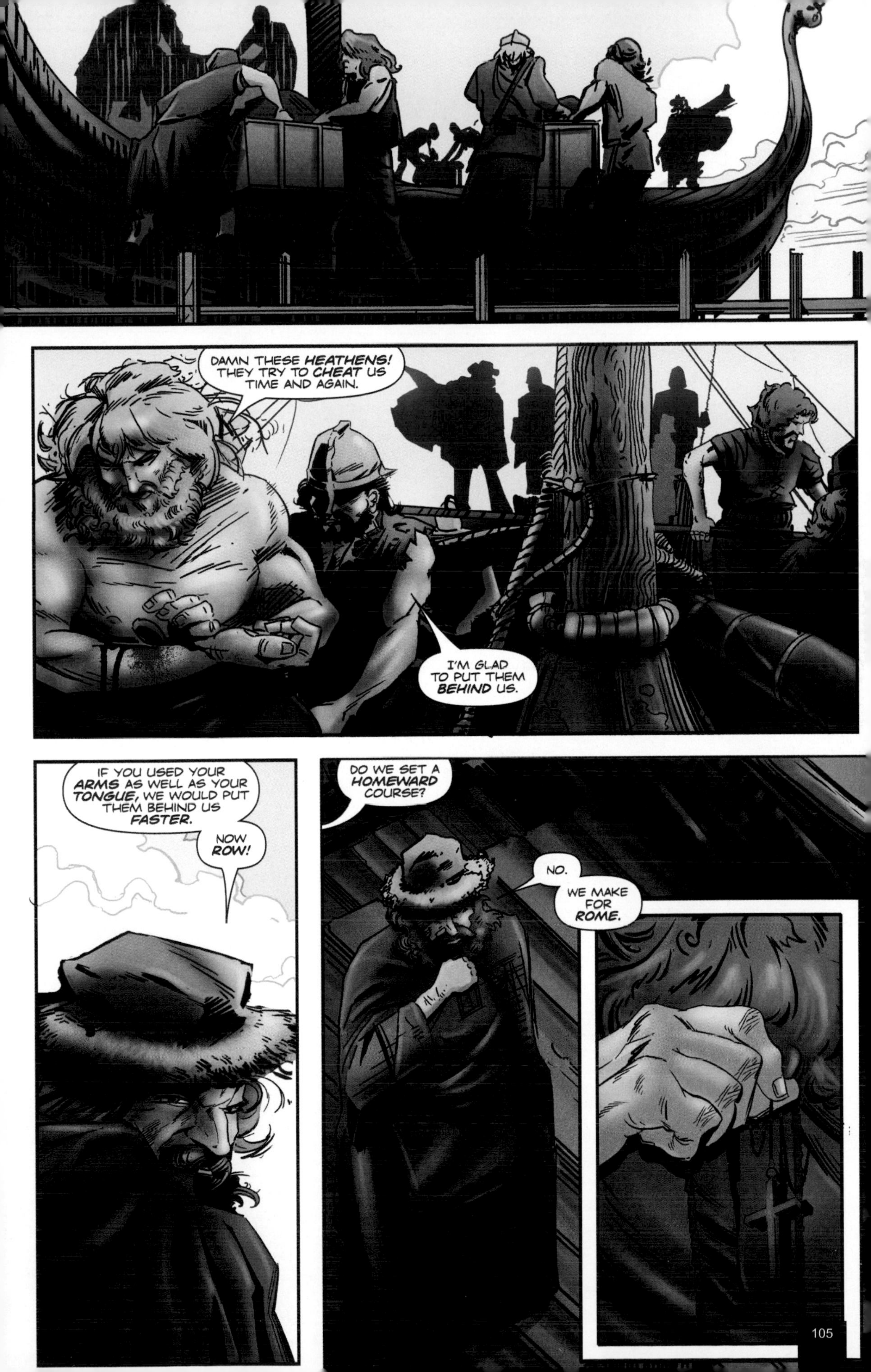
DAMN THESE HEATHENS! THEY TRY TO CHEAT US TIME AND AGAIN.
I'M GLAD TO PUT THEM BEHIND US.
IF YOU USED YOUR ARMS AS WELL AS YOUR TONGUE, WE WOULD PUT THEM BEHIND US FASTER.
NOW ROW!
DO WE SET A HOMEWARD COURSE?
NO.
WE MAKE FOR ROME.

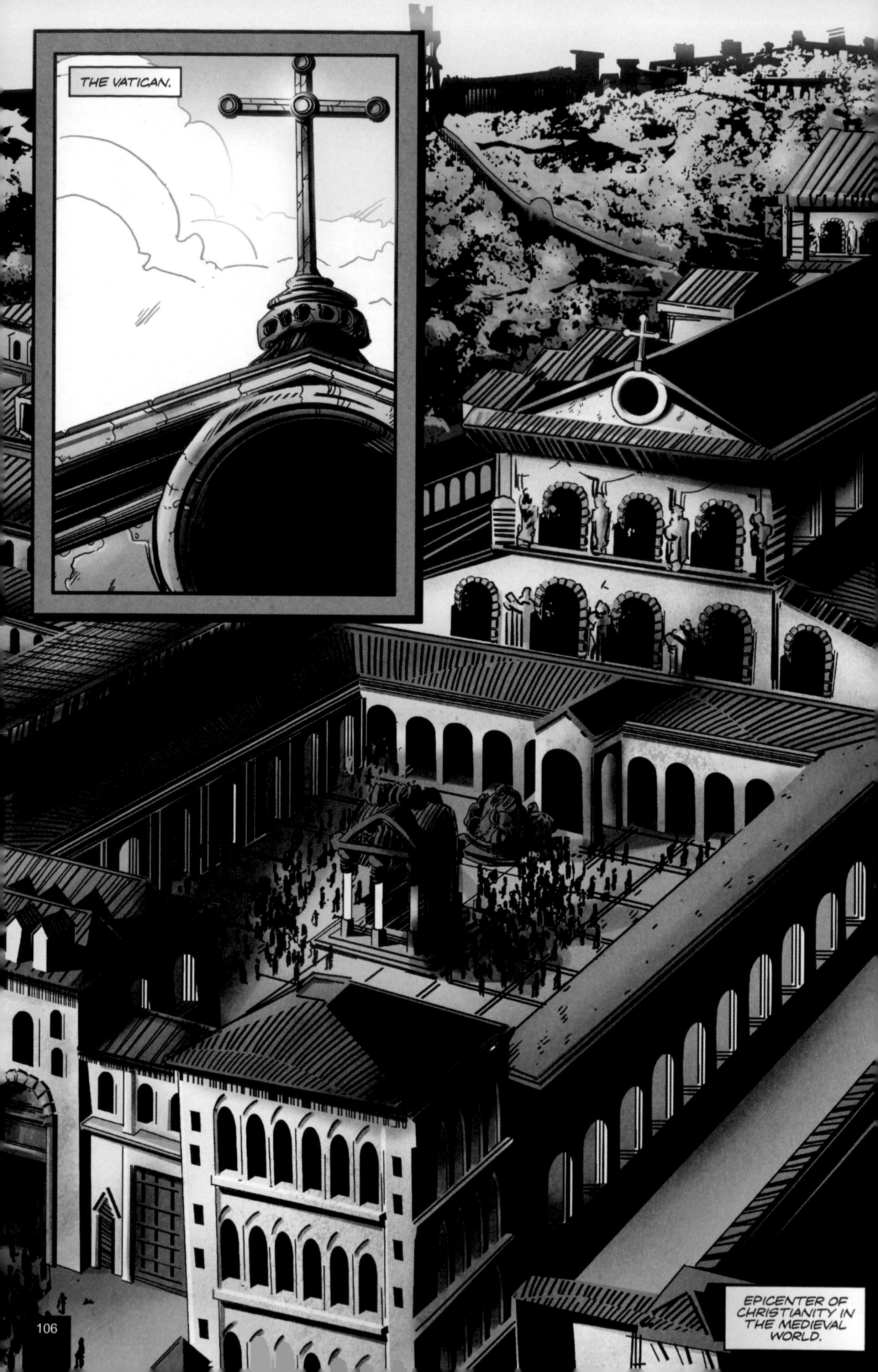
THE VATICAN.
EPICENTER OF CHRISTIANITY IN THE MEDIEVAL WORLD.

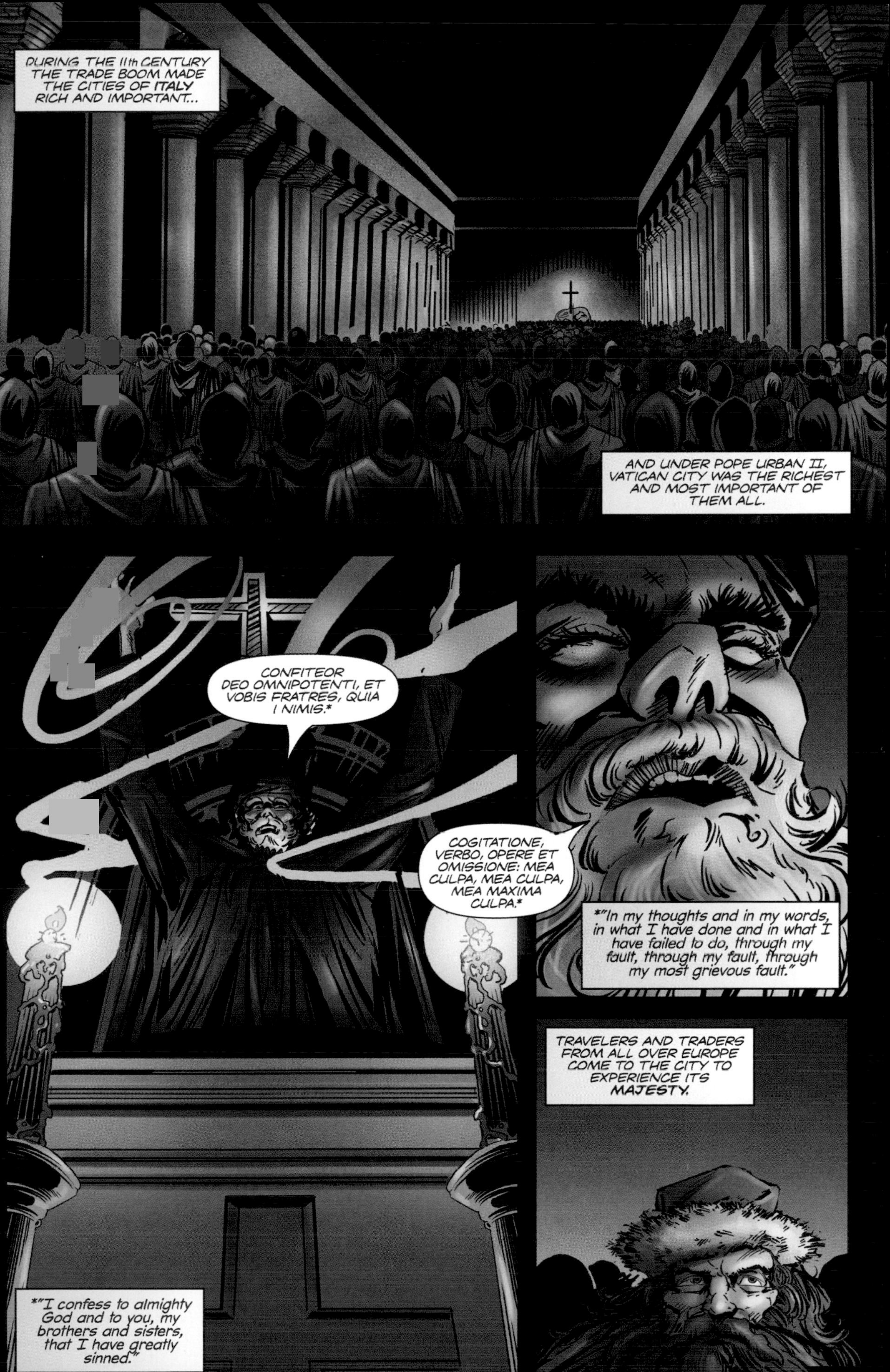
DURING THE 11th CENTURY THE TRADE BOOM MADE THE CITIES OF ITALY RICH AND IMPORTANT...
AND UNDER POPE URBAN II, VATICAN CITY WAS THE RICHEST AND MOST IMPORTANT OF THEM ALL.
CONFITEOR DEO OMNIPOTENTI, ET VOBIS FRATRES, QUIA I NIMIS.*
*"I confess to almighty God and to you, my brothers and sisters, that I have greatly sinned."
COGITATIONE, VERBO, OPERE ET OMISSIONE: MEA CULPA, MEA CULPA, MEA MAXIMA CULPA.*
*"In my thoughts and in my words, in what I have done and in what I have failed to do, through my fault, through my fault, through my most grievous fault."
TRAVELERS AND TRADERS FROM ALL OVER EUROPE COME TO THE CITY TO EXPERIENCE ITS MAJESTY.

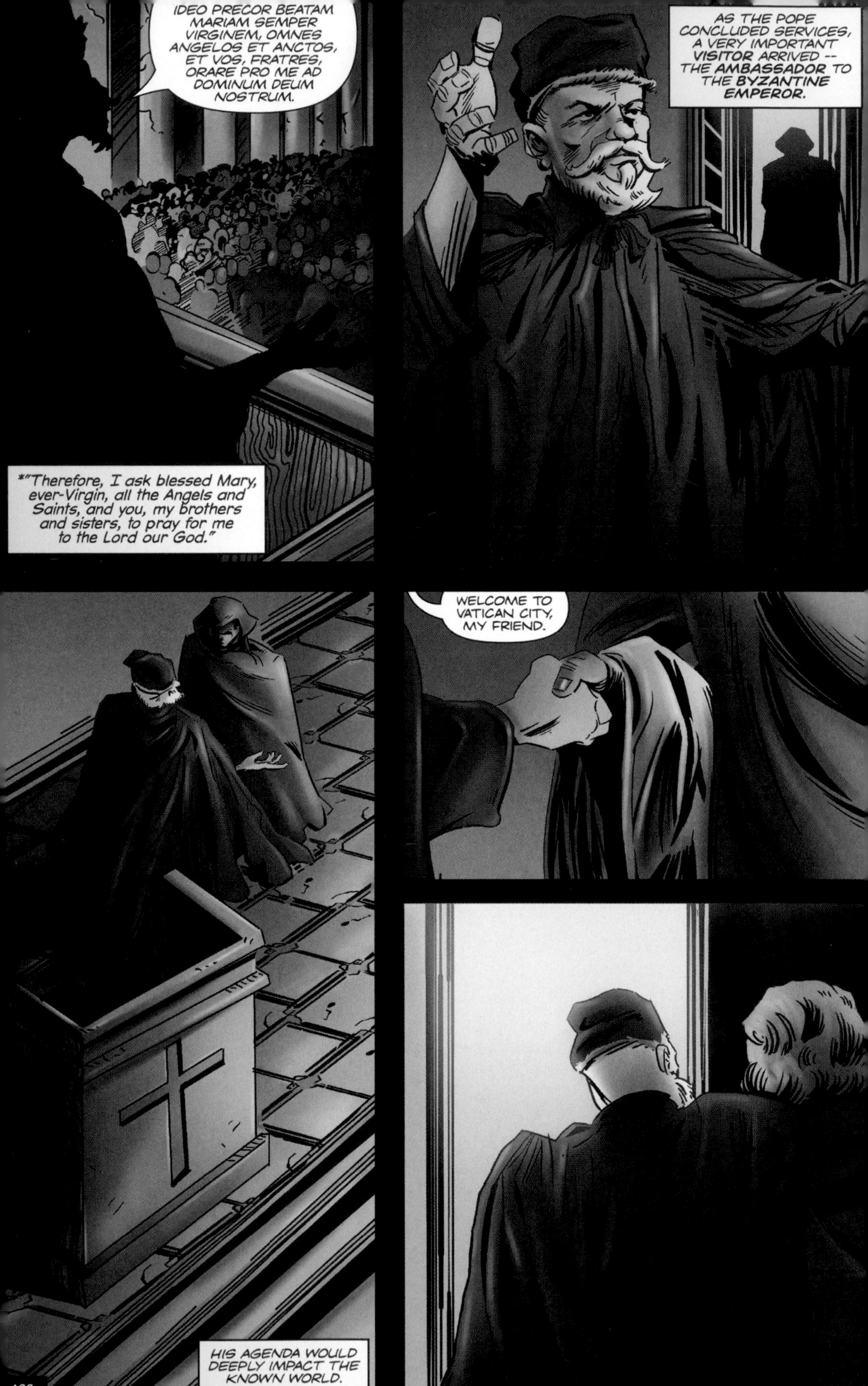
IDEO PRECOR BEATAM MARIAM SEMPER VIRGINEM, OMNES ANGELOS ET ANCTOS, ET VOS, FRATRES, ORARE PRO ME AD DOMINUM DEUM NOSTRUM.
*"Therefore, I ask blessed Mary, ever-Virgin, all the Angels and Saints, and you, my brothers and sisters, to pray for me to the Lord our God."
AS THE POPE CONCLUDED SERVICES, A VERY IMPORTANT **VISITOR** ARRIVED -- THE **AMBASSADOR** TO THE **BYZANTINE EMPEROR.**
WELCOME TO VATICAN CITY, MY FRIEND.
HIS AGENDA WOULD DEEPLY IMPACT THE KNOWN WORLD.

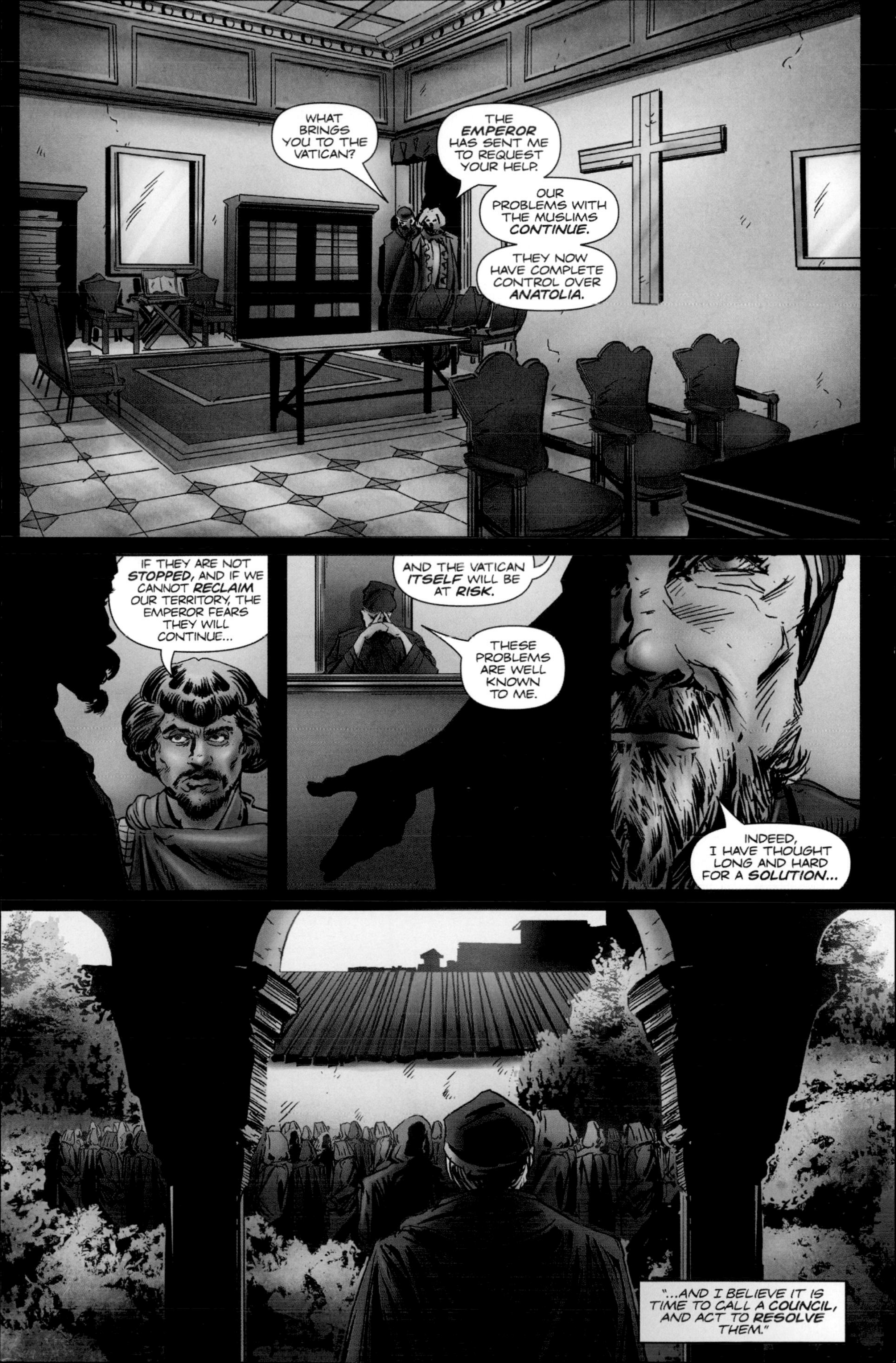
WHAT BRINGS YOU TO THE VATICAN?
THE EMPEROR HAS SENT ME TO REQUEST YOUR HELP.
OUR PROBLEMS WITH THE MUSLIMS CONTINUE.
THEY NOW HAVE COMPLETE CONTROL OVER ANATOLIA.
IF THEY ARE NOT STOPPED, AND IF WE CANNOT RECLAIM OUR TERRITORY, THE EMPEROR FEARS THEY WILL CONTINUE...
AND THE VATICAN ITSELF WILL BE AT RISK.
THESE PROBLEMS ARE WELL KNOWN TO ME.
INDEED, I HAVE THOUGHT LONG AND HARD FOR A SOLUTION...
"...AND I BELIEVE IT IS TIME TO CALL A COUNCIL, AND ACT TO RESOLVE THEM."

MARCH 5, 1095 C.E.

THE COUNCIL OF PIACENZA.

OVER 4,000 CHURCH OFFICIALS AND 30,000 LAYMEN ATTEND THE COUNCIL, AS WELL AS 200 BISHOPS FROM ITALY AND FRANCE.

FOR FIVE LONG DAYS, POPE URBAN II HEARS THE COMPLAINTS AND PROBLEMS OF FELLOW CHRISTIANS.

HE HEARS A RECENT CONVERT **CONRAD**, THE SON OF HENRY IV, THE HOLY ROMAN EMPEROR. ALONG WITH **EUPRAXIA**, DAUGHTER OF THE PRINCE OF KIEV.

HE TELLS OF HORRIBLE **ATROCITIES** COMMITTED BY HIS FATHER AGAINST THE CHRISTIAN FAITH, INCLUDING THE PERFORMANCE OF A **BLACK MASS** ON THE PRINCESS'S NAKED BODY.

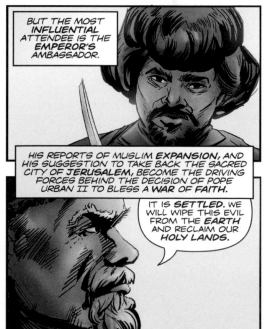

BUT THE MOST **INFLUENTIAL** ATTENDEE IS THE **EMPEROR'S** AMBASSADOR.

HIS REPORTS OF MUSLIM **EXPANSION**, AND HIS SUGGESTION TO TAKE BACK THE SACRED CITY OF **JERUSALEM**, BECOME THE DRIVING FORCES BEHIND THE DECISION OF POPE URBAN II TO BLESS A **WAR OF FAITH**.

IT IS **SETTLED**. WE WILL WIPE THIS EVIL FROM THE **EARTH** AND RECLAIM OUR **HOLY LANDS**.

110

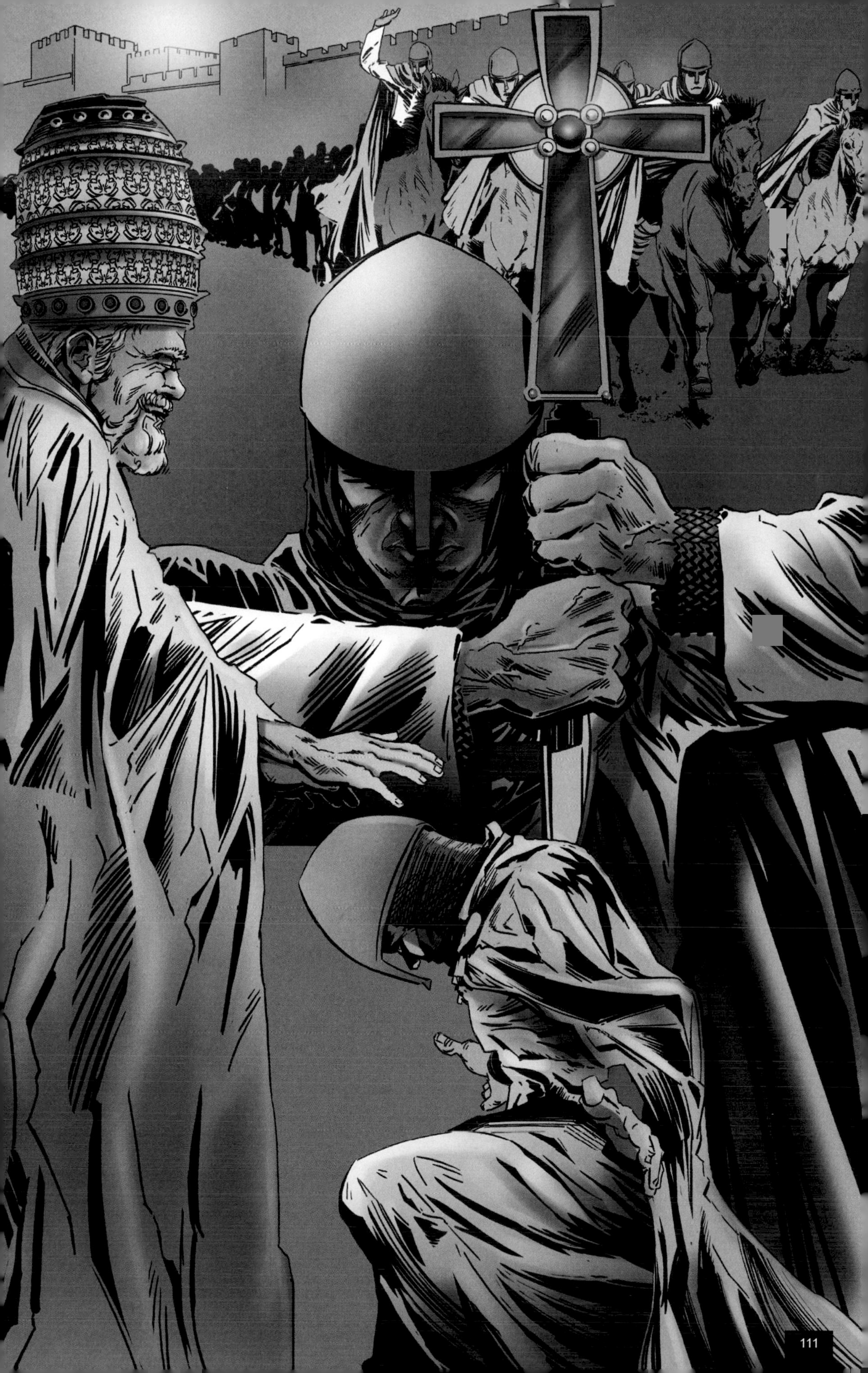

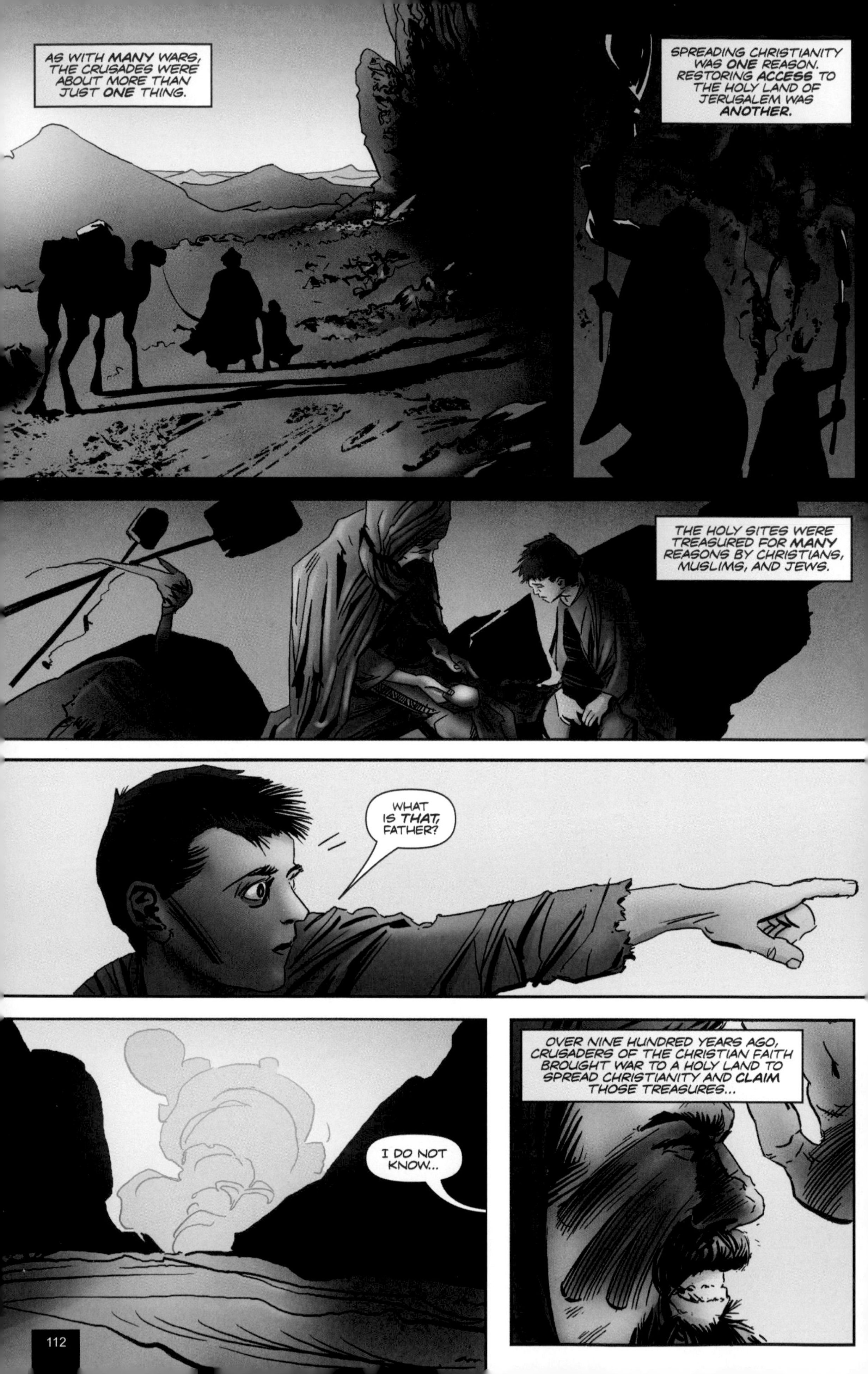
AS WITH MANY WARS, THE CRUSADES WERE ABOUT MORE THAN JUST ONE THING.
SPREADING CHRISTIANITY WAS ONE REASON. RESTORING ACCESS TO THE HOLY LAND OF JERUSALEM WAS ANOTHER.
THE HOLY SITES WERE TREASURED FOR MANY REASONS BY CHRISTIANS, MUSLIMS, AND JEWS.
WHAT IS THAT, FATHER?
I DO NOT KNOW...
OVER NINE HUNDRED YEARS AGO, CRUSADERS OF THE CHRISTIAN FAITH BROUGHT WAR TO A HOLY LAND TO SPREAD CHRISTIANITY AND CLAIM THOSE TREASURES...

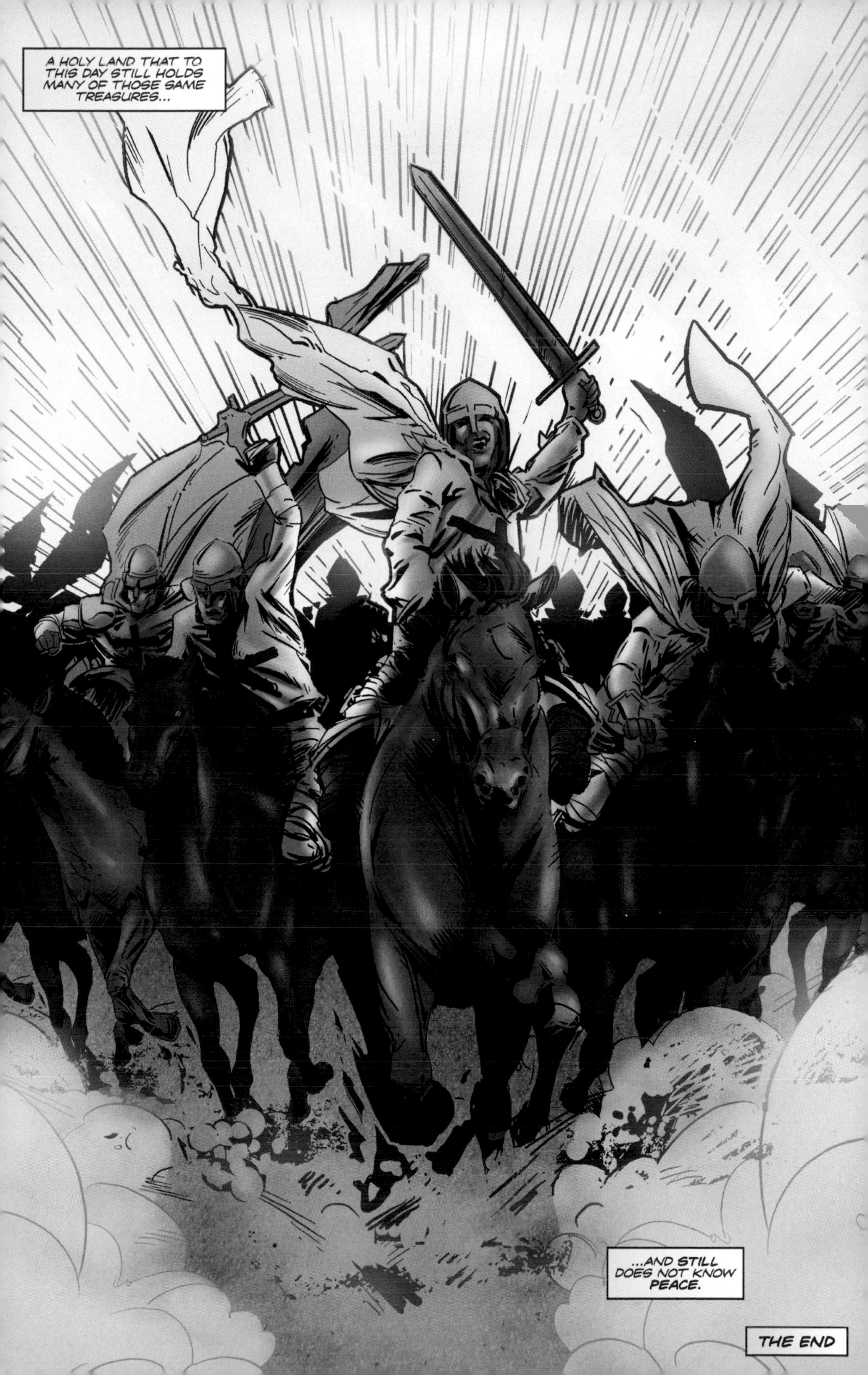
A HOLY LAND THAT TO THIS DAY STILL HOLDS MANY OF THOSE SAME TREASURES...
...AND STILL DOES NOT KNOW PEACE.
THE END

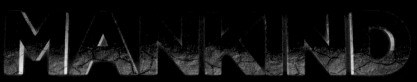

MANKIND

THE OFFICIAL ART

Ancient Athens was clearly the toughest part of drawing this story, but also the most satisfying.

While I was working on it, I had two monitors in front of me: one with various pictures and paintings of the city, and the other with google earth opened over Athens.

Being an Italian, I felt very close to this material. Ideally, I would have drawn it as a double page spread, spending hours on every single temple, but I believed that the final result on this single panel conveyed the landscape just as well.

From the layout to the pencil stage, there was only one revision to this page. I originally had sketched the runner, Pheidippides, standing upright on the mountaintop as he looked at Athens; I thought he would feel proud seeing his great city, chest out and head held high.

My editor pointed out that after all that fighting and running, Pheidippides was barely alive. As a result, I drew him falling to his knees to show how much this journey has physically and emotionally worn on him.

-GIOVANNI TIMPANO

STANDARD CLASICAL LAYOUT. IT WORKS BUT BORING.
MANKIND
MEN COMING TOWARD US
MAMMOTH
OUT OF ICE AGE
GROWING GRAINS
KING AND ASSISTANT
BUILDING PYRAMIDS
HORSES CHARIOTS OVERCOME

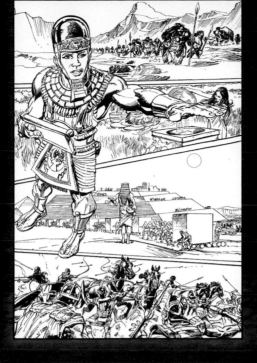

Neal Adams went above and beyond the call of duty for the cover. Using extensive reference, Neal rendered four spectacular, separate images showing early human history's sweep towards a pivotal event: the battle of Megiddo, history's first reliably recorded battle and one that anchored the greatest expanse of the Egyptian empire.

Experimenting at the sketch stage with great designs and greater leaders- Cleopatra and Tuthmosis III- Neal made it a challenge to choose just one design. "Your call," Neal wrote in the margin notes. With Bill Sienkiewicz's gorgeous inks, I call it a cover for the ages!

-Joan Hilty, Executive Editor

③ SAME BORDER BREAKUP.. AND CLEO (OR TUTMOSIS III
3 ERRUPTING 3-DIMENSIONALLY UP TOWARD US. BEST. MORE
MANKIND

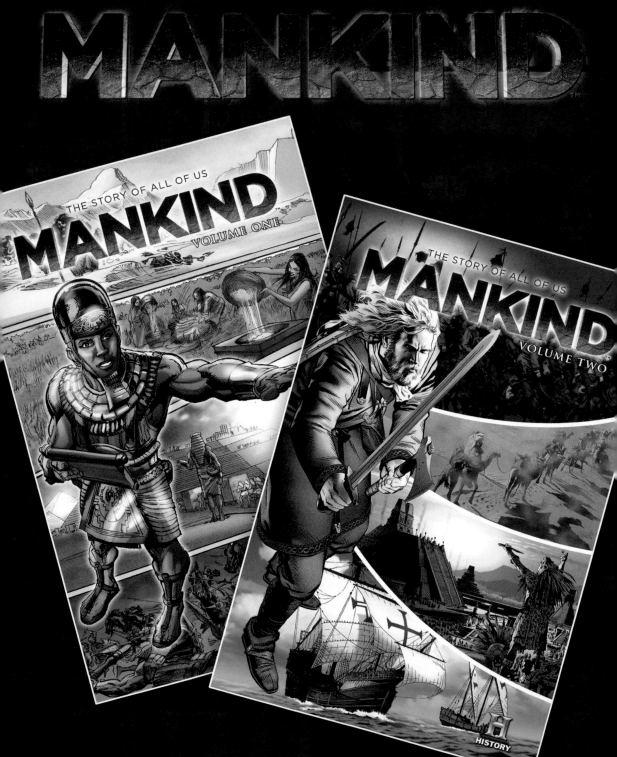

EXPERIENCE MORE
MANKIND
THE STORY OF ALL OF US
MANKIND
HISTORY
by Pamela D. Toler, PhD
Foreword by Ian Morris
Blu-ray and DVD
Available December 11TH
Companion Book
and eBook
Available Now
Television series available via **digital download** starting November 14TH.
HISTORY

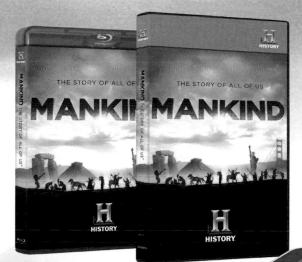

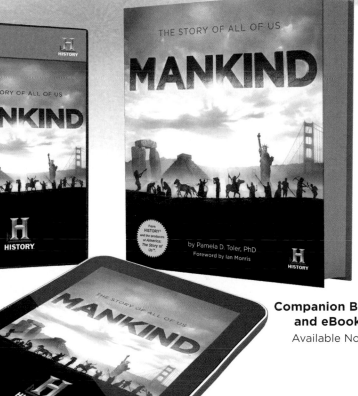

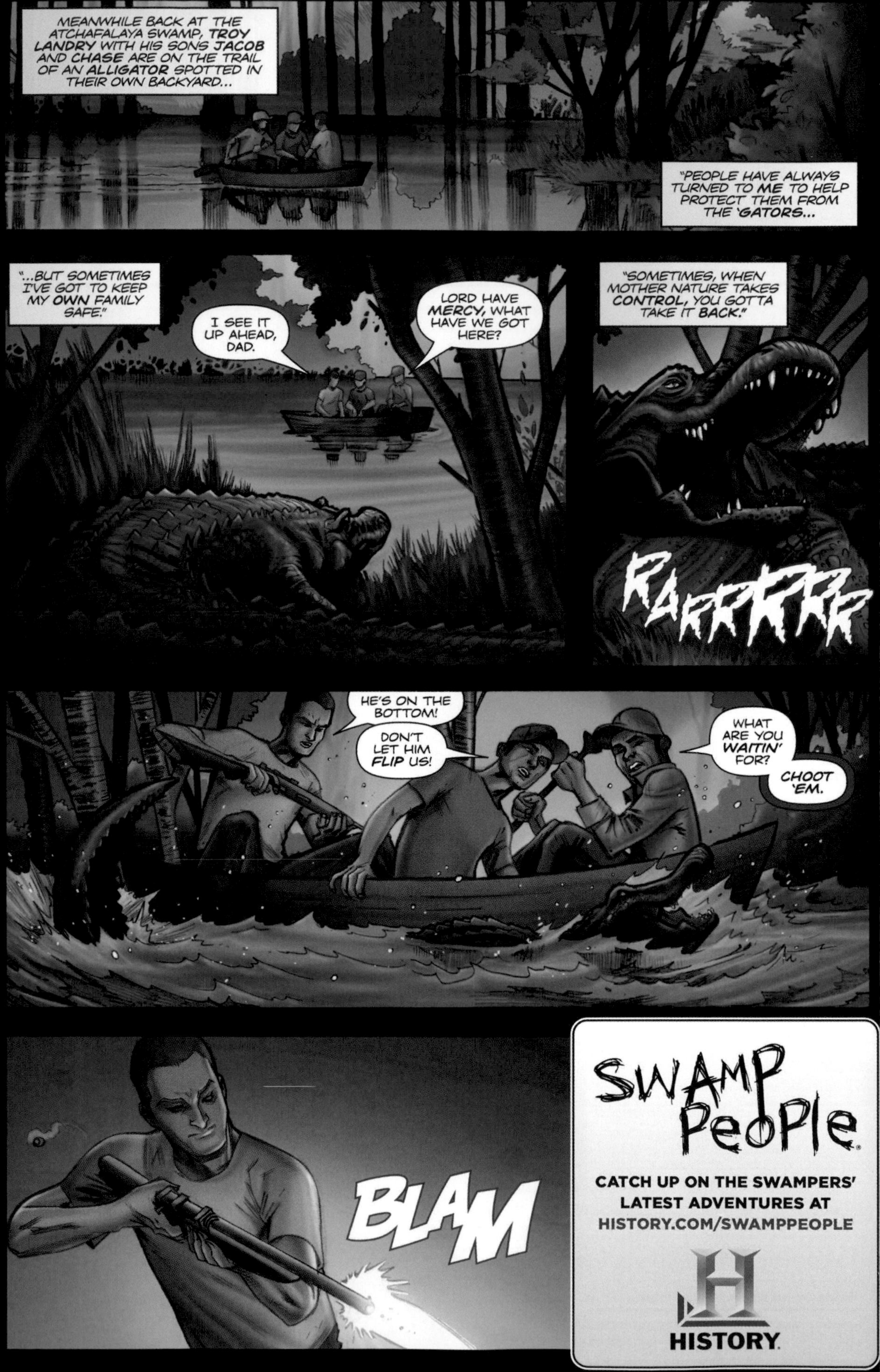
MEANWHILE BACK AT THE ATCHAFALAYA SWAMP, TROY LANDRY WITH HIS SONS JACOB AND CHASE ARE ON THE TRAIL OF AN ALLIGATOR SPOTTED IN THEIR OWN BACKYARD...
"PEOPLE HAVE ALWAYS TURNED TO ME TO HELP PROTECT THEM FROM THE 'GATORS...
"...BUT SOMETIMES I'VE GOT TO KEEP MY OWN FAMILY SAFE."
I SEE IT UP AHEAD, DAD.
LORD HAVE MERCY, WHAT HAVE WE GOT HERE?
"SOMETIMES, WHEN MOTHER NATURE TAKES CONTROL, YOU GOTTA TAKE IT BACK."
RARRRRRR
HE'S ON THE BOTTOM!
DON'T LET HIM FLIP US!
WHAT ARE YOU WAITIN' FOR?
CHOOT 'EM.
BLAM
SWAMP PeoPle
CATCH UP ON THE SWAMPERS' LATEST ADVENTURES AT HISTORY.COM/SWAMPPEOPLE
HISTORY

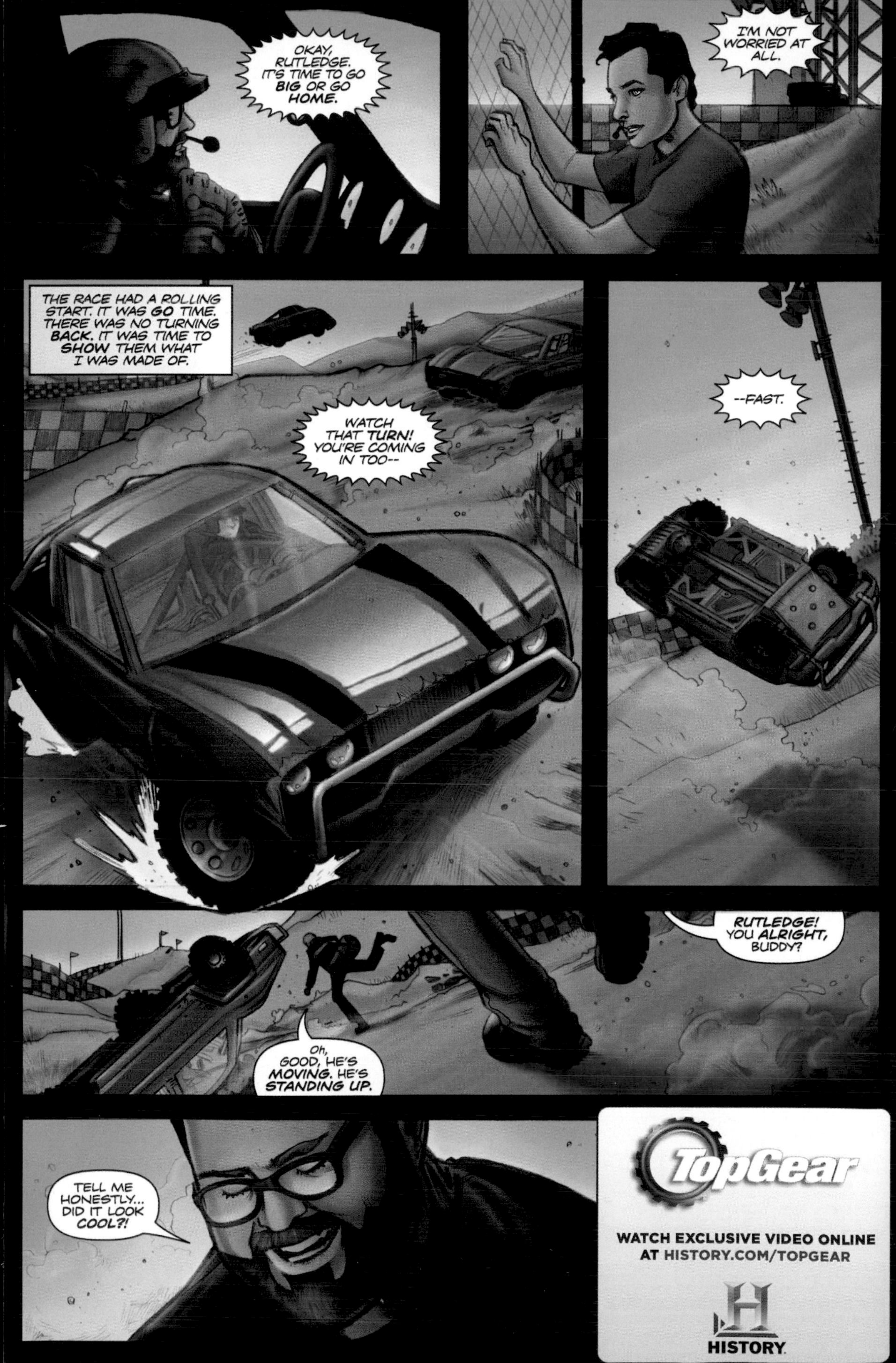
OKAY, RUTLEDGE. IT'S TIME TO GO BIG OR GO HOME.
I'M NOT WORRIED AT ALL.
THE RACE HAD A ROLLING START. IT WAS GO TIME. THERE WAS NO TURNING BACK. IT WAS TIME TO SHOW THEM WHAT I WAS MADE OF.
WATCH THAT TURN! YOU'RE COMING IN TOO--
--FAST.
RUTLEDGE! YOU ALRIGHT, BUDDY?
Oh, GOOD, HE'S MOVING. HE'S STANDING UP.
TELL ME HONESTLY... DID IT LOOK COOL?!
TopGear
WATCH EXCLUSIVE VIDEO ONLINE AT HISTORY.COM/TOPGEAR
HISTORY

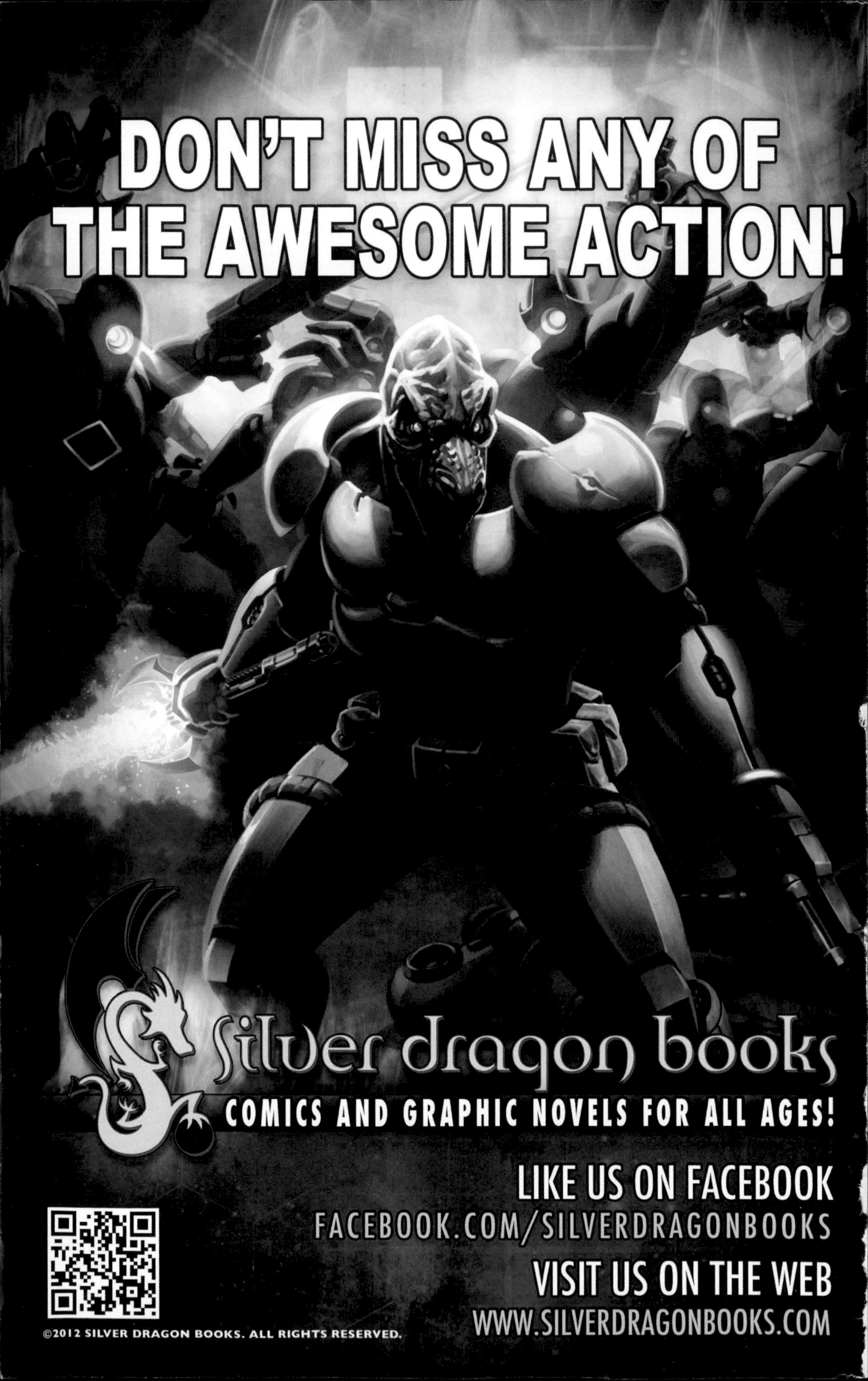
DON'T MISS ANY OF THE AWESOME ACTION!
silver dragon books
COMICS AND GRAPHIC NOVELS FOR ALL AGES!
LIKE US ON FACEBOOK
FACEBOOK.COM/SILVERDRAGONBOOKS
VISIT US ON THE WEB
WWW.SILVERDRAGONBOOKS.COM
©2012 SILVER DRAGON BOOKS. ALL RIGHTS RESERVED.